# RESENTMENTS
# KILL

CHARLES ROBINSON

# RESENTMENTS KILL

LifeRich Publishing is a registered trademark of The Reader's Digest Association, Inc.

LifeRich Publishing books may be ordered through booksellers or by contacting:

LifeRich Publishing
1663 Liberty Drive
Bloomington, IN 47403
www.liferichpublishing.com
1 (888) 238-8637

ISBN: 978-1-4897-2000-9 (sc)
ISBN: 978-1-4897-2001-6 (hc)
ISBN: 978-1-4897-2002-3 (e)

Library of Congress Control Number: 2018913522

Print information available on the last page.

LifeRich Publishing rev. date: 11/8/2018

# PROLOGUE

Four-thirty p.m. The petite, teenage girl lay bound and gagged on the twin bed in her room, whimpering behind her bonds, terror in her young eyes. The two men were in the master bedroom. One was on top of the woman in that room, who was also bound. He was inside her, riding her, finding self-gratification at the expense of her degradation.

When he had finished violating her, he got off, and his partner straddled her, desecrating her again, grinning at the horrific and obvious pain she felt. The duct tape on her mouth prevented her from screaming out in the pain, rage and humility she felt. When they had fulfilled their own perverted desires, the tall one shot her three times and, without any obvious remorse, moved on to the daughter's bedroom.

She was not there, and they ran down the hall looking for her. The other bedrooms were empty, but the bathroom door was closed and locked. The taller of the two, lanky with long hair and a scruffy beard, beat on the door and then began kicking it until the jamb splintered, and the door gave way. The youngster cowered against the tub, knowing, knowing this was the worst day, and possibly the last day, she would ever have. She sobbed as they drug her down onto the floor and ripped away her clothes. Their debauchery was savage and, to her, endless. They laughed at her pleading, ignoring her cries of pain at their savagery.

When they were done, as with her mother, the lanky one shot her and left her dying on the cold tile of the bathroom floor. They then went through the house with reckless abandon, pulling out drawers, opening closets, and throwing around anything they didn't like. When they had collected everything they thought valuable, the smaller of the two, went back to the bedroom of the mother and ripped the wedding and engagement rings from her finger.

Satisfied they had left nothing they could sell or pawn, they went out and climbed into the van they had parked in the driveway and squalled the tires as they swung out onto the street and passed the car coming in the opposite direction.

# CHAPTER 1

Henry Jenkins, five-feet-eleven-inches, 180 pounds, with already thinning blond hair at thirty-eight years old, leaned back on the vinyl chair and stretched is arms as he looked across his desk at the office clock on the far wall. 3:45 p.m. Fifteen more minutes and another day shot to hell. He pushed the wire-framed reading glasses up onto his forehead and ran his fingers through his hair. Then, massaging his tired, blue eyes momentarily, he straightened and began putting papers and folders in the desk drawers. By the time he finished, it would be time to go home. And he still had a couple of things to do.

Henry had worked at Blaycock Manufacturing, a company of 500 employees in Clarksville, PA, for twelve of this thirty-eight years. But as personnel manager, he knew little of the plant's actual operation nor did he really have a need to know. His was strictly personnel management: interviewing, hiring, firing, counseling, etc. He picked up the folder that he had left out and carried it to the office next door, where he laid it on the desk next to the nameplate that said George Williams, V.P.

George was on the phone, so Henry nodded and left the office, stopping by the secretary's desk. The middle-aged and slightly overweight woman looked up from her typing and smiled. Henry returned the smile and said, "Marge, George is on the phone. When he gets off, would you remind him the reps from AMCO will be here in the morning, and he needs to review the information I put on his desk." "Yes, Henry," she acknowledged while she continued typing. "Thanks, Marge," Henry said as he walked away from the desk. "I'll see you in the morning."

Henry retrieved his coat from his office and headed for the door. His job was not the best paying job in the world, but it was certainly adequate. Also, the two-point-five-million-dollar inheritance he got from his half of his parents' estate eight years ago made life more than comfortable for himself, his wife, and his daughter. It even provided a few luxuries. Thinking of luxuries, Henry remembered that today, June twelfth, was his daughter Linda's birthday. Henry smiled. It didn't seem like fifteen years since he had held the small bundle in his very nervous arms.

At 3:55, Henry retraced the steps to his office, picked up the phone, and dialed his home number. As he waited for the connection to be made, he got his checkbook from his pocket and looked at the balance to ensure that he had adequate funds for a present. As the phone was picked up at the other end, he heard the familiar voice of his wife, Mary, say hello. He said, "Honey, I'm going to be a little late. I've got to find something for Linda's birthday."

He listened to her response and said, "I shouldn't be more than an hour or so. I love you, too. Tell Linda I'll see her in a bit. Bye-bye."

Henry returned the phone to the cradle and once more left his office, this time shutting off the lights. As he stepped into the bright sunlight of the August afternoon, he realized that he had no idea what to get for his daughter. Fifteen-year-old young ladies could be difficult to buy for. He figured he'd browse through a few stores until he found something he thought she'd like. Up until this point in her life, he'd never bought her anything that had failed to please her.

At the risk of strangers on the street thinking him nuts, Henry smiled. He and Linda were very close. It was a closeness that he knew Mary envied, although she denied it. Yet, if Linda had a problem or was bothered by something, other than feminine issues, she would always come to Henry at a time when her Mother was busy elsewhere.

They would resolve most of the things that bother a fourteen . . . now fifteen-year old, young lady.

Henry did see her as a young lady. She had a good sense of responsibility, was very level-headed, and though it may one day cause them a headache or two, was very pretty and physically mature for her age.

Driving downtown, he located the store he wanted and put aside other thoughts as he searched for an appropriate gift. One hour and five presents later, with two hundred twenty-five dollars less in his checking account, Henry got into his two-year-old Cadillac and started home. Mary always got a little angry at him for his extravagance with presents. "Honey, don't get so upset," he would say. "Birthdays come but once a year. It's not like we don't have the money." Yet, he appreciated where his wife was coming from. Until they had received the inheritance, things had been pretty tight with just his salary, especially with the large house payment each month. However, the inheritance and wise investments had made life not only better but much easier.

The drive home from work usually took thirty-five minutes. This evening, however, Henry pushed it and made the last turn onto Euclid Street in twenty-seven minutes. It was now 5:30 p.m.

As he neared his house, he noticed the black, customized van with the heart-shaped side windows pull quickly out of the driveway. He winced as he heard the whining tires. It was not unusual for people to turn at his driveway for his was the last house on the dead-end street. He also remembered that his driveway received a lot of damage from squealing tires.

As the van roared past, quickly picking up speed, he first noted a curious "Q" shaped dent in the bumper beneath the left headlight and then the shadow of two occupants behind the dark tinted glass. Henry would not have normally noticed such an insignificant detail because he really didn't care much about cars. But the dent seemed to mar the otherwise perfect condition of the beautiful vehicle. The van flew around the corner and out of sight as Henry turned into his driveway.

He mused that the van would have a lot more dents if they continued driving like that. Henry then put the incident out of his mind.

Retrieving the packages from the back seat, Henry walked up the steps to the front door. Noticing the door standing ajar, he made a mental note to say something to Linda about leaving the door open when the air conditioning was on. But, it was August, and they would not be needing the air conditioning much longer. "I'm home," he said as he placed the presents on the coffee table. Hearing no answer, he called out again. "Mary, Linda, I'm home." Still hearing nothing, he started toward the kitchen where he always found Mary cooking dinner. "Honey, I'm home," he said as he pushed open the door. No one was there.

The kitchen was a mess. Drawers pulled out, utensils strewn all over the floor, and cabinet doors open.

"Mary, where are you? Linda!" Henry quickly walked into the dining room and found the same disarray. The china cupboard stood open and some of the dishes lay broken on the floor. He stepped over to an open drawer of the hutch. The silver that he had bought for Mary for their tenth anniversary was missing.

Had they been robbed? Where the hell was his family? With his heart pounding and a sick feeling in the pit of his stomach, he walked then ran toward the stairway leading to the bedrooms upstairs.

They hadn't needed a house this big for just the three of them, but they had gotten a damned good deal on it, and it was, or had been, a great neighborhood to rear a child.

"Mary, Linda!" Henry climbed the stairs two at a time, noticing an acrid smell that he hadn't noticed before. "Mary, is anyone home?" What the hell was that smell? He reached the top of the stairs. Mary knew when he would be home, and he knew that she would not take off without leaving a note. That smell . . . it was vaguely familiar.

"Mary, are you up here?" He turned left at the top of the stairs toward their bedroom. He and Mary had met seventeen years ago in college when she was nineteen.

Henry had only known her a few months when he asked her to

marry him, and she accepted. She was a pretty little thing, Henry thought. Still is. The sixteen years of marriage had, if anything, improved his five-foot-three-inch, blue-eyed, blonde wife. If Henry was any judge at all, their daughter would be just as pretty, though taller and a little more well-endowed. Henry walked hastily toward the master bedroom. What the hell was that smell?

Turning the knob of the bedroom door, he pushed it open and gasped out loud. Their bedroom was in complete shambles. The dresser drawers were pulled out, and the contents strewn all over the floor. Mary and Linda were not there. Had they gone out and someone taken the opportunity to rob the house, or had they heard prowlers and slipped out to the neighbor's to call the police?

Standing in the doorway, he surveyed the mess. The mirror on Mary's vanity was shattered. Her jewelry box lay open on the floor with what was left of its contents scattered.

Henry's eyes switched to the picture where the wall safe was. The picture was still in place. His eyes went to the bed where he noticed a brownish red stain. "What the hell is that," he exclaimed aloud as he started toward the bed for a closer inspection.

Paying no attention to what was underfoot, he tripped over one of the drawers. Attempting to stop his fall, he allowed his full weight to come down on his left arm. He heard the bone in his wrist snap just before he crashed onto the floor. He lay there slightly stunned, waiting for the pain to catch up with the noise of the broken bone.

Slowly at first, then with growing intensity, the pain came. Henry gritted his teeth and rolled off of his arm. As he did, he saw something that caused him to cry out in anguish. He now understood the brownish red stain he had seen on the bed and the pungent smell in the air.

From his vantage point on the floor, Henry could see under the bed, and there, he saw something that was not visible from the doorway. His beautiful wife was lying on the floor with three bleeding holes in her chest and stomach. Her dress was around her hips, exposing torn and ragged panties. The smell was gunpowder.

The scream welled from deep in his throat and came out tortured and ragged from his mouth. "Mary! Oh my God! Mary!" Ignoring the pain in his wrist, Henry struggled to his feet amid the mess on the floor and stumbled around the bed to his wife. "Mary! Oh God! Mary," he wailed. His voice reached a crescendo as he knelt and picked up the limp, still body of his wife and placed her tenderly on the bed. "What happened, honey? Please answer me." He felt for a pulse in her wrist and then on her neck, knowing that he would find none but still hoping for a miracle. Henry lifted her gently and held her against him. He kissed her cheeks, her brow, and as the tears came, he buried his face in her soft blonde hair and wept openly.

"Oh, Mary, not now. It's not time. What will I do? What will Linda do without you? We are supposed to raise her together, darling. I can't do it without you." Again, his voice raised with the agony of his loss. "How could you? God! How could you? Damn you! Damn you! Please give her back. I need her. We need her."

Henry sat holding his wife. A thought gnawing at him, trying to get through . . . a word. What word? Something he said . . . what was it? Sudden realization struck him. He had said "we need you." We. Where was Linda?

"Oh, God no!" Henry looked at his wife. "Don't let it be so." He got up, ignoring the swollen, useless left wrist, which was throbbing incessantly, and lay his wife gently back on the pillow, absently pulling up the sheet over her torn skirt and panties.

Stumbling across the debris on the floor, he ran down the hall to his daughter's room and threw open the door. "Linda . . . honey?" He looked around the room. It looked much like the one he had just left with empty and broken drawers with clothing strewn all over the floor but no Linda. "Maybe she's not at home," he whispered. But the gnawing pain in the back of his head told him differently. He softly closed the door and ran to the next room. Same results. The room was a mess, but Linda was not there. He hurried to the last room, not wanting to open the door but knowing that he must. Turning the knob and taking a deep ragged breath, he entered the room.

The mattress lay on the floor. There were great slashes in it where a knife had been pulled through. Drawers lay smashed on the floor. The full-length mirror fastened to the closet door was smashed. Henry picked his way through the room to the opposite side of the bed. Nothing.

Maybe, he thought, just maybe, she wasn't here. Maybe she had gone somewhere. Maybe she'd be coming in the door any minute.

Henry couldn't let her come upstairs. He'd go down, call the police and an ambulance. Then, he'd wait, so she wouldn't see her mother the way she was now. He picked his way back to the door and closed it behind him.

The walk down the hallway back to the staircase was extraordinarily long. The pain in his wrist was like fire. His head was throbbing. Then he heard it . . . a low, soft moan that shattered his hope. A moan, so soft, yet so loud . . . so full of pain that the color left his face, and the strength drained from his body. If the newel post had not been at hand, he would have fallen. The word that forced from his throat was more a strangled gasp. "Linda."

Henry looked at the door. He had not opened the bathroom door with the wood splintered around the lock. He forced himself away from the stairs and in two steps was pushing open the door.

Falling on his knees beside his daughter, he pulled her up into his arms. Her clothes were torn from her once flawless young body and were strewn around the small room. Large scratches encrusted with blood covered her legs, stomach, and breasts. Seeing the pool of blood on the floor, Henry looked at her back. There were two bullet holes . . . one near her shoulder and the other in the small of her back that welled blood.

Again, ignoring the broken wrist, Henry picked her up and carried her to her bed. At least she is alive, he thought as he picked up the phone. After dialing the operator, he picked up a pillow and pulled off the case. The operator answered, and Henry said, "There has been a shooting on the second floor of my home. I need an ambulance and the police. My name is Henry Jenkins, and I live at 325 Euclid Street. Do you understand?" The operator repeated the information, and Henry replaced the receiver. Holding the pillowcase in his right hand, he tore it into two pieces with his teeth while cursing the broken wrist. He next tore two strips from the sheet in the same manner. Folding the pieces of the pillowcase, he made compresses for the wounds, using the strips from the sheet to bind them tightly into place. It was a difficult task as he used only his "good" hand and his teeth. He turned his daughter gently onto her back and pulled the rest of the sheet over her.

Linda coughed and a hint of blood welled in the corner of her mouth, causing Henry's heart to sink. She opened her eyes. Tears filled them, the pain that Henry knew she must feel. "Oh, Daddy."

He kissed her gently, trying desperately to hold back his own tears. . . . tears of sorrow, despair, and anguish. "Rest baby. The ambulance will be here in just a few minutes." He held her against him.

"Daddy, please don't leave me."

"I won't darling . . . never again."

"Daddy," Linda's eyes searched her father's. Her voice barely audible, she asked, "Daddy, why?"

Henry's eyes again filled with tears, and he wished he had an answer. "I don't know, honey. I wish to God I did." "They hurt me, Daddy. Momma told me to run, and I did, but they broke down the door."

"I know, love. You tried." Henry stroked his daughter's long blonde hair. Linda was so proud of her hair. She brushed it every day so that it gleamed. He buried his face in that hair so that she wouldn't see him cry.

"Daddy, where's Momma? Did they hurt her, too?" Henry held back the shuddering sob that nearly escaped his lips. "She's in her room, honey. They hurt her, but she's all right now. She doesn't hurt anymore." Before Linda could ask any more questions about her mother, he continued, "Right now, we've got to take care of you, honey. We've got to get you to the hospital so that they can take care of you."

He silently cursed the damned ambulance even though he knew they hadn't had the time to get there yet.

"Daddy?" Linda coughed again, and Henry wiped the blood from the corner of her lips. "It hurts so much, Daddy. Am I going to die?" Henry waited a moment to make sure he had control of his voice, and then through trembling lips, he softly said, "No darling. We'll get the doctor to fix you up; you'll see."

Henry knew that he was lying, but he couldn't tell the truth, not even to himself. Failing miserably at making his voice light, he said, "Besides, it's your birthday, and tomorrow, I'll bring your presents to the hospital. We will open them there."

"Will Momma be able to come, too?"

"Yes, Momma will be there, too."

The police arrived first. When they reached the room, they saw Henry weeping softly and rocking back and forth with the lifeless body of his daughter held tightly in his arms.

# CHAPTER 2

B right light coming through the window jolted Henry out of a vivid nightmare. In the dream, two men in a black van were raping a woman. Henry was chained to a telephone phone and could do nothing. Sweat rolled off of his forehead and chest as he reached up to shield his eyes against the light. The pain in his head was horrendous. How long had he been here? The cast on his wrist looked grungy, and he smelled like a distillery. He had been drunk for weeks, but how many weeks? He tried, unsuccessfully, to piece together the events of his life since the double funeral.

The police had tried to question him about the incident, but Henry was in no condition to talk to them. He had ridden in the ambulance with Mary and Linda and had been sedated almost as soon as he got to the hospital. After that, everything went in slow motion. They had x-rayed and set his fractured wrist and wanted to keep him at the hospital for observation, but he refused. They asked him to at least talk to the hospital psychiatrist. Within the deep recesses of his mind, Henry recalled saying, "I don't need a fucking shrink. I need to kill someone!" Immediately, he received another injection. Henry spent two sedated days in the hospital, of which he remembered virtually nothing.

Though heavily sedated, he vaguely recalled attending the double funeral where people ... relatives, friends, co-workers, and some people that Henry didn't even know, drifted by offering condolences. "I just want it to be over and for everyone to leave me alone," he murmured softly. The hospital shrink had gone with him and spoke soothingly to him when he appeared to be getting edgy.

Then it was over . . . all over. Two thirds of his life was buried under six feet of dirt, rocks, and sod. Henry was numb.

The hospital released him a day after the funeral. Just before he left, the police had come to question him. Henry told them that he'd get with them later. The plainclothes detective, who had introduced himself as Lt. Cameron, said, "Mr. Jenkins, we need a statement now if you know anything. The longer we wait, the more difficult is becomes to locate the perpetrators."

Henry looked coldly at the detective. "I'll find them." The lieutenant looked somber. "I understand your feelings, Mr. Jenkins. But this is . . ."

Henry jumped up, his eyes mere slits. "You don't understand shit. That wasn't your wife and baby. It was mine. Now get the fuck out. I'll call you or come by the station in a couple of days." He strode into the bathroom, slammed the door, and urinated. When he came out, the police were gone.

Henry had phoned for a taxi, and when he was picked up fifteen minutes later, he gave his address to the driver. Reaching his house, he paid the driver and started up the drive as the cab pulled away. He suddenly realized that he couldn't go in. He knew that the house had probably been thoroughly cleaned and straightened up, but the thought of going inside repulsed him.

Three cars besides his own sat in the driveway. They were friends who had come to help out. Henry stood in the drive several minutes, just staring at the house. The headache started at his temples, seemingly growing worse the longer he stood there. He dug his keys out of his pocket and got into the Cadillac. As he was backing out of the drive, he saw Sheila Mackenzie, a next-door neighbor, open the front door, but he didn't acknowledge her wave. Turning the car, he headed for the interstate.

Now, two months and many fifths of bourbon later, he woke up in this motel with a raging hangover. The sun glared through drapes that he had forgotten to close. He sat up in the bed and groaned audibly when a fresh wave of pain ricocheted through his head. He stumbled to the window and pulled the drapery cord, closing out the sun. Next, he went to the bathroom and turned on the faucets, adjusting the water until it was tepid. With one hand, he shoved his skivvies down his legs and off. Then pulling the plunger for the shower, he stepped in and winced at the coolness of the water. He cursed the cast on his left wrist, which he had to hold outside the shower curtain to keep it dry. As he got used to the temperature of the water, he turned the hot tap down gradually until the sting of the icy needles seemed to drill into his throbbing brain.

Thirty minutes later, feeling something other than dead and red from the cold, stinging spray, he stepped out of the shower stall. He rubbed himself with the motel towel, which was too small and thin to be considered a bath towel. He dressed in the same clothes that he had obviously been wearing since . . . since when? The slacks and shirt both look and smelled as if they had been slept in for a year. He'd have to get fresh clothes.

Thinking back, or trying to think back, he remembered very little since that Friday. Going home . . . finding Mary and Linda . . . the hospital . . . police . . . shrink . . . funeral . . . drunk . . . and now. He tried to piece the middles together but couldn't. Had he called his brother, Fred? Had he called his boss? He didn't remember seeing either at the funeral. But, he supposed there was a lot between the tranquilizers and the booze of which he had no recollection. What did they call that? A blackout? He called the motel desk for the time, date, and location and found out that it was 7:30 a.m. on August 12, two months since the murders, and he was in Alabama. Henry checked the room to assure himself he hadn't left anything of value. There were three empty whiskey bottles, twelve coke cans, and a pretzel bag. He picked up a small suitcase (where did that come from?) then went to the office and checked out.

After searching for his car, he finally found it around the end of the building. It was 8:00 a.m., and he had probably fourteen hours of driving ahead of him. It certainly would give him time for thought and time for planning. After filling the gas tank, he pulled onto the interstate and started the long drive home.

The first two hours were taken up with thoughts of Mary and Linda. Tears and gut-wrenching sobs burst forward as he thought of his monumental loss. Eventually, there were no more tears, just hatred.

The cruise control was set for seventy, and Henry now relaxed in the car with his thoughts turning to the two people in the back van with a "Q" shaped dent in the bumper. He wished now that he had noted the license number. He knew it was Pennsylvania. "You've got a friend in . . . tag number . . . Pennsylvania," (You've got . . . excellent grammar, he thought) but he couldn't remember the numbers. How to find them? A private detective? That was no good. Henry had special things in mind for these people when he found them. Therefore, he couldn't involve anyone else in the situation: certainly not the police. Thoughts of the police reminded him that he had to go to the police station to answer some questions when he got back to Clarksville. The answer to this problem was that he would have to find it himself. Find them he would, and then they would pay.

Henry wondered if he was crazy. Did rational people think the way he was thinking? Probably, but did rational people really do what he was going to do? Probably not. What was he going to do when he found them? What was the plan?

"Vengeance is mine, sayeth the Lord," (or Jack Maccabee). The quote from the Bible flashed through Henry's mind as he drove. His thoughts drifted to his and Mary's college days back in Salem, West Virginia. During their time in college, that area had made national news because of a series of rape/murders. Henry couldn't remember now how many there were, but he did recall some of the conversations that buzzed through the college at that time.

In one particular rap session, just after a fifteen-year-old (the same age as Linda, he reflected) was raped and killed. Henry recalled the dialogue. One of the guys said that the person that did it should be hunted down and shot. Henry had rebutted that with, "I'll tell you what I think. Killing them is too easy. To me, rape is worse than murder because if the person lives, they have to live with the emotional scars and degradation of the experience for the rest of their lives. I think that they should torture the guy, and make him feel what those girls must have felt."

A guy named Jack Maccabee had joined the conversation. Henry didn't like Jack, though he seemed to be the pride of the townsfolk, college, and the church in Salem. Jack seemed to be uniquely wholesome. But as much as he was doted on by virtually everyone else, Henry thought him to be "too good to be true." As a matter of fact, Henry wasn't so sure (a bane on Henry by anyone he should tell) that Jack wasn't capable of those deeds himself. Henry had seen the way Jack eyed a girl's boobs and legs when he thought that no one was looking.

Jack had said it was not up to man but to God to punish the person responsible. Henry had replied, "Bullshit! Maybe God has that option at the millennium, but that guy should know what it's like to be humiliated, degraded, and hurt beyond repair now. Retribution should be swift, not when the guy dies of old age."

In his soft, nauseating voice, Jack replied, "Vengeance is mine, sayeth the Lord. It is not up to us but Him who reigns supreme to make those judgements."

"You think your way, Jack," Henry had replied, "and I'll think my way. But there is one thing sure. If society doesn't start taking appropriate and more drastic action in these situations, they'll get worse and not better. I believe that torture would accomplish a hell of a lot more in dissuading such behavior than forgiveness ever will." Jack looked at Henry with more of a sneer than a smile. "I'll pray for you Henry; you need it."

Returning to the present, Henry thought it didn't matter if the police caught them, if they went to trial and were convicted, or if the case wasn't thrown out because someone forgot to read them their rights, they would conceivably get no more than a life sentence, which meant they would be out in three to seven years. There were too many "ifs" and too many chances under present laws that they would be freed. Mary and Linda would never again walk the streets, so why should the ones who brutalized, raped, and killed them? Even death by lethal injection, in the very unlikely event they should get it, was not a fitting punishment. Mary and Linda had suffered horribly at their hands. They, likewise, should die horribly.

Henry had all of the money he would need to bring about a solution, but what was the solution? How would he find them? How could he catch them? What would he do with them once he had them? Henry wasn't a detective. He wasn't even sure how a detective went about looking for perpetrators, but he would find out in time.

A car passed Henry going what appeared to be over ninety miles per hour. It then cut in front of Henry so closely that he ran off the right shoulder to avoid being hit. The Cadillac slid sideways and then jolted back onto the blacktop. Henry fought for control of the car and finally won, though he left long rubber streaks on the pavement.

"Bastards," he growled through clenched teeth. "If I had a semi, I'd take care of you." The curses continued against the faceless driver for several moments, even when he was out of sight and probably three miles down the road.

Henry had never been the macho type, and violence was something he stayed far, far away from. As a matter of fact, he hadn't had a physical confrontation since he was fifteen years old. At that time, even though he had "whipped" the other kid initially, he lost in the end. When he turned to leave, the other kid hit him in the back of the head with a rock, and while Henry lay on the ground dazed, the kid had turned his face into a bloody mess.

Some people would call backing away from a fist fight cowardice. Henry called it good sense. There were ways to correct 'problems' other than by fists. Besides, after the last fight, Henry had decided that the only fair fight was the one you win, regardless of the way you went about it. Since that time, Henry had won a few without ever being touched. Like the kid who had beat him. Henry had ultimately won.

CHARLES ROBINSON

The kid, Rick Devericks, had just taken Dr. Greenstein's Lincoln to do a little joy riding. He'd done this before and with other peoples' cars. Along with others, his buddies, they'd hotwire a car and drive the backwoods half the night. Then, they would return the cars to where they were parked so the owners (unless they checked the mileage or gas gauge) never knew they had been moved. Henry had been out one night alone, as he often was in his youth, and saw Devericks turn up Layman's road in the Lincoln. Henry anonymously called the police, who caught him three miles outside of town. Devericks spent the next two years in a school for juvenile delinquents. Henry never told anyone what he had done, but he laughed his ass off when the kid got sent up.

Anyway, Henry reflected, with the guy who had just forced him off the road, if he had a semi, he would show the guy what force was. How would he like it if someone forced him over? Well, not just over but off the road and down the embankment. The thought grew slowly in his mind. But not a semi. A semi was too big and bulky and didn't have the acceleration. Maybe a car, a big car, a heavy car, modified. A car that would take a jolt with little or no damage. Like the one in that old TV series. What was it, 'Blackrider,' or something like that? Maybe not some miracle age Metal, or whatever that was supposed to be, but heavy, heavy steel, armored with special bumpers and seats and other amenities. "Maybe, just maybe . . ." Henry mused aloud. What else, a gun? Yeah, he'd need one of those. Maybe a stun gun. Probably weren't legal, but, "When guns are outlawed, only outlaws will have guns."

The thoughts skittered through Henry's mind as the miles flashed by. A car, weapons, a safe secluded place, not his home, to take the scum who killed his wife and daughter if, no when, he caught them. What would he need when he caught them, and he would get them, either before the police did or after the justice system was done with them. It might take a week or a month or a year. He didn't much care. He had time. What was the bumper sticker he had seen a few days ago? Resentments Kill? Well, maybe he was taking the slogan out of context, but he had a resentment, and when the time came, he would kill. Or would he? Could he?

16

It was ten o'clock in the evening when Henry got to Clarksville. Clarksville, Pennsylvania was not a large town. Just over five thousand people and nestled in a valley in the foothills of the Appalachians near the Allegheny national forest. Blaycock Manufacturing was its largest industry. The streets didn't roll up at dark as they did in a lot of smaller towns, but aside from some strip shops, a fast food joint, and a few lounges, in town activity was at a minimum.

Henry started to turn toward home then decided he wasn't quite ready to face that hurdle. He instead drove to Hobart's lounge on Pride Avenue. Parking and locking his car, he went inside the dimly lit bar and ordered a draft. He had had enough of the hard stuff to last him a while.

"Henry?"

Henry turned to see George Williams come up beside him. "Hello, George," he said, dreading the words he knew were coming from his boss. "God, Henry, we were really devastated at the office when we got the news. We are really sorry for your loss."

"Thanks, George." Henry didn't know what else to say in the situation as he didn't know what to say when someone else died. He respected George. He thought he was a relatively good vice president even though he didn't care for his overall management system. Right now, however, Henry didn't want to talk to anyone, at least on this subject. George patted his shoulder. "If there is anything we can do, I can do, you let me know."

Henry tried to smile, failed horribly, and suddenly realized George was as uncomfortable as he. "Thank you, George. I appreciate your thoughtfulness. I'll keep it in mind. By the way, I'll be in on Monday, but it may be to tell you I need more time." George shook his head but frowned, the wavy, gray, well-coiffed hair never moving. "Well, Henry, you've already been out over two months . . . but we'll discuss that on Monday." He put his hand on Henry's shoulder. Henry could tell he was not particularly enamored by his attire or the body odor he emitted after his two-month drinking binge. "I've got some people over at my table, so I have to get back. You're welcome to join us if you like."

17

Henry knew it was only a gesture and wondered what George would do if he accepted. "No thanks, George. I won't dampen your evening. I just wanted to stop in for a quiet drink. But, thanks anyway."

George moved away looking relieved. "All right, Henry, but remember, anything you need . . ."

Henry raised his hand in a half-hearted wave as George bustled back to his table. He probably just wanted to get away from the stench Henry exuded. Looking down, Henry thought, well I guess I can't blame him.

Henry sat at the bar for half an hour. Three more acquaintances came by to offer condolences. When the third went away, he paid his tab and left before someone had him crying. He knew he would have to endure this type of conversation for a while but certainly not all in one night.

He got his car, again started home and again changed his mind. Driving the four blocks to the police station, he decided he might as well get that over with if anyone cared at this time of evening. Parking his car in a spot that said Police Only, he went inside to the desk. The desk officer looked up with an expression that said, "Oh, God, let's not have a problem." Then, in a tired voice that matched the expression, said, "Yes, can I help you?" Henry thought, screw you too, and said, "Yes, I'm Henry Jenkins. I'm here to see Lieutenant Cameron if he's still here." "Oh, yes, Mr. Jenkins," the sergeant said, appearing a little more awake. "If you'll have a seat over there, I'll see if he's in." Henry nodded and walked across the room to sit in one of the hard plastic chairs not made for comfort. Twenty minutes later, an uncomfortable Henry was thinking about leaving when Lieutenant Cameron strode into the room looking slightly disheveled. "Good evening, Mr. Jenkins," Cameron said extending his hand. "Sorry for the delay. They had to reach me at home. Can't work all the time, you know. I've been by your house several times, but it seems no one knew where you were. Didn't it occur to you that you might be considered a suspect by leaving like that?" He looked at Henry's clothes and raised an eyebrow.

18

Henry looked up at the six-foot-three detective that looked more like a football player than a police officer. "No, I guess not. I just had to get away for a while . . . try to get my thoughts together. And, by the way, I apologize for the way I acted toward you before. I . . ."

Cameron waved his hand. "I can appreciate your thinking, Mr. Jenkins. Under the circumstances I may have said worse. But, thanks for the apology. Now, why don't you come to my office so we might discuss the situation."

Once at his desk, Cameron removed a notepad from a drawer and sat with pencil poised. "Now, Mr. Jenkins, may I call you Henry? I need to get some information from you since you were first on the scene. Let me explain, before I do that, that we have gone through your house thoroughly. We have dusted for fingerprints, and as much as we could, tried to piece things together to help us solve this crime." Henry nodded, looking down at his hands clasped between his knees. "Were you able to find anything useful?" Cameron shrugged his shoulders. "Well, they left no fingerprints, indicating they wore gloves. During the autopsy on your wife and daughter, we did find that one had long brown hair and a different individual had 'A' negative blood." Henry winced at the thought of the knives dissecting his beautiful wife and daughter. "And they couldn't have come from the same person?"

"No sir," Cameron shook his head. "We have done thorough DNA testing. Those tests indicate two different individuals. Unfortunately, those individuals are not in the system. As such, Henry, anything you can tell us at this point will be helpful."

Henry nodded, "Okay, how can I help?" "When was the last time you saw your wife a . . . When was the last time you talked to you wife?"

Henry thought back to his last conversation with Mary. "It was 3:58 p.m. on Friday." Cameron made a note on his pad. "How do you know the precise time?" "I leave work at four o'clock. I called home just before I left to let Mary know," a sob caught in Henry's throat, ". . . to let Mary know I was going to stop on my way home to buy Linda . . ." another catch in his voice, ". . . to buy Linda a birthday present. It was her birthday."

Cameron nodded. "Did she sound upset? Maybe like something was wrong?" Henry shook his head. "No. I would have noticed it in her voice." "All right, Henry. What time did you get home?" Henry sighed, choked back tears he felt might start any moment, and continued to stare at his hands. "I turned into my street at just about 5:30. Normally, I'm home by 4:30, but as I said, I stopped to buy the birthday present. He paused for several seconds. "God, if I had only gone straight home, I might have been able to . . ."

Cameron stopped writing for a second and interrupted him. "If you had been there, you may also have been killed. There was a .357 magnum used in the crime. I don't believe there is anything you could have done to stop it, and it would, in all probability, have resulted in your death as well." He let that soak in for a moment then said, "Lets continue if you can. Did you notice anything as you drove up to the house? See anyone suspicious?" Henry nodded. "A black van, customized. There was a Q-shaped dent in the front bumper under the left headlight. It had Pennsylvania tags, but I don't know the number." Cameron looked more interested. "What made you notice the van?" "I live at the end of a dead-end street. We're . . . I'm used to people turning in my drive, but the van was spinning its tires on my driveway, and it irritated me."

"All right, you said a Q-shaped dent? Explain that." "You know, a circle with a slash in the right side. I only noticed it because it was the only mark on the otherwise pristine vehicle."

Cameron continued to write in his note pad. "Do you know the make and year?" "It was a Dodge. I saw the emblem on the front, but I have no idea of the age. I don't know much about vans." Cameron wrote. "Single or dual headlights?"

"Two on each side." More note taking. "That means it's relatively old." He looked up from the notebook. "Okay. Any other features you may have noticed?" "Yeah, one more thing. It had heart-shaped windows near the back on the sides."

"Anything else?" "No. That's all I remember." "All right. Now if you can continue, what happened when you got home?"

Henry shook his head. "You probably know more than I do. I went in, saw the house was torn up. I went looking for my family. When I went into the bedroom, I tripped over a drawer and fell." Henry held up his casted arm. "That's how I got this. That's when I saw M-M-Mary." He stopped, breathed deeply, and continued. "She was on the far side of the bed on the floor. I picked her up and put her on the bed. And, I guess I pulled the sheet up over her legs. I knew she was d-d-dead. I went to look for Linda. I found her in the bathroom. She was alive . . ." Tears formed in Henry's eyes. ". . . alive when I found her. I took her in to her bed and tried to stop the bleeding while I called for help. She d-d-died while I was waiting."

Cameron sat quietly until Henry regained his composure. "I know this is difficult, and I'm sorry we have to do it, but just a couple of more questions, and I'll be done. Could you see how many people were in the van?" Henry, felt the resentment rise deep inside. "I'm not sure. The van only had the small windows in the back, so I couldn't see into there. The front windows were dark tinted, so I couldn't get any definition, but I could tell there were two people in the front seats. I guess there could have been more, though."

"All right, one more question. Try to think back. Do you recall any numbers or letters on the license plate?" Henry shook his head. "No, none. I've tried a hundred times to remember if I even looked at it for that reason. The only thing I can remember was it was a Pennsylvania tag."

"Do you recall if there was any tag on the front?" "I don't know. I just remember looking in my rear-view mirror in time to note it was a PA tag."

Cameron laid down his pencil. "All right, Henry. I'll need a list of any items missing from your home. And, I guess that's all I have for right now. Are you going to be in town if I need to get in touch or have a cell phone?"

Henry shook his head. "I don't know when I'll be in or out of town. If you need to get in touch with me, you can call my next-door neighbor. Her name is Sheila Mackenzie. I'll try to keep her posted as to where I am."

"Very good." Cameron put his note pad back in the desk drawer and slid it shut. "Unless you can think of anything else, I guess we're finished for now."

For the first time since the interview began, Henry sat back in his chair.

"As a matter of fact, I do have something on my mind, and I feel it is only fair to you to share it." Henry paused until Cameron sat back to listen. "You see, Lieutenant, when I came here this evening, I had every intention of lying to you and telling you I had seen nothing, knew nothing. While I was sitting there waiting, I decided I was going to give the bastards responsible for this a chance they never gave my wife or daughter. I'm going to give you a chance to catch them before I do."

Cameron leaned forward, and Henry held up his hand. "Let me talk. I'm not going to sit on my laurels while you do your investigation. I'm going to be looking for them too. I'll use every avenue and every cent I have to find them first. I have well over a million dollars from an inheritance plus what I've made through investments, which is sizeable. I don't mind spending it all to make sure that scum never walks the street again."

"As I said, I'm giving those two, if it was two, a chance they never gave my wife and child. I figure if you get them first and they stand trial, they may go to prison. Without the death penalty, they might get life, about seven years or, with a good lawyer, two or three years for manslaughter if they are convicted at all. If they get life, they probably have seven years before it's my turn. Less I get them sooner. Whichever the case, when the justice system is done with them, it's my turn. I will make sure they never walk the streets or do anything like this again."

Cameron started to say something, but Henry held up his hand again. "Let me finish, and then you can talk. If I get to them first they will never come to trial. I will give them the justice they deserve. I may even let them live, but if they live, they will spend every day of the rest of their lives feeling what Mary and Linda must have felt before they died."

Looking at Henry, Cameron sighed. "Mr. Jenkins, I want these people as much as you do. I would like to see them get a death sentence. I'd like to be that Eastwood fellow and blow them away, but we can't do that. If you take the law into your own hands, then I'll be after you. You'll go to prison with, or instead, of them. Is that what you want?"

"No," Henry said, "that's not what I want. What I want is the legal system to be just, but it isn't. I want the ACLU to protect the victims and not the criminals, but they don't. Look at the record. How many criminals get nothing more than a slap on the wrist because they have, and I use the term loosely, good lawyers or deep pockets? How many cases are dismissed because of some bullshit technicality? How many are back on the streets in just months or a few years only to do the same or worse?

"My wife and baby were brutalized and raped before they were killed, Lieutenant. Is your legal system even going to come close to making the punishment fit the crime? Don't bullshit me, Lieutenant. What are the chances of the punishment being even one-tenth the severity of the crime? What about the recidivism rate? What is it, 80 percent? So much for rehabilitation."

Cameron quietly shook his head. "I won't kid you Mr. Jenkins. I know the justice system can leave something to be desired. The police want better enforcement too. However, I don't want you to be the one we're out there hunting. Besides, what you are proposing is a premediated act, and for that, the punishment is worse."

Henry stood to leave. "Are you saying what they did to my family was not premediated? That they were out for an afternoon drive and, on the spur of the moment, robbed, brutalized, raped, and killed two innocent people? And that on a seventy-five degree day, they just happened to be wearing gloves?"

Henry walked to the door and turned. "I'll get you the list of things missing from the house as you requested, probably in a couple of days." Cameron nodded. "Thank you, Mr. Jenkins . . . Henry." He paused. "Just think it over. It's not worth it." Henry opened the door. "Then you find them first, Lieutenant." He turned and strode from the station.

# CHAPTER 3

After leaving the police station, Henry stopped, picked up a pint of bourbon, and drank half of it. When he pulled up in front of his garage, he was starting to feel the effects of the alcohol.

Maybe this was good. It would help take the edge off. But, he didn't want to get drunk. If he got drunk, he'd just sit and cry and bemoan his losses. He needed to be straight to accomplish some chores. Henry grabbed the keys from the ignition, walked quickly to the front door, opened it, and went in before he changed his mind again.

He flipped on the light and closed the door, looking around him. The living room and what he could see of the dining room were spotlessly clean. Thank you, crime scene clean-up and neighbors. He walked slowly through the downstairs, noticing that the rooms were neat again. They looked just as Mary always kept them. Dreading what came next, he walked up the stairs, though he really didn't want to. In fact, he hated to go but knew that he must.

Henry was at the landing when the doorbell rang. It felt as if a weight was lifted off him as he went back down the steps to answer it. When he opened the door, Sheila MacKenzie put her arms around his neck and started crying against his shoulder.

He held her, letting her cry. Tears came to his own eyes as she said over and over, "Oh Henry. I'm so sorry." Sheila and her husband had moved next door to the Jenkins three years ago. She and Mary had been very close friends. Mary had also been aware of the problems between Sheila and Bob, her now ex-husband. They had gotten a divorce about a year ago. Henry liked Sheila. Not only was she pretty but also intelligent with a good sense of humor. He, Mary, and Sheila had spent many evenings together, either out or just sitting at home watching T.V. Sheila was never an unwelcome guest. He gently stroked her back until her sobs quieted to an occasional hiccup. Giving her a gentle squeeze, he held her back at arm's length. "You don't have to say anything, Sheila. There's nothing to say. We both know and care and hurt because of it. We'll both get through it, one day at a time."

"Thank you for coming over, I really don't want to be here alone. Also, thanks for cleaning up. I don't think that I could have come back to the way it was." Sheila hiccupped again and said, "Oh, Henry..." and was silent. Henry took her hand. "Will you go upstairs with me please? I guess I'm a little apprehensive about going alone."

Sheila nodded, and they went up the steps to the second floor. He noticed that the battered bathroom door had been removed, but he didn't ask where it went. He gave a labored sigh and squeezed Sheila's hand. They walked down the hall to his and Mary's . . . no . . . his bedroom. He looked at the door for what seemed to be several minutes but was actually a few seconds. Taking a deep breath, he opened the door. He didn't know what he expected to see, but the room was neat, almost sterile. The carpeting was gone, exposing the hardwood floor beneath.

Sheila let him survey the room, and then in a slightly more than a whisper said, "We had to take the carpet out Henry. It . . . it was . . . we couldn't get the stains out. Oh, Henry. I'm so sorry . . . " and she began to cry again, burying her face against his chest.

He consoled her. "Sheila, you did just fine. You did everything just right. I will never be able to thank you enough or repay you. Come on, let's go back downstairs." He took her hand, and they walked back to the living room.

"I can't stay here, Sheila. I'm going to get some clothes. God knows

I need some. Then, I'm going to a motel. Would you wait here until I grab a couple of things from upstairs?"

Sheila squeezed his arm. "I'll get them for you if you want. It might be easier."

"No, I know what I want. Just give me a couple of minutes." He returned to the bedroom and got a suitcase and hanging bag. He quickly filled them with suits, slacks, shirts, shoes, underwear, and other necessities. Zipping the bags shut, he carried them both downstairs.

Sheila was still standing where he had left her. She looked up. "Henry, why don't you stay at my house tonight? It's late, and you don't need to be alone."

Henry smiled at her. "I appreciate the thought, Sheila. But I really shouldn't."

Sheila took the hanging bag with his suits in it. "Don't worry about the neighbors. I would hope they aren't that narrow-minded, although as we discussed before, they probably are. Come on anyway. You can go to a motel in the morning." Henry conceded. "Okay, if you're sure that I won't be putting you out."

Sheila shook her head. "Don't be silly. You know better."

With each of them carrying a suitcase, Henry closed and locked the house. They walked across the lawns to Sheila's house, and fifteen minutes later, they were sitting in her kitchen drinking coffee. Henry related as much of his last two months as he could remember and then told her about his trip to the police station for questioning. He omitted what he had told Cameron after the questioning, as well as his thoughts on the road as he was driving back to Clarksville. He knew that he could have told Sheila about his plans and she would go along with him. But for now, anyway, and until he could better formulate his plans, it was best that he just let it go. Maybe he'd tell her later. Maybe never.

Henry glanced at his watch. It was 2:15 in the morning. "What the heck are you doing up so late? Do you know what time it is?" Sheila smiled looking like a scolded child.

"I knew that you had to come home sometime. I just didn't want you to be alone, at least not for the first night. Besides even though I was already in bed, I couldn't sleep well so when I saw your car I came over."

Henry took her hand and squeezed gently. "You're sweet, but you know that." She smiled. "You're nuts, but then we know that." Her smile changed to a troubled frown. "I guess I shouldn't be joking now . . . I mean . . ."

Henry shook his head and interrupted her. "No, maybe that's just what we both need. Maybe we should get drunk and have an Irish wake. I expect that I've cried and cursed and been depressed for long enough. You make me laugh, and I love you for it."

Sheila smiled again. "I guess you're right. I just don't want you to think I'm being callous." "I know how you felt about Mary and Linda better than anyone else. I know, too, how much Mary liked you. I would never think you callous. The three of us had some terrific times together. I just hope, since things have changed, that we don't lose sight of those times and our friendship."

"We never will, Henry. You're stuck with me, I guess."

Henry smiled. "Good. I wouldn't have it any other way."

Sheila fixed them another cup of coffee, and Henry remembered the bottle in his jacket. He retrieved it and poured some whiskey into each cup. "Takes the edge off," he said. "Helps you sleep."

Sheila sipped hers and looked over at Henry. "What now? What do you plan to do?"

Henry set his cup down and held up his left arm. "First, I get this damn cast off my arm. Then, I really don't know for sure. I have some thoughts muddling around in my head, but that's all they are, just thoughts. Considering the time, I think I need to take a shower and get some sleep. Probably wouldn't hurt you either." Henry smile. "The sleep, I mean, and not the shower." "Come on. I'll show you where you're sleeping, and you make yourself at home. I mean that."

He finished his coffee, and they stood. "I know that, and thanks." They carried his luggage into the bedroom, and Sheila left to go to her own room. He found clean underwear among the things he had thrown into the suitcase and went into the bathroom. He shaved and was just getting ready to undress when there was a knock on the door. He pulled it open and Sheila stood there. Not looking directly at him, she held out a plastic bag and rubber band. Henry laughed. "I'm dressed."

Sheila turned toward him and blushed. "I thought that you might need this." Henry took the offering and stared at it. "What's it for?"

"To put over your cast," she replied. "So it doesn't get wet while you're in the shower."

"Hey, thanks. Good idea." Henry closed the door, stripped, donned the plastic bag, and showered. When he came out of the bathroom, he saw the light under Sheila's bedroom door. He went softly into his own room and closed the door. The cool sheets felt good against his skin. He pulled them up around him, feeling the tiredness brought about by the long drive and even longer day. Moments later, he slept.

In his dream, the black van pulled up beside him, crowding him toward the edge of the road and the cliff. Over the edge, he noted the menacing rocks far below. He fought to pull back onto the road, but the van was pushing against the side of the car. As his car started over the edge of the abyss, he looked up at the window of the van. All he saw was a huge grin, like that of the Cheshire cat from Alice in Wonderland. Henry awoke, startled. A cold sweat ran from his forehead. He lay thinking about the house next door. He no longer wanted it and didn't want to even look at it. He lay in bed staring into the darkness and conceiving a plan. Switching on the bedside light, he glanced at his watch, 4:30 a.m. It was probably at least an hour before daylight. He slipped out of bed and rummaged through his clothes. He donned jeans, a sweatshirt, and sneakers. Walking softly down the hall so he wouldn't wake Sheila, he went into the kitchen and slipped quietly out the back door. Before he pulled the door shut, he flipped the latch to open so he could get back in when he had finished next door.

Going quickly across the back lawns, Henry realized for the first time that the October air had a definite coolness in it. He opened the back door to the garage and felt his way around Mary's Buick in the dark. He didn't want to turn on the lights. Found what he was looking for. It was a two and a half gallon plastic gas can, almost full. Going from the garage through the connecting door to the kitchen, he went down the kitchen stairs to the basement. There, he turned on a dim light over his workbench.

The small workroom of his basement had not been ransacked by the intruders, so Henry felt relatively sure that no one would question him on how the gas can got there. He got a small pan from under the workbench and poured it half full of gasoline. Into this, he set a lawn mower carburetor. He picked up the can of gasoline. Then, a thought came into his mind. He set down the can and ran upstairs.

Locating the thermostat for the furnace in the darkened hallway, he rolled the dial back and forth several times. Listening to the furnace ignite, then go out, ignite, then go out. He rolled the dial back until he heard it shut off, then past the shut off about five degrees. Satisfied with the setting, he went back to the basement and got the gas can. He poured a line of gasoline from the furnace and across the basement into the workshop. He then poured gasoline liberally on the workbench. Surveying his work, he sat the can on the bench and hastily went back upstairs. He started for the door then remembered something. Running to the living room, he jammed his leg against the coffee table in the darkness. Cursing, he rounded the table and grabbed the two photo albums from the bookcase. Limping, his leg hurt like hell. Henry retraced his steps to the back door and closed the door behind him, making sure it was locked. Suddenly, he remembered the safe in their bedroom, but decided that since it was fireproof, it was okay. He disregarded going back in to empty it. Besides, he didn't know how long it would be until the furnace clicked on.

When he reached the border between his lawn and Sheila's, he turned and stared at the house for a long time. As he stood, tears welled up in his eyes. He clutched the photo albums to his chest, breathing in the cold night air. "Mary . . . Linda . . ." he said no louder than a whisper. "They'll pay. If it takes the rest of my life, they'll pay. Goodbye, darlings."

Henry turned and hurried to Sheila's back door. He slipped in, locked the door, and returned to his bedroom, turning on the light. He placed both photo albums in the suitcase under his clothes and closed the cover. Then, he shed his clothes and sneakers and climbed back between the sheets.

He was reaching for the light switch when there was a light knock on the door. "Come in." Sheila opened the door and stuck her head around. "Are you okay? I was going to the bathroom and saw your light on."

Henry smiled. "Just couldn't sleep, I guess I was laying here thinking."

Sheila looked at him sorrowfully. "Would you like some company for a while?"

Henry nodded. "Sure, that sounds good."

Sheila motioned toward the light. "Why don't you turn that off. I don't have too much on."

Henry turned off the light and heard her footsteps pad across the floor. Then, he felt her wright as she slid into the bed beside him. She drew up next to him, and he put his arm around her, realizing that she was nude. "Don't think me horrid, Henry, but if you need me, you may."

He kissed her forehead and hugged her to him, caressing her back. "I love you for that, and I hope that the offer holds for the future. Right now, just let me hold you."

Sheila nestled into his arms, putting her head against his chest. They both slept. It was 5:25 a.m.

At 6:05, there was a muffled explosion at 325 Euclid Street, the big house at the end of the road. No one heard the explosion.

At 6:35, Ed Bell walked out of his house to go hunting and saw the flames breaking through the upper floor and the roof. When the firetrucks came to the end of the street at 6:47 a.m., the sirens woke up Henry and Sheila. Dressing quickly, they went out and watched as the fire was slowly, and much, much too late, brought under control. By the time the fire was out, the roof and second story, as well as the main floor, were gone. Henry had tears in his eyes as he realized that now it was all gone. The Fire Chief told Henry how sorry he was, but "if only we had been called sooner."

Henry waved it away. "It's not your fault." Later, the fire investigator told him, "May never know what caused it. It appears to have started in the lower part of the house, probably the kitchen. But it's so far gone . . ."

Henry sat in the living room at Sheila's sometime later. She brought him a cup of coffee and sat beside him. "Henry, you have nothing left now. Nothing to remember them by."

He shook his head. "Well, at least I have the photo albums." Then, reflecting on what he had said, he quickly added, "I got them when I went over before."

Sheila looked at him quizzically and sipped her coffee. She sat quietly for a long while. Then said, "Henry?"

Henry sighed. She knew. "Yes."

"I don't know how to ask this, but . . ." She paused, and Henry let her search for the words, ". . . did you . . . what I'm asking is, when did you get the albums? I mean, when we were straightening up the house they were in . . ." Her voice trailed off.

Henry sat for a moment reflecting on the situation. Would she understand . . . really understand? Henry sighed and decided that she would. "I don't think that's your question. You're trying to ask if I had something to do with the house burning down, aren't you?"

"Well," Sheila replied, "It's just that I saw, I saw . . . Yes, I guess it is."

Henry took her hand in his. She gripped his and looked at him. "I was lying in bed last night. A bad dream had woke me up. I lay there thinking about Mary and Linda and what happened. I was thinking about how I hadn't wanted to go to the house and didn't want to be in it once I was there. And while I was lying there, I knew that feeling would be there every time I walked through the door."

Sheila squeezed his hand. "But why not just sell it?"

Henry smiled. The smile looked tired. "That was Mary's house, Sheila. If, and maybe it was stupid reasoning, I sold it, every time I saw it, I would be reminded of that. I don't want to be reminded. Now, if I look up, and another house is there, I won't have that thought. Do you understand?"

Sheila put her arms around him and hugged him. "Yes, I do. The way you put it, it sounds like a nice gesture." She then leaned back in the chair, concern crossing her face. "But, what if they find out?"

Henry shook his head. "They won't. I was talking to the Fire Marshall. He thinks it started in the kitchen. But even if they find the cause, I have an explanation. Don't you be concerned. But, I do have a request. May I stay here with you for a few days, just until I find a place?"

"You know you don't have to ask that," she said in mock anger. "Of course you can. You can stay as long as you want."

Henry kissed her cheek. "You're a sweetheart, but I've got some things to do, and this would not be a good place to do them from."

Sheila again looked concerned. "You're going to try to find them, aren't you?"

Henry laughed. "Very perceptive, my dear Watson . . ."

"Henry, I don't think you should . . ."

"Uh-uh," Henry quieted her.

"But you might get ki—"

Henry put his fingers against her lips. "Sheila, I won't try to explain why nor how. But, I've got an idea. I won't be in danger. This is just something that, as insane as it sounds, I'm going . . . I have to do. Please try to understand. I know you can't understand, just believe in me."

"Henry, I do believe in you, but I don't understand . . ."

Henry interrupted. "That's all I ask now. Let's not hear any more about it."

The rest of the day was taken up with phone calls to his insurance company. An insurance adjuster came by to look at the remains of the house. He went for a quick appointment to his doctor to have that infernal cast off of his left wrist. After that, there were calls to his life insurance company to get the policies and paperwork together for Mary and Linda. Overall, the day took an emotional toll on Henry, and he was glad when the clock finally told him he could go to bed.

# CHAPTER 4

The clock said 9:30 a.m. Henry rolled out of bed and, after showering and dressing, went into the kitchen where Sheila had a cup of coffee waiting for him.

"Good morning," he said. "Sorry I slept so late."

"Oh, it's not late," Sheila replied. "Besides, I just got up a few minutes ago. Would you like some breakfast?"

"No thanks," Henry said as he sipped his coffee. "Maybe later. I want to take care of some things today, and I need to get started."

Sheila looked at Henry inquisitively. "May I ask what they are?"

Henry shook his head. "It's best you don't. It's either I don't tell you, or I lie, and I don't want to lie to you."

Sheila took a drink of her coffee. "Anything I can help with?"

Henry smiled at her persistence. "I've got some shopping to do, but it's shopping by phone. I hope you don't mind."

Sheila saw the conversation was at an end even though she was worried. "No, of course not. While you're doing that, I'll fix some breakfast."

Henry got his wallet out. "I've got a better idea. I'm going to be quite a while on the phone. Why don't you go shopping?" He handed her a couple of credit cards. "And when I'm done, we'll go out for something to eat."

Sheila looked at the charge cards she now held in her hand. "What are these for?"

Henry smiled. "They're unlimited. Enjoy yourself."

Sheila smiled in return. "How do you know I won't break you?"

"Either I trust you, or I'm really naïve. Now scoot. I'll be the one here."

Sheila went down the hall toward the bedroom and, twenty minutes later, came back with her coat on and her car keys in hand. She smiled as she went by Henry, who was pushing buttons on his phone. "I'll be back in a couple of hours."

Henry nodded as she went out closing the door and heard the connection being made at his brother's house in Denver.

A woman's voice came on the line. "Hello?"

"Hello, Midge. This is Henry. Is Fred home?" He looked at his watch—10:00.

"Oh, hi Henry," the phone said. "How are you?" Her voice sounded condescending as it usually did when Henry called.

"Fine," Henry replied. He didn't much like phones and liked Midge less. "Is Fred home?"

Ignoring his question, Midge continued, "How is Mary and your girl?"

Henry hadn't notified them, and apparently, it wasn't news worthy in Denver.

"Is Fred Home, Midge?"

Midge was persistent. "But haven't you talked to her?"

"For God's sake, Midge, is Fred home or not?"

"Just a minute, Henry, I was just trying to be nice."

Or nosey, Henry thought. "Please, put Fred on."

Henry didn't like Midge. She was a domineering, opinionated bitch who only valued her own opinion to Henry's way of thinking. Her normally condescending attitude was more than he cared to tolerate.

"Hello, Hank." Fred came on the line with his usual gusto. "Wasn't expecting to hear from you. What's happening?" Fred had always called Henry Hank though no one else did.

"Hi, Fred. Sorry I haven't been in touch. Just a lot on my plate. Anyway, I have a desire, shall we say, to have some unusual work done on a car for me and wondered if you might know anyone?"

"Well, maybe," Fred replied. "What is it you're looking to have done?"

"I'm really not sure, Fred, and don't know if what I'm thinking is just a pipe dream. I can give you a general idea though. I'm looking for someone who can mold heavy metal, do extensive wiring, knows electronics, and so on."

"Damn, Hank," Fred sounded perplexed. "Let me think for a minute." There was silence on the phone, and Henry glanced at his 'wish' list. He didn't want to tell Fred about his crusade. The less anyone knew, the better it was.

Fred's voice came back on the line. "I might know a couple of places you can get that type of thing done, Henry. I don't know if any one place can do it all. The only thing is they're out here."

Henry shrugged his shoulders as if Fred could see him. "That's fine. I can come out there for a while if needed. I just need you to give me the names and phone numbers, so I can call those places and make an appointment. I'd hate to come out and find they couldn't do what I want."

"Okay, Henry, let me look here for a minute."

Henry heard rustling over the phone and figured Fred was going through the phone book.

"What's the matter, Hank? Decide to spend some of that money you've been hoarding away on a new toy? Or are you slipping into your second childhood?"

Henry laughed. "Yeah, I guess you could say that. To use a worn out cliché, 'You can't take it with you.'"

"Well," Fred asked, "if you come out this way, you will stay with us, won't you?"

"Fred," Henry voiced his reservations, "you know Midge and I don't get along. No, I'll see you if I come out that way, but it would be better if I stay at a motel. Midge and I get along better the less we see each other."

"Yeah, I know," Fred replied. "Wishful thinking on my part. I just wish you two got along better. Oh, here's that number. Got a pencil handy?"

Henry poised the pen over the paper. "Yes, go ahead."

Fred relayed the information to Henry then said, "By the way, that first name I gave you, Frank, the metal and body work guy. He may be a bit shady. Not that he'd cheat you, but he has been known to bend the law a bit. Does damned good work, though, if he doesn't go to jail in the middle of it."

Henry nodded to the phone. "Okay, Fred. Thanks. Listen, if I decide to come out, I'll give you a call when I get there."

"Yeah, fine," Fred responded. "It'll be good to see you." Pause, "Sure you can't tell me what's going on?"

"Yeah, I'm sure. Not now anyway. Perhaps later, all right?"

"Okay, Hank. Give me a call." The line disconnected.

Henry set the receiver back in its cradle and rejoiced at his good fortune. Fred had said the guy was shady, and that's just what he needed. If, that is, the guy could also keep his mouth shut. Well, Henry would find out. He picked up the receiver and dialed the second number Fred had given him, drumming the pen against his knee while waiting for a reply. He was ready to hang up after seven rings when the line connected at the other end.

"Baker Electronics. May I help you?"

"Hello, and perhaps," Henry said. "I need some information on having an electronic display board installed in a car. Could you connect me with someone that does that sort of work?"

"Just a moment," the phone replied. "I'll connect you."

A man's voice answered almost immediately. "May I help you?"

"I'm hoping you might. I'm interested in having an electronic message board installed in my car. Can you do that?" Henry asked.

"Well, sir, could you be more specific?"

"Sure," Henry replied. "On several buildings around here there are digital electronic message boards where the message either flashes on and off or seems to run across the board from right to left. Do you know what I mean?"

"Yes, sir," came the response. "You say you want it in a car?"

"That's what I said," Henry stated, slightly annoyed. "I want the display board across the back window with three to four inch lettering and the programming board or control panel where the driver can reach it. Can you do that?"

The voice at the other end chuckled. "Yes, sir. But it will be expensive."

"I'm not asking the expense," Henry said, annoyed. "Could you give me an educated guess or a W.A.G. on the cost?"

"Well, sir, what type of car do you want this in?"

Henry hadn't thought about the car. "Let's say a Buick or a Cadillac."

"Just a moment, I'll give you a guesstimate." The phone went dead as Henry drummed the pen against his knee, growing impatient. After what seemed an exorbitant amount of time, the connection was reestablished.

"Sir, you must know that this is a very rough estimate, but I would guess about two, maybe three, thousand dollars depending on the vehicle."

That sounded high to Henry, but with installation, it might be that much.

"Okay, that would have to be firmed up before the work is done. And you're sure you can do it?"

"Yes, sir," was the response. "Of course, it may take some time. By the way, what company is this for?"

"This is for personal use, not a company." Henry knew what was coming next.

"I see. Then, of course, the work will have to be paid for in advance."

"Of course. I understand. I'll check back with you in a couple of days if I want you to do the work. Do I need an appointment?"

"Yes, sir. Just a moment." There was a pause. "When would you like to come in?"

Henry thought about prior needs. He would have to talk to the other guy Fred had told him about, buy a car, go to Denver (not necessarily in that order), and then make a decision. "Would next Friday be all right?"

"That's fine," came the response. "About ten a.m.?"

"That sounds good right now," Henry said. "I'll let you know if that changes."

"Good enough. Can I have your name?"

"He ... Harold Daniels," Henry said quickly regrouping his thoughts. He didn't know that providing his own name would be prudent, and he would be paying cash for the service anyway, so his name wasn't important.

"Very well, Mr. Daniels. We will see you Friday."

"Goodbye." Henry disconnected the call. That part was started, but if he couldn't get the rest, it wasn't worth a tinker's dam.

He picked up the phone and dialed the first of the numbers Fred had given him.

"Frank's."

Damn, couldn't people answer a telephone properly anymore? What happened to 'Hello?' What happened to, 'This is so and so's business?'

"Hello?" Henry waited.

There were a few moments of silence then, "Yeah? This is Frank's Metal and Auto. You need something?"

Henry hoped this was not the person he would have to deal with. "Yes. May I speak with the proprietor, please?"

"Yeah, buddy. Just a minute."

Henry ran his fingers through his hair, and as a thought came to him, he added another item to his list.

"Hello. This is Frank. May I help you?"

At least this guy sounded a little more intelligent than the first one. "Yes, sir. I was referred to you by a friend who told me you might be able to do some extensive—shall I say—remodeling on a car for me."

"Well, that depends on what you want done and the amount you are willing to pay for it," came the reply.

"Of course," Henry said. "I'd prefer not to get into details on the phone, but I can give you an idea of what I want, and if you feel you can do it, I'll come out there and go through everything with you."

Henry picked up the list he had written and ran his eyes over the items. "All right, I need the body replaced with something like quarter to half inch metal, maybe thicker, but still looks like the original. I would need something like three inch thick bumpers mounted on hydraulic struts that can extend them out about eighteen inches. Also, I would want a couple of tanks mounted in the trunk or maybe under the rear seat. The tanks would need to have control switches that would allow them to be opened from the driver's seat to dump the contents on the ground behind the rear wheels."

Henry looked down the list and decided that was enough for the moment. "That gives you an idea of what I'm looking for. I can tell you more when or if we meet face to face. When these things are done, the car has to look as it did when I brought it in. Do you think you can do it?"

"Sure, we can do it," Frank said. "The question is do you want to spend as much as it will cost?" There was a chuckle on the line. "Sounds like a 'James Bond' car."

"Well," Henry said, ignoring Frank's last statement. "I'm sure we can come to a figure that will be acceptable to both of us if we decide to do this. As I said, however, there are additional items I would want that we can discuss later. I do have a question, though. What type of vehicle would be the easiest to work with?"

"That depends on the other items you want." Frank responded. "If I might make a suggestion, why don't you come in next week, say Monday, and we'll discuss it."

"Yes," Henry replied. "I suppose that is the best idea. Very well, Monday it is." Then, as an afterthought, "I can assume everything is payable in advance?"

"Yes, but we will discuss that on Monday as well. Now, can I get a name to go with this?"

"Oh, of course. Daniels, Harold Daniels," Henry said.

"Very good, Mr. Daniels, I'll expect you Monday, say around ten o'clock. I may need some references, by the way."

Henry winced. "I'm sure we can work that out as well. I'll see you Monday. Goodbye."

Henry put the phone down and leaned back on the sofa, crossing his ankles on top of the coffee table. Then, remembering he wasn't home, put his feet back on the floor and picked up the phone book.

Thumbing through the book, he found the number he wanted and punched in the appropriate buttons on the phone.

"United Airlines. May we help you?"

"Yes, thank you," Henry said. "I would like to make reservations for a round trip flight to Denver, Colorado."

"Of course, sir. And when would you be flying with us?"

"I'll be flying out on Sunday if that's available."

"Just a moment, please." The phone went to music, and a moment later, the pleasant voice came back on. "Sir, we have a flight to Denver leaving at 10:05 Sunday morning."

"That's fine," Henry said and gave the voice on the phone the information requested and a credit card number.

"You will pick up your boarding pass at the arrival counter. It is suggested you arrive two hours early to assure you will get through to your gate in time."

"Very good," Henry said, "and have a nice day."

"Thank you, sir. Goodbye."

Henry hung up the phone and went to the bedroom. Removing his bank books from his suitcase, he sorted through them and found one that had First National Bank of Clarksville printed on it. He flipped through it to the total, $382,110.47. Probably not enough, but it would do for now. He closed the book, slipped it into his pocket, and went to the mirror to assure he was presentable.

Deciding his reflection was good enough, he dumped his change and keys into his pockets. Switching off the lights, he went out of the house, locking the door behind him.

Walking across the lawn toward the car, he remembered he had not left Sheila a note. No problem. He probably wouldn't be gone that long anyway.

He opened the door to his car and got in, looking at the soot and ash that covered his car. Starting the engine, he backed out of the drive and headed for the bank on Danville Drive. He would have the car washed later.

# CHAPTER 5

The bank loomed ahead, and Henry slowed, put on his right turn signal, and entered the parking area. Pulling his car into a slot, he turned off the ignition and, locking the door, went into the bank. Going up to a teller's window, the middle-aged, pleasant-looking woman gave him a polite smile. "How may I help you?"

Henry returned the smile and withdrew his account book from his pocket and slid it toward her. "Yes. I would like to withdraw my savings from this account, please."

The teller took the book, opened it, and looked at Henry. "All right, Mr. Jenkins, how much would you like to withdraw?"

"All of it," Henry replied.

The teller gave him a tight smile. "If you will wait just a moment, sir."

She left Henry standing at the counter and disappeared through a door at the end of the counter. A few moments later, she reappeared and beckoned Henry. "Could you come with me, Mr. Jenkins?"

Henry walked behind her through the door she had previously taken and followed her into an office.

"Mr. Randolph, this is Mr. Jenkins. Mr. Jenkins," she turned to Henry, "Mr. Randolph will help you with your transaction." She gave Henry another tight smile and left the room.

"Mr. Jenkins," Randolph said, holding Henry's bank book in his hand and displaying a mouth full of false teeth and a very bad excuse for a toupee. "Would you take a seat, please?" He pointed to the two chairs on the opposite side of his desk. Henry didn't want to sit, but he knew, with the size of the withdrawal he wanted to make, there were certain preliminaries and procedures that had to be followed, and he didn't want to spend all day here standing.

He sat down in the brown vinyl-covered chair that matched the rest of the brown vinyl-covered office and crossed his legs.

"Now, Mr. Jenkins, I understand we want to make a sizeable withdrawal. May I ask why?"

I don't know about WE, but I know I do, Henry thought. To Randolph he said, "My reason doesn't concern the bank, sir."

"No, sir, Mr. Jenkins," Randolph said looking slightly embarrassed. "I didn't mean to imply that it did. It is just that we want to assure that it is not a problem with the bank or that you are in any way being coerced in any way to withdraw such a large amount."

Henry knew his last statement was uncalled for, but he couldn't resist it. Showing more tact now in answering the obviously embarrassed Randolph, he replied, "No, sir. The service with the bank has been excellent." He didn't know if that was true or not. He never came into the bank except when he opened the account, always made his deposits through the night deposit drawer, and had never made any withdrawals. "I just have some personal business that will take a great deal of cash, and your bank is closest to my home. Let me assure you, Mr. Randolph, I will transfer money back into the account as soon as possible."

"Yes, yes, of course." Randolph sounded somewhat, if not totally, appeased. "Well, Mr. Jenkins, we'll need you to sign some documents, and I will need your identification." He added quickly, "Just a formality, you understand."

Henry smiled, "Yes, of course. I understand."

Randolph pushed a button on the intercom on his desk. "Miss Philips, could you bring me a triplicate withdrawal form for Henry Jenkins, account number F3071163, please."

The intercom answered, and Randolph released the button.

Henry took his wallet from his pocket and removed his driver's license, two credit cards, social security card, and his concealed carry permit. "I trust this will suffice?"

Randolph looked at the cards, more the signatures than anything else, and said, "Yes, fine. This will do nicely."

Henry watched a mini-skirt-clad girl bring the forms in, lay them on the desk, and retreat. Randolph confirmed the information on the forms and handed them to Henry.

"If you would sign these, please, we will get you your money. Any particular denominations?"

Henry shook his head. "The bigger, the better."

Randolph watched Henry sign the necessary forms then said, "Two things. Do you have something to carry it in?"

Henry nodded. "I have a briefcase in my car. I'll get it while you clear things here."

"Fine," Randolph replied. "And secondly, do you have, or would you like an escort when you leave?"

"I don't believe so," Henry answered negatively. Then to appease the banker, he said, "Perhaps to my car. That will be good enough."

Henry stood and walked out of the bank to his car. He emptied the contents of the briefcase on the passenger seat and, locking the car, returned to the bank going directly to Randolph's office.

Randolph, on the telephone, motioned Henry to sit down.

"Yes, that's fine. Large bills, thank you. Very well." He put the phone back in its cradle and turned to Henry.

"Your money is on the way, Mr. Jenkins." He slid Henry's license and other cards across the desk, and Henry returned them to his wallet. Luckily, the wait was short, and in a few minutes, the door opened and a bank official and a bank guard entered the room.

"Ah, here we are," Randolph said. Standing and going around the desk, he took the container with the money and thanked the bank official who nodded and left the room, closing the door behind him.

The guard stood at the door while Randolph counted out the bills, placing the wrapped bills into Henry's briefcase. "Three hundred eighty two thousand five hundred three dollars and ninety-two cents."

"Correct," Henry said, doing some fast mental calculations in his head. That is the figure he came up with after adding the current interest. Closing the case and picking it up, he turned and shook hands with Randolph. "Thank you, sir. It has been a pleasure."

Randolph smiled. "We will look forward to future business with you, Mr. Jenkins."

He took Henry's arm and led him to the door. "The guard will escort you to your car."

Henry thanked him again and followed the guard through the bank and out to his car. He unlocked the door, got in, and thanked the guard who tipped his hat and walked back to the bank.

After locking his door and looking around, Henry opened the briefcase and reinserted the previously removed papers and documents he had dumped on the seat back into the case. He then closed and locked the case and placed it on the floor in front of the passenger seat.

Starting the car, he pulled away from the bank and drove back to Sheila's house.

# CHAPTER 6

Henry pulled into the driveway just behind Sheila as she was returning home and getting out of her car. She waited while he parked, got his briefcase, left the car, and walked around to her.

She smiled and said, "When I came back and saw your car gone, I thought you were trying to get out of buying me breakfast."

Henry smiled in return. "Dream on, kid. You couldn't be so lucky."

Sheila held out her keys. "Since you've only got one hand free, why don't you open the front door, and I'll bring in the packages."

Henry, assenting, took the keys and, going ahead, opened the front door. He held the storm door as Sheila came in with several totes. "I wanted to spend more," she smiled, "but I ran out of time."

Henry laughed. "Why do you think I said two hours? I didn't want to go broke."

Sheila smiled as Henry sat the briefcase on the coffee table. "Want to see what I bought?"

Henry sat down on the sofa. "Sure. Are you going to model it for me?"

Sheila started removing the clothing from the bags and boxes. "If you would like, but for the most part, I don't think they would look real good on me."

She started laying out her purchases: slacks, sweaters, shirts, suits, socks, underwear, shoes, and toiletries. All men's.

Henry looked more and more displeased as the unveiling took place.

"I really expected you to go shopping for you, not me."

Sheila got a pouting expression on her face. "I was hoping you would be happy. Besides, I have everything I need, and yours got burned up in the fire."

Henry shook his head. "Why do I feel like I'm on the losing end of this conversation? The idea was for you to go shopping for you, not for me. Besides, how do you know they're the right size?"

Sheila grinned. "Because, before I left, I went in your room and checked the sizes in your clothes."

"Okay, you win," Henry conceded. "Now, let's go get something to eat, and I'll try them on later. But first . . ." He popped open the briefcase and extracted two thousand dollars. Of this, he handed fifteen hundred to Sheila and put the rest in his pocket.

Sheila looked at the bills in her hand. "What's this for? And why do you have so much money in there?"

Henry slid the briefcase under the couch and, taking Sheila's arm, steered here toward the door. "The answers are, one, kicks. And, two, because I like it. In other words, don't ask questions I am not willing to answer right now."

Sheila persisted as they got in her car with Henry driving. His car was too dirty. He pulled around his car and headed down the street.

"I agree," Sheila stated. "It's none of my business. But why do you have all this money, and why did you give me this?" She held forward the bills she still held in her hand.

"First," Henry said, "Put that in your purse before someone sees it. The reason I gave it to you is because I am staying in your house. I owe you for that."

Sheila, putting the money in her purse, argued, "That's a nice gesture, but it's too much unless you're planning to stay for a year. Are you planning on staying for a year?"

Henry laughed, "Well, maybe not that long. Besides you may kick me out well before I'm ready to leave anyway. But if you'll allow it, I'll at least stay through the weekend."

Sheila was immediately concerned. "Where are you going? Did you find another place to stay?"

"No. I just have to fly out to Denver for a few days. I've got some things to take care of, and I have my brother out there. I should probably visit him for a bit."

"How long will you be gone?"

"Well, Sheila, right now, I don't know. I may be there a few days or a week. The thing is I think I'm going to have to make several trips out there in the next few weeks."

Sheila was not appeased. "Can I ask what you're going for?"

When the light they had stopped for changed, Henry made a right turn. "I would, but I think that would be a conversation for another time. Let's just say it's to visit my brother for right now. Really, nothing nefarious and certainly nothing to be concerned about."

Sheila frowned. "It's about your family, isn't it?"

Henry nodded as he pulled into the parking lot of "The Olde Inn," one of the better restaurants in Clarksville. "I will say this much. Yes, it's about them."

Sheila laid her hand on his arm. "Henry, I don't want you to do this. I think I understand why you want to do it, and I'm not saying I disagree with the thought. But you'll get hurt, or . . . or killed. I don't think I could handle that Henry. And I . . . I'm scared."

Henry, finding an open spot, pulled in and shifted into park. He shut off the ignition and turned to Sheila. "I don't expect you to completely understand, Sheila. And I don't have all the answers right now. Just rest assured that I am in no danger. You'll just have to trust me in what I am doing and going to do. I promise you, I will never be in any danger."

Shelia stared into Henry's eyes. Then sighing in resignation, said, "I guess I'll have to trust you. You won't tell me anything. But when will I see you?"

Henry got out of the car, closed his door, and walking around the car, opened the passenger door then closed it when Sheila got out. As they walked toward the restaurant, he said, "I won't say I'll see you every day. I will give you a call when I get back from Denver, and I'll see you whenever it's practical and when you have time."

Henry opened the restaurant door and as they went inside, said, "Now, enough of this talk. Smile for me, and let's get something to eat."

Sheila took Henry's arm. "Okay, you win." She smiled. "For now."

Seated at a table, they ordered. When breakfast came quickly, they devoured a couple of bites of ham, eggs, hash browns, and toast and washed it down with orange juice. He swallowed and said, "I do have a couple of favors to ask, if I might?"

Sheila nodded as she too swallowed a bite of pancake. "Of course you can. What is it?"

"Well, I'm going to need a ride to the airport in Pittsburg because I would prefer not to leave my car there. Second, may I leave my car at your house for a while?"

"You know I will, and you know you can for as long as you want."

Henry continued. "I just think it's a good idea having the car there. It gives the impression there is more than one person in the house. I'll feel better knowing that after what happened to Mary and Linda."

Sheila nodded. "You're thoughtful. That's nice."

Henry took another bite. He wondered if the people he would be looking for would think him thoughtful if . . . no, when, he found them?

"Another thing," he questioned as the thought occurred to him, "can I have my mail sent to your address? I don't seem to have one as present."

"Sure," she said. "We'll pick up the change of address cards at the post office when we leave here. The post office is still open, and I'll send them in on Monday." She smiled impishly. "Anything else, sir?"

"Just that I really appreciate you and how kind you have been."

When they had finished eating, they stopped at the post office, got the cards, and then drove back to Sheila's house.

Henry filled out the change of address cards, signed them, and laid them on the kitchen counter to be posted on Monday. After finishing that task and the coffee Sheila had brewed when they got home, he walked into the den. Sheila was watching TV and ironing one of the shirts she had purchased for him.

"What, the heck, are you doing?"

Sheila looked up from the ironing board. "These shirts are creased from being folded, and I didn't want to hang them in the closet like that."

"You don't need to do that. I can take them to the cleaners."

Sheila shook her head. "That's silly. Besides, I haven't got anything else to do right now anyway."

Henry smiled. "Well, I do. I've got to go out for a while."

Sheila paused her ironing. "Would you like company?"

"No. Not this time. But thanks for the offer. And thanks for the presents."

"It was your money."

Henry kissed her on the cheek. "Yes, but it was your thoughtfulness. You did all the work. So, anyway. I don't know how long I'll be out. I'll try to be back in time to take you to dinner, but it may be late."

Sheila shook her head. "No, don't worry about that. You take your time. I'll fix dinner here, and if you're late, I can keep it warm or warm it up.

"Oh, please. I don't want to take advantage."

"You're not," Sheila said. It's been a while since I've even nuked more than a frozen dinner. It will be a nice change. Now, you scoot."

# CHAPTER 7

Henry retrieved his briefcase from under the couch and put it in the car. Then, backing the Cadillac out of the drive, he gave some thought to what he needed. And what he needed was a house (sorry, Sheila). But he was unsure where. He was sixty-five miles from Pittsburgh, and he really wanted to be closer to the larger city. He would be much less conspicuous there than in the smaller city of Clarksville.

Stopping at the corner 'Byer Street News Center,' he picked up a Pittsburg map and newspaper. Then, going to the carwash, he sat in the waiting room and scanned the real estate ads as he waited for his car to be cleaned inside and out.

There were three houses that appeared interesting. One ad, larger than the others, had a certain appeal. Henry tore the page out of the paper just as the attendant told him his car was ready. He folded the page he had removed, leaving the rest of the paper, and paid for the wash. Thanking the attendant, he started the car and pulled to the corner of the lot. Unfolding the paper, he pulled out his phone and punched in the number of the real estate agent listed in the ad.

As he waited for a connection, he looked at the other two ads. All three were through the same realtor. Good, he thought. This will take less time if one of the houses fit his criteria.

On the third ring, a voice said, "Greene Realty, Don Greene speaking. May I help you?"

Henry turned his attention to the phone. "Yes, sir. I noticed three homes you have listed in the paper. I'd be interested in looking at them this afternoon if someone is available to show them."

"Of course, sir, of course, and which homes would that be Mr. . . . ?"

"Jenkins, Henry Jenkins," Henry responded and read him the listings.

"Well, Mr. Jenkins, the home on Halethorpe has been sold, but the other two are available. Also, I'm not sure what you are looking for, but I do have another one available that I would hate not to show you instead. Now, you said you wanted to see them today. Could I meet you somewhere at, say, two o'clock?"

Henry looked at his watch. It was 12:30. "Well, I'm about an hour or so away. Why don't we make it two-thirty to be on the safe side?"

"That's fine, Mr. Jenkins. I . . ."

Henry interrupted, "By the way, why don't I meet you at your office? Just give me the address, and I'll log it into my GPS." Henry acknowledged the address and disconnected the call.

Arriving at the office at quarter past two, Henry was greeted by a small, fiftyish, balding man in thick, dark-rimmed glasses. "Yes, sir, Don Greene at your service. May I help you?"

"Yes," Henry shook the extended hand. "I'm Henry Jenkins. We spoke."

"Ah, Mr. Jenkins, shortly after we spoke, a gentleman contacted me to say he had a house for sale that I think you might be interested in. It is comparable to the ones you saw in the ads, and I think from the way he was talking, the price may be negotiable. If, of course, you are interested."

Henry nodded. "Sure. I'll be happy to see any that may suit my needs."

"Very well," the agent said. "We can take my car."

In the car, Greene kept up a continual dialogue explaining the house they were going to see.

Henry let him ramble. There was only one major aspect of a house, as Greene explained them, that Henry was interested in.

The first house they visited was about twenty-five miles from Pittsburgh on a street called Peachtree Drive. The house was situated on an acre of land and, to Henry, the most interesting aspect was that only the front and one side were visible from the road. The rest was buried in the side of the hill, behind and to the left of the house. He continued to listen to the ramblings of the agent as he meandered through the interior.

After fifteen minutes, he was done with his inspection and said, "It's an interesting house Mr. Greene . . ."

"Oh, call me Don," Greene said. "And may I call you Henry?"

"Sure," Henry replied. "As I was starting to say, Don, the house is interesting, but I'm not sure it's what I'm looking for."

"No problem, Henry. The next one is the one that just came on the market. So I don't know a whole lot about it except for what the owner told me." He chuckled, "I guess we will learn about it as . . ."

Henry, half listening, let him continue his spiel as they rode, nodding at the appropriate times, agreeing when necessary. His thoughts, however, were on other things. The house they just looked at was just under three hundred thousand. The one they were going to see, according to Don, was three hundred eighty. He knew he could probably get either for less.

The second house was ten miles from the first and ten miles nearer Pittsburgh on a road called Hunters Trail. Henry smiled to himself, a fitting name.

Turning onto Hunters Trail, the first thing Henry noticed was he did not see any houses but did see an occasional mailbox. The house they were to see was in the middle of a seven-acre plot and hidden from the view of the road. About two acres had been cleared of trees in the middle of the wooded plot, and the drive up to the house angled such that the house was not visible from the road. It might be partially visible in winter when the trees were barren, but right now, it was totally hidden from view.

The house itself was a four-bedroom ranch with a two-stall attached garage. Henry had noted that the closest drive was about a quarter of a mile down the road, and he saw no mailboxes in the other direction. They went inside, and Henry followed Greene through the house as he explained the wonderful attributes of country living and only ten miles from the city. As they went room to room, he commented on the spacious rooms, walk-in closet in the master bedroom, large full-sized baths, and the cabinetry in the spacious kitchen.

Henry agreed the house was beautiful and responded without hesitation to Greene's questions. No, his wife couldn't come with him, but she trusted his judgement . . . they had two boys and one girl . . . yes, his job was transferring him to Pittsburg . . . shopping was important, and he was glad they had an excellent high school with bus service . . . The lies came automatically.

After the barrage of questions, Henry said, "This is pretty nice, Don, and I know my wife would find it acceptable, but you mentioned a shelter somewhere?"

"Of course, of course. The owner said there was an old fall-out shelter out back. And according to him, there is also a workshop and den in the basement. Which would you like to see first?"

Henry motioned toward the back door. "Let's see the shelter."

"Of course, of course," Greene said. "As I said, there is a den and workshop in the basement, but we can see them later." He headed to and out the back door onto the lawn behind the house with Henry following.

Greene laughed. "Ha-ha, are you afraid of the big one?"

Henry returned a smile. "No, not at all, but the wife would really like it as a root cellar," he lied.

Greene looked around and found the door. "The owner said there was a key hidden here somewhere," he said feeling around and above the door until he produced the key. "He said it was really an elaborate shelter. Of course, at the time it was built, I guess a lot of people were into that sort of thing. I never was, you understand, but . . ." He let the thought trail off.

He unlocked the door that was situated in the side of a rise and probably two hundred feet from the house and swung the heavy metal door outward. Henry noticed the door was about two inches thick and at least metal covered, if not solid metal. In any case, it appeared extremely heavy.

Following the never-ceasing dialogue of Greene, they went down; Henry didn't count but estimated twenty steps and through another key search and another door into a very spacious room that looked to be about thirty feet square. The room's walls and ceiling appeared to have lead shielding. There were shelving and cabinets along two of the walls, a bathroom in the far corner, and another massive door that appeared to go toward the house.

Greene continued to explain what the owner had told him. "As you can see, they didn't take the stuff out of here when they moved. I guess they didn't have a need for a shelter where they were going. Ha-ha. But if you want the place, I'll make sure it is removed, if you want. Some people don't like . . ."

Henry ignored him as he looked around. The shelves were indeed stocked with food stuffs, as he was sure the cabinets were also. There were some army cots folded on one shelf, along with army blankets and sheets wrapped in plastic. There was a tall metal cabinet in one corner, which Henry guessed probably held tools, and another cabinet next to it that was locked.

Henry pointed to the locked cabinet. "Do you have a key for that?"

"Well, as a matter of fact," Greene looked injured, "no. You see, I . . ."

Henry waved it away. "No matter, just curious. I expect just tools." He continued to survey the room: battery operated radio, AM/FM; walkie-talkie, Army; an old television, probably eighties; and an icebox. He looked at the ceiling noticing a ventilation shaft.

". . . they were getting older," Greene was saying. "I guess they figured it didn't matter if the big one came. Ha-ha. No disrespect, you understand. I'm getting older myself and . . ."

"All right, Don," Henry interrupted. "Let's see the basement, and then we can go."

"Of course, of course." Greene started toward the door they had entered when Henry stopped him. "Wait a second, Don. Doesn't that door in the far wall lead back toward the house?"

Greene looked slightly embarrassed. "Oh, sorry, didn't see that one. It may just do that."

He bustled to the door that looked as large as the first. This door was unlocked. He pushed it open and, feeling for a light switch, lit up a long, narrow hallway. They went up several steps to the basement level of the house and continued to a second, more familiar looking, door at the end of the hallway. Opening it, they stepped into the basement workshop. Henry reached behind him and flipped off the hall lights then closed the door. In doing so, he noticed the workshop side of the door did not look like a door but was instead a peg board wall.

Greene laughed. "Well, that's interesting. Wonder how you open it from this side?"

Henry smiled. "No problem, we can go now. I've seen all I need to see."

Greene looked perplexed. "We still haven't seen the rec room. I'm sure you will want to see it. You . . ."

Henry held up his hand. "I think we'll pass through it on the way upstairs. And I am rather in a hurry. We can discuss the price on the way back to your office."

Greene looked somewhat relieved. "Does that mean you want the house?"

"That means we can discuss it on the way back," Henry replied.

They climbed the stairs to the main floor, exited and locked the front door, and returned to the car. Greene slid the key into the ignition and started the engine. "Well, we do have one more house to see."

Henry shook his head. "That won't be necessary. I've decided that I will buy this one. It's now just a matter of settling on a price that is agreeable to me and the owner."

Green looked obviously relieved. "Of course, of course. I'm sure we can come to an agreement with the owner on the price. He did seem quite anxious to sell. Of course, you must understand that the house is worth a good bit more than the asking price, so he may not be willing to drop down."

Henry shrugged. "Then I'm not interested," Henry said fastening his seat belt.

Greene, flustered, "Well, let me call when we get back to the office. Perhaps they'll negotiate on the price a little." He put the car in gear and headed toward Pittsburg. "What were you thinking of offering, Henry? It is quite a stunning home, and I'm sure your wife would love it."

"I will pay three fifty. That includes taxes, title search, points, and any other costs," Henry said.

Greene looked hurt. "But that's thirty thousand less than they are asking just for the house. I don't think they would come down that..."

Henry interrupted. "They will have to meet my price. It should not be a problem for you. At 7 percent, you will still make close to twenty-five thousand on the sale. If they want to unload the house, it will not be a problem for them."

"Oh, Mr. Jenkins," guess it was not Henry anymore, "I don't believe they..."

Henry again interrupted Greene. "They, or you, will also have to assume any other costs associated with the sale. I don't want to be bothered with them. If they, and you, are truly interested in selling me the house, the deal will go through."

Greene sighed. "Oh, Mr. Jenkins, I can't think they would even consider..."

Henry ignored him. "Tell them I will have cash or a cashier's cheque for them next Wednesday."

Henry knew that meant he would have to come back from Denver on Tuesday. But no matter. He'd do what he had to do.

Greene looked at Henry astonished. "I don't know if you can get that much in so short..."

Henry was getting annoyed with the realtor. "You just finalize the deal with them. I'll take care of the finances."

When they got back to the realtor's office and were seated, Greene made a phone call to the owner of the Hunters Trail house. He explained Henry's proposal to the phone. Then, putting his hand over the mouthpiece, said, "Mr. Hampstead asked if you would consider either three-seventy or you paying the points and closing costs?"

Henry reached out his hand. "May I?"

Greene spoke into the phone. "Mr. Hampstead, Mr. Jenkins would like to talk directly with you if you are willing." He listened for a moment. "Of course, of course." He handed the phone to Henry.

"Mr. Hampstead, Henry Jenkins here." He paused as he acknowledged the response. "Sir, this is the only proposition I have. I can have you three hundred fifty thousand cash or cashier's check next Wednesday. I would say sooner, but I will be out of town. My offer is final, and there are not any options. I realize that is pretty cut and dried, but the house is an older home, and even though it has been well taken care of, I will need to make several upgrades and will need any money left for that purpose. I will give you back to Mr. Greene."

Henry handed the phone back to the realtor. "Discuss it with him. I need to go out to my car for a moment. I'll be right back." He stood and went out of the office.

Getting his briefcase out of the Cadillac, he tarried for a moment to give Greene time for his conversation with Hampstead then went back inside.

Greene was off the phone.

Henry sat down and opened his briefcase, the lid between him and Greene so Greene could not see the contents. "I assume things are as I anticipated," he said, counting out a number of bills.

Greene nodded, if not enthusiastically, but pleased that he had made a sale without even marketing it, even if he had lost the extra commission.

"Of course, of course . . ."

Henry laid twenty thousand dollars on the desk and closed the briefcase. "There is twenty thousand dollars for a deposit. I'm sure that is more than enough. I'll need a receipt, of course."

Greene eyed the money. "Of course, of course." He began looking for his receipt book. "I will, however, need you to sign the contract at this time."

"That's fine," Henry responded. "Otherwise, you can take care of the necessary paperwork for me. Put the deed in the name of Henry D. Jenkins. Use the address of the house on Hunters Trail as my address. Don't mess it up. I'll have my attorney look at it before I sign it. Also, take care of the additional monetary costs. That will be included in the total."

Henry picked up the receipt Greene filled out and put it in his briefcase. Closing it, he stood up. "Make sure everything is complete by Wednesday, and oh yes, give me the keys to the house. I don't believe you need them, and Mr. Hampstead said I could have access to the house."

Greene, looking astonished, handed Henry the keys without questioning the dubious transaction.

Putting the keys in the briefcase and closing it, he stood and stuck out his hand. "Mr. Greene, it has been a pleasure doing business with you. I will see you on Wednesday." He wondered how long it would be before Greene realized he gave him the keys to a house he didn't own yet.

Henry walked out of the office and to his car, leaving the astonished Greene staring after him.

# CHAPTER 8

Henry climbed into his car and glanced at his watch, 6:40. It would be after eight when he got back to Sheila's house. Not bad for having just bought a house, or almost. He smiled to himself as he pulled out of the realtor's parking lot and aimed the car for Clarksville. The drive back was filled with thoughts and ideas for the house on Hunters Trail.

Henry pulled into Sheila's driveway at 8:05 and cut the lights and ignition. He sat for a moment, thinking about his purpose for going to Denver. Then, grabbing the briefcase, he went into the house.

Entering, he called to Sheila and then heard the shower running in her bedroom. He set the briefcase on the coffee table and went to the kitchen for a glass of water. On the way, he noticed the dining room table had place settings and water and wine glasses with a bottle of wine, but he saw nothing on the stove in the way of food.

Going into his bedroom, he undressed, took a quick shower, and then dressed in the slacks and shirt Sheila had bought and ironed. Checking his appearance in the mirror, he went back down the hall.

Sheila met him in the living room and, smiling, handed him a glass of wine. "Welcome back."

He accepted the glass, looking at the woman in front of him. Sheila was wearing a black dress that shimmered in the dim lights of the room. The V at the neck came down to reveal some cleavage and was seductively appealing. The skirt was split to mid-thigh. The attire and lighting made her dark hair appear almost black. Henry looked into her sparkling brown eyes and returned the smile. "Looking at you, I'm certainly glad to be back." He realized their eyes were almost level and, casting his down, saw she was wearing heels that brought her five-feet-eight-inches almost up to his height.

"You don't like it?" she asked.

Henry laughed. "If I didn't, I would most certainly be either blind or insane. You look absolutely fantastic."

Sheila, obviously pleased, held up her glass and touched it to his, making a light ring as they clinked together. "To us."

Sipping his drink, he looked over the rim and into her dark eyes, wondering . . .

Taking his arm, Sheila led him into the dining room. The candles had been lit and cast a soft glow across the table settings. Henry sat in the chair Sheila indicated, while she went to the kitchen. After a few moments of doors and drawers opening and closing in the kitchen, he thought he heard a knock at the back door.

Moments later, she carried several dishes in and sat them on the table: soup, salad, then lobster thermidor. Henry ate, not realizing until he started how hungry he was. The conversation was light, and Henry felt somehow better than he had in days and weeks. He wondered if he should, considering the newness of events, then discounted the thought. He would avenge Mary and Linda. He would accomplish what the law would not. But he wouldn't/couldn't do it tonight.

"Henry?" Sheila cut into his reverie. "Is something wrong?"

Henry shook his head. "No, of course not, just a passing thought. I'm sorry. What were you saying?"

Sheila looked downcast. "Henry, I'm sorry. Maybe I shouldn't have done this. I . . ."

Henry leaned over and, pulling her closer, kissed her lightly. "You couldn't have done it better. This is just, you are just, what I need right now. Thank you."

Sheila gazed into his eyes for a moment, decided he was telling her the truth, and her smile returned.

Henry took another bite, relishing the taste. "This is really fantastic. If I had known you cooked like this, I would have been coming over here for dinner occasionally."

Sheila laughed. "You have been over here for dinner, and if you must know, I didn't do this. You see, this guy I know gave me a wad of money, so I had it catered."

Henry grinned. "You're amazing."

Sheila returned the grin. "I called earlier today and placed the order with the restaurant. I didn't know when you would be back. So, when I saw you pull in the drive, I called them to bring it over, to the back door, and jumped into the shower real quick."

"Okay, but what if I had not gotten back 'til eleven or twelve?"

"Hey," she replied with levity, "for what you paid for this, I wouldn't have cared if they had to stay open 'til two in the morning. Of course, you would have been dining with someone in cold cream and a flannel nightgown if you got back that late."

Henry laughed. "Now, why don't I believe that?"

By the time dinner was over, it was after eleven. Henry helped Sheila clean up the dishes, and when the young man came from the restaurant to collect them, Henry gave him a generous tip.

Later, they watched TV until Sheila fell asleep while leaning against Henry's shoulder. He nudged her gently awake. "Hey, sleepyhead, looks like it's bedtime."

She sat up. "Oh, Henry, I'm sorry. I didn't mean to fall asleep."

"You don't have to apologize. It is rather late, and we've both had a long day."

Henry walked with her down the hall and paused at her door, saying goodnight.

"Henry?"

"What?"

"Will you sleep in my room? With me?"

Henry looked at her a long moment, then still saying nothing, turned and went into her room behind her.

Sheila didn't turn on the bedroom light. Instead, she turned on the bathroom light then pulled the door until it was slightly ajar, leaving the room in semi-darkness. Henry undressed and climbed into the bed. Sheila slipped out of her dress and laid it across the back of the nearby chair. She then padded across and slid in beside Henry. She had had nothing on under the dress, and even though they didn't make love, Henry liked the feel of her naked body against his.

# CHAPTER 9

The soft light filtering through the bedroom drapes woke Henry. He lay on his side with Sheila cradled in the curve of his body. His arm was around her with his hand cupping the warm firmness of her breast. He wanted to keep it there, feel her beauty, but he gently moved his hand away and rolled on his back. When he did, Sheila turned over with him, putting her hand on his chest as she snuggled against him. He gently pushed her hair back from her cheek, letting his hand linger in her tresses.

"How long have you been awake?" he asked.

"A while," she said softly. "I didn't want to move because I didn't want you to . . . didn't want you to move."

Henry stroked her hair and stared at the ceiling. "Sheila, I'm going to tell you something, and I don't know if it will come out right, but I'll try.

"I think you're beautiful, one of the most attractive women I know. When you used to come over to the house, I would look at you and think if I ever thought of cheating on Mary, it would be with you. Besides your looks, you're intelligent, you've got a great sense of humor, and we, I think, think alike on a lot of subjects. Anyway, I've slept with you now, and I love the way you feel in my arms. I love feeling your body next to me. It's just that . . . well, I guess I feel guilty about making love with you right now."

Henry paused and then laughed. "Shoot, I don't even know that you would want me to do that."

Sheila playfully slapped his chest in mock anger as she rose up and glared at him. She looked at him for several seconds before laying her head back on his chest. "I've thought several times that if you weren't Mary's husband, I'd grab you in a heartbeat. Because you were, I couldn't. I wouldn't. I loved Mary, Henry. You know that. I realize it hasn't been a long time since your tragedy, and I understand how you feel. I just want you to know that I am here if, or when, you do want me. I want to be a part of your life now, not to replace Mary or Linda but to be the one you want to be with since they're gone, if you'll let me. I want to make love with you when you're ready. If that is today, next week, or a year, it doesn't matter. Whenever that is, it will not be out of disrespect for Mary or you, and I will love you for it. Whenever . . . if we do."

Henry lay for a long while stroking her hair. Finally, a thought struck him, and he laughed. "Does that mean you will respect me in the morning?"

Sheila laughed and rolled out of bed. She walked toward the bathroom then stopped and wiggled her bottom sassily. "Why don't you try me and find out, big boy." She went into the bathroom and closed the door.

Henry, smiling, watched her until the door closed. He stared at the ceiling and listened as the shower was turned on, ran for several minutes, and then shut off. Moments later, Sheila opened the door and reentered the bedroom wrapped in a bath towel.

She looked at Henry watching her as she went to the dresser and opened a drawer. "Are you going to watch me get dressed?"

Henry looked stunned. "You mean you're going to put clothes on?"

Sheila let the towel drop to the floor and stood facing Henry. "Do you like me better this way?"

Henry sighed. "More than you know, and with the curtains open, the neighbors do too."

She glanced quickly at the closed drapes then picked up the towel and threw it at Henry. She dressed as Henry lay watching her and then went to the door. "When you are done ogling naked women," she laughed, "get dressed, and I'll fix you some breakfast." She slipped out and closed the door.

Henry folded his hands behind his head and stared at the ceiling. What he had told Sheila was true. He did want her, all of her. Yet, he was also afraid to get too close to her while he planned his moves elsewhere. He had told Sheila he would not be hurt in any of his endeavors, but he was going out against at least two animals—no, not animals; animals wouldn't do what these scumbags did. Anyway, he was going after them, and they had guns and knives. Henry getting shot could be a very real possibility if he wasn't careful. They had already proven they had no qualms about rape or murder.

His would be no different for them.

Now, when he was with Sheila, she kept his mind off it for the most part, or at least relegated to the back of his mind. But he couldn't take her with him, couldn't tell her about it, and certainly wouldn't involve her in it. Maybe when everything was over, he could work on a relationship with her, but that seemed way down the road right now.

Sheila opened the door, interrupting his thoughts. Concern showed on her face. "Henry, there are a couple of people over at your place. I saw them out there yesterday and figured it was insurance people, but they're over there again digging around."

Henry sat up. "Don't worry. They're probably with the fire department. They have to try to determine the cause for the insurance company. I'll get dressed and mosey over there in a little bit."

He showered and dressed then went in to find Sheila gazing out the window. Henry went up behind her and, glancing out the window, patted her bottom.

Sheila jumped. "Jesus, you scared me. I almost peed myself."

Henry laughed. "Sorry about that. Now, you stop worrying about those men. They're just doing their job."

"Henry, what if they find something?"

"I'm sure they might but nothing of any value. Tell you what. Let me get a cup of coffee, and then I'll go talk to them. Okay?"

Sheila squeezed his arm and then went to pour two cups of coffee. Henry watched the two men pawing around at the back of the house for a few seconds then turned away from the window.

Henry, though he would never let on, was a little concerned. They were pawing around the kitchen area, just above the workbench in the basement. He forced himself to drink the coffee slowly and carry on light conversation with Sheila until the coffee was gone. Then, acting as if he was going only because of her concern, he went out and across the street.

When Henry walked over to where he could see what was going on, the two men were staring down into the basement through what use to be the kitchen floor but was now just a huge hole.

Henry walked up to them. "Hello. I'm Henry Jenkins, the owner of this, or what's left of it."

They looked up, and the larger of the two said, "Oh, yes, Mr. Jenkins. I'm William Hillcrest of the fire marshal's office. I would shake your hand, but mine are a mess. I do think we have found the culprit or the cause."

Henry felt his heart rate increase in expectation of his finding. "Oh, you did? That's good. Can you tell me?"

"Sure," Hillcrest replied. "You see, yesterday we took some samples from where we thought the ignition point of the fire was. We found the fire was started by a petroleum based accelerant. So, we immediately thought arson."

Henry felt his heart thud wildly in his chest.

"No reason not to think that," Hillcrest continue. "If you lean over here, I'll show you what I mean."

Henry leaned in and looked down into the hole where Hillcrest pointed.

"You see that piece of pipe sticking out of the wall right there?"

Henry nodded.

"Well, your house had an oil fired furnace, which I'm sure you know. Anyway, that pipe had what, for our purposes, I'll call plastic tubing that went from it, around the wall, and then connected to another metal pipe at the furnace. As I see it, it looks like the plastic pipe got a hole punched in it some way and enough oil leaked out that when the furnace kicked on, it ignited the spilled oil or the fumes. I don't understand why anyone would use that plastic for a fuel line. Anyway, once the fire started, the plastic melted, and the fuel in the tank just started pouring out onto the floor and feeding the fire. If that had been a metal line, there would probably have been a lot better chance of saving the house. As it were, once the line melted and the fuel started pouring out, it would be almost impossible to put it out. Surprises me the whole thing isn't ash."

Henry felt his heart leave his throat and return to his chest. Breathing much easier, he said, "Well, I hadn't had the tank filled yet. I think they were supposed to come out next week."

Hillcrest nodded. "Yep, that's it. It wasn't full. Probably about half, I'd say, from the looks of things." He looked at the report in his hand. "Didn't you have smoke detectors? This report says the house had been burning for quite a while before the fire department was called."

Henry wondered if questions would raise more questions and the answers would incriminate him. Well, he had to answer truthfully. It would be easy to check it out. "Yes, I did have smoke detectors, but I wasn't home."

Hillcrest looked back at the report. "It says here that you were on the scene at the time of the fire."

Henry sighed. "Let me explain. My wife and daughter were murdered here not long ago. My neighbor has been kind enough to let me stay next door until the house was cleaned up. I don't see how that has any bearing anyway. You just said . . ."

Hillcrest interrupted, "I am really sorry, Mr. Jenkins. I read about the mur . . . incident in the papers. I didn't relate the two, and I should have. From what I read, they did a lot of damage to the house too."

A thought apparently crossed the inspector's mind like an aha moment. "That's probably what happened to that oil line. It probably got punctured when they were ransacking the place." He looked pleased with himself. "Yes, sir. That must be it. Look, I'm sorry if I upset you, Mr. Jenkins. Ah, under the circumstances and all. Just trying to do my job and didn't tie the two incidents together."

Henry nodded. "I understand, sir. So what is your final conclusion . . . for the report, that is."

Hillcrest shrugged. "I'll just show it as accidental. They probably did it, but that's just a guess on my part. Nothing I can prove short of a confession."

"I suppose," Henry asked, "that you will send a copy of your report to my insurance company? They'll need it, I'm sure."

"Yes, sir, we sure will. That's policy. They'll need it anyway before they'll pay out."

Henry, appeased, was ready to go back to Sheila's and was searching for an excuse when Hillcrest provided it for him.

"Well, Mr. Jenkins, I guess we're finished here. I'll complete my report and send it out on Monday. So you should hear from your insurance company shortly after that. As I said before, I would shake your hand, but mine are filthy. Well, part of the job, I guess."

They walked toward the front of the lot where their vehicle was parked. "And I just want to say again how sorry I am about your family. I hope it doesn't take too long to catch those guys and put them where they belong."

Henry started back across the street. "I hope that too, Mr. Hillcrest. I hope that too."

When Henry stepped in the door, Sheila was there to meet him. "What did they want? What did they say?"

Henry laughed and said, "You worry too much. As I told you, it was just a routine inspection, so they can send a report to the insurance company."

He didn't tell her of his apprehension when he first talked to Hillcrest. He did tell her what Hillcrest's answer to the cause of the fire was and most of their conversation. In thinking about it, Henry decided he could not have started the fire in a better place. The plastic oil line

Hillcrest mentioned ran right along the underside of the workbench top. Henry had forgotten that when he planned the house's demise. He wondered what happened to the gas can and figured it was buried in the rubble somewhere. Still, it was a plastic container, so it may have melted right along with the oil line.

# CHAPTER 10

Henry and Sheila ate a late breakfast, after which Henry went to pack for his trip to Denver. As he was packing, an idea came to him. He finished packing and went into the kitchen where Sheila sat drinking a cup of coffee.

"You know, I had this great idea while I was packing," he said. "My flight is at 10:30 in the morning, and it's shy of a couple of hours to the airport in Pittsburgh from here. Why don't we drive there this afternoon? That way, we won't have to get up so early tomorrow."

Sheila leaned back as though pondering the idea. "On one condition."

"That being?"

"I can stay there with you tonight and see you off in the morning."

Henry acted as though he had to think about it before answering. "Well, it puts a cramp in me seeing my other girlfriends, but I think I can forgo them if I have you."

Sheila picked up her coffee cup. "Hey, fella. I have a dangerous weapon here. You don't want to get on my bad side."

Henry smiled. "Okay. Why don't you throw some things in a bag while I see about reservations."

She held up her index finger. "One room."

"Hey, lady, are you trying to seduce me?"

Sheila laughed. "One room," she repeated.

"Yes, ma'am," he said as he picked up the phone.

Dialing the eight hundred number for Holiday Inn, he made a reservation, gave them a credit card number, and told them he needed a late arrival guarantee. By the time he finished, Sheila had finished packing, and within half an hour, they were on the road to Pittsburgh.

The Cadillac, Sheila told Henry, did not impress her. "It's way bigger than my Subaru. I'm afraid I might ding it."

"Nonsense," Henry retorted. "It's just a car, and in five miles of driving it, you'll be perfectly comfortable with it. I only ask that if you do dent it, you don't dent you in the process."

"Henry, you know what I mean."

"Yes, I do, but it's just a car, as I said. Besides, when I have to be away, you'll need to drive it occasionally anyway. It's not good for them to just sit without starting them once in a while."

She frowned. "Do you have any idea how long you'll be gone? You said before that you . . ."

"Oh, I'm sorry. I've got so many things running through my mind, I forgot. I have to be back in Clarksville Wednesday morning to take care of some financial business. So I'll be coming back Tuesday afternoon. I'll let you know what time as soon as I can. See," he smiled, "and you thought you were getting rid of me."

Sheila was obviously pleased, but Henry didn't want her to get the impression that he was going to be around all that long, or that often. "It's just for a day or two, then I have to make another trip."

She was not to be discouraged. "That's a day or two where I might encourage you to stay."

Henry let the subject drop, instead saying, "Do you think you can pick me up Tuesday? It's okay if you can't. I can rent a car and drive back."

"No. Of course I'll come get you. Just don't forget to call and let me know when you'll be arriving."

When they arrived in Pittsburgh, Henry found the motel, and they registered. Getting the keycard for room 238, they carried their bags to the elevator and rode to up to the second floor. As the door opened, Sheila asked, "Oh, do you have your briefcase?"

"It's in the trunk of the car. I thought about bringing it up, but I don't need it, and I think it will be safe where I parked."

"If someone doesn't steal the car," Sheila said.

"Good point," he said. "Remind me when we come back from dinner, and I'll bring it up. I don't think I need to carry it back and forth. By the way, you know that seafood restaurant we passed on the way here?"

Sheila nodded.

"I was thinking we could go there for dinner if you would like. It looked like a pretty nice place."

"Whatever you like is fine with me. I like seafood."

Henry picked up the motel's entertainment magazine and flipped through it. "And if you want, after dinner, we could take in some of the local talent."

Sheila fluffed a pillow and leaned seductively back on the bed. "Let's see how we feel after dinner. We may want to make our own entertainment."

Henry smiled. "Sure. Let me make a phone call and we'll go to dinner."

Getting the phone book, he looked up the listing for the restaurant and called, making a reservation. Hanging up, he said, "It's good I called. Our reservation is for 9:30. Why don't we go down to the lounge and have a drink while we are killing time?"

"Good idea," Sheila said getting off the bed. "Just let me check my make-up."

She looked in the mirror, applied fresh lipstick, and apparently satisfied, turned to Henry. "Well, good enough. I guess we can go."

Henry opened the door. "You'll be the most beautiful woman there."

They sat in the lounge sipping cocktails and chatting over mundane issues until 9:00 then drove over to the restaurant where Henry had a combination seafood platter, and Sheila had lobster dipped in butter.

After the meal, they drove back to the motel, and Sheila suggested they stop again in the lounge for a nightcap.

Henry looked at Sheila with mock sternness. "Excuse me, lady, are you trying to get me drunk?"

Sheila grinning devilishly, leaned over, and flicked his earlobe with her tongue. Then with a very bad Spanish accent said, "Si, Senor, and then I am going to seduce you."

Henry laughed loudly. "I hope your seduction is better than that accent."

Sheila put her finger to his lips. "Shush. You'll draw attention."

Henry sipped his drink, but leaving it unfinished, he paid the tab, and they took the elevator back to the second floor and their room. When there, Sheila went to take a shower, and Henry ordered a magnum of champagne from room service. The bottle and glasses arrived. He gave the man a tip and finished pouring just as he heard the shower shut off. The door opened, and he handed a glass to a very pretty, very naked Sheila.

Henry raised his glass. "Let me offer a salute to nudity," he said admiring the woman in front of him, "which you accomplish so very beautifully."

Sheila smiled coyly as they clinked glasses, and she sipped from hers. "I hope so. I really want to please you, and I've really ruined the moment if you think otherwise."

Henry took her glass and sat both on the table. Pulling her to him and enveloping her in his arms, he caressed her back and bottom. "Sugar, you do please me. Believe me, you are the most beautiful thing in my world now and the most important." He stepped back. "Now, if you'll unhand me for a few minutes, I'll go take a shower."

Sheila released him, smiling. "You know, we could have saved time and water if you had showered with me. And it might have been even more enjoyable."

Henry kissed her cheek and headed for the bath. "Maybe next time, but I expect it would take a lot longer to shower if you were in there with me. So even though it would be fantastic, I'm not sure it would be a water-saving experience."

As he was closing the door, he turned to her and grinned. "If I'm too long, just go ahead and start without me."

He heard Sheila laughing as he turned on the shower.

When he came out a few minutes later, Sheila lay seductively on the bed. Henry acted as if he was going to get in the other bed, and Sheila grabbed the towel he had around his waist and pulled it off.

"If you get in that bed, you'll have a broken leg to go with that broken arm," she said menacingly.

He climbed onto the bed with Sheila. He realized he might feel guilty tomorrow, but for now, his physical need and desire for Sheila outweighed his emotional loss. He put his arms around her and pulled her to him . . . feeling . . . wanting . . . needing her firm, yet supple, body against his.

She clung to him. Her hand moved on him, exciting him, as he, in return, touched her, caressing, manipulating and listening to the soft, sexy noises she made in response. He moved into her and felt the frenzy that accompanied their heightening movements.

Later, much later, she laid quietly against him, her head on his chest, her hand gently stroking his arm as he did her back.

"Henry?"

"Umm?"

"Would I scare you if I said something?"

"You know better."

"Would it be terrible if I told you, I love you?"

Henry hoped she did not feel or hear the increase in his heart rate. He moved her over on her back and rose up on one elbow, so he could see her in the semi-darkness of the room. "I think that's great, sweetheart. In time, I hope to tell you the same. It's not that I don't . . . I just can't right now. Maybe some time . . . when I'm done . . . I can."

Sheila looked into his eyes. "I think I understand. I can be patient."

Henry held her, kissed her, and fell asleep, as did she nestled closely in his arms.

# CHAPTER 11

The phone rang and Henry reached for it. "Hello?"

The automated voice informed him that it was his wake-up call. He put the phone back.

Sheila tightened her grip around his rib cage. "I've decided you can't go."

"Okay, sugar," Henry chuckled. "We'll just stay here."

She snuggled closer. "Good."

He laid there another ten minutes, enjoying the feel of her naked body against his, then extracting himself from her grip, he went in and showered, washing the sleep and sex from his body.

When he returned, Sheila sat on the edge of the bed. Henry looked at the long legs, firm breasts, and flat stomach and thought it would be nice to have a repeat of last night. Instead, he kissed her forehead and pulled her to her feet.

"Come on, sleepyhead, time to move your body."

She put her arms around his neck and buried her face against his neck. "One more time?"

Henry patted her bottom playfully. "When I get back."

As he got out clothes to wear, Sheila went to shower. He slipped into slacks and a shirt then called room service for coffee and a local newspaper.

The coffee and paper were delivered while Sheila was still in the shower, and he scanned it as he sipped the hot brew. On page three of the paper, he read that police in Clarksville still had no clues as to the rape/murders that had taken place.

Secretly, Henry was not disappointed.

It went on to say that in addition to the loss of his family, Henry Jenkins, on Thursday, suffered the loss of the home where his family was slain to a fire caused by a ruptured oil line leading to the home heating unit in the basement. It further stated that Jenkins was not home when the fire occurred, and the fire marshal declared the total loss of the home accidental.

Sheila came out of the bathroom as Henry turned to the comic section to see what Doonesbury had to say. Sheila leaned over him, and he felt the moist warmth of her breasts against his back. Her tongue found his earlobe as she said, "One more time, Senor?"

Henry smiled and tousled her hair. "When I come back. I really needed you last night, and I do want you now, but I would miss my flight if we got back in that bed, and I really need to make that flight."

Sheila sighed, pushing her lower lip out in a pout. "Well, okay then, but I will hold you to it when you get back."

Henry folded the paper and laid it on his suitcase. He could work the crossword and Sudoku puzzles during the flight. "Hey, kiddo, you say that now, but later on, you will be telling me to get away from you or, 'not tonight, sweetheart. I have a headache.'"

She laughed. "You couldn't get so lucky."

With dressing completed, hair coiffed, and make-up sparingly applied, Sheila announced she was ready to go. They went down to the restaurant, ate breakfast, and then, suitcases stowed, they made the short drive to the airport.

Parking in the short-term parking garage, Henry gave the car keys to Sheila, and retrieving his bag and briefcase, they walked to the terminal. He picked up his boarding pass and, scanning it, told Sheila the flight number and time of the return flight.

Checking his bag, he turned to her. "Well, I guess I will see you Tuesday."

Sheila put her arms around his waist. "Are you going to call me when you get there?"

Henry started to say yes then reconsidered. "I doubt that I will, but I will call you if something comes up, and I can't make the return flight." He didn't want to give her the impression that his whereabouts would be known all the time, and it was best to start now. There would be days, and maybe weeks, he wouldn't want her to know where he was . . . couldn't let her know where he was. As much as he wanted a close relationship with her, he could not allow a dependency to develop between them, at least not in the near future.

"It's best this way," he said to the hurt look that clouded her face.

Sheila nodded, but the look remained. "Please be careful."

"Honey," Henry laughed, "I'm just going to buy some things. That's not dangerous."

Henry checked the time. "I better go, sugar. I'll see you Tuesday." He kissed Sheila as she gave him a long hug. He returned the embrace then stepped away, picked up the briefcase, and smiled. "I'm gonna miss you."

Sheila returned the smile. "I'll be here when you get back. Have a safe flight."

Henry went through security and shortly afterward boarded the plane. As the jet was backed away from the gate, Henry could see Sheila standing at the large windows of the departure lounge. He would have to maintain some distance between them. Her feelings for him, his for her for that matter, could screw up his plans if he got too close. His feelings for her were strong, but he had made a vow to Mary, to Linda. Regardless of anything else in his life, he would avenge them.

# CHAPTER 12

With the airplane lifting off, and with Sheila behind him, Henry opened the newspaper to the puzzles. He absently filled in the words as his thoughts went to Mary and the love he had for her that, perhaps, he didn't express as much as he should have. The sense of pride he had for both her and Linda that he should have shown a little better. The profound loss and despair that they were gone, and as expected, the guilt of sleeping with Sheila before he had avenged them. He thought about Linda lying in his arms as she died. Dying needlessly and horribly, dying in fear and pain, and not even understanding why.

For them, for him, and possibly for potential future victims, Henry would stop them, forever. Screw the people who were against capital punishment. It was not their families who were assaulted, bludgeoned, raped, and murdered. If it had been, Henry wondered, would they continue to be against it, or would they be screaming for their heads on a spike?

He remembered hearing about one of those activists, not long ago, on the evening news. What was the spokesman's name, Lawrence Reynolds? Reynolds had been saying, "The death of another human being as punishment is amoral and against the laws of God. You who sanction the death penalty are as guilty as the man who throws the switch or inserts the needle, and you will burn in Hell as surely as they will burn in Hell."

Henry hadn't particularly disagreed with Reynolds' idea at the time. Really, he didn't even consider it relevant to his life. He had never (before this) been an advocate of an eye for an eye. Of course, he had never been against it either. It had just been one of those things where it didn't involve him one way or the other. So he didn't care one way or the other.

But now, he wondered how old Larry would feel if it had been his wife and daughter. Henry could see it in his mind now. Good old Larry, standing in front of the news cameras with the microphones stuck in his face, saying "Yes, gentlemen and ladies, they raped my fifteen-year-old daughter before they brutalized her and shot her twice to leave her on the floor dying. Oh, no, they raped her right there on the tile floor. They didn't undress her. They just kicked in the bathroom door, cut her clothes off her defenseless body, and brutalized her repeatedly right there on the floor, viciously, repeatedly, sadistically."

"And my wife, gentlemen and ladies, they tore off her clothes and raped her too. Not only that, they brutalized her too. They broke off three of her teeth when they pistol whipped her and fractured her skull before they shot her three times."

"But, ladies and gentlemen of the press, I don't think these men should be executed. Not at all. I think they should be punished, but that punishment should be aimed toward rehabilitation so these young men will be able to again walk in society. Yes, we should be able to rehabilitate those misguided youths in the three to seven years they'll probably serve if convicted. And let me reiterate, if they are convicted.

"I do not believe in capital punishment, ladies and gentlemen of the press. I think, with the right guidance and help, we will be able to trust those men in a room, alone, with your fifteen-year-old daughters or your wives."

Henry suddenly wanted to choke good old Larry and all his following. That was the problem with the judicial system. Life in prison was not life in prison. It was twenty-five years and with time off for good behavior maybe seven. In all probability, it would be less, and they would be out in three or four years. Hell, they could do three years standing on their heads.

And what rehabilitation? They had overworked prison psychiatrists dealing with too many criminals under adverse conditions in a place akin to hell. And the psychiatrists were probably just out of school and never dealt with anyone under normal circumstances. It was one thing if someone wanted help and sought out a licensed and reputable counselor. It was entirely another when one was forced to see a pimply faced kid with a tie when they didn't want to be there. Shit, they would say anything the shrink wanted to hear to be released a little earlier. You didn't have to be a damned genius to be able to determine the answers they wanted to hear or the type of response you were supposed to make. If the shrink said, "Are you going to rape, brutalize, or kill anyone again if we let you out?" What was the criminal going to say?

"Yes, sir, Mr. Shrink, as soon as I can get out of this hellhole and find me another fifteen-year-old girl and her mother, I'm going to fuck them 'til I'm satiated, and then I'm going to do the most horrible things imaginable to them."

Hell no. He was going to tell Mr. Shrink how he had found Jesus in those three long years in prison. He would tell him how he got down on his knees, every night, and begged God to forgive him for the horrid and unspeakable acts he had committed during a drug or alcohol blackout. He would tell how he was now drug and alcohol free and was helping the prison Chaplin because he now realized the gravity of his sins and wanted, had strived for, and finally achieved a rapport with God.

The young, overworked psychiatrist was going to go to the parole board with that malarkey. The parole board was going to buy it because the learned Doctor of Psychiatry professed it to be true, and they would turn the depraved bastard loose. Then, in six months or a year, they would wonder why this pervert (who had laughed his ass off that they let him out) had again done the same thing again or even worse. That is, if they even thought about it at all.

And good old Larry Reynolds would, once more, be in front of the cameras saying, "I think he can be rehabilitated."

Well, screw good old Larry and the police and the justice system with their corrupt defense attorneys and underpaid prosecutors. Screw the ACLU. What had he heard it called, The American Criminal Liberties Union? Screw the system that depended on the size of one's wallet as to the justice they were warranted, Henry thought. My justice will put the situation in the right perspective, and my punishment will fit the crime. Larry might think God would frown on such punishment, but the bible also said, "An eye for an eye and a tooth for a tooth."

When the plane touched down in Denver, the sky was cloudy when Henry walked into the terminal. However, when he collected his suitcase from the baggage area and went outside, the weather was warm, so he carried his coat over his arm. He went to the Avis counter and gave his name for the reservation he had made before he left home. Moments later, he walked outside and climbed into the rented Cadillac Sonata and headed for his motel.

Once situated in his room at the Ramada Inn, Henry found the addresses for Frank's Automobile Customizing and Baker's Electronics in the phone book. Then, he called his brother and arranged to meet him in the motel lounge at 7:30.

It was after 6:00 when he got off the phone with Fred, so Henry went down to the restaurant and ate a leisurely dinner then strolled into the lounge to wait for his brother.

When 7:45 and then 8:00 rolled by and Fred had not shown, Henry knew, when he did, Midge would be with him. Two things Henry knew about Midge, aside from the fact that she was a bitch. One, she believed in being 'fashionably' late. Henry wondered about her funeral. Two, when it was Henry, she believed she needed to be even later because it goaded him. As it happened, it was almost 8:40 when they entered the lounge. Henry told himself he would try to be nice to Midge, even if it killed him.

"Hank!" Fred's voice boomed as he located Henry at the bar.

Henry stood and turned. As he knew she would be, Midge was

at his side. "How are you, Fred," he said taking is brother's hand. He paused looking toward his sister-in-law. "Midge."

"Just great, little brother. It's good to see you. I was just telling Midge on the way here that it's been, what, four years? Anyway, sorry we are running so late. Midge had trouble finding the appropriate attire. You know how women are. Ha-ha."

Henry smiled. He did know how women were. Mary had always been punctual and, if she felt she'd have trouble finding the right garment to wear somewhere, she would start preparing earlier in the day, so she wouldn't be late. "Yes, I certainly do. And how are you Midge?" God, he wished Mary could be here.

"I'm just sooo wonderful," she said in her nasal twang that grated on Henry's nerves. "How are Mary and your daughter? What's her name, Lydia, Linda? Oh, yes, Linda. I was hoping they were with you. Why didn't you bring them? You know how much I love those dear people." She pronounced dear as deah.

Yeah, Henry thought. Whenever they did get together, Midge talked, Mary listened, and Linda (she couldn't even remember her name, or chose not to) was ignored. And all the talk was about Midge. How horrendous her day was, her aches and pains, her Dior and Gucci or other fashions, the celebrities she knew, and on and on. Fortunately, Mary had had more patience than Henry and could tolerate that continuous drivel. Unfortunately, she would never be around to hear it again.

Henry ignored her and turned to Fred. "I was hoping you would come alone, Fred. Not that it's not nice to see you both," he lied, "but I need to talk to you alone."

He saw from the corner of his eye that Midge was teed off by what he had just said, and suddenly, he didn't care.

"Well, I was going to," Fred said, trying to smooth ruffled feathers, "but I knew Midge hadn't seen you either and . . . well, I tell Midge everything anyway. So I thought . . ." He let the thought trail off unfinished.

Henry knew Fred was lying. Fred hadn't asked Midge to come;

Midge had insisted upon it. And Fred had always backed down, eventually, to Midge's demands. Also, Fred only told things to Midge that she absolutely needed to know or that she found out about and browbeat out of him.

"Well, whatever the case," Henry stated, "I can't talk to you with Midge here. So if you'll take her home and come back, we can talk."

Midge was obviously and totally pissed off now. Henry didn't want to put Fred in the middle, as he was doing, but he had put off this heart-felt confrontation with Midge for far too long.

Midge glared at Henry but tried to put on a show of being pained that he would not want her included. "Henry, I am really hurt by that. You know how I've always felt that you and I had a good rapport. Why, I'm crushed to think that . . ."

"Cut the bullshit, Midge," Henry interrupted. "You don't like me. I have tolerated you because you're my brother's wife. It's as simple as that. You're here because you're nosey and afraid Fred won't tell you what we talked about. Go home, Midge. I phoned because I needed to talk to my brother, not to you."

Midge stood in stunned silence that anyone would deign to speak to her that way. Regaining her voice, she said, "Well, fuck you, Henry Jenkins." She grabbed Fred's arm. "Fred, take me home."

Fred started laughing as if he was watching a comedy skit. He held his sides, tears running down his cheeks as he sat down on a chair and gasped for breath between chortles.

Midge, her face scarlet with anger, pinched the soft underside of Fred's upper arm. Henry flinched, imagining the pain Fred must have felt.

"Fred," she almost screeched, "I said take me home!"

Fred, now over the laughing bout, probably because of the painful pinch to his arm, extracted his keys from his pocket and held them out to his wife. "Here, you can take the car and go home. Hank can bring me home later."

He turned to Henry, "You do have a car, don't you, Hank?"

Henry nodded. "Yeah. I'll get you home."

Midge again pinched Fred's arm. "I want you to take me home."

Fred jerked his arm away, flinching in pain. As if drawing strength from the recent confrontation between Henry and Midge, he turned to his wife. "Midge, I've never hit a woman in my life, nor do I ever want to do that. But I swear to God, if you ever pinch me again, I'm going to hit you dead in your fucking teeth."

He again held out the car keys. "Now, you take these keys, get the car, and go home. Hank and I need to talk."

Midge, who outweighed Fred's one hundred and fifty pounds by probably another fifty, stood glaring at the brothers for several seconds, searching for the words to, as Fred would say, "put them lower than whale shit."

Finding nothing appropriate for their putdowns, she spat, "Well, fuck you both!" Snatching the keys from Fred's hand, she spun and stomped out.

Fred looked after her with mock consternation. "Bad attitude, she needs to correct that." And he started laughing again.

"Fred," Henry said. "I need to apologize for my outburst with Midge. It's just that I . . ."

Fred grabbed his arm and headed to the bar. "No, you don't. I should apologize to you for the way she has been with your family. Don't give it another thought. I should have done something about it years ago, but it was just easier to go along to get along. Someone once said, 'If you want to know what your wife will be like in twenty years, look at her mother.' I didn't believe that at the time. When Midge and I got married, she was sweet, petite, and the opposite of my mother-in-law. Now, it seems, she has become her. Anyway, no worries, I'm sure things are going to be better in the future. Now, let's you and I do some catching up over a drink or two."

Henry ordered an old-fashioned and Fred got a double shot and a beer, then they found a table away from the main traffic.

"However," Fred continued when they were seated, "we didn't come here to talk about Midge. That's my problem. What's happening on your side of the world?"

Henry gazed into his glass for a long while then up to Fred. "Well, Fred, some very bad news. Mary and Linda were mur . . . died a few months ago."

Fred's face went ashen in the dim light and downed the double shot. "My God, Hank! My God! I don't know what to say. What happened? Why didn't you call?"

Henry shook his head. "I know I should have called you Fred, but when it happened, I kind of lost it. I was under sedation for a while because of the shock, and then I lost myself in a bottle for a couple of months."

Fred gripped his brother's hand across the table. "My God, Hank," he said again. I am so sorry. God knows I am. I wish I had known. For God's sake, what happened, car accident, fire?"

Henry took a long breath and then related the details of the grizzly episode to Fred. He told him a lot of what had happened since, leaving out the real cause of the house fire and his plans for the perpetrators.

Fred absorbed the story as he sat staring at his empty whisky glass. Then, after again expressing his sorrow, said, "So, tell me, Hank, is that why you're out here? Something to do with their mur . . . deaths?" He ordered another double when the server came by the table.

Henry thought about telling Fred his plans, but he wasn't sure how much Midge would know if she kept nagging him. So he said, "Well, Fred, as a matter of fact, it's not. It's more like what you said when I called. I've decided to spend some of the money I've been hoarding. I've always wanted a really snazzy sports car, and since I'm on my own again, I decided to buy one and have it customized to my tastes. As I told you before, I just don't know anyone who does customizing, so I called you."

"Well, Hank," Fred said skeptically, "it's just that I know you and know the way you think, or thought when you were growing up. I remember the time Gary Berkshire killed your kitten when you were nine or ten years old. You waited almost six months to get revenge. Then, one day, you saw his bike parked next to his front porch. When you saw it there, you sneaked over and sabotaged his brakes. Then you just sauntered off like you didn't have a care in the world."

"Later that day," Fred continued, "Berkshire jumped on the bike and, riding down the street, flew in front of a car because he couldn't stop. If I remember correctly, he ended up with a broken leg, fractured wrist, and three or four busted ribs. You were perfectly happy about it. Karma, I think you said."

"Ah, come on, Fred." Henry looked chagrinned that his brother even remembered the incident, even though he was there. "That was twenty-five years ago. I was just a kid. Kids do a lot of things that adults know are irrational behavior. They don't carry those things into adulthood with them."

"Hank," Fred paused and looked at Henry for several seconds before continuing. "That was just one example and certainly not the last. I know when you married and had Linda you settled down, became a responsible husband and father. But, somehow, I think that young kid is still in there."

Henry cringed at Fred's past tense usage "were a good father," but Fred was right. Henry was no longer a father or a husband. He could never again watch as Mary padded naked across the bedroom to the bath after they made love. He could never again hear Linda's bubbling laughter or, when she became a teenager, groans after one of his terrible jokes. His family, his loves, his life with them was past tense.

Fred continued, "I'm just saying . . . I'm just saying be careful, Hank. You aren't playing with bicycles or barbed wire anymore. The hurt, this time, is a lot harder. I guess devastating is a more accurate word. The stakes are a lot higher and resentments can kill. Be sure they don't kill you."

Henry thought again of the bumper sticker.

"And Hank," Fred gripped Henry's arm. "Just do me a favor. Think long and hard before you do anything like I think . . . no, like I know you're thinking. I know you were always kind of a loner Hank, and I won't interfere. I never have. But, if you need me . . . Well, if you need me for anything, you know I'm here for you."

Henry smiled. "I know Fred, and I appreciate it. I really do. If I find I have a need, believe me, I know I can trust you with my life."

"So, Hank," Fred changed the subject, "what kind of car are you getting?"

Henry chuckled. "That's a good question and one I don't have an answer for right now. The guy, Frank's, that's going to do the work, needs to know what I want before I know the best car to get."

Henry and Fred, reducing the conversation to small talk, reminisced until after midnight. Then after taking Fred home, Henry returned to the motel and went to bed and to sleep.

In his dream, Henry was tied to a post. His arms were behind him, lashed firmly to the pole so that he couldn't move. He was tied facing the rear of the black van with its doors open. In the back, cloaked in shadow, were three figures, two men and a female. One of the men was holding the female down while the other assaulted her.

Henry strained at the unrelenting bonds that held him.

Then, the men changed place as the second savagely used her.

When they were done, laughing hideously, they threw the girl, bloody and beaten almost to unconsciousness, out of the van onto the asphalt in front of Henry. Then, squealing the tires, they tore out of the alley and were gone. The girl turned her tear streaked face up toward Henry. She was just a teenager, maybe thirteen or fourteen years old. Sobbing through the tears and bloodied lips, she sobbed, "Why didn't you help me, mister? Why wouldn't you help me?"

The phone rang, jerking a sweating Henry back to wakefulness and reality. The phone told Henry it was seven o'clock. As he showered and shaved, the dream slowly faded into the back of his mind. But the hatred that he felt in his heart grew.

# CHAPTER 13

Henry arrived at Frank's promptly at 8:30 as he had planned. That was even though he had made a wrong turn and gone several miles out of his way thanks to a rental with no GPS. He pulled into what was once a service station and parked. The pumps had been removed, but the pump islands remained, harkening back to earlier days. The difference was the relatively new building attached to the back that appeared to cover about two acres and stood over two stories high.

Henry, taking his briefcase, walked into the station and told the apparent receptionist sitting behind a desk that he was there to see Frank.

The woman gave Henry a professional smile, saying, "May I tell him who it is that wishes to see him?"

Henry did not return the smile. "Yes, Henry Jenkins."

The woman picked up a phone and, hitting the first button, spoke into the phone. She then looked at Henry and said, "Mr. Alessio said he doesn't know you, and he has no appointments with a Henry Jenkins."

Henry immediately realized his mistake. "Oh, I'm sorry. Tell him Harold Daniels. I do have an appointment."

The woman again spoke into, and then hung up, the phone. "Mr. Alessio said he would be here shortly." She didn't offer Henry a seat and eyed him suspiciously.

Well, it was his own fault for giving a fictitious name in the first place. He turned his back to her annoying gaze and pretended to look at a drab, unrealistic seascape that hung on the paneled wall. Several minutes later, a door at the back opened, and Henry turned as a voice said, "Daniels, or Jenkins, or whatever your name is. I'm Frank Alessio. What do you want?"

Frank was huge. He was probably six-five, three-hundred pounds and looked like a football player. He had unruly, thick, black hair that matched his name, and he did not look particularly happy.

Henry started to put out his hand then thought better of it. "Yes, sir, Mr. Alessio. I'm Henry Jenkins. I called you last week to inquire as to whether you could do some work for me."

Frank growled, "Yeah, and you used a different name."

"Well, sir," Henry asked, "is there somewhere we can talk privately? I'll explain that."

Frank eyed Henry again and then motioned toward a glass enclosure on the right side of the station. "In there."

Henry stepped into the room and then stood until Frank closed the door and seated himself behind a massive desk that seemed to be appropriate for his massive bulk. He then motioned Henry to sit opposite.

Frank eyed Henry for, what seemed to Henry, forever but was probably only a few seconds. "What you need to know, Mr. Jenkins, is that if you are to do business with me, you never, ever lie to me. That is an excellent way to destroy a business relationship, and it could be worse. Do we understand one another?"

Henry nodded. "Yes, sir, I do understand. If I might explain, I did not know you or if you could do what I want done when I called. I felt the less you knew about me, the better if I didn't want to use your services. As it is, I feel you can help. Therefore, I have no need to give you false information. I believe you can understand I need to protect my interests just as you do yours."

Frank looked at him thoughtfully for a moment. "Yes, I suppose you do. Now, on the phone you said you needed some work done on a car. What kind of work do you need that a regular mechanic can't do, aside from what you told me on the phone?"

Henry opened his briefcase and extracted the list he had compiled. "I want the things on this list installed in and on a car." He slid the paper across the desk to Frank. "As I think I mentioned previously, when completed, the car should look like it did when it was manufactured."

Frank ignored him as he perused the items on the list. When he finished, he raised his gaze to Henry. "I have nothing to say concerning this at the present. Right now, I need some information from you. If that information pans out, so to speak, I will get back in touch with you."

"Fair enough," Henry replied. "I understand. You tell me what you need, and I'll provide it."

Frank pulled a form containing several pages from his desk and slid them to Henry. "You need to fill this out. Don't second guess what I need. It will be clear later on."

The form looked as complicated as a loan application and had about as many pages. Frank stood. "Just fill it in. It will probably take about an hour. Also, I will need a driver's license and six-thousand in cash. Fill in the paper. I'll be back." He rounded the desk and left the room.

Henry retrieved a pen from his pocket and began the arduous task of completing the expansive form.

Exactly sixty minutes later, Frank opened the door and resumed his seat behind the desk. "I don't run a bank here. For the type of work you want done, I want to know who I'm dealing with. The 6k is to let me find out more about you than you know about yourself. And I will." He tapped the list Henry had given him. "I noticed you have an item here for a Baker Electronics. If we are to do this work, we will do it all. Don't involve anyone else."

"Well, I just thought . . ." Henry started to say.

Frank interrupted. "And don't think. I'll do the thinking. All I need from you right now are the things I mentioned earlier."

Henry obediently handed Frank the completed form and, reaching for his wallet, extracted his driver's license, which he slid across the desk. Next, he opened the briefcase on his lap and counted out six-thousand dollars, which also went across the desk.

Frank counted the money then said, "I'm not going to give you a receipt for this. Less written items mean less items to come back and bite you in the ass later. You'll just have to trust that I'll always be above board with you."

He called the receptionist who took his license, copied it, and returned it to Henry. With that completed, Frank walked over, opened the door, and beckoned Henry.

Henry closed his briefcase and stood, moving toward the door.

"This may take a little time, maybe a month. If I need further information, I'll call you. I prefer you not call here questioning our timeline. It just slows things down. Rest assured, we will get back to you, and now, sir," he continued, "I have another appointment, so I will let you see yourself out."

This time, Henry shook hands with him and headed for the exit. He did not, in passing, bother to look at the receptionist.

Climbing into the rental, he started the engine and pulled out into traffic. And that, my friend, is that, he thought. Wham, bam, thank you ma'am, and hit the road. Oh, and on your way out, give me six grand. Henry scratched his head. What the hell was he going to do with six grand, investigate Henry back to conception?

Well, that meeting with Frank had only taken a couple of hours, and now, I have nothing to do until my flight tomorrow. As a matter of fact, I apparently have nothing to do for a month on this end. Well, at least, by that time, I'll have my plans together. Hopefully, there would be no problems with Frank's. Still, if he didn't pull the rest together, it would be back to square one anyway. Also, the police had a big head start on him because they were looking, and he was still planning. Well, no matter, he had chosen to give them a chance. If the cops catch them, and they get the death penalty, I can accept that. If no death penalty, I'm only thirty-eight. I can wait. As for the next month, I can renovate the house on Hunters Lane, or at least part of it.

He thought about the house.

Maybe I can get an interior decorator. I'm certainly not into that sort of thing. That was Mary's forte. But if I could get a flight back to Pittsburg today, it would give me tomorrow to get things started on that end.

Sheila wasn't expecting his flight in until six-thirty.

Parking in the motel parking lot, he went to his room and reached for the phone.

# CHAPTER 14

At 3:45, Henry, lucky enough to catch a direct flight out of Denver, sat in the Pittsburgh airport searching his phone for interior decorators. The fourth call was the one he wanted. Patience had never been one of Henry's virtues. When he wanted something done, especially when it was going to cost a lot of money, he didn't want to wait until Thursday or Monday or next month as the first three calls had suggested.

"Andre's Interiors," said the feminine voice. "May I help you?"

"Yes, I hope so," Henry responded. "My name is Henry Jenkins. I am looking to have my home decorated and the interior possibly redone and furnished and . . ."

"Just a moment, sir. I'll connect you with Ms. Cartier."

The phone went to elevator music and was picked up a moment later by another feminine voice. "Brenda Cartier. May I help you?" The voice was assertive yet pleasant, authoritative without being overbearing.

"Ms. Cartier, I hope you can. I recently purchased a home just outside Pittsburgh which I hope to have redecorated and furnished. My problem is I'm very restricted on time and cannot be available after about five tomorrow afternoon."

"I quite understand, Mr. Jenkins. Let me check my schedule."

There was a pause, then, "Mr. Jenkins, Helen tells me I just had a

93

cancellation for this afternoon. Do you think we could meet in about an hour, or would tomorrow morning be better?"

"No, today is great if you have time. I just flew in from Denver, so I'm at the airport. Let me get a rental car and I can meet you wherever you want."

"Let me see if I can make this easier," Cartier replied. "I'm just outside the airport. How about I pick you up at the baggage claim area, and we can drive out to see the house?"

"That would be great, if it's not too much of an imposition. Just so you know who I am, I'm wearing a blue suit with a print shirt and blue tie. I'll be carrying a tan suitcase and a briefcase."

"Very good, Mr. Jenkins. I don't think I'll have any trouble finding you, but I'm driving a red Trans-Am and I will see you shortly."

Henry had barely gotten through the airport, picked up his bag, and went out through the door when the red car pulled up in front of him. "Mr. Jenkins?"

Henry smiled, extending his hand through the passenger window. "Yes, and you would be Ms. Cartier?" It was more a statement than a question.

He took the slender hand and shook it, noticing it was firm, not mealy like some he had grasped. Tossing his bag and briefcase in the back, he climbed in—well, more like down—into the car and closed the door.

Sitting in the car, Henry judged the attractive woman next to him to be about thirty, five-foot-six or so, probably one-hundred-thirty pounds with shoulder length red hair and blue eyes. She wore a professional gray suit that came to mid-thigh on nicely shaped legs. She wore high heels, but they were relatively short, not stilettos.

"I hope I didn't make you wait long. I am Brenda, by the way. If we decide to work together, I don't think we need to be so formal."

"You can call me Henry, and no, I barely got out the door when you pulled up. Thank you, by the way, for doing this on such short notice."

Brenda pulled the car away from the curb and swung into the

traffic lane. "You're quite welcome. You sounded like this is something that is a priority, so if you point me in the right direction, we can discuss your intentions for the house on the way there."

Henry gave her directions to the house on Hunters Trail, then said, "To tell you the truth, I have no idea at all as to what I want. I am hoping you can use your expertise and knowledge to come up with ideas and solutions."

She glanced at Henry and back to the road. "Do you have a figure to work with?"

"No, I don't. There again, I will have to trust your better judgement."

The light ahead turned red and Brenda eased to a stop. "Mr. Jenkins, I don't mean to be harsh, but could you show me some identification? I hope you . . ."

"No, not at all," Henry said retrieving his license and handing it to her. "As a matter of fact, it surprised me that you didn't ask for it before you allowed me in your car."

Brenda looked at the license and handed it back, pulling forward as the light turned green. "I should have." She smiled. "I didn't mind picking you up, but when you didn't know what you wanted, and you didn't have a figure in mind for the work, I started to get worried. I hope you understand?"

Henry shook his head. "No, please, don't apologize. I understand completely, and I owe you an explanation. You see, my house burned down not long ago, and I bought this one to replace it. I would have had my wife do the interior, but she was ki . . . she di . . ."

Brenda's head swung quickly to look at Henry, this time interrupting him. "Oh, I know who you are now. There were write-ups in the paper about your wife and daughter and your house up in Clarksville. I am so sorry. I should have connected it when I heard your name."

She continued, "I read in the paper this morning that they were holding two persons of interest in connection with the case. I expect that makes . . ."

"What!?" Henry responded loud enough and quickly enough that Brenda jumped for the brake pedal. "What did you say?"

Brenda eased off the brake and resumed her speed. "The newspaper this morning, it said they had two suspects in custody for the murders."

Henry looked around at the scenery. "Can you pull over? I need to make a phone call."

"Sure, Henry, I'm sorry if I upset you. I just figured . . ."

Henry shook his head. "No, I'm sorry. I didn't mean to startle you. It's just that being out of town, I had not heard the news. It's important to me to know more information, so I need to call the detective in charge of the case."

Brenda found a place to pull onto the shoulder away from the traffic lane and came to a stop. "There you go. Take your time."

"Thank you. I'll be right back," Henry said, getting out of the car.

He pulled his phone from his pocket and punched the number for the Clarksville police.

"Clarksville Police."

"This is Henry Jenkins. May I speak to Detective Cameron, please? It's important." Henry' heart was pounding so heavily that his chest hurt, and he thought wouldn't it be great if I had a heart attack?

"Lieutenant Cameron. May I help you?"

"Lieutenant, this is Henry Jenkins. I've been out of town, and I just heard you had arrested two people in my wife's case. Is that true?"

"I'm sorry, Mr. Jenkins. Reporters like to jump the gun on reporting things before they are fact. That was false."

Henry's heart slowed immediately, and the ache in his chest disappeared.

Cameron continued. "We did bring in two guys, but they were in a stolen van. It turned out to be the wrong van anyway. It seems it belonged to a senior citizen in Philadelphia and was just stolen a week ago."

Henry said, "Oh, that's too bad. Just got my hopes up, I guess." But he breathed a sigh of relief in knowing he still had time.

Cameron coughed. "I hope you mean that, Mr. Jenkins. I really do, but for some reason, I don't feel that's the case. In any event, I'm sorry the news had to jump on shit like this before we had time to do our job. It just makes things more difficult."

Henry nodded as if Cameron could see him. "Yes, you're right. Well, maybe next time."

"Mr. Jenkins, Henry, just remember what I said before. Don't make me come after you too."

"Right, Lieutenant. I'll be talking to you." Henry disconnected and returned to the car, sliding in and closing the door.

Brenda shifted into gear and pulled back on the highway. "Well, did they get them?"

"No, wrong guys," Henry said, trying to make is voice sound depressed. "Newspapers just got ahead of themselves."

"I am so sorry," she said compassionately. "I know you must feel terrible. I wish there was something I could say or do . . ."

"Yeah," Henry said. "Well, maybe they will find them soon. Anyway, it's nice of you to say. And if you can make this house look like something, you will have done plenty."

Following Henry's directions, they were soon at Hunters Trail. Henry pointed to a mailbox further up the road. "Turn in at that next driveway next to the mailbox."

Brenda pulled in the drive and angled back to the house. Getting out, she admired the brick and stone structure for a moment before following Henry to the house.

Henry unlocked the door to the house he did not yet own and turned on the lights even though they weren't needed in the well-lit foyer.

"As I said, I know nothing from nothing. So if you need help, yell. If not, I'll stay out of your way while you do your thing."

Brenda sat the briefcase she had carried in from the car on the floor and took out a digital tape measure, a sketch pad, and a pencil. "Well, what I have to do first is measure each room and sketch the layout. That will help me determine what I have to work with. So I guess I'll just take measurements for a while and sketch. When I get to full room dimensions, I may want your help, but that will probably be a while."

"That's fine," Henry said. "You take your time. I'm going to go meander around outside and in the basement to look around. If you need help, just yell, and if I don't hear you, just hang tight. I won't be far away."

"Okay," Brenda said, heading for the stairs. "I'll start in the back and work my way forward."

Henry nodded, smiling. "By the way, if you haven't made plans, I'll treat you to dinner when you're finished here."

Brenda returned the smile. "No, I haven't any plans, and dinner sounds like a lovely idea. I'll even drive," she said with a laugh.

Henry laughed in return and exited the living room heading for the basement and the shelter, which he had a keen interest in exploring.

At least the heat had been left on in the house. It kept the chill out. That reminded him, when he took the money to Greene on Wednesday, he would have to have the utilities transferred to his name.

He exited the back door and stood on the porch. It was a real porch, not a stoop as was the case on many houses. He looked across the lawn to the shelter entrance. The knoll into which the door was set looked like a small, manmade hill. Striding across the lawn and unlocking the door, he went in and turned on the light switch at the entrance.

At the bottom of the stairs, he found another door identical to the one at the top that opened into the shelter. He had not noticed this one as it stood open in the darkened stairwell. He checked the hinges, found them good, and fitted the key into the lock. It was the same as the top door lock. Good, he only had the one key. Turning on the fluorescent lights spaced evenly in the ceiling, he decided to take inventory of the items in the shelter.

After standing and surveilling the room for a minute, he began to walk around the perimeter. The shelving ran the length of two of the walls and was about eighteen inches deep. There were five tiers of shelving, and all were laden with an assortment of items.

Henry started with the food section of the shelves. He idly picked up various cans and boxes, reading the labels and expiration dates on them, then returned them to the spots from which he had taken them. He noticed two things in his browsing. One, all the food was relatively new, and two, it was arranged in alphabetical order with apple sauce and asparagus on the left followed by beans, corn, and so on, down to canned zucchini on the right. All in all, Henry figured there was enough food to last a family of four five or six months, longer if it were rationed.

He went on to inspect the cots, blankets, sheets, and pillows he had seen on his first visit, along with the battery-operated radio and uniquely battery-operated television (how good would they operate within the lead shielding of the room?). Henry guessed there was an outside antenna somewhere. There were two walkie-talkies, flashlights, and boxes of batteries that were new with guarantees of five years.

He would have to ask the realtor when Hampstead had moved and why they had replenished everything so shortly before.

He moved along the shelves, coils of rope—probably ten about a hundred feet long—a chain saw, bar oil, and four cans marked gasoline. Henry hefted one to find it was full and marked Sept. 27. Then on to regular hand saws, a log splitter, wedges, and four boxes of books. Henry picked up a few and looked at the authors, Poe, Hart, Hemingway, Twain, and King, some psychology books, and a library dictionary.

Henry replaced the books and closed the lids to the boxes. There were enough books in the boxes to stock a small library, he thought, or at least the bookmobile that came into Clarksville on Fridays when he was a young lad.

He moved to the next wall. Near the end and next to the shelves were several folded director's chairs—the ones with the canvas seats and backs. Next to those were three folding tables a little larger than a card table and made of plastic. Near that was the large icebox Henry had seen on his last visit. He opened the door. The box was constructed so as to operate either by electric or with a large block of ice in the top bin. Now there was a block of ice in the bin and the electric was on to keep it frozen.

To the right of the icebox was a generator. It looked like a gas generator, but there was a large box next to it that revealed a lot of electrical equipment that, Henry figured, kept it running even when the electric was off. It was probably configured before the modern automatic whole-house generators of today.

In the corner was, as Henry had guessed, a bathroom complete with a small shower that was probably operated with an underground well and powered by the generator.

Along the fourth wall, between the bathroom and the door leading to the basement were the six-foot-tall, double-wide wall lockers he had seen before. He walked over to them and looked at the locks. Whoever had put them on didn't want anyone to get into them. They were huge, and the shackles that went through the loops in the door were about three eights of an inch thick. There were two locks on each cabinet. The cabinets themselves were not standard office equipment. They appeared, to Henry, to be about a quarter of an inch thick steel.

Henry fingered one of the locks wondering about the Latin inscription on the side, 'Finem Respice,' Consider the end!

"Good evening, Mr. Jenkins."

Henry jumped; the hair on the back of his neck prickling. His heart beat wildly in his chest. He swung around to stare at the tall, white-haired figure standing in the shadow of the hallway to the house.

"What in Christ's name . . . ? Who are you, and what are you doing in here?"

The man stepped into the shelter. He was probably six-four and very thin. The trench coat he had on seemed to hang from his frame rather than him wearing it. His skin had a pasty pallor, almost ashen gray.

"Well, Mr. Jenkins, I should really ask you what you are doing here as I technically still own this house until Wednesday. Allow me to introduce myself, Mr. Jenkins. I am Bartholomew Jephthah

Hampstead. I'm sorry for startling you. I thought you would have heard the door opening."

Henry shook the offered hand and willed his heart back to its normal rhythm, at the same time forcing himself to smile. "I guess I was just engrossed in my thoughts. How did you get in?"

Hampstead swung his head back toward the house. "The young lady upstairs allowed me in. She called for you, but as you are now aware, you can't here from in here. So, I expected I would find you in here. This room is lead lined and soundproof, almost tomb-like you might say." He smiled.

Henry suddenly didn't like Hampstead, although he was not sure why. Intuition, Mary would call it, gut feeling to Henry. "I didn't know for sure, but I figured it was lead lined if it was a bomb shelter."

Henry motioned to the tables and chairs. "I'm glad you came by, Mr. Hampstead. I have several questions for you. Shall I grab a table and a couple of chairs?"

Hampstead helping, they set up a table and two chairs in the family room portion of the basement. He then went back through the workshop to close the door to the shelter. He reminded himself to ask Hampstead how to open it.

Returning to the family room, he said, "Hopefully, the next time you come, I'll have more comfortable furnishings."

"There won't be a next time, Mr. Jenkins," Hampstead said sitting on the chair facing the empty fireplace in the large L-shaped family room. "I'm afraid I only came today to drop off some more keys. I knew with a little sleuthing you would be able to figure them out. I didn't realize you would be here since our deal closes next week, but since you are, I will try to answer your questions and, perhaps, offer a little advice."

Henry was glad he wasn't coming back and wondered what the advice was, but he decided he would do as Hampstead requested and ask his questions. Besides, the man gave Henry the creeps. He looked like death warmed over. Henry would be glad to get this over with and see the last of him. Also, what kind of name was Jephthah? Hebrew?

CHARLES ROBINSON

"Well, I guess my first question is how did you know I'd be here? I believe you did know I would be here. Don Greene probably told you I had taken the keys. But, how did you know it would be today?"

Hampstead smiled (his eyes didn't), showing a glimpse of yellowed dentures. "Deductive reasoning, you might say. You're right; Greene did tell me you had taken the keys. So, I figured you were in a hurry to get started. I did miscalculate, however. I stopped by earlier as I figured you'd be here this morning."

"Yes," Henry replied, "I just got back into town."

"I know," Hampstead interjected. "From out west somewhere, I think."

Henry was becoming unnerved by the man sitting across from him. How did he know he was out west? Did he know about his flight? He started to ask Hampstead how he knew that, but the piercing eyes took his courage, and he remained silent.

Instead, he asked, "Can you tell me why, if you were moving and selling the house, you stocked the shelter with supplies? I noticed all the food, water, and gasoline was stocked in September or later of this year.

Hampstead's gaze did not waiver from Henry. "Yes, it's quite simple. My wife had a stroke in June."

Henry jerked, and Hampstead nodded. "Yes, Mr. Jenkins, the same month as your tragedy."

"How did you know about that?" Henry asked suspiciously.

Hampstead laughed, and it was almost a cackle. "Don't be alarmed, Mr. Jenkins. It's no great mystery. I do read the newspapers you know, and it was just simple arithmetic. Your house burned. You needed another. My wife stroked. I needed to get rid of one."

Hampstead watched as Henry relaxed and then continued. "As I was saying, my dear wife had a stroke in June. I continued to supply the shelter until the doctors told me she would not recover to any great extent and that she would need my care. Because of that and the layout of this house, I decided to buy one on one level and sell this one. The one I bought is smaller, so I had no need for and no room for all the things I had put in the shelter."

Henry felt somewhat better but not completely at ease with Hampstead's answer. Hampstead seemed to look through him, into him. And it made Henry jittery.

"Also," Henry said, "I noticed a bathroom with a shower, deep sink, and toilet. Where is the water supply and where is the power to supply it if the gasoline runs out?"

"Good questions." Hampstead smiled without smiling. "There is a well in the floor of the entry out back. It goes down six hundred-eighty-three feet. That's to stay below the effects of radioactive fallout. The pump is powered by the generator I'm sure you saw in the shelter. As you probably already know, the gasoline is only to start the generator. Once it is running, the electronic and electrical system keeps it running until it is shut off manually.

Henry didn't like that Hampstead seemed to know what he knew, but said, "I noticed two large cabinets. What's in them?"

"That is a question I will answer shortly. Any others?"

Henry nodded. "Just one, how do you get from the house into the shelter? I noticed you came in that way, so there must be a way to access it from the basement."

Hampstead stood, "That I will show you and then answer your previous question." He strode toward the peg board wall with Henry following. Pulling what looked like a laser pointer from his pocket, he stood gazing at the door. Henry wasn't sure if he was praying or looking for something in the peg board.

A moment later he aimed the pointer at the peg board. Henry heard an audible click, and the door swung open.

He released the button on the pointer and handed it to Henry. "That is a laser key, Mr. Jenkins. It is set at a frequency to operate the locking mechanism of the door. You just have to know where to aim it. If you count in six holes from the right and twelve holes down from that blue line on the peg board, that is the lock. Then you just aim the key at that hole and push the button. The numbers should be easy for you to remember, Mr. Jenkins. Six and twelve, June, twelve."

Henry again felt his skin crawl. June twelfth, the day Mary and Linda died. Hampstead pulled the door open, and Henry followed him into the shelter.

Once inside, Hampstead pulled four keys from his pocket and handed them to Henry. "Those," he said, "fit the locks to the cabinets."

Henry held the keys and gazed at them uncomfortably. On one side of each key was a coiled serpent in bas relief, and on the other, the French inscription 'Ils ne passeront pas,' they shall not get past. The keys were two inches in length to match the size of the locks.

Henry started to ask Hampstead about the inscriptions when he said, "I believe, Mr. Jenkins, that in those cabinets, you will find everything you will need for your planned endeavors."

Again, Henry felt the hair on the nape of his neck rise, and he had a fervent desire to reach up and smooth it down. "I'm afraid I don't understand what you mean, Mr. Hampstead."

Hampstead's eyes drilled into Henrys. "I believe you do, Mr. Jenkins. Allow me to explain. In some circles, I am believed to have certain psychic abilities. As a result of those, shall we say, powers, I am able or perceive events before they happen. Sometimes, those premonitions are not of my choosing, but I do not always have the liberty of selecting what I wish. As such, when you spoke to me at the realtor's office, I began to receive subliminal messages, or visions, whatever you wish to call them. So please let me explain what I envisioned of your situation.

"You are looking for," Hampstead continued, "or more correctly, will be looking for, the perpetrators of the murders of your wife and daughter. This shelter is your reason for wanting to buy this particular house. You will, in time, probably find those who are the object of your search. However, Mr. Jenkins, one will be elusive to you."

"Your plan is to use this room and the items in those cabinets to carry out your deeds. One word of caution, Mr. Jenkins, if you carry out your plans, you will pay dearly for your resentments."

Hampstead buttoned the too large trench coat around his lank frame and walked toward the door.

"Mr. Hampstead," he called after the departing figure as he followed him into the family room. "If what you say is true, or even partially true, and if I am going to do what you say, will I catch them?"

Hampstead did not stop or turn but said, "I don't know. That's all I see. Goodnight and goodbye, Mr. Jenkins." Hampstead strode up the basement stairs and was gone.

Henry listened to the closing of the front door. He didn't believe in psychics and wondered how Hampstead knew what he knew. Had he been talking to Cameron? If so, how did he know him, and why would Cameron be talking to a civilian about an open investigation anyway? Maybe he needed to do a little research on Hampstead. The man was, to say the least, eerie. Henry shivered involuntarily. He absently put the four keys in his pocket.

Henry closed the door to the shelter and was standing in the family room when Brenda Cartier came down the stairs. She looked at him, and the smile she wore faded when she looked at him. "Are you okay? You look like you've seen a ghost."

Henry wondered if he was all right but smiled and said, "Yeah, I'm fine. I guess that guy just gave me the creeps."

"I'm sorry. Maybe I shouldn't have let him in," she said. "It's just that he said he was the previous owner, and I . . ."

Henry laughed. "No, that was fine. Technically, he is still the owner until next Wednesday, and I needed to see him anyway. He just seemed a little weird, that's all."

"Well," she said, "I finished upstairs. If this is the only room down here, I will get the measurements, do my sketch, and we'll be finished."

Henry nodded. "I believe that will be good. There's a bathroom, but I don't think it will need anything, and there's a workshop that you don't need to worry about." He didn't mention the shelter.

She quickly got the measurements of the room, sketched them on her pad and turned to Henry. "Okay, I'm all done."

"Good," he replied. "Let's go get some dinner. It's late and I'm famished."

They retreated upstairs where Brenda returned her work to her briefcase and snapped it shut. They then exited the house, got in the car, and headed back toward Pittsburgh.

"I'm afraid," he apologized, "that I am going to have to depend on you as to where we will eat. I know very little about this town."

"No problem," she said shaking her head and making the red curls bounce. "You tell me what you are in the mood for, and I'll find the place."

I'm in the mood for a redhead, Henry thought. Then thought he shouldn't think that. Aloud he said, "Well, a filet mignon sounds pretty good unless you have something better in mind."

She smiled. "No, that sounds perfect, and I know just the place."

An hour and a half later, they sat at the table, dinner over, discussing the house on Hunters Trail.

"Is there any particular style you prefer," Brenda asked. "Mediterranean, French Provincial, Early American, Conventional?"

Henry smiled, "Like I would know. No, I will have to trust you as to what will look best and trust your judgement and your good taste."

Brenda laughed. "Thank you for your confidence in me. That's very kind of you. I'll tell you what. Are you going to be around tomorrow?"

Henry nodded. "I will be, until about one o'clock anyway."

"Good," Brenda replied, "I'll put some ideas together with some pictures and bring them to your motel in the morning, if that's okay. That will give me a chance to see what style you like."

"That will be fine," Henry said. "The only problem is, I don't have a motel and didn't even think of it until you mentioned it."

"No problem," she replied. "We'll get you settled in somewhere."

An hour later, Brenda dropped him off at a Red Roof Inn with a promise to be there by nine o'clock the next morning.

Henry got to his room and went to bed to lay there to think about Bartholomew Jephthah Hampstead until the wee hours of the morning.

# CHAPTER 15

The phone rang letting Henry know it was eight o'clock. He picked the receiver up, sat it back down, and swinging his legs around, sat up. It felt like he had only gotten a couple of hours' sleep, and then he remembered that it had been little more than that. Thank you, Bartholomew Jephthah Hampstead.

He showered, letting the tepid water bring him slowly to life. Dressing, he went to the lobby, had a continental breakfast, picked up a newspaper and a cup of coffee, and went back to his room. Scanning the paper, he saw there was nothing about Clarksville and had half the crossword puzzle filled in when a knock at the door told him Brenda had arrived.

He opened the door, and she came in flashing a smile. "Good morning."

She had on a pale blue dress, under her coat, that came a couple of inches above the knee. She took off her coat and tossed it on the bed and placed her briefcase on the table under the window. "I found some really nice pictures that I hope will give you some ideas. I know pictures are not as good as the actual items, but it will give you the differences between the styles we might use. Want to look?"

"Sure," Henry replied.

She sat down, the dress riding up to mid-thigh. It did not go unnoticed by Henry, but he glanced away and sat at the table. She passed pictures to him, explaining the types, styles and guesstimated costs, placing the pictures in piles of likes, dislikes, and no opinion.

When she had gone through the entire stack, she had narrowed the 'likes' down to about a tenth of the original size. These, she clipped together and tossed back into the briefcase.

Smiling again, she said, "Well, now I have a pretty good idea of what you want the house to look like. And I must say you have pretty good taste."

"Thank you," Henry replied, "even if it is not true. Now, let's discuss money. How much do you think you'll need to get started?"

"At this moment," she said, tugging her earlobe, "I can't even give you a guess. Now that you have provided me with some ideas, I will need to do some pricing, check on availability, and where I will have to go for items before I can even give you an educated guess."

Henry reached for his briefcase. "Okay, let's do it this way." He counted out several bills and slid them across to her. "There is thirty thousand. That should get you going."

Brenda whistled. "I'll say. Are you sure you want to entrust me with this? I might run off to Mexico and retire."

He laughed. "If you're going to retire on that, you better use it to find a rich boyfriend. No, seriously, the way my time and availability is right now, and things I have to do, it will not allow me to be in touch very often. So with that, you can get a start. I'll check back with you occasionally to see when you will need more." He paused, "I can't give you a number to reach me, because of my work, but I will be in touch."

"All right." She wrote out a receipt and handed it to him. "Do you prefer Henry or Hank?"

"Henry is fine. I don't think anyone besides my brother has ever called me Hank."

"What is your middle name, if I might be so bold?"

"David. I was named after Thoreau."

"Oh," Brenda smiled. "I like that. Anyway, I'll get started on your project this afternoon and will try to have it finished as soon as possible."

"You can take your time," Henry replied. "I won't be ready to move in for a month at the earliest and maybe a good bit longer."

He gave her the key to the front door. He could always get in through the shelter if need be. "And I guess you shouldn't be in the house before next Wednesday. That is when I take ownership."

"No problem. I will be in the planning stage until then."

Henry looked at his watch. It was already past twelve, and Sheila was to meet him at the airport at two o'clock.

"Could I," he asked, "impose on you to drive me out to the airport? I'm supposed to meet someone there at two."

"Certainly," Brenda said, "and it's not an imposition. I'm more than happy to take you back."

Henry smiled. "You're a sweetheart. Let me grab my things, and we can go."

Brenda dropped Henry at the baggage claim area as he requested with a promise that he would love the house when she was finished.

At exactly two o'clock, Sheila walked into the doors looking for Henry, who was standing just to the side. She stopped surveying the area when he walked up and patted her on the bottom. She turned swiftly, swinging her purse in an arc as she did so.

Henry ducked below the weapon, laughing. "Boy, I'm glad I didn't do more than pat your butt. I'd be dead."

Sheila laughed in return, putting her arms around him. "I thought you were a masher. It's been a long time since anyone patted my bottom out in public."

"Just goes to show," he responded, kissing her, " there are a lot of people who have no taste."

Sheila took his arm, and they headed for the exit with Henry carrying his bag and Sheila his briefcase.

"Are you saying you assault all the ladies?"

"No, not at all," he said. "Just the pretty ones."

Sheila acted as though she was going to hit him again, and he grabbed her hand. "Let's change the subject before you kill me."

Retrieving the car, with Henry driving, they made the trip back to

Clarksville and Sheila's. The conversation was light both through the drive and through the delicious dinner Sheila prepared for them. Later, they sat together on the couch watching TV.

Sheila looked up and asked, "So are you just passing through, or are you going to stay awhile?"

"Well, my dear," he said, thinking about what he had upcoming, "I Guess, if you can tolerate me, I'll be around town this week, but I'll be gone most of the next week and maybe longer."

Sheila considered the possibilities and smiled. "Good. That's that long I can try to change your mind about staying."

Henry winced inwardly, but said, "I don't think that is in the cards, but I understand your feelings. Now, rather than get into any heavy conversation, why don't we call it a day?"

Sheila leaned against him. "On one condition."

"What's that?"

"We sleep in my room."

Henry stood and pulled her to her feet. "I think that is doable. I'll race you to the bedroom."

Henry, lying on his back and drifting off after they had made love, tried to remember if making love with Mary had been like this. He was grateful he couldn't remember and felt guilty for trying to make the comparison.

# CHAPTER 16

Henry woke. Sheila lay on her back, one hand raised above her head. The sheet had been kicked off during the night, and Henry rose up on one elbow to relish the beautiful, naked figure beside him for a moment and then pulled the sheet up over her breasts and rolled out of bed.

He had a lot to do today. He was already two days late in his promise to go to the office, and he still had to get a cashier's check and drive to Pittsburgh.

By the time he had showered, shaved, and dressed, Sheila had roused and lay on the bed stretching.

Henry leaned down and kissed her. "Good morning, sleepyhead."

Sheila yawned and stretched again, the sheet sliding off her breasts. She didn't bother to pull it back up. "Why didn't you wake me?"

"Well, when I woke and you were laying there naked, I decided would rather admire you than wake you." He grinned.

"So you covered me," Sheila pouted. "That doesn't sound much like admiration to me."

He laughed. "It was either cover you or attack you, and since I have a lot to do today, I opted for the first."

She reached up her arms. "I would prefer the second."

Henry kissed her and stood. "Under other circumstances, I would too. However, for now, I'll have to settle for memories of last night and get my body out of here."

Sheila propped a pillow against the headboard and leaned back against it. The sheet fell to her waist, and she left it there as concern wrinkled her brow. "Would I be out of line if I asked what you were doing today?"

Henry smiled, "Relax. I'm just going to the office, the bank, stuff like that."

She nodded smiling. "Well, in that case, I won't make you come back to bed."

Henry leaned, kissed her once more, and started for the door. "I'll see you this evening, imp."

He drove to his office, and placing his briefcase under his desk, walked down the hall to George Williams' office where he rapped on the open door.

Williams looked up, recognized who it was, and said, "Come in Henry. Have a seat. I thought you were going to be back on Monday."

He didn't look particularly happy.

Henry took a seat opposite Williams and crossed his legs. "Well, George, I had every intention of being here on Monday, but I ran into a situation that required me to be out of town. As it were, I didn't get back until yesterday."

George tapped his pencil against the pad on his desk pad. "You know the old expression, Henry. 'The road to Hell is paved with good intentions.'"

Henry knew Williams was right, but it did not negate the beginning of his anger at the tone of the man's voice. "Yes, I realize I could have, should have, but I made the decision to go on the weekend, and with the nature of the business, it slipped my mind to call on Monday."

Williams gave him a knowing look, tapping his pencil. "Yes, well, I guess now that you're back at work, we can put this little incident behind us and move on."

Henry cleared his throat and stared at the tapping pencil. He wanted to jerk it out of Williams' hand and throw it across the room.

Instead, he said, "As a matter of fact, George, I'm not going to be able to return to work right now. I came in to tell you I'm going to be off a while longer."

The pencil tapped faster. "How much time are we talking about, Henry?"

Henry shrugged. "At this particular time, I'm not sure. I've got things to get in order. I've got to find another place to live since my house burned down and some other things I need to take care of before I return."

The pencil tapping slowed but didn't stop. "What are we talking about here? A day, a week?"

The urge to grab the pencil from his hand grew. "I don't know. I know it will take longer than a couple of weeks. It may be a month, six months, or a year."

The tapping again picked up speed. "I'm afraid that is unacceptable, Henry. As a matter of fact, the time you have taken already is too much. You will have to make a decision, Jenkins. Either return to work today, or I'll have to let you go."

And it's Jenkins now, Henry thought then said, "Then, I guess, under the circumstances, I'm fired."

George stared at him, tapping, tapping. "You mean that you are willing to give up twelve years and your retirement with Blaycock on a whim?"

Henry suddenly detested Williams and his tapping pencil. "Well, with twelve years, I'm vested, and would you stop with the damned pencil?"

He grabbed it from the man's hand and, snapping it into two pieces, threw it on the desk. "Yes, I am willing to give it up! I don't need this job and haven't since an inheritance and my investments have more than doubled over the years. Furthermore, the things I wanted the time off for are, to me, more important than this company or your patronizing, asinine attitude and your pencil tapping."

Williams looked aghast, and as if it had suddenly grown hot in the office, reddened. "Then I believe, Mr. Jenkins, that this conversation is at an end. I will call security, who will escort you as you clean out your desk and vacate the premises."

Henry rose from this chair. He had never burned his bridges behind him before, but in this case, he relished it. "Goodbye, sir, and I use that in reference to your age, not out of respect." He walked back to clear out his office smiling. At least he got him to stop tapping the damned pencil.

Henry removed his personal belongings from his desk under the watchful eye of a security guard and put them in a box. The guard, standing in his office door, pissed him off. What was he going to do, steal his desk? The company didn't have anything he would have wanted. Still, the guard was only doing as he had been directed by someone. So Henry placed his belongings in the box and said nothing.

Next, he stopped by his secretary's desk where the news of his departure had already landed. "Kathy." He smiled. "It has been really special to have you as my secretary. I could have asked for no one better. If you are interested, when I get to my next job, I will have a place for you."

The thirty-three-year-old secretary, not beautiful but not really plain either, smiled while holding back tears. "Thank you, Henry. I'll remember that. I'm really sorry that you're leaving though. I've enjoyed working with you."

Henry leaned and kissed her cheek. "And I could have picked no one better. You take care." He started toward the door and said over his shoulder, "And, don't forget what I said. When I have a job, you have one with me, if you want."

Kathy reached for a Kleenex. "I won't forget. Goodbye, Henry."

# CHAPTER 17

Henry got in his car with mixed feelings. He was glad he had quit, glad about what he had said to Williams who really was, always had been, a jerk. Yet, he was sad he would no longer be working with Kathy, or for that matter, many of the others, to whom he hadn't said goodbye.

He backed the Cadillac out of the parking space and looked at the sign in front—Henry Jenkins, Personnel Mgr. (soon to be removed).

As he drove to the Clarksville Savings and Loan, his next stop, he thought about his next withdrawal. He had given Brenda thirty thousand. Six thousand had gone to Frank's Auto. Then there was the cash he had used for Sheila and himself. He would have to withdraw enough additional to pay for the house, and who knew how much he would need for the car.

He decided it would be best to get a cashier's check for the house and keep the cash for the car since that was a cash only deal.

Once inside the savings and loan, he hoped it would take less time than his previous banking transaction. Yet even though he had more money in this bank and was not closing the account, it took longer. As a result, by the time he had completed the withdrawal and drove to Greene Realty, it was three o'clock.

"Ah, Mr. Jenkins," Don Greene said as Henry stepped into the realtor's office. "Here with the money I see."

"Of course, of course," Henry said mimicking the realtor. It went unnoticed by Greene.

"If we can step into the conference room," Greene said, "the necessary people from the title company are here to complete the paperwork."

They entered, and Henry was introduced to the other two people in the room. Seated, the appropriate legal papers were passed to Henry for signature. While the title attorney explained each, Henry read each page of the contract, sometimes rereading clauses for clarity. Greene fidgeted occasionally, wishing he would hurry along, but Henry ignored him, absorbing the entire document. When he had finished, he signed and/or initialed each page as required, and the title people left.

"There is one more thing I will require," Henry said.

"Of course, of course, Mr. Jenkins, and what would that be?"

Henry wanted to punch him in his 'Of Course'. Instead, he smiled, "I will need the utilities transferred into my name. I'm sure Mr. Hampstead no longer wants them in his."

Greene nodded. "Of course, no, he would not want that. I'll get that done first thing in the morning. Of course."

"Of course," Henry responded. At least he spread them out that time. He picked up the check and stood to go. "Let me know when that is taken care of, and I'll be back with your check."

"Just a moment, Mr. Jenkins!"

Henry thought Greene was going to jump across the table to keep him from leaving. "Perhaps I can get in touch with them right now and save you an additional trip down here. If you don't mind sitting, I will go to my office and make some calls."

Henry smiled. "Of course, Mr. Greene, you are absolutely right. There is no need at all." He sat and waited while Greene went to his office to make the necessary calls.

When he returned and assured Henry that everything had been completed satisfactorily, Henry pulled the cashier's check from his briefcase and handed it to the realtor. "That is for three hundred forty thousand dollars. With the twenty thousand I gave you before, that takes care of our transaction. I see that Mr. Hampstead has completed his portion of the sale, so if you will give me my copies, we can consider it complete, and I will be on my way."

"Of course, Mr. Jenkins, of course." Greene hesitated, "Of course, there is one thing. It is your responsibility to pay for the title search. It is just routine."

Henry whirled toward the realtor. "You mean to tell me that for some lawyer's secretary to call a courthouse and ask if a deed is clear costs three hundred dollars?"

"Yes, Sir, Mr. Jenkins. It sure does. Three hundred dollars. That's what it will cost you."

Henry threw his briefcase on the table, flipped it open, and removing the paperwork for the house, held it out to Greene. "Give me back that Cashier's check and the twenty grand. I told you up front that three sixty was it. Not one penny more. Three hundred dollars is more. Therefore, I don't want it."

Greene looked panicked "No, no, Mr. Jenkins. Don't you worry. I'll absorb that cost. I'll take the loss personally."

Henry laughed. "Loss? At seven percent, you made over twenty-four thousand on this sale. Don't you mean a reduction in your gain? Oh, and I will need your receipt for that. I don't want it to come back on me later."

Greene grabbed a receipt book and scrawled the information. Signing it, he handed the paper to Henry, ignoring his comment.

Henry put the paperwork and the receipt in the briefcase and closed it. Putting out his hand and smiling, he said, "Mr. Greene, it has been a pleasure doing business with you. If I decide to move in the future, I will be sure to list the house with you."

Greene, moments before flustered, now beamed as he shook Henry's hand and watched as his most recent sale went out the door.

When Henry pulled into Sheila's driveway, it was seven-thirty and after dark. He locked the car and, carrying his briefcase, went inside.

He had wanted to sift through the debris next door in search of the wall safe but decided it could wait until tomorrow.

Upon entering, he caught the aroma of dinner wafting through the house from the kitchen. Just like coming home to Mary from work, he thought sadly. Then pushing the thought aside, he called to tell Sheila he was home.

"In the kitchen," she yelled back.

When he entered the kitchen, he was met with a hug and deep kiss. He held her back at arm's length and turned her slowly around. She was attired in a ruffled apron that covered most of her breasts and came barely below the tops of her thighs. It came about six inches from meeting in the back, exposing her bottom in a provocative manner.

"You look delicious." He smiled.

"Delicious is an expression for something you eat," she responded.

He grinned. "Yes, I know. Are you what I'm having for dinner?"

"I believe," she said, "that I have created a monster."

"And you love it," he retorted, pulling her back against him and caressing her derriere.

As it were, the chicken that had been roasting burned to something akin to a cinder while they explored the various ways to bring Sheila to a climax in the bedroom. Later, they had pizza delivered and watched TV as they ate their alternate dinner.

By Friday, Henry had retrieved the wall safe from the ashes next door, deposited Mary's jewelry, some files, and other items in a safe deposit box and made arrangements with a local company to clean up the lot and dispose of the debris. They would also haul in fill dirt and topsoil and fill in the hole that had been the basement. Also by that time, he had received checks from the insurance for the house and Mary's car that had been in the garage. Of the proceeds, he redeposited three hundred eighty thousand in the Clarksville National Bank, which made Mr. Randolph very happy. The rest he deposited in the Savings and Loan he had recently visited.

By Monday, he had tied up all his loose ends in Clarksville. Though

Sheila was not at all enthusiastic about it, Henry decided to go (he told her to Denver to go over family business with Fred) back to Pittsburgh.

No, he didn't know how long he would be gone. Yes, he would call her when he knew when he was coming back. Yes, he had packed enough for the trip and could get more there if need be.

# CHAPTER 18

Henry pulled into the drive at Hunters Trail at nine o'clock. Although Sheila had wanted to, again, drive him to the airport for his flight to Denver, he persuaded her to remain at home this time, and he would just park in long term parking, as he was unsure when or what time he would be returning.

When he went in, he saw there was still no furniture, but the interior had been painted and new wall coverings had been assigned to the bedrooms. Henry wasn't especially fond of wall paper, or vinyl, but it was tastefully done, so not a problem. He thought, even without furniture, the place looked significantly better. New carpeting had been installed in the bedrooms that coordinated well with the walls, and the hardwood in the rest of the house had been sanded and recoated. Brenda was doing an excellent job, and Sheila would really like it.

Sheila? He thought. Then, well, after this is all over, why not. If they stayed together, he could do a lot worse.

After walking through the rooms upstairs, he opened the basement door, went through, and shut it behind him. He found the light switch on the wall, lit the stairwell, and went down to and through the family room and the workshop to the peg board wall at the end. Then pulling the laser key from his inside jacket pocket, he started counting. Over six from the right, down twelve from the horizontal line, he thought.

Six-twelve, June twelve, easy for him to remember as Hampstead had reminded him. He pointed the laser at the appropriate hole and pushed the button. There was an audible click, and the door swung open two inches.

Sticking the key back in his pocket, he thought he needed to find a place in the workshop to leave it so he didn't have to carry it around with him. He stepped into the hallway and closed the door behind him. Feeling in the dark for a light switch, he chided himself for not locating it before he closed the door. Throwing the switch, he flooded the interior with the lights that lined the ceiling, going down the steps and along the tunnel to the shelter. He was amazed at the cost someone must have paid to put the elaborate shelter in.

Once inside, he went directly to the cabinets and trying the keys found those that opened the locks on the one in front of him. He removed the locks and opened the doors. At first, he saw a pile of what looked like huge logging chains on the floor of the cabinet. Rusty chains that appeared very old. Then a circlet of metal caught his eye and, reaching in, he pulled it to him.

One side of the metal hoop was hinged and attached to a chain. The other side, opposite the hinge, had been made with a locking mechanism to secure it. Henry turned what was obviously an antique leg iron over in his hand, wondering how old it was, where Hampstead (if it was Hampstead and not the previous owner) had acquired it, and why he even had it. Inscribed around the side of the leg iron was the Latin 'exitus acta probat' 'The event justifies the deed.'

He pulled the entire chain out of the cabinet. It was about fifteen feet long, half the length of the room, and at the other end was a ring about two inches in diameter. He pulled out another chain identical to the first. The third and fourth chains he removed had smaller shackles, probably for a wrist. The inscriptions on those were different, 'pro lege, et greege,' 'For the law and the people.'

There was one more chain lying in the cabinet, and as he retrieved it, he saw a much larger shackle, this one about five or six inches and probably for a neck. The shackle was designed like the others with a hinge and lock. It was an inch wide and probably three eighths of an inch thick. The chain on this one was somewhat longer, about twenty feet, and the small ring at the other end also had a lock. The inscription on this shackle read, 'ooderint dum metuant' 'Let them hate, so long as they fear.'

Henry laid the shackle on the floor with the others and turned back to the cabinet. On the shelf above the chains, he found what looked like mortar or concrete tools in a large metal pan that, from the looks of residue, was used to mix concrete.

Henry, looking at the items, was already beginning to formulate ideas as he browsed through the cabinet. On the next shelf, he found a drill, power saw, mortar bits, and saw blades. He also found a box containing four enormous eyebolts with a four-inch steel plate welded to the bottom of each. The bolts were a half-inch thick with a two-inch eye.

On the next shelf were several pieces of reinforcing bar, Henry thought it was called rebar, each one two feet long. On the top and last shelf, he found only a small metal box the size of an index card file. It had a conventional hasp lock on it, and Henry was looking for something to break it open when he spotted the key for it taped to the inside of the right door.

Removing the key, he unlocked the box and lifted the lid. Inside, he found seven keys. Six appeared similar and one different. He guessed, and trying one proved him right, that they were for the locks on the restraints. That accounted for six of the keys, one for each of the leg restraints, one for each wrist restraint and two for the locks of the neck restraint. He put the six similar keys back in the box and returned it to the cabinet. The odd one he put in his pocket. Maybe the other cabinet would reveal its use. He put the chains back and closed the doors, relocking it.

Opening the second cabinet, he was amazed at the contents and again wondered about the previous owner(s). He thought about calling Hampstead to ask about his intended use of the items then immediately discounted the idea. Hampstead was weird and, frankly, gave Henry the jitters. He would just have to live with his curiosity.

The first item that drew his attention was a rifle of some kind. Henry was not a long gun enthusiast, but he did know this one was not a conventional weapon. It looked more bulky than a regular shotgun or rifle, and the bore size was different. Whatever it was, it was a single shot, bolt action weapon. He replaced it on the shelf and picked up one of two identical handguns that lay on the shelf. This weapon also was not the ordinary variety Henry was used to seeing. The bore was the same as the rifle. It, like the rifle, was a single shot, bolt action. He laid that back on the shelf and picked up a box next to it. When he opened the box, he realized what the weapons were. In the box were twenty tranquilizer darts of the kind used by the game commission or veterinarians to sedate animals.

Henry picked up one of the handguns and, opening the bolt, slid a dart into the chamber and slid the bolt home. He aimed the gun at the far wall and pulled the trigger. The noise sounded extremely loud in the enclosed space of the room, but he figured it was really no louder than a twenty-two caliber round. The dart stuck in the lead shielding and liquid ran down the wall. "Well, it works," he said to no one, placing the gun back on the shelf. The ringing in his ears from firing the gun was already starting to recede.

Also on that shelf, he found a set of handcuffs and leg irons. These had keys inserted into the locks and neither, he checked to be sure, matched the key in his pocket.

On the next shelf was what appeared to be twenty packages of modeling clay. Each package was about eight inches by four inches by three inches. He wondered why Hampstead would need modeling clay and why he stored it in the cabinet. It seemed out of place with the other items stored there.

He next retrieved and opened a large box next to the clay. When he looked inside, he realized the clay was not clay at all but was plastic explosive materials. The items contained in the box were detonator caps, probably twenty-five or thirty of them. Next to that was a roll of electrical wire, according to the label, two-hundred-fifty-feet.

On the next shelf were numerous pharmaceutical bottles and containers. Most were five to seven inches tall and three inches in diameter. Henry scanned the labels: valium, heroin, phencyclidine, morphine, dextroamphetamine, opium, cocaine, lysergic acid diethylamide, hemp, and cannabis. Some of the labels Henry recognized for their street names: PCP, LSD, marijuana, and hashish.

There were also hypodermic syringes, spoons, clips, pipes, matches, and other drug user related paraphernalia. There must be enough stuff here to keep the population of Clarksville stoned for a month, he thought. Was Hampstead a dealer? Why would he have this stuff otherwise? And if not him, who? Henry only knew he was going to have to get rid of this stuff before some drug agency raided the house.

On the top shelf was a variety of more conventional drugs: aspirin, antacids, antihistamines, antibiotics, and more. There were also several surgical instruments, suture thread and needles, bandages, and antiseptics, stuff one might expect to find. Last but not least were four cases of assorted alcoholic beverages.

Henry was flabbergasted by the things he found in the cabinets. What could Hampstead have had in his mind when he put this stuff here, especially the illegal drugs? What was the idea of the shackles? Why would a man, even a man afraid of the big one, ha-ha, want these items? Was Hampstead a drug dealer? Henry didn't think so. He would have taken that stuff with him. Why the tranquilizer guns? After "The Big One," wouldn't someone want more conventional weapons, rifles, shotguns, pistols?

Next, Henry thought, why did he leave it here? The drugs alone probably had a street value worth more than the house. How does he know I won't call the police and turn him in? Was he just crazy as hell, or were the things in the cabinet even his? If not his, who did they belong to?

He closed and locked the cabinet with the drugs inside and turned his mind back to the seventh key. Pulling it from his pocket, he examined it. It, like the other keys, bore a coiled snake insignia on one side and on the other was the Latin word 'Aeternum,' 'Forever.' Walking around the room, he looked at various items in the shelter for the elusive lock to no avail.

Why would there be a seventh key, he thought, that fit nothing? Had there been something else in the shelter that Hampstead had thrown away but forgot about the key? Henry didn't think so. Whatever lock it fits is still in the room, but where? He spent another fifteen minutes searching then decided to go get a drink of water.

As he was leaving the room, he reached for the light switch and glanced up toward the fluorescent lights. That's when he saw it. In the center of the ceiling was a small, square panel about five inches across. At the opposite end of the hinges was a place for a key. In the side was a slot extending about halfway to the middle of the panel. He got one of the folding tables from against the wall and set it up under the panel, hoping it was strong enough to hold his weight. Then climbing on it, he fit the key into the slot and turned. The panel swung down out of the way, and Henry looked into the cavity above but could see nothing. Jumping off the table, he got a flashlight from the shelf, checked to be sure it worked, and climbed back up on the table to shine it into the recess.

The only thing in the ceiling cavity was a metal pipe two inches in diameter and about fifteen inches up. "What the hell . . ." Henry muttered. He tapped the pipe with the key. The tone told him the pipe was, in fact, a solid steel bar that extended into the concrete on both sides of the recess.

Henry stared into the hole for several moments, reaching up to tug on the bar, put his weight on it. Then a thought came. He got off the table and went back to the cabinet with the chains. Pulling out the one with the neck shackle and taking the box of keys, he went back to the table and once more up to the recess. Finding the appropriate key, he unlocked the small ring, fit it around the bar, and with difficulty, relocked it. In the small opening, it had been hard to maneuver, but he imagined that was by design, so one could not readily get in and jimmy the lock. The space below the bar was large enough to store the chain and neck shackle in, so he pulled them up, shoved them into the hole and, closing the panel, relocked it.

Jumping down from the table, he refolded it and replaced it against the wall. Next, he put the key box back in the cabinet, relocked it, and went to get a drink of water.

# CHAPTER 19

When he opened the door to go into the workshop, Henry heard voices coming from the family room. He thought about going to see who it was, but if it was Brenda, he would have a hard time explaining how he had been in the workshop and just now heard them, especially if they had been there for any length of time. Also, if they had looked in the door of the shop and not seen him, how would he explain that?

Very quietly, he stepped back into the tunnel and closed the door. Hearing the lock click shut, he went back through the shelter and exited through the door into the back yard.

As he crossed toward the back of the house, he saw Brenda watching him through the kitchen window. He smiled and waved as he walked across the lawn and up onto the porch.

Brenda opened the door just as he was reaching for it. "Good morning, Henry. I saw your car out front when I got here, but when I called out, you didn't answer."

Henry smiled. "I'm sorry. I was out meandering. I guess I didn't hear you." Before she could ask where, he asked, "How long have you been here?"

Brenda looked at her watch. "Over an hour, I guess. Part of your furniture arrived, and we're getting the family room set up. Have you looked at the house?"

He nodded. "Yes, it really looks fantastic. You're doing an excellent job." He smiled. "I knew when we met I had picked just the right person for the project."

Brenda smiled, pleased. "I just knew you would like it. It fits your personality." Then she changed subjects. "What was that thing I saw you come out of in the back yard?"

Henry nodded toward the shelter door. "That? It's just an old root cellar." He lied. "I just thought I'd see what was in it."

"Oh, really?" Sheila asked inquisitively. "That's interesting. Did you find any treasures?"

Henry laughed. "Hardly." Then to quell any interest added, "As a matter of fact, it looks pretty dangerous. The beams and top are rotten, and I expect I'll have it filled in before someone gets in there and gets hurt or worse, buried alive."

"That's really a shame," she said. "Those old root cellars are going the way of covered bridges. Pretty soon, there won't be any."

Henry changed the subject. "So, we got furniture. Do I get to see?"

Brenda took his arm. "Can I get you to wait? To answer your first question, we have part of the furniture: the baths, the master bedroom, and the rec room in the basement. For your second question, could we wait just an hour or so until those rooms are done?"

"Sure," Henry said. Then, looking at his watch, he asked, "Have you had lunch? We could get some lunch then come back later, unless of course, you have to be here with your workers."

Brenda shook her head. "No, as a matter of fact, I think lunch is a great idea. Let me run downstairs to see how things are going, and I'll meet you at your car."

As he sat in the car, waiting for Brenda, he thought about work he wanted to do in the shelter. He wondered if the noise he would be making would be heard in the house then discounted it. He had fired the gun while they were in the house, and Brenda had said nothing about hearing anything. He did know one thing, however. He would have to be careful about entering and leaving the shelter. If she was going to be around, he didn't want to raise any unnecessary or hard-to-answer questions.

He watched a man come out of the house, get a large—apparently heavy— carton from the truck sitting in front of Brenda's car, and trudge back inside. A moment later, Brenda emerged and slid into the passenger seat beside him. He noticed that today she wore jeans and sneakers, and he missed the short skirt that showed her well-formed legs and thighs.

She smiled. "Okay, I'm ready."

Henry started the car and drove out of the driveway. During the short trip to the restaurant and during lunch, they discussed the house and the progress Brenda was making way ahead of schedule. He also found that Brenda had no plans for the evening after she was finished for the day at Hunters Trail, so he made a date with her for later.

When they returned to the house, the truck had departed, and they went in to inspect the completed work.

Henry was delighted with the look and with Brenda's eye for decorating. She obviously had good taste and ability. The room was tastefully decorated and emitted a comfortable, welcoming, atmosphere.

The workers, at Brenda's direction, had even built a fire in the enormous fireplace, and it cast a warm glow across the room and reflected light off the biggest 'U' shaped sectional couch Henry had ever seen. There were also two large recliners, two easy chairs, a cocktail table, assorted side tables, and aesthetically pleasing lamps. Near the fireplace, on the floor, was a large animal-skin rug. Several tasteful oil paintings decorated the walls.

Around the corner of the L-shaped room, there was a wet bar with an octagonal table and chairs around it. Henry smiled broadly and put his arm around her shoulder. "You've done a fantastic job."

Brenda beamed as she placed her arm around his waist. "I knew you would like it. I thought the animal skin in front of the fireplace was a nice touch, considering the name of the road leading here." Then, more seriously, "I am afraid it is going to cost more than what you have already given me."

Henry shook his head. "Don't worry about the money. From the looks of this room, it will be well worth the cost, whatever it is. I am really impressed and pleased."

He walked to the bookcase at the end of the room. The shelves, except for the top two, had been stocked with various old classics, mysteries, thrillers, political, newer authors, and more. The bindings were matched for each type. He pointed to the top shelves, smiling. "Did you run out of books?"

Brenda laughed. "No, I wanted to leave space, so you would have room for your favorites."

He groaned. "Oh, good, you made this really great effect, and you're encouraging me to ruin it."

They moved on, looking at the bathrooms and the master bedroom. The bedroom had been decorated with a Hollywood King bed, walnut furnishings, and more of the tasteful oil paintings. Soft drapes decorated the windows that, when closed, would put the room in semi-darkness even with bright sunlight. The bed had even been made with decorative bed coverings.

Brenda pointed to the bed. "I thought maybe you would want to stay here when you came, so I took the liberty of having the bed ready."

Henry smiled. "I really appreciate that. However," he lied, "I have already made reservations in town, so I won't wreck your work until it is all done."

After their tour of the completed work, and having made arrangement for meeting at her house later, Brenda got in her car and left.

Henry called and made reservations at the Holiday Inn on Tenth Street and let them know he would be arriving shortly. Then, getting in his car, he drove directly there while thinking about his evening and the date he had planned with Brenda.

He hadn't really wanted to leave the house because he needed to get started on the work in the shelter. However, he didn't want Brenda to know what he was doing, or equally important, where he was doing it. So the motel was really a better base of operations.

Getting the keycard from the desk, he went to his room, wondering why he had made the date with her. She was a very attractive woman. He certainly couldn't deny that, but he had not come here to form attachments. He had extremely significant things he wanted to accomplish. Also, with Brenda and her crews in the house during the day, he would be ahead to do his work during the evening and night.

Making a cup of coffee he had brewed in the provided in-room coffee pot, he sipped it as he thought about his options and which plan was more important. Then picking up his phone, he dialed Brenda's home. Getting no answer there, he called her office. She picked up on the third ring.

After their greetings, Henry said, "Brenda, I really hate to have to tell you this, but I'm afraid I'm going to have to cancel our plans for this evening. I am sorry. I was really looking forward to it."

"Oh, I'm sorry too, Henry. I was hoping to have the time with you. Is anything wrong?"

"Well, having to cancel is certainly wrong but no. It's just that I had a message when I got to the motel," he lied. "I have to run up to Erie this evening. I really am sorry. I know it is unfair to you. I'm hoping I can have a raincheck for some time later."

"Don't be sorry," Brenda replied. "Things pop up. I understand, and I'll look forward to redeeming that raincheck."

"Thank you, so much," he said. "I'll make it up to you."

They said their goodbyes and Henry hung up. That completed, he changed into dungarees, sneakers and a sweatshirt. Grabbing a burger and fries at a nearby Burger King drive-thru, he ate on his way back to Hunters Trail.

Once more ensconced in the shelter, he found a pencil and a carpenter's square and marked off four one-foot squares on the concrete floor. The four squares made up a larger square of about five feet and were centered around the panel in the ceiling where the neck restraint was now hidden.

Going to the cabinets, he opened the one on the right and removing the power saw; he inserted a mortar blade. He set the blade at an angle so the holes would be smaller at the top, expanding as they went down. As such, when new concrete was poured, it could not be readily removed. Placing the blade above the line he had previously drawn, he pulled the trigger on the saw and lowered it onto the concrete. The saw made a deafening noise in the room when the blade contacted the concrete floor.

Stopping, he got some cotton balls from the cabinet to abate the sound. Thus prepared, with cotton stuffed in each ear, and again lowering the saw, he began the arduous task of cutting the concrete. He immediately realized he would need something better than cotton to protect his ears. He would have to pick up some hearing protectors tomorrow before he returned to the house.

He had sawn only a short time until he had to stop and tie a cloth around his nose and mouth because of the dust he was raising.

He sawed on the lines he had previously drawn until he had completed the cuts for one hole. The task was going to be bigger than he had first thought. By two in the morning, he had sawn one hole, and by six, he had finished the second. But now, he was so tired from the exertion of holding the saw that he could do no more that night. Besides, with the new dawn soon to arrive, he would have to leave before Brenda showed up and found his car in the driveway.

He didn't bother to put the tools away. He brushed off as much dust as he could from his clothes so as not to track it into the house. He coughed and tasted the concrete dust that he knew coated his lungs and nasal passages. He would have to pick up dust masks and goggles, as well as the ear protectors before he did any more work. For now, however, he just needed a hot shower and some sleep. He closed the door, assured it was locked, and went back to the motel.

# CHAPTER 20

Henry had thought about going back to Clarksville for the weekend, but by the end of Thursday night, really Friday morning, all he had accomplished was getting the four holes sawed into the concrete floor. Thankfully, with the aid of the goggles, dust masks, and ear plugs he had purchased at the local Home Depot, it had made the job at least tolerable if not easier. However, with the time it was taking, he would never finish before the middle of next week. And that was if he continued his work every day until then.

After leaving the house, he stopped at a nondescript diner and had breakfast. At nine o'clock, he called Sheila. After the preliminary greetings, he answered her questions. "Yes, his brother was fine. No, he wouldn't be home before next week sometime. Yes, he could hardly wait to see her again, probably next Wednesday or Thursday. Yes, he had missed her a lot [not really, he had been too busy] and would be very happy to get home and to her."

Those things out of the way, he asked, "Have you heard of any progress in my case, either by the police or in the newspapers?"

"No, Henry, not a thing. Oh, wait, there was a call from a man named Frank something. He wants you to call him. He said you have his number."

"Okay. Thanks, sugar, and as I said, I should be home Wednesday or Thursday."

"If I must wait that long, I guess I will," she said mournfully. "Should I wear something sexy for you?"

Henry laughed. "You'd be sexy in a potato sack. See you later."

He heard her say goodbye, hung up.

Why would Frank be calling this soon, he wondered. Was something wrong that he wasn't going to do the work? Had he found something Henry had done in the past that dissuaded him or made him leery? Had someone said something to scare him off?

Henry searched through his briefcase and found Frank's number. Dialing, he sat down on the bed and waited for a connection.

"Frank's."

"Yes, Frank left a message for me to call," Henry said.

"Hold on a second. May I ask who's calling?"

"Henry Jenkins. I'm returning his call."

"Just a moment." Henry was put on hold.

Seconds later, the phone clicked, and Frank's voice boomed into the earpiece. "Mr. Jenkins, Frank here. Can you come in?"

"Well, yes," Henry responded, hesitantly." I can come in the week of the first. Is there something wrong?"

"Our discussions will always be face to face, Mr. Jenkins. That may require you to come here occasionally. When will you be here?"

Henry hesitated. "Well, I was just wondering if there was anything wrong or if you would be able to do the . . ."

"Mr. Jenkins," Frank interrupted, "I don't discuss business on the phone. I will make an appointment for you for nine o'clock on November fourth. Can you be here?"

"Fine," Henry replied. "I'll be there."

"Good. I'll see you then."

Henry said goodbye to a dead line. Frank had already hung up.

Henry was beginning to not like Frank. Caution was one thing, but the guy wouldn't say shit, and it pissed Henry off. Besides, he thought, what if I fly out there just to find out he won't do the job. I'm out an airline ticket and six grand. Henry had always been something of a worrier, and he didn't need bullshit people adding to it. Well, he would just have to wait until the fourth to find out.

Right now, he was dog tired and needed to get some sleep. He wasn't used to the manual labor he was doing in the shelter, and he was dragging.

# CHAPTER 21

He was back in the shelter, but he wasn't alone. There were others in the shadowy room. The lights were on, but they were dimmed down to the point he couldn't make out the faces of the men. One of the figures was holding Brenda by the arms. The other had a long knife in his hand. He was slowly, methodically, cutting the buttons from the frock she wore. Henry tried to yell at them to stop, but tape was stretched tightly across his mouth, preventing him from screaming his objection.

The buttons slowly fell to the floor as the thread of each one was severed. He cursed them behind the gag as the last button was cut, and the dress was pulled from her shoulders and fell to the floor. The knife came up again, first slicing her bra straps, and then cutting the bra apart, exposing her breasts to the two men. She screamed, beseeching Henry to save her.

He started forward, but the four squares he had cut into the floor were now five feet wide and connected so that he was standing on a small, one-foot square of concrete in the center of a bottomless pit.

The knife whipped forward, cutting the thin fabric of the silk panties from her hips as she again pleaded with Henry for help. He groaned and felt the tears of uselessness in his throat as Brenda cried, looking at him pleadingly, begging him to stop the men assaulting her.

The men pushed her to the cold, concrete floor and one of them straddled her. Henry, beyond hate, jumped, trying to cross the abyss below him. However, the weight of the iron restraint around his neck and the chain attached to it pulled him down into the pit. As he fell, he heard the cruel laughter and Brenda's desperate cries for him to help her.

Henry struggled for wakefulness, fighting the sheet that had become twisted around his face and neck as he slept. He sat up, wiping sweat from his forehead and breathing rapidly. His heart felt like a jackhammer in his chest, and he forced his breathing to slow until he was calm. He wanted to call Brenda, assure himself that she was all right. He knew he wouldn't and fought down the impulse. If he called someone every time he had the dream, he would be on the phone every morning. For the dreams, no, nightmares, had become an every night occurrence. They were never the same but always the same, never different but always different. There were different women, different ages, different locations, but always the men, always the rape scene, and he, restrained, useless, watching, unable to help.

He pushed the appalling dream to the back of his mind and went to shower. As the needles of water hit him, he could feel the tightness in his arms from holding the power saw dissipate, and he stood, letting the powerful spray wash away the soreness and the dream.

Toweling off, he went to get dressed and looked at the clock. Six p.m. He had slept the whole day away. By the time he dressed and got something to eat, it would be seven o'clock. Brenda would have left the house for the day.

After eating a hearty dinner, he drove back to the house and the unfinished task ahead of him.

Once in the shelter, he stood looking at the squares he had cut in the concrete. Since he had cut the concrete at an angle, he could not just lift it out of the hole. He would have to break it up to extract it. He went to the shelves and located a sledge hammer. That in hand, he began swinging the heavy tool at the first of the squares. He felt the toll it took on his shoulders, back and arms with each blow. By the time he had the first block broken up, almost two hours had passed. The second took longer, and the rest periods came more often.

When he had finally broken the last into pieces, it was almost six a.m. His arms felt like lead weights hanging from his shoulders, and Henry realized the toll his sedentary life as a personnel manager had taken on his muscles and his stamina.

He didn't bother with clean-up. That would be for his next trip. He needed to figure out where he was going to dump the debris he took from the holes. He certainly couldn't leave it here. Also, he would need to go to Home Depot and get several bags of concrete to finish this project. For now, however, sleep and rejuvenation was what he needed most.

Within thirty minutes of leaving the house, he was back at the motel and sound asleep.

# CHAPTER 22

The phone rang, waking him. It was Brenda telling him the phones had been installed, and even though it was Sunday, she thought she would try them by calling him. Besides, she was just loafing and thought she would drive up to Hunters Trail to assess the work.

"I hope I didn't interrupt anything," she said. "Did I wake you? You sound sleepy."

"Yes," he replied. "I had a long night and didn't get to bed until almost seven this morning. What time is it?"

"It's four o'clock," she said. Then, "I'm sorry I woke you. I shouldn't have called."

"No, no, it's fine," he lied. "I slept way too long anyway."

He shifted, and the movement reminded him of the shape he was in. "Listen, I don't have anything planned for this evening. May I make up for the other evening and take you to dinner?"

"I'd love that," she answered.

"Okay, where should I pick you up and what time?"

"I'll tell you what. Since you don't know where I live, and I am already out here, why don't we meet at the house? That way, we can go to dinner, and you can see what we've got done here. Also, it will give me time to set things up for your inspection. Say about seven?"

"That sounds good to me," Henry said. "I'll see you then."

He hung up the phone and lay back on the bedspread where he

had fallen that morning. At least he had taken off his clothes, but he could still see concrete dust on the spread. He got up and brushed it off and onto the carpeting. He didn't want the housekeepers to think him a complete animal.

A shower did little to ease his aches, and he felt more like going back to bed than out to dinner, but it, at least, made him feel a little more human.

At six-thirty, he drove out to Hunters Trail. A couple of ibuprofen made the aches tolerable. When he pulled up to the house, Brenda came out. She was again wearing a short skirt and blouse, and Henry admired her legs as she walked to the car. She really was a stunning, beautiful woman.

She got in the car smiling. "I thought we might have dinner first and then see the house."

"You're the boss." Henry smiled.

At dinner, they discussed the progress at the house. It was shaping up nicely and would probably be finished in a couple of weeks. Some of the furniture for the other bedrooms had been back ordered but should be there in seven to ten days. Henry gave her what she said was more than enough money to complete the project, and she assured him he would love the results.

Switching from that, they talked about Brenda's career choice. She had wanted to be an interior decorator since she bedecked her doll house when she was six years old. She had then, as a young woman, taken courses in interior design to enhance her skills. She had planned to open her own boutique by the time she was twenty-one, but it had taken a little longer than that. Henry assured her she would be successful from what he had seen of her work.

Then, Henry discussed the events of his life the last few months from the murder to the house burning to quitting his job to now, when he was, with Brenda's help, getting reestablished. Yes, things were better with each passing day. Yes, he was sure the police would be successful in catching the perpetrators. No, he wasn't concerned about being unemployed. It was something he should have done long ago. No, he wasn't looking for another job right now; his financial situation was sound, and he wanted to do some traveling before he began another career, if ever.

Dinner over, they drove back to Hunters Trail. Henry really didn't give a damn about the house, only the shelter. He did, however, show the right amount of enthusiasm and interest as Brenda guided him through. He had to admit she was doing a fantastic job, and even if he never lived in it, he would more than recoup his investment if he sold it. Brenda held his arm throughout the tour, most of which he had seen and which ended at the door to the master bedroom.

Brenda pushed open the double doors to the suite and led Henry inside. While waiting for him to arrive, she had apparently been busy. There was a fire in the gas fireplace across from the bed. Soft music wafted from the speakers hidden somewhere in the room. The bed linens had been turned down, and a magnum of champagne with two glasses sat on the table next to the bed.

"I hope I have not overstepped or been too forward," she said. "I know there is still a lot to be done, but I thought we could celebrate what we have accomplished so far. Also, if you don't feel like driving back to your motel, everything is ready for you here, including food in the fridge."

Henry put his arm around her and smiled. "Does that include you?"

She returned the smile. "I know we have not known each other long, but I feel a very pleasant connection with you. So, if you want, yes, it does include me."

Henry closed his arms around the sultry redhead and they kissed deeply, his tongue exploring hers as he ran his hands down to caress her bottom. He unbuttoned her blouse and dropped it to the floor, along with her bra, exposing her firm breasts. Then unzipping her skirt, he slid it, along with her panties, down to the floor, and she stepped out of them to stand naked in front of him.

She kissed him and stepped back, reaching for his belt buckle. "I hope I'm not the only one naked in this venture."

Henry smiled. "I just wanted to admire this beautiful vision in front of me for a moment."

He undressed, and they climbed onto the bed to explore, caress, and drink in the euphoric feelings of their intensive passion.

Later, exhausted from their amorous romp, they lay back sipping champagne from the flukes and basking in the warmth of their closeness. Henry knew he would feel guilty later because of both Sheila and Mary. For right now, however, he savored the emotional freedom with the beautiful woman lying with him, bodies touching.

"You are going to spend the night, aren't you?" he asked.

"I can, if you like," she said. "If I do I will have to get up early, get this room straighten up, and go home to change then get back before my people get here."

Henry smiled. "I think we can manage that. Although, I just don't know if I am done with you yet."

Brenda laughed. "I hope not."

Later, they made love again, and then fell asleep with Henry's arm under her head and her leg across his thighs.

# CHAPTER 23

Brenda was up and out of the house by five thirty Monday morning, having roused Henry, putting the bed back together, and depositing the wine flukes and the empty champagne bottle in her car.

Henry drove back to the motel, showered, changed into jeans and a sweatshirt, and ate a leisurely breakfast. He perused the newspaper for any word on his case [there was none] and worked the crossword puzzle. That done, he got in his car and went to Home Depot.

Going to the lumber desk, Henry beckoned an employee. "I have a question."

The young man nodded. "Yes, sir. I'll be glad to help."

"I have some holes I would like to fill with concrete," Henry said, "and I'm not sure what I need to get."

"How big are the holes?"

Henry spread his hands apart, approximating twelve inches. "About this big and about a foot deep."

"Well sir, if this is a home project, I would suggest 'Quickrete.' It's easier to use because you don't have to mix the cement, sand, and gravel, and it sets up just as hard."

"That sounds like just what I need."

The man led him to the shelves containing the bags of ready-mix concrete, and Henry, guesstimating the amount he would need, loaded sixteen bags onto a wagon. He pushed it to the front where he paid and then to his car where an attendant loaded it into his car trunk.

That done, Henry went back to the motel to sleep until time to go back to the house. He didn't bother to undress, instead lying atop the coverlets and dozing off. Apparently, his age was telling. A couple of bouts of love making and an early morning chore had worn him out.

Waking at five thirty, he visited the Burger King for a couple of cheeseburgers, fries, and a milkshake and ate them as he drove to Hunters Trail. By the time he got there, Brenda and the workers were gone, so he began unloading and carrying the bags of concrete to the shelter. Having stacked it out of the way, he buckled to his next task of removing the broken concrete chunks and dirt below from each hole and placing that in bags he found on a shelf.

When he had excavated each hole to the depth he wanted, about twelve inches, he carried the bags of waste to his car and put them in the trunk to be disposed of when he got back to Clarksville. He didn't want to dump it out back to have it possibly questioned later.

Next, he removed the rebar from the cabinet, and dividing the rods into four equal piles, he began to place them crisscrossed into each hole at the three, six, and nine inch levels.

With that completed he got the eyebolts and chains from the cabinet and carried them to the holes. He fitted an anchor ring of each chain into an eyebolt, mashed the eye closed with the sledge hammer and placed each eyebolt in a hole.

Going to the shelves containing the canned goods, Henry selected four cans of green beans. Opening and dumping the contents in the toilet, he flushed them and took the cans over to his work area. He then removed the bottom and split the side of each can and placed them around the eyebolt and chain. Surveying his work, he found it acceptable, and the time told him it was time to quit.

Calling it a day, or in this case a night, he went back to the motel for a shower and then to sleep.

He woke at two and wondered what Brenda was doing. He called her cell, and she answered on the first ring. "Are you coming over?"

Henry smiled. "Great minds and all that. I was just wondering if we might get together this evening."

"Well, I have done about all I can for today, and the guys have left, so I'm alone. Why don't you come over here if you aren't busy?"

"Give me half an hour?"

"That will be great. It will give me time to take a shower in your shower."

Henry hung up, thinking the guilt was not nearly as strong as the desire. He dressed in his jeans and headed for Hunters Trail.

He pulled into the drive twenty-seven minutes later and went into the house. He called for Brenda and heard her answer from the bedroom. When he opened the door, he found her lying on the bed naked with a glass of wine in each hand, one held out for him.

She smiled up at him as he accepted the glass with one hand and caressed her stomach and breasts with the other. He kissed her while sliding his hand down between her legs, which she had parted acceptingly for his caress.

She moaned softly at his touch. "I guess you didn't give me time to get dressed before you got here."

"If that is the case," he smiled, continuing to caress her, "I should never give you that time."

"Are you saying I should be naked whenever you come to see me?"

He smiled as he stripped off his clothes to climb onto the bed beside her. "You would never get an argument from me."

They kissed again, and then Henry began kissing first her neck and slowly kissing down, kissing and nibbling at her nipples as she moaned, "You're making me very wet."

He stopped long enough to say, "Isn't that the idea," before he continued slowly down across her stomach and to the softness between her legs.

When she had climaxed twice, he moved back up and entered

her as she thrust against him. "Please, don't ever stop," she whispered ardently.

As she reached another climax, Henry joined her, and they both shuddered in unison.

Afterward, they lay sipping wine, basking in the afterglow of their passionate union.

"I could really learn to like this," Brenda murmured softly.

"Learn to like it?" Henry questioned, smiling. "I got there yesterday."

"Yeah," she said, "me too. That is why I was so happy when you called today."

She rose up and kissed him. "Does that mean we get to do it again tomorrow?"

Henry laughed. "The idea is really appealing, but I have to head out tomorrow. Can I get another raincheck?"

"As many as you want," she said sipping her wine. "As many as you want."

# CHAPTER 24

At five o'clock, Brenda indicated she would have to leave because she needed to go to her office before going home. Henry watched her as she dressed, again becoming aroused at the sight of the beautiful, naked redhead as she wiggled into her pants.

She noticed his look. "You know you can call me if you have a need before you have to leave."

Henry smiled. "I may hold you to that."

Brenda finished dressing, and giving Henry a kiss, she made her way out of the house and the drive.

Henry waited until he was sure she was gone then got up and got dressed.

Once more in the shelter, and rejuvenated by his tryst with Brenda, he retrieved the large mixing pan from the cabinet and carried it to the first hole he would fill. Opening the first bag of concrete, he dumped it into the pan, along with enough water to make what he figured was the right consistency and stirred it until it looked like a slightly stiff cake mix batter. Dumping this into the hole, he repeated the process three more times.

Before mixing the fourth batch, he drove an eyebolt into the slurry and placed the tin can around the bolt. The fourth dump brought the new concrete up and level with the floor. He retrieved a trowel from the cabinet and smoothed and leveled the concrete even with the existing floor. The color was different, but that was an insignificant detail. He cleaned around the eyebolt until only the top portion was exposed.

Stepping back, he inspected his work and, finding it acceptable, began the task of doing the other three holes. Those took less time as he was now efficient in making concrete.

When he had finished, he looked around the shelter. He had a good bit of clean-up to do, and as much as he wanted to quit for the evening, he knew he needed to get it done. He picked up the concrete bags and putting them in a garbage bag carried them to the car. Next, he got a broom and swept up the concrete dust. He couldn't believe the mess he had made cutting the holes. He looked around and noticed the dust had covered everything in the shelter. He found an indoor/outdoor vacuum cleaner on a shelf and cleaned as much as he could with that. More effective cleaning would have to be another time, if at all.

He looked around. There were several tools in the shelter that could be used to chip away at the concrete. Those would have to be removed. Going first to the shelves, he took down all the tools and put them in the workshop. Then, he went to the cabinets and removed the power tools and any other tools there. These also went to the workshop.

Looking in the cabinets, he decided the handcuffs and shackles could remain for the present. He dropped the cuffs he had picked up, and when he did, a small black item fell from under the shelf. He picked it up, turning it over in his hand. It was one of those magnetic key holders used to hide spare automobile keys. He shook it. Hearing the rattle inside, he opened it and extracted a key similar to the one for the panel in the ceiling. He knew the key, as all the others he had, had to have a use, but an abbreviated search turned up nothing. Putting the key back in the magnetic holder, he placed it back under the shelf where it had been. He would determine its use on another day. Locking the cabinets, he left the shelter and went back upstairs. Even though his muscles were getting used to the activity, he was still tired from his efforts and decided that was enough for that day.

He looked at his watch, 12:15. It hadn't taken near as long as he thought it would and was he really too tired? He wondered if Brenda would like to be awakened in the middle of the night. He pondered that thought for several minutes and then dialed her number.

"Hi, Henry," she said sleepily apparently reading his name off the caller ID. "Do you miss me already?"

"As a matter of fact," and then, "Did I wake you?"

"No, I was lying here reading, but if you had called ten minutes later, I might have been."

"Are you too sleepy?" He asked suggestively.

"Never." She laughed. "What do you have in mind?"

"I was just thinking, I'm not asleep, and if you're not asleep, maybe we could get involved in something to make us sleepy. What do you think?"

She chuckled, "I think that's a lovely idea. Where would you like this 'something' to take place?"

"Your choice. I'm game for anything that puts my body next to yours."

"Well, then," she suggested, "I'm about as far from Hunters Trail as your motel is. Why don't I meet you there in, say, forty-five minutes?"

"That's a wonderful idea," Henry said, not telling her he was already there. "I'll see you then."

He hung up and jumped in the shower. Feeling less tired, he found wine in the wine cooler in the kitchen and two glasses in the dining room hutch. Uncorking the wine, he carried the items to the bedroom. He lit the fireplace, turned the lights down to a warm glow, and turned on the TV above the fireplace. Turning down the coverlet, he leaned against the pillows to watch a comedy rerun until Brenda got there.

When he heard the front door open, then shut, he sat up, turned off the TV, and was pouring the wine as Brenda came into the room. She looked at Henry with a pouting expression. "Gee, I got naked for you."

Henry laughed. "Yeah, but you have a body to die for. I don't."

She smiled as she unbelted then unbuttoned her knee-length coat. As she let it slide to the floor, Henry's eyes widened in surprise at her naked elegance in front of him. "And I thought that only happened in the movies." He said, obviously pleased.

He set the glasses on the nightstand and reached for her, pulling her to him. He held her gently, first tenderly kissing her mouth and then kissing her beautiful breasts that were at eye level as he sat on the bed, his hands cupping the fullness of her bottom.

She hugged him to her breasts, relishing the feel of his lips and tongue on her nipples. "Well, you certainly make it worth my while to make a midnight run."

"Hey," he returned, "I have had several hours to think about this, and I just found I couldn't leave without seeing you one more time."

Brenda swung around and laid back on the bed, her arms outstretched. "Then why don't you get undressed and show me what you want?"

Henry undressed and lay next to her. "Are you sure you're ready for what I want?"

"I'm sure anything you do is only going to leave me wanting more. I expect after you leave, just fantasizing about us is going to make me cum."

"Wow," he exclaimed, "you sure do give me a lot of credit."

She smiled, "Maybe you should have seen what I was doing when you called."

He laughed. "Okay, if you keep that up, I'll climax before I even get inside of you."

She rubbed him seductively. "Well if you do, I'll bet I can get you ready again."

He laid back and pulled her on top of him. "Yeah, I bet you could."

He entered her, and while she moved back and forth above him, he teased her nipples, helping to arouse her even further. When they both climaxed and lay back, Brenda said, "I have to go pee, but my knees are so weak right now, I don't know if I can walk."

Henry roller over and stroked her cheek. "Don't worry; I'll be glad to pick you up if you fall." He continued to gaze into her radiant green eyes until she reached up, kissed him, and scuttled off to the bathroom.

When she returned, he pulled her to him. "So are you sleepy now?"

She licked the lobe of his ear. "Not yet, but maybe if we went one more time?"

Henry, chuckling, ran his hand up between her legs, gently kneading. "I think you are familiar with the expression 'The spirit's willing, but the flesh is weak.' I can probably make you very contented, but I don't think I will be ready for a while."

Brenda buried her face between his neck and shoulder, moaning softly. "I'll just give you an hour to quit that."

"Good, that's all I'll need before you, again, make me a very happy and satisfied man."

He teased her with his hand and fingers for several more minutes and then slid down to satisfy her again orally. She groaned and held his head against her, her hips rocking with his motions.

When he finally moved back up beside her, she grabbed him and hugged him tightly. "I don't ever want to get out of this bed. You just made me cum five times. I've never cum five times. That was wonderful."

"I'm glad. And now, do you get back on top or do I?"

Smiling broadly, she pushed him down on the bed and straddled him for a longer, but no less explosive, orgasmic conclusion for them both.

Afterward, they drank a glass of wine, and then they both fell into a totally satisfied, if exhausted, sleep.

# CHAPTER 25

Henry sat in the front of Frank Alessio's shop waiting for him to show. It was the fourth, and he was fifteen minutes early.

Sheila had not been extremely happy when he came in Wednesday afternoon to tell her he had to go back to Denver. She was more hurt than angry, and hurt that he didn't have more time for her. Hurt that his compulsion, his resentment, drove his agenda, and she could not dissuade him from it.

He tried to explain to her that he was only going to look at a car that he was interested in buying. Though she believed that to be the case, she was still not overjoyed with him leaving so soon after just getting home.

There were several other things too. He didn't have to drive to the airport. She could take him and pick him up.

Yes, but that was four trips instead of two.

She could go to Denver with him.

That wasn't the best idea because he was just going to fly out, look at the car, and come back. She would just be sitting in the motel waiting. Also, if he could get a flight, he would be back the same day.

He finally appeased her by telling her that when he returned, they could go somewhere for the weekend, and that before very long [another lie] he would be finished with his escapades.

Where would they go?

It was a surprise. He would tell her later. (He had no idea.)

In bed, later that evening, they made love and then slept with Sheila snuggled against him.

"Mr. Jenkins?"

Henry looked up from his reverie. Frank Alessio stood in the doorway leading into the rear and new part of the building behind.

He stood up. "Yes, sir. Good morning."

Frank ignored the greeting. "Will you follow me?"

Henry picked up his briefcase and followed Frank into the expansive building behind the service station. He wasn't sure what he expected, maybe an assembly line, but that was not the case. The business was definitely a factory, though. It had paint shops, a machine shop with enormous metal forming equipment, welding shops, drop hammers (for metal forming, Frank said), assembly areas, mechanics shops, and more. There was activity in all the areas.

Henry guessed there were about thirty-five vehicles in the building in various stages of assembly or disassembly. There looked to be as many, or more, people working on or around them.

They went about halfway through the factory and then got on an elevator. Frank used a keycard to operate the car that took them to a penthouse office above the second floor. Henry figured not just anyone could get to that office without authorization, and Frank indicated it was the only access to his office.

Henry ventured a question. "What if it gets stuck on the way up, or won't go back down?"

Frank grinned. "Well, I guess you either jump or wait for someone to fix it. The idea is no one comes up here unless I say so, or they land a helicopter on the roof. And with all the wiring on the roof, I don't think that would be a wise idea. They'd end up getting electrocuted."

They stepped off the elevator into Frank's office. He pointed to a seat for Henry and asked him what he would like to drink.

Henry looked at his watch. "It's too early for me, but you go ahead."

Frank walked behind the large mahogany desk and sat down. "I don't drink. It's just there for those who do. It also tells me the caliber of the person I'm dealing with."

He pulled a sheaf of papers toward him then looked up. "As I told you I would, I had some investigation done on you. It didn't take as long as it does for some people because, it seems, you have an overall criminal-free and uneventful past. Of course, I did find a couple of things. Let's see, just before you turned eighteen, you went for psychiatric therapy for several months for something having to do with trying to electrocute someone with a lawn mower?"

Henry smiled. He had. When he was fifteen, he built a hunting cabin back in the woods on his grandmother's forty-eight acre farm. He used to go there during hunting season for two or three days at a time. During the summer, he would improve upon the place. He had put in a fireplace, so he could cook. He had built two sets of bunk beds along one wall, lacing them with rope for the springs and getting old mattresses people were discarding to put on them. He had carried all the materials there by himself.

Over time, he collected utensils, dishes, pots and pans, a few old chairs, and other items to furnish the place. He had built a table because he couldn't find a discarded one and shelves for his kitchenware. He had even built a couch and found old cushions to put on it.

By the time he turned seventeen, the place really looked good. His dad even went with him one weekend, and they stayed at the cabin. His dad certainly found his share of things to criticize about the place, but Henry had bagged an eight-point whitetail and really didn't give a shit. He knew the place looked good.

Fred had liked it, as did Randy Breathed, his brother, and his only buddy respectively. Randy had been killed in the summer of his seventeenth year when he rounded a turn too fast in the vintage Karman Ghia his dad had bought him for his birthday. He slid off the road and rolled into the creek below. He was found with his car upside down in the creek the next morning. He had drowned because he couldn't get his seatbelt unbuckled. (So much for seatbelt safety; the catch had jammed.)

A couple of months after that, and a few months before his birthday, someone had vandalized the cabin. They had broken the windows, smashed the furniture, and scattered stuff all over it. Henry was pissed, but he repaired and replaced everything that had been damaged or broken.

Then two weeks later, it happened again. Once again, Henry did the necessary repairs, but this time, he did a little more. He got the Gravely tractor out of the shed at home and took it up to the cabin. It was just a two-wheeled job he had bought used when he was fourteen with money he had saved mowing yards, but it was big and a bitch to get to the cabin, even though he had removed the mower deck. He manhandled it into the corner of the cabin and anchored it in place with metal straps and fencing staples.

Later that morning, he went to the hardware store where he bought a hundred feet of barbed wire, twenty feet of electrical wire, and some electrical insulators. Again at the cabin, he ran wires from the tractor through two holes he drilled above the door. These he ran through the insulators and up to a hinged board and catch he fastened to the eave. Next, he attached a rope to that board and down to the door. When he opened the door, it released the catch, and the hinged board swung down as designed. He reset the board and unspooling the barbed wire so that it was a very loose coil he hung it on the board. Now, if his calculations were correct, anyone opening the door would be entangled in a hundred feet of the barbs. Although very obvious in the daytime, Henry didn't think anyone would see it at night.

Once satisfied with his trap, he stocked the cabin with enough food to last three weeks and some books to read during his vigil. He didn't want to turn on the radio and scare off any approaching vandals. If he had to go out, he could exit and reenter the window in the back. It wasn't huge but neither was he.

For eleven days and nights (his parents thought he was staying with friends) he sat in the cabin eating cold food from cans because he didn't want to light a fire and read novels to entertain himself. He went to bed when it got dark, slept very lightly, and rose with the first rays of light.

It was the night of the eleventh day, and he was starting to give up hope of catching the vandal. At one thirty in the morning, he was awakened by a thud and then shrieks of pain.

Henry jumped up, pulled the choke out half way, and jerked the cord on the Gravely, which shuddered and then roared to life. The shrieks turned into screams. He moved the accelerator knob up a notch and heard the screams go up an octave. Henry moved to a gun port near the door of the cabin and looked out. He didn't know the guy, although he had seen him around town in a chopped fifty-six Chevy. He had heard he sold drugs to the locals, but he had never contacted Henry or Fred.

Henry backed away from the port, and getting a flashlight, he moved quietly to and out of the back window. Walking in the darkness, he went down the hill until he was out of sight of the cabin, flicked on the light, and made the fifteen minute trek home. He certainly didn't want to stay and listen to the screams. Randy Breathed would have loved it, but he had died six weeks beforehand.

The Gravely did not have a full tank of gas, but it did have enough to run two hours or so. At two forty-five, Mr. Stonehouse, the neighboring farmer, was awakened by the distant screams. At first, he thought it was a wildcat and conveyed as much to his wife, who had also woke to the noise. However, when the incessant screams continued, he became concerned. He woke his eldest son and, saddling a couple of horses, they rode out shortly after three o'clock. By the time they reached the cabin, the Gravely had run out of gas and shut down. It took them thirty minutes to cut the man out of the barbed wire and another fifteen minutes to get him down to a waiting ambulance.

The police picked Henry up at ten o'clock that morning. Since he was a minor and had no previous record, he was released into the custody of his parents.

It had required over one hundred and fifty stitches to sew up the cuts from, it was determined later, George Merrill's body, and they had to replace over a pint of blood. George, as far as Henry knew, was still stumbling around town, drooling and mumbling to himself. He didn't drive anymore, couldn't remember how or even that he had had a car.

Henry felt he had done the community a service. The kids who were supplied the drugs thought Henry was scum. Others thought him a hero. The adults thought he was sadistic.

The courts found him guilty of assault and battery with intent to maim, but they gave him probation before judgement if he completed 250 hours of community service and saw a shrink.

The psychiatrist thought he was seeking attention he didn't get during his formative years.

Henry didn't give a good damn what they thought. Merrill never vandalized his cabin again, and no one else, except Fred, would go anywhere near it.

"That," he said to Frank, returning his thoughts to the present, "was just a small misunderstanding. I felt the situation was entirely justified."

Frank nodded. "I'm sure it was. You also got fifteen points under California's twelve point motor vehicle system just after you got out of the military. Yet, you didn't apparently lose your license. Explain that."

Henry had moved to the San Leandro area of California when he got out of the Navy. While there, he couldn't seem to go anywhere without being stopped for some speeding infraction. He had left California to move back east before the last six points caught up with him and he lost his license.

"I guess I just had a lead foot for a while and left before the points caught up with me. I had moved back east and got another driver's license before California's system caught up with me and pulled my license. I guess my awakening came when I collected nine points soon after I got back east, and my insurance rates went through the roof."

Henry shrugged. "But that was all a long time ago. It certainly has nothing to do with the present, and it's been years since I've been stopped for any infraction. So, my question is, are you going to be able to do the work for me?"

Frank closed his folder and looked up at Henry. "Well, you aren't a cop or a Fed. You'll be safe to work with according to my people, and you have more than enough in various banking institutions to pay for the work. So, yes, I'll do the job. It will take about a month, barring any glitches to complete the work. We'll be ready to start as soon as you get the money to me."

Henry picked up his briefcase and set it on his lap. "Okay, how much do you need?"

Frank gave him a figure, and Henry whistled. "Wow, I wasn't expecting that. I don't have that much with me."

"How much do you have?"

Henry did some fast mental calculations. "I can give you three hundred thousand right now and wire the rest later."

Frank shook his head. "I told you before, I don't do anything that leaves a paper trail. We'll work it this way. Give me the three hundred now. I have it on good authority that you will be good for the rest. Bring me the rest, in cash, within the next month. I will get the work started in the next few days."

Henry counted out the money and slid it across the desk. "I'll have it here. Now, what kind of car do I need to get?"

Frank counted the money and slid it into a drawer locking it. "I'll take care of everything. I have your list. If you have the money here on time, the car will be ready around the middle of December. Don't call to ask questions. I know what I'm doing, and if you have anything else you want, tell me now. It's too late once I've begun work."

Henry shook his head. "No, I believe that is everything."

Frank pointed to a picture on the wall, and Henry looked at the painting of a ten-point buck lying in a glade. "Nice picture."

Frank smiled. "Thanks, and you just had your picture taken. I'll need it, and you'll need it later."

Gesturing toward the elevator, he took Henry back down and back to the front. "Just remember, the rest within the month."

Henry caught the next flight to Pittsburgh. He called a disappointed Brenda to tell her he would not be back to Hunters Trail until sometime in December but would call her when he got there. Back in Pittsburg, he picked up two tickets to San Francisco with a stop in Denver.

On Wednesday, he and a very pleasantly surprised Sheila went for a vacation to the west coast with a stop in Denver to drop off the balance of the money to Frank. He told her it was a business stop, and she remained at the motel, napping, for the two hours he was out. The next day, they flew to their destination to enjoy the ambiance, the food, and visiting the city's many tourist attractions and clubs, and according to Sheila, the sex wasn't too bad either.

# CHAPTER 26

The Boeing 747 touched down in Pittsburgh, and they deplaned. The flight had been uneventful, and the vacation fantastic for them both, but Henry had noticed that Sheila had gotten progressively quieter as they neared Pittsburgh.

Driving toward Clarksville after they had retrieved the luggage, souvenirs, and the car, Henry turned to Sheila. "You've been awful quiet for a while. Want to tell me about it?"

Sheila stared at the road, stroking Henry's leg as he drove. "Well, I've had a fabulous time and everything was fantastic. I've come to realize that you mean more to me than I can even imagine, and I love being with you and want to make you happy. I want you with me because that is when I am the happiest." She sat quietly.

"I feel a but coming," Henry said.

She stared out the window for several seconds. "It's just that, now that we're back, I'm afraid you're going to be gone again for various lengths of time, and I don't want you to go. I guess I'm scared. I really care about you, and I don't want anything to happen to you."

Henry took her hand and squeezed gently. "Sheila, I have a few things to do that are necessary for my peace of mind and for the good of society. If the same thing happened to someone else, some other family, because I did nothing, I don't know that I could live with myself. I made myself, and Mary and Linda, a promise that I would see this through. If I don't, I will have lied to them and, more importantly, to myself. I can't, I won't, do that."

Sheila continued to stare out the window. "I understand your thoughts, Henry. I admire you for your integrity. I guess I even understand your desire, but why? Why not just let the police and the justice system take care of them? Or if you do find them, just call the police and report it, and let them handle it."

Henry sighed. "Sheila, I just may do that," he lied. "My intentions are not etched in stone. I'm not out to get myself hurt or killed. I just want to make sure, if possible, that they hurt no one else like they hurt Mary and Linda, if they have not already done so. Statistics show that this was not their first foray into this quarter and, in all likelihood, will not be their last if they aren't stopped."

"Then why does it take so much of your time away if you are just going to turn them over to the police?"

Henry laughed. "Listen, you don't even know what I do when I'm away. I think, when all is said and done, you will be pleasantly surprised and also realize that your fears are totally groundless."

She looked at him, slightly more interested. "Do I get any hints?"

"Nope, sorry, it would ruin the surprise."

"Not even one?" she chided.

He squeezed her hand. "Not even one."

She took his hand and guided it up the inside of her thigh. "I could make it worth your while, mister."

Henry laughed. "You have been wearing me out for a month, and you think that is going to work? He moved his hand further up her leg. "Well, maybe it will."

But it didn't. Even after the weekend and several hours naked in bed, he revealed nothing about the house on Hunters Trail or anything that was happening in Denver, and Sheila didn't bring up the subject again.

Sunday evening, with little objection from Sheila, he drove to Pittsburgh and caught a flight to Denver. He promised Sheila he would try to be back by Friday.

Monday morning at nine o'clock, he sat in the station at the front of Frank's browsing a month-old Newsweek. He was halfway through the old news before Frank came through the door.

"Mr. Jenkins, you're punctual. I like that. Sorry I couldn't be, but I was trying to get things set up in the back to demonstrate your car. That said, if you will follow me, we'll get started."

Henry rose, putting down the magazine, and followed Alessio's hulk through the door an out through the plant in the direction they had gone before. This time they did not stop at the elevator but continued on to the end of the building and into one of the three large rooms situated there.

The car, a gray Lincoln, sat in the center of the room gleaming under the overhead lights. The windows tinted so dark Henry could not see the interior.

"Look it over." Frank said. Start it up and listen to it run. However, don't touch anything else until Ray here," he pointed to a sandy haired, middle aged man standing slightly behind him, "goes through and explains everything to you. I've got to go upstairs, but I'll be back in half an hour to answer any questions."

Frank left and Henry walked over to the car and began inspecting the contours and paint. It certainly did look like a Lincoln one would find on the show room floor. The only difference Henry noted, was the solid sound when he rapped on the metal of the door and fenders with his knuckles. The sound was muted and solid, not like the tinny sound of the original car.

"The metal," Ray explained, "runs anywhere from seven-eighths of an inch thick to one and a quarter, depending on the location and need. You could roll this baby ten times and it would never dent. The paint is five coats or Emron topped with what is called flip-flop. That's a real hard clear coat that appears to change color with different lighting. The Emron is the hardest paint available. It is expensive but well worth it. It will take a hell of a lot to scratch or chip it.

"Let me show you." He said, picking up a hammer. He swung the hammer, hitting the fender twice as Henry winced. Then he took a cloth and wiped the surface where he had struck the car.

Henry looked at and rubbed his hand over the struck surface. He was pleased to see there had been no damage as a result of the hammer strikes. "That's really good." He said. "How much impact will it take?"

Ray stuck the cloth back in his pocket. "Well, if you are shot at, it will nick the paint or put a chip in the windows, which are bullet resistant. If you roll it, it will probably scratch the paint, but normal wear and tear won't mar it."

Henry took a couple of more minutes inspecting the exterior and then opened the driver's door. The door made a clicking noise then a soft hissing sound as it opened. "What is that?"

Ray stepped up beside Henry. "These doors are hydraulically actuated and electronically controlled. If they weren't, you wouldn't be able to open them except on level ground. The weight wouldn't allow it."

Henry gave a slight shove on the door, and with another slight click and the hiss, it glided closed with a solid thunk. "So what happens if your fingers get in the way of the door closing?"

Ray shrugged his shoulders. "I guess you lose some fingers."

At Henry's surprised look, he laughed. "Just joking. It has a safety mechanism built in to the computer in the dash. If the door meets any resistance in its travel, it immediately reverses direction and goes the other way."

He opened the door and, once open, he shoved it shut. As it was closing, he put his hand against the door frame. When the door came in contact with his hand, it immediately opened.

Henry nodded, impressed, but he didn't know that he trusted the system enough to stick his hand there on purpose.

He asked, "What if someone broke into the car?"

"That's virtually impossible unless they have a bomb. The locks have electric overrides. Even if someone could get a shim between the door frame and glass, the override would hold the lock down. Also, the clearance between the door and glass would not even allow a grain of sand between them. The only way the locks will work is with a key or with the key in the ignition. There is one other way to open the door if you inadvertently leave the keys inside." He pointed to what looked like a small smudge in the bottom corner of the windshield. "Put your left thumb against that smudge."

Henry placed his thumb on the indicated spot and heard the door lock on the driver's door click. Ray explained, "That will only work with your thumbprint which, by the way, we got from Frank's desk where you touched it. You might want to keep that in mind when you're out and about."

Henry nodded. "That's a great feature, but what if someone breaks the window?"

Ray laughed. "Good luck with that. That's one-and-a-quarter-inch bullet resistant glass. A .357 caliber shell wouldn't penetrate it."

Henry was pleased, so far. "How about the hood and trunk; how do they open?"

Ray, opening the door, reached in and pushed two buttons near the bottom left of the dash beside the steering column. Henry heard the locks click and watched the lids open on hydraulic struts. "They open and close on the same principle as the doors. To close them, you just apply pressure, or you can push the respective button again."

He walked to the front of the car, Henry following. "Now, if you are familiar with engines, you will notice this is nothing like the factory motor. The original would never perform with the weight of this vehicle. This one has a lot more torque and horsepower, but when it is running, the average person would never know the difference. It will, like the original, accelerate from zero to sixty in about eight seconds and purr at a hundred forty miles an hour. It's a diesel, so there is some slight valve tap, but with the thick body and insulation, it won't be noticeable. We had to reconfigure the inner fenders to accommodate the larger engine and the special tires needed because of the weight. That large bundle of wires on the firewall is to operate the various electrical systems."

He turned to Henry. "Now, a word of warning, if the car ever stops or needs maintenance, you never open the hood or trunk for some local mechanic. If there is an issue, you call us. We will take care of any problems. That includes preventative maintenance or something as simple as a flat tire, which you will never have, or a burnt out headlight."

Henry, looking down, noticed two round ports, one under each headlight. "What are those?"

Ray smiled. "Well, to tell the truth, they're gun ports. We already had the molds made for your car because of a similar one we built several months ago for an oil rich Saudi. They wanted guns mounted in the fenders. You don't have them because they weren't requested, but you still got the ports, which I might add, are inoperative. One more thing, if we had had to make new molds for your car, it would have cost a lot more."

"Now to the trunk." He moved around the car to the rear. "If you look in here, you will see the trunk is about six inches shorter that factory. That is due to the hydraulic system and additional electronic and computer equipment we needed to install. There is also an extra battery in there due to all the electrical equipment."

He pointed to the sides of the trunk. "There are compartments on each side of the car that are operated by switches on the dash, which I will show you shortly. We had to do some work on the inner fenders to accommodate them. Each one is about three cubic feet. They are filled with oil on one side and tetrahedrons on the other, per your list of instructions."

He reached up and pulled gently on the lid. Henry watched it glide gently home on the hydraulic struts and click into the locked position.

"One more thing, never hide an ignition key on the outside of the car. Someone will find it. And even though we can locate this car anywhere in the world, we don't want to go looking for it. If you lose your key, call us, and we will provide another."

Ray walked toward the passenger side. "Now, if you will get in the driver's side, I'll explain the console to you."

Henry climbed in, immediately noticing the added height of the vehicle. He sat down on the comfortable leather bucket seat and looked at the console, noticing it appeared to be an unimpressive smoked gray plastic panel. Ray slid into the passenger seat. "All right, Henry," he said, handing Henry the key, "turn the key to accessory, and I'll explain the interior controls."

Henry inserted the key and turned it as instructed. When he did, the instrument panel came alive, showing digital information for the speedometer, odometer, fuel gauge, oil, heat and coolant, clock, radio/cd, and GPS navigational panel. Ray pointed to a green light about an inch square beside the speedometer readout. "Place your left thumb against that light. You don't have to push; it will read your thumbprint. You are the only one who can operate it outside of this building."

Henry placed his thumb on the light. He heard a click, and the top of the center console raised and revolved revealing an assortment of gauges, switches, and a miniature keyboard, as well as ports to plug in a cell phone, laptop, or other equipment. It lit up in red and green lights, reminding Henry of an airplane cockpit.

Ray flipped a toggle switch beside the keyboard. "This is to operate your message board in the back window. You type in the message you want displayed then push the flash or run button to display the message. 'For those in Rio Linda,' to quote Rush Limbaugh, the flash will cause the message to blink on and off, and the run will cause it to run right to left across the display area."

Henry typed, Turn right at the next street, and pressed the flash button. Then, he walked to the back of the car to see the message flash on and off. Next, he pushed the run button and viewed that display before shutting the message off.

Back in the car, Ray explained the working of a police siren and the buttons that controlled the siren's wail, hi-lo, and whelp settings. "Next," he said, opening another compartment, "is a secure car phone which also serves as a CB and a PA system. "This knob switches it to the particular system you want to use. The phone cannot be traced back to you. The toggle switch next to it switches the PA sound to the front or back outside speakers of the car, as you choose." Pointing to two covered switches, he continued, "These two guarded switches control the tanks of oil and tetrahedrons. If you flip the switch on the one chosen, it will dump the contents on the ground to the rear of your back wheels. The switch on the left is for the oil. The one on the right is for the tetrahedrons or spiked jacks if you prefer. The gauges next to the switches tell you if the containers are full. This gauge," he said, pointing to a gauge slightly below and centered between the others, "tells you how much hydraulic pressure you have. It should always be above twenty-five PSI. If it drops below, let us know. It controls the brakes, steering, doors, and trunk and hood. Ignoring it could have dire consequences."

"Now one more thing," Ray said, pointing to two yellow switches with a knob between. "These switches control the bumpers, and the knob in the center the license plate holder. The one on the left is the front bumper, the one on the right is the rear bumper, and the knob in the middle rotates the license plate holder. If you will get out and go to the rear of the car, I'll show you the operation."

When Henry was at the rear and to the side of the vehicle, Ray flipped the switch. The rear bumper shot out with a solid thunk to about eighteen inches from the car. He flipped the switch again, and the bumper returned to its original position. Next, he turned the knob. The California license plate rotated to show an Iowa license plate. Ray turned the knob again and revealed a Maryland plate. Lastly, he revealed a Pennsylvania plate. He then beckoned Henry back to the driver's seat.

"When you rotate the plates, there are four of them, as you saw; the particular state and plate number show up for ten seconds on the navigation screen. Just make sure the registration you show anyone matches that plate. The registrations are in this compartment." He pushed a button, and a small, inconspicuous compartment opened at the bottom of the dash. "They are all registered to you, and there is a corresponding driver's license with your picture and an associated address for each one. Make sure you use the right one. A mistake would, in all likelihood, land you in jail, the fake IDs confiscated, and the vehicle impounded."

Frank leaned into the car, arriving before Henry even knew he was around. "Well, what do you think?"

Henry grinned. "It's fantastic. When I first envisioned this, I wasn't sure it could be done."

Frank chuckled. "For the right amount of money, anything can be done."

He leaned back and straightened up. "Now, if you will follow me up to the office, we'll take care of any remaining questions and some minor details."

Henry got out of the car and followed Frank across the factory floor to the elevator and up to his office. When they were seated, Frank said, "Now, I will field any questions you have."

Henry nodded. "Just out of curiosity, if I get a scratch on my thumb, how do I open the door?"

"A minor cut or scratch is no problem. The computer looks at a fourteen point reading. That would not deter you from entering the vehicle or using the console. If there was major damage, like you lost your thumb or the print was obliterated, I would send a man to reprogram the computer for another of your prints."

"Okay," Henry said satisfied. "What about the gun ports? Could I have guns put in later if I wanted?"

Frank shook his head. "As Ray probably told you, the drop hammer forge molds were already made, but that was for much thinner metal than you requested. Because of the weight of the car, we had to go to a larger, specially designed tire and wheel, therefore not allowing room for large weapons. With the redesign of the inner fender, we could get nothing larger than a handgun in there, and that would be both totally useless and therefore stupid. Also, and as I told you up front, once we started, there could be no design changes. If that is what you wanted, it should have been on your list."

Henry coughed, slightly embarrassed. "Yes, you're absolutely right, and it's not important. Just one more question, if I may. If I come up with any 'special needs' in the future, can you fill them?"

Frank shrugged. "Like what?"

"Nothing at the moment," Henry replied. "Just an offhand question."

Frank scratched his chin. "As I said before, for the right price, anything can be done. But I might caution you; don't ask for something unless you are absolutely sure you want it. You might not like the result. Now, any other questions?"

Henry shook his head. "No, not at the moment, anyway."

"Good." Frank leaned back and crossed his legs. "Let me take a moment and explain a couple of things about the car. Ray probably went over them, but repetition is the best teacher, so to speak."

"The first thing is you obviously don't want anyone around Pittsburgh to know about the unique qualities of the car, or you would have had the work done there. If someone sees that console or under the hood, it won't take but a few days for a thousand people to know about it. For that reason, if you don't know how to change the oil or plugs or fill the hydraulic reservoir, have Ray explain it before you leave. If anything goes wrong with the car or you have issues you can't resolve, call me. We'll get someone out there to fix any problems within a few hours. It will cost you, but no one else will know about it."

"Second," Frank continued, "the diesel fill opening is the same as a conventional car. As such, a gas jockey won't know the difference between your car and any other unless he's damned good. Also, I would suggest you don't park beside a like car. Your car is three inches higher and is six inches longer. Although not noticeable by itself because we designed it that way, the difference would be obvious next to another one."

"Next, I would offer that no one sit in the back seat. Though it looks standard, it has been modified to accommodate the rear portion of the added tanks and filler openings. The seat is hinged, and there is a release at the bottom and right behind the driver's seat to gain access to the tanks. However, due to the configuration, there is very little padding or springs, so it would be uncomfortable."

Frank shifted in his chair and continued. "There are four license plates on the rotating holders. One is legal and registered to you on Hunters Trail in Pittsburgh. One is for a Harold Daniels, I'm sure you recognize that name, of San Leandro, California. One is for George Williams of Ames, Iowa, and the last if for a William Donaldson of Fallston, Maryland. There are associated registration cards, insurance cards, and driver's licenses to go with each plate. They will pass any inspection if you happen to get stopped. However, if you do get stopped in, say, Maryland, you should probably use the Iowa or California ID.

"One final thing, Mr. Jenkins. If you fuck up, you don't know me, and you don't know who did the work on the car. If you feel you might forget that, know one thing, my reach is long. Do you understand what I mean?"

Henry smiled. "I'm sorry, who are you?"

Frank stood and Henry followed suit, saying, "I really appreciate the work and prompt turnaround."

Frank put his hand on Henry's shoulder as they got on the elevator. "You paid for it."

"Yeah, but just the same . . ." He let it trail off then asked, "If I wanted some work done in the future, nothing that immediately comes to mind, but I would like to keep that door open?"

"Henry, it is your money. I am available to help in many things."

The elevator slid to a stop, and Henry stepped off, extending his hand. "Thank you, again."

Frank took the proffered hand. "Goodbye, Mr. Jenkins, and good hunting." The elevator door shut.

Henry felt a chill course up his spine. "Goodbye, Frank," he said to the closed door.

He walked back toward his car, and Ray joined him to go over items suggested by Frank and a few last minute instructions. Forty-five minutes later, he was pushing the monstrous car east.

The project phase was over. It was time to put his plan in action.

# CHAPTER 27

February twelfth. It had been exactly six months since Mary and Linda had died. Six months in which the police were no closer to finding the killers than they had been the first day. It had also been six months in which Henry had done nothing as far as learning the art of finding the killers.

He sat on the edge of the bed. Perspiration beaded on his forehead from the recurring nightmare that had jolted him awake. He looked across the bed to Sheila sleeping on the other side and eased off the bed so as not to wake her.

After showering and dressing, he sat at the kitchen table and sipped at the coffee left from yesterday and warmed in the microwave. He pored through his memory files of that fatal day, which seemed so long ago, yet as fresh as yesterday, and he wondered how he was going to proceed.

One thing was sure. He wasn't going to find them by spending all his time here and in bed with Sheila, and he was beginning to find that to be a very comfortable place to be.

Well, the first thing to do, he mused, was to start looking for the black van. There were several possibilities for the police not having found it. One, the men did not live in or around Clarksville. Two, the van had been junked and possibly crushed. Three, it had been repainted. If the vehicle had been crushed, he was back to square one. Anything else, and he had a chance, even if a small one, of finding it.

He decided the first thing he would do was check the junk yards in, what, fifty miles, a hundred miles? He rubbed his chin. That was a lot of junk yards and a lot of vans. He sighed; at least it was a start.

He swallowed the last of the coffee and rising, put the cup in the dishwasher. Turning, he found Sheila standing in the doorway looking at him. A frown creased her brow. "You're going to leave, aren't you?"

Henry nodded. "It's time."

"Do you have to?"

"You know I do."

"Why, Henry?"

"We've been through this before. You know I have to go."

Sheila came to him and circled his waist with her arms. "I'm afraid."

"There's no need to be scared. All I'm going to do is drive around and look."

"I know that's what you say, but what if they find out you're looking for them? They'll try to stop you."

"They won't find out." That, however, is a good question, he thought. What if they did find out? Then, yes, he would be in danger. He could quite conceivably be killed by the very ones he hunted.

A thought came to mind, and he logged it in his mental file. He would need to see his attorney, and in the very near future. To Sheila, he lied, "Don't you worry about me. I'll be safe. All I'm going to do is drive around and look. If I see anything or find out anything, I'll turn it over to the police."

She looked at Henry's smile but did not return it. "I know I can't talk you out of this, but I don't have to like it. How long will you be gone?"

"I honestly don't know. As long as it takes."

"Where are you going?"

"Well, for today, I'll be around here, checking some things out. If I don't find anything, then I'll start branching out. So I'll be here to pester you tonight, but if you don't turn me loose, I'll never get out of here."

This time, she smiled. "If I thought that was the case, I'd never let you go, and if you stay, I will most definitely make it worth your while."

He kissed her forehead. "I know you would, and that certainly gives me the incentive to see this through and get back here. Now, though, let me get out of here. I need to get something done, or I'll never get back."

He started out of the kitchen. "Henry?"

He turned back. Sheila stood, holding her robe open to reveal her gorgeous naked body. "Hurry back."

He grinned broadly. "That is undoubtedly the incentive I need. Thanks, sugar."

He went out and got in the Cadillac. Upon his return from Denver, he had taken the Lincoln to Hunters Trail and parked it in the garage. He didn't want people to know he had it just yet, and the car, sitting in Sheila's driveway, would surely raise questions and eyebrows as his living with her did.

Once the car was safely locked in the garage, Henry had called a cab for a ride to the airport to get the Cadillac and then drove back to Clarksville.

Now, he drove downtown to the Clarksville Professional Building, and parking in the 'Clients Only' area, went inside. His attorney was located on the second floor, and Henry took the stairs instead of the elevator. He needed the exercise anyway, he told himself.

Walking to the door for Daniel Gaston Doumergue IV, Attorney at Law, he entered and went over to the gray haired receptionist. "Hi, Marie, is Dan in? I know I should have called, but I was downtown and thought it would be a good time to take care of a little business if he's available."

"Yes, sir, Mr. Jenkins." She smiled. "Have a seat, and I'll buzz him."

Henry sat and picked up a Sports Illustrated, swimsuit addition, to browse through, but the inner office door opened before he even had a chance to open the magazine cover.

"Henry, how are you." The tall, silver-haired lawyer greeted him. "How's the golf game? I haven't seen you on the course lately." Doumergue was in his late sixties, five-eleven, and probably two hundred pounds. He had been Henry's attorney since Henry had received his inheritance after the death of his parents. They had, on many occasions over the years, gotten together to play eighteen holes.

"Fine, to the first question," Henry replied. "To the second, I haven't played since . . . since August, last year."

"Oh, God, Henry, bad question. I'm sorry." He and Henry had played a foursome on the eleventh. "I was devastated by the news. How are things going now, for you, that is?"

"Everything is coming back together, and thanks for the flowers and your attendance at the funeral home."

Dan waved it away. "So what brings you to my humble office today?"

Henry smiled. Humble? Bullshit. The office was furnished with leather chairs and couch, mahogany desk and tables, and expensive artwork on the walls. There was a bar hidden behind one of the bookshelves behind Dan's desk and stocked with some very expensive liquor. "Well, I was just thinking earlier that, with my life-changing events, I need to change my will."

Dan waved him into his office. "Excellent idea. Come on in. I don't have to be in court until this afternoon, so now's as good a time as any."

Seated, and with a legal pad in front of him, Dan said, "Okay, before it all went to Mary and Linda. Now, I would assume you would want it to go to . . . let's see, you have a brother don't you?"

"I do, but I want everything to go to Sheila M. MacKenzie."

Dan raised an eyebrow. "Sheila MacKenzie, isn't she the pretty brunette I handled a divorce for a couple of years ago?"

Henry smiled. "That's the one. You did. I'd forgotten that."

"You two have something serious going on, huh?"

"In a way," Henry responded. "The thing is she doesn't know anything about this, so we'll keep it that way, for the present at least."

"You're the boss," Dan said writing on his pad. "Now, I know you don't have the house anymore. Any other changes?"

"Yes. I bought a house in Pittsburgh." He gave Dan the address. "And I have a Lincoln you might list."

Dan looked up. "Well, the Lincoln doesn't really have to be listed individually. Those things are usually changed after a few years. Maybe you just want to say the current vehicle."

Henry shook his head. "No, not this one. This one does need to be listed."

Dan looked at him again. "Something special?"

Henry knew he could trust Dan with confidentiality. Also, if things went awry, he would probably need his services. "Yeah, as a matter of fact, well over a quarter of a million."

Dan whistled and put his pen down. "What the hell is it? Gold?"

He told Dan his plan to catch Mary and Linda's killers and the intended use of the car, if necessary, in doing so. When he finished, he added, "You see, I'm not as confident in hunting these guys as Chuck Norris or Steven Segal. So, I got the car."

Dan leaned back and ran his fingers through his hair. "Have you considered what the ramifications of your actions could be, Henry? We're looking at people here who have done horrific acts and would willing do so again rather than go to prison. We're looking at monsters who put no value on human life and would kill you in a heartbeat if they thought you could identify them. My advice to you, my friend—and I mean this as a friend and not just your attorney—is that you let the police handle it."

Henry shook his head. "They've been handling it for six months and gotten nowhere. Also, you know as well, or better, than I do what would happen if they are caught by the judicial system, next to nothing. No, Dan. This is my plan, and I plan to carry it to fruition."

Dan put his elbows on the arms of his chair and put his fingers together. "And what happens if you catch them, or do I want to know?"

"I don't know at present. I have some ideas, but for now, just ideas."

Again the raised eyebrow. "Are any of those ideas legal?"

CHARLES ROBINSON

"Probably not. Will you represent me if things get screwed up?"

"Oh, hell yes. I can probably get you off with ten to life, you dummy."

Henry smiled. "What about temporary insanity?"

Dan shook his head. "That's bullshit, and you know it. If you do something to those men, and the prosecuting attorney finds out about that decked out car, it will be premeditation, big time. And that house you bought. It must have something to do with this hair-brained scheme of yours, or you wouldn't have gone to Pittsburgh to buy it. You would have bought something here in Clarksville. What's in that house that will incriminate you?"

"Damn! Is it that obvious?" Henry asked.

"Only if you carry out this obtuse idea. I'm telling you, Henry, what you're doing is dangerous; it's illegal and downright stupid. As your attorney, I recommend you give it a lot more thought before you make a decision that you might get to die with or end up in prison for."

"Sure, Dan. I'll think it through. I just need to know you'll be there for me if I need representation."

"You know I will. Just don't be impetuous." He turned to his legal pad. "Now, this isn't a complicated will. Let me have Marie run it through the computer, and we'll get it signed before you leave."

He buzzed Marie, who got the legal pad and instructions and disappeared back to her desk.

"So, where are you off to from here?" Dan asked.

"Just meandering around town and the area for today. See what's happening in our fair city."

Dan nodded. "On vacation?"

"No. I am presently unemployed."

"What! What happened?"

Henry explained his activities after the murders and his conversation with his boss. "I guess George doesn't like his employees taking long bereavement leaves."

Dan shook his head. "I know you don't need the money, Henry, but I think, if you aren't careful, you're going to fuck up your life. That job kept you grounded and was something constructive in your life. Now, it looks to me you're heading for some self-destructive morass."

"No lectures, Dan. I'm a big boy. I'll think things through before I take any action."

Dan sighed as Marie returned with the will. "I hope so, Henry. I hope so."

Henry signed the will with Marie and Dan's partner, Ralph Dennison, as witnesses. When it was completed, Marie made copies and handed Henry his.

Dan looked at his watch. "I have to get to court in a while, but I have time for lunch if you want."

Henry shook his head, "No, thanks. I'll take a raincheck. I've got chores to do, and the day doesn't wait for me."

Dan stood and shook hands. "As my friend, Henry, just do me a favor. Take a little time to think."

"Sure, Dan. I will. You take care now. I'll see you later."

Henry walked out with Dan staring after the departing figure. You dumb shit, Dan thought. You'd better be careful, or you'll be joining Mary and Linda a lot sooner than you think.

Leaving the law office, Henry stopped at the bank to deposit the will in his safe deposit box. He then had authorization to open the box changed from him and Mary to him and Sheila.

That completed, he spent the rest of the day cruising the streets, alleys, and junk yards in and around Clarksville looking for a van with heart-shaped windows. He had never noticed a lot of vans before, but now that he was looking for one, they seemed to be coming out of the proverbial woodwork. He saw all kinds: window vans, utility vans, windowless vans, raised tops, extended, plain, and decorated. It seemed there were hundreds of vans but none with heart-shaped windows.

At seven-thirty and weary from driving, Henry decided to call it a day and headed for Sheila's. Tomorrow, he would browse some junk yards further out and see what he could find there.

# CHAPTER 28

Henry was at the local AAA office when it opened the next morning. He got maps of Clarksville and surrounding areas and ordered county maps for the surrounding counties within a hundred miles. Those were to be sent to the address on Hunters Trail. Triple A was not extremely pleased with the order, but as Frank had said, anything could be done if you have the money.

Taking the available maps and the yellow pages he had brought with him from Sheila's, he selected the closest used auto parts lot and drove there. With no luck at that one, and an hour wasted, he drove to the second lot with the same results. Few Dodge vans, fewer black vans, and none with heart-shaped windows.

It was four o'clock on Saturday afternoon, and Henry had time for one more lot for the day. He picked a lot fifteen miles from Clarksville and drove there in as many minutes.

Walking into the office, a dilapidated trailer, Henry went to the potbellied man sitting beside a potbellied stove. Henry thought humorously that they looked like brothers, both well rounded and both grungy.

"Help you buddy?" the live brother asked.

"I hope so," Henry responded. "I'm looking for a Dodge van with heart-shaped windows."

The guy scratched his massive gut with grime encrusted fingernails and played, almost fondly, Henry thought, with his navel. "Well, I don't know as I got any with heart-shaped windows. I got a couple with ovals and one with spades or clubs, but don't rightly remember which. You're welcome to look. Too friggin' cold for me to go out there."

"Thanks," Henry said starting for the door.

"Wantin' to change windows, huh?"

Henry stopped and turned back. "Change windows?"

"Yeah," the guy said, opening the door to the stove and chunking a piece of wood inside. "A lot of the kids, they switch the windows if they find something they like better."

Henry felt three days of searching going down the tubes. "But what about the hole where they take the old window out? That has a different configuration."

"Shit man, that ain't no problem." He closed the door to the stove. "They just weld in new metal or cut the hole bigger. Hell, some of those little assholes are better at body work than the body shops are."

Henry felt drained. Three days of running around the countryside and now this. What else did he have to go on? Windows now out, paint color iffy. The only thing left was the Q-shaped dent in the bumper, and they could just as easily have replaced that.

He sighed. "Well, if you don't mind, I'll go ahead and look around for a little bit."

"Help yourself, man. If you find anything you like, just bring it up here to the office. Too damned cold for me to go out there."

Henry went out and closed the door. The guy was right; it was colder than a witch's tit, but he meandered up and down the rows of twisted and rusted metal anyway, finding nothing that could have been the vehicle he sought.

Getting in his car, he drove back toward Clarksville. He'd have to recheck all the lots he had gone to and drive the streets again. This time doing a closer inspection.

He stopped at O'Shannon's bar, just outside town, and drank a Sam Adams draft, then got a six pack to go. Back in the car, he drove the streets until midnight. When he saw a Dodge van, he would stop, get out, and look it over, checking the sides for indications of body work and the bumper for the dent. He was careful that there was no one around to see him. He certainly didn't want any confrontation.

When he got home, he explained to Sheila that on Monday he would be leaving for a while. He wasn't sure how long, but he would call her occasionally to let her know he was safe.

That night and Sunday, he stayed with her, consoling, appeasing, trying to make her understand. Also, on Sunday, he wrote detailed instructions for Sheila, in case anything happened. This he sealed in an envelope and gave it to her.

She held the envelope in her hand, her feet planted against the coffee table as she slouched against the back of the couch. "What is this for?"

He sat beside her and put his arm around her. "Now don't be jumping to any morbid conclusions. It just makes good sense, in any situation, to prepare for the unexpected. With Mary and Linda gone, I just needed to change some of my affairs around, and you are my choice."

Sheila continued to stare at the envelope. "What about your brother? Won't he be hurt if you have me taking care of your things?"

"Whoa," he exclaimed, sitting up and laughing. "I'm not going to walk out the door and disappear. I'm just trying to keep my life straight. I made a will fifteen years ago and didn't die."

Sheila looked at him and a touch of a smile made the dimples in her cheeks deepen. "I guess it does sound silly when you say it out loud. I just think about what you are doing, and it scares me. I guess I should be happy that you think enough of me to want to include me in your life."

"Honey," Henry said putting his arm around her again, "I think a lot more of you than 'enough' but enough of this. Like I said, it's just normal actions for a realistic situation and certainly not a death wish. Just accept the idea that I think enough of you, of us, to want to include you in my life and kiss me."

Sheila turned and embraced him, kissing him deeply, lovingly, holding him tightly. "Make love to me, Henry. Make love to me all night and never stop."

Henry stood and, picking her up, carried her to the bedroom. Their lovemaking was intense with Sheila taking command. First with her mouth on him, she brought him to a full arousal, and then she turned so that he could delight her the same way. Next she climbed on him, straddling him as he entered her. After she had reached a climax, and before he could, she rolled over and pulled him atop her where they felt the crescendo of their passions collide.

Sometime later, far into the night, they fell into an exhausted but totally contented sleep and, for Henry, the first dreamless sleep in months.

# CHAPTER 29

Monday morning. After once more assuring Sheila he would be safe and would return as soon as possible, and with a promise to call at least weekly, he pulled from the driveway and headed toward Pittsburgh. The drive, though less than an hour, seemed endless to Henry.

Nearing Pittsburgh, he called Brenda. He told the receptionist who he was, and a moment later, Brenda answered. "Good morning. I was beginning to think you had got lost somewhere. Are you in Pittsburgh?"

"Yes. I'm sorry I haven't been in touch with you sooner. I had to go out to the west coast and didn't get back until a short time ago. I thought that now that I'm back, and if you have time, we could go look at the house."

"Absolutely. I'm in the middle of something right now, but I will be available in about an hour. Are you at the airport? I can pick you up."

"No, I'm driving. Why don't I meet you at the house, say about ten thirty?

"Oh, that's fine." Then she lowered her voice. "Should I change into something you like?"

Henry laughed. "As cold as it is, that's probably not a good idea."

She changed the subject. "By the way, did you know there is a car in your garage?"

"Yeah, I know. I had it put there. I figured it would be safer there than in the driveway, but I promise, I did not go in the house."

"Oh, good. I've been keeping an eye on the place since you aren't there and found the car there. I was a little concerned because it has out of state tags."

Henry grimaced. He had forgotten to turn the license plates. That kind of deficit could cost him his life or his freedom. He would not do it again. "No," he said to Brenda, "I just bought it out of state and needed the plates to get it back here. As a matter of fact, I just got the registration changed and am going to change the plates when I get to the house."

He laughed, "You didn't call the police, did you?"

"No, of course I didn't. I thought I'd wait until I had a chance to ask you about it."

Henry breathed a sigh of relief. "Okay, well listen, let me get off the phone, and I'll see you shortly."

"Great. I'll be there at ten thirty." She chuckled. "Don't start without me."

Stupid, damned mistake, he thought when he got off the phone. He couldn't afford mistakes. Even little ones like that. What if she remembered the number? Well, he'd have to change to the Pennsylvania plates and hope she didn't remember. Also, there was his connection with her. He couldn't have her coming by the house uninvited, and with his relationship with Sheila, his affair with her was irresponsible and possibly hazardous. What if, in the middle of sexual excitation, he called Sheila Brenda? Granted he had never told Sheila their situation was exclusive, but he was sure she wouldn't look at it that way. It was also irresponsible having an affair with an employee. He had never believed in employer/employee relationships. He never had one, and he should have kept this one strictly business like. Still, he thought, justifying his actions, it was a short term contract, and she did have an incredibly irresistible body. Well, he thought, no matter how irresistible she is, I need to end it.

Getting to the house shortly before her, he went in and rotated the plates to reflect Pennsylvania and put the Pennsylvania registration and insurance cards in the glove compartment. Removing the California information, he put it in the compartment under the dash and closed it. Then, he started the car to let it run and charge the batteries that had probably depleted some over a month of sitting. At 10:25, he shut off the engine, closed the garage door, and went to sit in the Cadillac to wait for Brenda.

When she arrived, she immediately threw her arms around Henry and kissed him. He returned the kiss and then held her back. "Why don't we go inside? I want to see what you've done, and we need to talk."

She looked at him quizzically but moved to the house. "That seemed a little subdued after our last kiss."

Henry smiled and put his arm around her shoulder. "I guess it does, but my situation has changed since we were together. You see, there is someone else in my life, and I feel a bit guilty carrying on two relationships. Also, and though we have not discussed it, I think she sees a marriage in our future."

"Oh. I'm happy for you. Maybe I could meet her sometime, to see what she thinks of the work we put into the house."

Henry shook his head and, as far as he knew, lied. "I don't know that that's a good idea. I've found she is a slightly jealous young lady, and seeing how beautiful you are, she would probably not receive you well."

"I see," she said reflectively.

After they got in the foyer, she took his arm and, turning him toward her, said, "Just one thing before we go in, Henry. I know it's none of my business, but I like you, a lot. My ex and I got a divorce because of his jealousy. He was just slightly jealous when we were going together, and I thought it was becoming. It even attracted me to him. Then we got married, and once we were married, it got progressively worse until it became abusive. Anyway, do you think it's a good idea to marry someone like that? I have heard many times that whatever trait you find in someone, you should magnify it ten times for when you marry them. I know that was true for me."

Henry smiled. "To tell you the truth, maybe it isn't, but I figure if I play my cards straight, she might eventually outgrow it."

She squeezed his arm gently. "I hope you're right, but I thought that too, and five years later, it was much worse. So we separated, and a year later, after a couple of bad reconciliations, we divorced. I've met his second ex-wife, and she has the scars to show he has gotten worse. I would just hate to see you get hurt."

Henry thought about saying, yeah, you're right. The hell with marriage, let's find the closest bedroom. Instead, he said, "I guess that's always a possibility, but when we're together, she's very loving, and, well, marriage may be worth a try if it gets that far. I do think it's nice of you to care, and you are definitely wonderful for caring."

"Now, let's get off that subject and see what you've done with the house."

Though he had seen most of the house before, she had added a flourish here, an embellishment there, and completed the other bedrooms. It was immaculate, the décor tasteful. It looked homey without being prudish. Later, the tour satisfactorily over, they sat in the family room sharing a celebratory glass of wine from the wine cooler. They shared small talk about decorating, and Brenda tried to return three thousand dollars she had not used. Henry was impressed, not only with her, but with her honesty and insisted she could keep it.

The conversation then returned to Henry's theoretical future marriage and Brenda's conclusion that it would not be a good idea to rush into such an arrangement for at least a year or two. In the meantime, she ventured, since he did not have an exclusive relationship with Sheila, maybe they could see each other occasionally because, according to Brenda, the sex was amazing. Henry could not disagree with her as she kissed him and pulled his hand over to cup her breast.

"Okay," he said, unbuttoning her blouse, "but we have to have some ground rules. You can't call me unless I ask you. I'll call you whenever we can get together, and you can't come by unannounced because you won't know who might be here. Promise?"

She smiled as he unhooked her bra and slid his hand around to tease her nipples. "Okay," she said rubbing her hand against his slacks, feeling him grow with her massage. "And I promise not to be jealous, even though I'll know you're having sex with someone else too. Now, let's go upstairs, because you've got me so hot I'm going to cum without you if we sit on this couch much longer."

He followed her up the stairs as she removed her blouse, bra, skirt, and panties. He wanted to grab her and have her right there on the steps but restrained himself until they got to the bed.

He stripped off his clothes and slid in beside her, moving his hand between her legs as she did the same to him. "I need you inside of me. I don't want to cum without you."

He continued his caress, kissing and teasing her nipples. "Go ahead. If I get inside you right now, I'm going to finish before you do."

She slid down and got him in her mouth. Seconds later, he reached a climax. "I told you that would happen."

She laughed as she moved back up to lay beside him. "I know, but the next time, you'll have more staying power. Besides, I had an orgasm while I was doing it, and I know you can keep me going until you're ready again."

He moved his hand back to her, kneading, caressing, inserting his fingers to heighten her pleasure. "Well, I don't want to make you sore before I'm ready."

She laughed again. "Sweetheart, you could do this all day, and I would only want more. If I start to get tender, you could always use your lips and tongue. I can assure you, you would never hear me complain."

This time, he slid down, sliding his fingers inside and pressing his lips to her until she moaned in ecstasy, and he was ready to go again.

Later, they lay bathing in the afterglow of their orgasmic romp, Henry with one hand behind his head and Brenda's head on his chest, her leg across his thighs. Well, he thought, truly, the spirit is willing, but the flesh is weak. There went the idea of not seeing her again.

Brenda padded naked out of the bedroom and returned shortly with the wine and glasses from the basement. She poured them each a glass, handing him one. "I just want to keep my doors open, in case things don't work out for you."

Henry smiled, caressing her leg. "And you have such enticing doors to keep open."

They lay for half an hour quietly relishing the ambiance of each other's company, then Brenda raised up on one elbow. "Are you hungry? I could make us something to eat."

"Wouldn't that require food in the house? I haven't been to the store."

She smiled. "No, but I have. There's frozen food in the freezer and canned and dried goods in the cabinets."

Henry hugged her. "Aren't you just the little Girl Scout? What do you have in mind?"

"Maybe a couple of steaks with mashed potatoes and asparagus. Of course, the potatoes are frozen. I could get the steaks out, and we could make love until they're thawed. Or we could just lay here and enjoy each other's company until they thawed. Then, we could eat and, afterward, fuck the rest of the night."

"Or both," he said and laughed when she started to roll on top of him. "No, I'm kidding, crazy lady. You might be able to go all night, but I have stuff to do tomorrow, and I want to be able to get off this bed. How about we rest a while, have dinner, and see where we go from there?"

She sat up. "How about we compromise. I'll get the steaks out, come back to bed, and you can make me cum a few times while we wait. Then, we can have some dinner and come back to bed to have a grand finale for a beautiful day."

"Deal," he said, "as long as you stay naked the entire time. I may need to have some dessert before dinner, or during dinner."

"I think that is an astounding idea," she grinned, "and I love being naked for you." She padded to the kitchen where Henry heard the freezer door open and close. Soon thereafter, she returned with a new bottle of wine. "Have you ever noticed how well wine and sex go together?"

Henry, to Brenda's vast enjoyment, brought her to a climax twice more, and then they both napped until the steaks were well thawed.

Brenda, to Henry's enjoyment, remained naked as she prepared dinner. Occasionally, she would come up to him for a kiss or caress, and he was more than happy to oblige.

After dining, she sat on his lap for a few minutes while he teased her, then they took the wine and returned to the bedroom.

Knowing he would only be good for one more time, he listened to her excited moans during two hours of foreplay before entering her and reaching the pinnacle of excitement for the final time that day.

She snuggled up against him. "Now, aren't you glad you changed your mind? I definitely know I am."

He hugged her to him. "You made me an offer I couldn't refuse." To himself, he thought, it's too bad we aren't Mormons so I could have both of them. Then, smiling, yeah, but that would end up in disaster, sure as hell.

The activities of the day had worn on both of them, and it was just a few minutes before they both fell into a deep, contented sleep.

# CHAPTER 30

The next morning, they rose, and Brenda showered before leaving. Henry declined the invitation to join her because he knew they would end up back in bed.

Then after a prolonged goodbye, she waved as she pulled out of the driveway. Henry promised to call her later if he had the evening free. When she had disappeared from view, Henry got his luggage from the Cadillac and hung his shirts and slacks in the closet, put his socks and underwear in a dresser, and his toiletries in the bathroom. Opening the linen closet, he found Brenda had even gone so far as to buy additional bed linens, towels, wash cloths, extra dental items, deodorants, bath products, and more. Henry smiled. She must have felt sorry for the bachelor who would probably forget to buy such items for himself. She had certainly gone above and beyond what Henry would have expected. He wondered if she did as much for all her clients but seriously doubted it.

After he had showered and shaved, he looked in the closet, selected slacks and a shirt and dressed. Then, thinking about the clothes he had brought with him, he decided he would delay his 'hunt' for the day and do some shopping. Of course, since Brenda would be here at times (now that they had decided they could maintain their relationship for a while), he should probably also have some fresh foods in the refrigerator. Eating frozen potatoes from a box was almost like eating paste.

He looked at his watch. Ten o'clock. The malls would be open by this time. He grabbed his jacket, wallet, and keys and headed for the door. He gave a thought to driving the Lincoln then decided against it. It was still early in his hunt, and he didn't need to protect himself against an enemy he didn't currently have.

He parked the car in the nearest mall parking lot and spent the next three hours browsing the stores to purchase slacks, shirts, underwear, flannel shirts, long johns (it got damned cold in Pennsylvania), additional foot wear, a heavier leather coat, and an overcoat.

With the purchases in the trunk of his car, he next went to a gun store and purchased a Kimber Classic Carry Elite forty-five-caliber handgun, which he had to put in the car before he could purchase the ammunition. He guessed the owner didn't want to get shot by a gun he had just sold. The weapon was a little pricey, but the proprietor assured him it was an excellent and accurate defense weapon. Henry was surprised he could purchase and take possession of the weapon on the same day but was told with the ability of the Feds to clear him in a few minutes, the three-day waiting period was no longer necessary. Henry guessed the Pennsylvania concealed carry permit he had didn't hurt either.

Once in the car, he loaded the weapon and placed it and the remaining ammunition in the concealed compartment and closed the door.

With that accomplished, he proceeded to a grocery store where he purchased milk, eggs, bacon, sausage, fresh vegetables, snack foods, and a variety of other things that, on an empty stomach, he found appealing. He had heard it was not good to food shop on an empty stomach because you bought things you didn't need. Henry had always thought one should always shop while hungry because then you stocked up on things you like to eat in the evening while watching TV.

By the time he was finished with his shopping excursion and got back to the house, over six hours had passed. He pulled the Cadillac into the garage beside the Lincoln and lowered the garage door. Then, he spent another hour carrying his purchases into the house and putting them in their respective receptacles.

Looking at the time, now after five, he dialed Brenda's number. He was, he thought, becoming addicted to the fiery redhead and her excitement at being in bed to enjoy their sexual escapades. "Hi, Henry," came the familiar voice when the call connected. "Are you home?"

"Yeah, I just got in a bit ago. I had to do some shopping. The larder was a tad empty, and so was my closet. I thought I should replenish the fridge, so we had something other than instant potatoes to eat. Anyway, I was thinking if you aren't doing anything special this evening, I could cook up something, and we could have dinner here."

Brenda laughed. "You cook too? If you cook like you make love, it's got to be quite elegant."

He chuckled. "I wouldn't get carried away with anticipation. However, I can probably throw something together that is palatable."

"And what time would you like me there, sir?"

"Well, it's five-thirty now, how about five-thirty?"

"Oh, I love the thought. However, I have some things to take care of here at the office. How about seven-ish?"

"If I must. See you then."

Henry hung up and started preparing. Clams casino as an appetizer, then prime rib with baked potato and salad for an entrée, and chocolate mousse for desert.

He had just put the prime rib in when he heard the front door open then close. There was rustling in the foyer and the thump of an overnight bag hitting the floor before Brenda padded into the kitchen naked. Smiling at the obviously pleased Henry, she spread her arms. "I didn't know if you had prepared a dessert, so I brought it with me."

Henry closed the oven door and took the exotic redhead in his arms. "Well, I have, but since you brought what appears to be the appetizer, entrée, and dessert, I could just throw all this in the trash and just go with your choice."

Brenda kissed him as he cupped her bottom and pulled her to him. "Or we could eat what you made first, and then what I brought second."

"Excellent idea," he said returning the kiss. "The problem is I need to let go of you to finish this, and you are a lot more delectable."

She shoved him away and went to sit on a chair at the table. "Well, you'll just have to wait. Besides, the longer you wait, the better the result."

Henry smiled and turned back to the stove. "Then I'll have to stop looking at you because you are really addictive."

She playfully crossed her arms and legs. "There, all gone until after dinner." Then, changing the subject, "So, did you do anything interesting today, besides obviously going to a grocery store?"

Henry shook his head as he put butter, sour cream, and chives on the baked potatoes. "No, I just went there and to the mall to pick up some extra duds. My closet and dresser looked a little barren."

Brenda nodding said, "I brought an overnight bag. I was tired of putting on the clothes of yesterday when I leave. It's a pain to have to go home to dress before I go to the office."

Henry carried the clams casino to the table and set half in front of Brenda, who immediately ate one. "Wow, this is good. Who taught you to cook?"

Henry smiled as they consumed the appetizer. "Well, my mom said I started cooking when I was so small I had to use a stool to reach the top of the stove. Apparently, I was so small I don't remember that, but I've always had an interest as long as I can remember."

He took the appetizer plates to the sink and replaced them with the entrée and, later, with the dessert. When they were finished, Brenda went to the sink to rinse the dishes before putting them in the dishwasher, and Henry stood behind her, against her, running his hands over her breasts and down to her pubic region.

Brenda laughed. "I can't do this with you doing that. Just give me five minutes, and then you can have all you want."

Henry smiled but stepped back. "Did it occur to you that all I want is still not enough?"

"Good," she returned. "The old adage is 'always leave them wanting more,' and I always want you to want more of me." Dishes properly disposed of, they moved to the bedroom where Henry, then Brenda, took control, each giving and receiving pleasure from their reciprocal activities. Afterward, they lay back sipping wine and enjoying the effect of their encounter.

"So, tell me," Henry asked, "how long do you think you could do this stay in bed, sex activity thing, before you needed a break?"

Brenda played her fingers across his chest. "Oh, I don't know, maybe two or three days. I guess, at some point, I would have to get up to eat and hydrate."

Henry laughed. "Well then, you're a better woman than I am a man. Two evenings of this is kicking my butt. As enjoyable as it is, and as delectable as you are, I think I need a little time to recuperate."

Brenda smiled, taking his hand and placing it between her legs. "You don't have to perform, sweetheart. The other things you do to me are beyond wonderful."

With the encounter pleasantly at an end, they snuggled together and slept.

# CHAPTER 31

Wednesday arrived much too early and much too cold outside. He roused Brenda by kissing her breasts and stomach and then jumped out of bed before she could grab him.

"That's not fair," she said stretching. "I should get to reciprocate."

Henry laughed. "And then we would be in bed all day. Thanks, sugar, but I think we both need to be up and about. Why don't you grab a shower, and then I will."

She threw off the coverlet to reveal her naked body and stretched again for Henry's benefit. "We could shower together. It would save water."

Henry grabbed her hand and pulled her off the bed. "That is wrong on so many levels. Scoot your bottom in there by yourself. If I survive the day, because of last night, there's always another time."

"Promises, promises," she pouted as she went to the bathroom. She showered and then dressed while Henry took his shower. After their morning rituals, they ate breakfast, which they prepared together, and then Brenda kissed him, offered herself to him once more, and left for her office.

Henry watched as she drove out of sight and shook his head. He wondered if he could keep up with her sexually over the long term. Hell, he wondered if she could keep up this rigor over the long run. He smiled. Well, it would be fun to find out.

Putting the thought aside for another time, he turned on the television and caught the weather. As he already knew, it was cold, cold, cold. He dressed accordingly and donned his new leather coat to bear the frigid temperatures.

Going into the garage, he got into the Lincoln, and pulling out, drove slowly out of the driveway, watching to make sure the garage door closed behind him. He drove gently the first few miles as the heavy Lincoln handled differently than the much lighter Cadillac. After five miles on the winding road and feeling comfortable with the car, he picked up speed as he drove into Pittsburgh.

While driving up and down the haphazard city streets, the GPS was no good, Henry found himself completely lost and totally disoriented. He detested Pittsburgh streets and was a little leery as crime was higher in the inner city. There seemed to be no order to the streets at all.

In four hours of driving, he had found a total of ninety-three vans. Sixteen had been Dodge vans. Three of those had dual headlights. None had been black, or were window vans, and none had the requisite dent in the bumper.

Pulling into the lot of a body shop, he opened a map of the Pittsburgh area and tried to figure out where he was. As he traced his finger across the map, trying to find the street he was on, he glanced up in time to see the roll up door closing behind the tail of a black van. He jumped out and went into the office area of the brick building. He was greeted by a tall, skinny guy in white paper coveralls who came through the door of the adjoining bay where the van was located.

The man looked at Henry through red-rimmed eyes. "We're closed, buddy. You'll have to come back tomorrow." The man talked with a slow, nasal slur and, Henry wondered if he was he was on something or if the paint fumes were getting to him.

"Oh, I don't need any work done. I was just wondering if I might ask you a couple of questions."

"Sure, man. I was on break anyway."

Henry pointed to the door the guy had just come through. "I noticed you had a van in there. I have a Dodge van that I am thinking of customizing," he lied. "And I was curious about the amount of work involved. Is that a Dodge you have in there?"

"Yeah, man. It's a Dodge Ram."

Henry's heartrate increased. "Really? That's what I have. Mind if I take a look?"

"Oh, I don't know man. The boss says the insurance don't cover people in the shop. He would kill me if he came in and saw you in there."

Henry found a twenty in his pocket and held it out. "Just a look, and I'll get out. Twenty bucks if you let me."

The guy eyed the twenty then snatched it from Henry's hand. "Okay, but make it quick, man. I don't wanna lose my job."

Henry stepped into the paint bay and looked at the van. It was similar to the one he was looking for, but the windows in the sides were different. Even though the bumper was dented, it too was different than what he was looking for.

"Tell me something," he began. "How much trouble would it be to change one of these into a window van or from a window van to one of these?"

The kid looked at him like he was stupid. "Are you kiddin' me? It wouldn't be worth it. You'd have to cut out the sides, put in different supports and redo the interior. It would be easier to get the box you want from a junk yard and switch them out. Or just trade it for the kind you want. It'd be cheaper too."

"How about the small decorator windows?"

"Nah, that ain't no problem. I've replaced 'em before. It's a piece of cake. Just weld in new metal, cut to the shape you want, and slap in the window. A little Bondo and paint and you're all done. Biggest thing is redoin' the interior if it's already finished."

Henry nodded. The porker at the junk yard had been correct. "Have you replaced any, say, heart-shaped ones with another kind in the last six months?"

The kid eyed him suspiciously. "Say, buddy, are you a cop or something?"

Henry laughed. "No, just curious. That's what my van has, and I'm just wondering how much it will cost me to replace them."

"Nah, I haven't replaced any. Listen, buddy, you better leave. The boss will be coming back, and I don't want him to find you in here."

Henry nodded. "Yeah, no problem. Mind if I look inside before I go?"

"Yeah, I do mind. You're gonna have to get the hell out of here."

Henry turned, walking toward the door. "Sure, man. No problem. I don't want to get you in trouble. Catch you later."

He returned to the Lincoln and pulled into the downtown traffic. He had found out one thing that made his hunt a little easier. It wasn't exactly feasible to completely change the van. However, if the windows had been changed, how could he tell if it wasn't obvious from the outside? Could one tell on the inside? He wished he had been able to see the interior of the van at the body shop too; he could have asked the kid. Well, he'd just have to find out somewhere else.

His driving was taking him toward the downtown section of the city when he saw a sign reading Vans Unlimited, buy, sell, or trade. He pulled into the lot and got out. The sign on the door indicated the lot was closed, but Henry wandered through the rows of vehicles, inspecting each one.

He was standing on the bumper of one, his hands cupping his eyes so he could see into the dark vehicle.

"What are you doing, fella?" the voice behind him said.

Henry, startled, slipped off the bumper, barking his shin painfully. He grimaced with the pain as he turned to see the police officer standing a few paces away.

"Cripes," he said rubbing the injured leg, "you scared the hell out of me."

The cop maintained his stance, his hand on the butt of his service pistol. Henry could see the safety strap for the weapon was unsnapped. "I asked you what you're doing here. This place is closed."

Henry smiled, continuing to rub the soreness from his shin. "I was just browsing, nothing illegal."

"Yeah. Well, like I said, the place is closed. You got some ID?"

Henry started to argue but decided that would only draw more attention to him. "Sure." He removed his driver's license and handed it to the officer. "Like I said, I was just looking."

The cop scanned the license and handed it back. "Well, Mr. Jenkins, I would suggest you look when the place is open. That way, you don't have to peer through the windows, and it will make my job a lot easier. Besides, this is a high crime area, and we get real leery in situations like this."

"I understand. Sorry." Henry put his license back in his wallet and returned to his car. He had already seen all the vehicles before the cop had shown up and was only trying to get an idea of the inside.

He spent another three hours cruising the streets. Then, noticing the hour, drove back to Hunters Trail. He thought about calling Brenda, and then discounted it. There was always tomorrow. He instead called Sheila.

"Hi Henry. I was beginning to wonder if I would hear from you this week."

"Well, I promised I'd call."

They passed pleasantries for a few minutes, then Henry asked, "Have you heard anything about the case?"

"No. I've watched the newspaper every day and listened to the local news on TV. There hasn't been a word."

"That's too bad," he lied. "I was hoping to hear something positive."

After a few more minutes of idle chatter, Henry begged fatigue and rang off. He retired to the bedroom and watched the news on cable television until he dozed off.

By Friday evening, he decided he had exhausted any hopes of finding the Dodge in Pittsburgh. He figured he could accomplish some necessary work in the shelter over the weekend. Then on Monday, he would begin searching the surrounding areas.

# CHAPTER 32

It was seven o'clock when Henry woke and 33 degrees outside. It was certainly not a day when he had any desire to be outside, but there was work to be done, and he was not going to accomplish it by staying in where it was warm. He donned long johns, jeans, a flannel shirt, and a sweater. While the coffee was brewing, he drug a waist-length coat, gloves, and cap from the closet. He drank the first cup of coffee then went to the workshop where he got a mattock, shovel, hammer, and screwdriver, which he carried to the back porch. When he finished his second cup of coffee, laced with a shot of brandy to ward off the cold, he put on the outer clothes and, gathering his tools, trekked across the back yard to the shelter entrance.

Laying the tools on the ground, he opened the entry door and stepped inside. He sighed. Sealing this entry and the steps was going to be a real pain in the ass. Going down the steps to the second door at the bottom, he flipped on the light and surveyed the job ahead of him. The entry and steps were not lead lined. At least he didn't have to contend with that heavy material. What I'll do, he thought, is drop the upper entry door and wood into the stairwell and shove dirt in on top of it.

Going back up, he checked the entry door by pulling it almost closed and looking at the overlap of the jamb. The door was about three inches wider and two inches taller than the overlap. Henry figured the threshold sat up about an inch, the entire thing effectively sealing the door when it was shut. He fished the key for the door out of his pocket and, fully closing the door, locked it. Then going to the lower door again, he reached for the handle.

That's when he saw the small panel. A rectangular piece of metal, three by six inches and hidden by the entry door when it was open. If Henry hadn't been looking at the door hinges, he would never have noticed it in the semi-darkness of the stairwell.

He got down on his knees and examined the panel. It was flush with the surrounding wall and held closed with a lock similar to the one in the ceiling that held the neck restraint. He studied the lock, wondering how to open it. Suddenly, he remembered the key under the shelf in the cabinet that he had replaced after it had fallen.

Hurriedly, he rushed to the cabinet.

Retrieving the key from the magnetic box, he returned to the stairwell and placed it in the lock. He was able to turn the key in the lock, but the panel did not open. He tried to get his fingers in the space between the panel and surrounding surface to no avail.

Going back into the shelter, he found a straight-slot screwdriver and, utilizing that, pried on the panel. The metal creaked as the rust let go, and the panel fell to the floor. Henry looked into the opening but could see nothing in the dark and was unwilling to stick his hand into the black opening. Going once more inside, he got a flashlight and, returning, shone it into the recess.

The beam fell on a plastic Ziploc bag, the only item in the recess. Henry pulled it out and turned it over. In that bag was a padded envelope like the one a person might buy at a post office to mail a small package. He carried it into the light of the shelter and opened the Ziploc bag, curious as to what Hampstead needed to secret in the stairwell instead of the shelter. He carefully opened the inner package and peered inside. What he saw both amazed and confused him. In the envelope were six keys identical to the keys for the restraints.

His mind whirled with his newfound discovery. Why two sets of keys? Why there, outside the shelter door? Why was the key to the panel hidden under the cabinet shelf? Henry would never have found it if he had not dropped a heavy item on the shelf above to knock it loose. There must be a reason. Hampstead did not seem to leave much to chance. The shelter was too well planned. He had laid it out and stocked it just the way it was with a purpose in mind.

Henry was beginning to get a headache. Carrying the envelope, he went upstairs where he got two aspirin (thank you, Brenda) and a cup of coffee. He was cold from being in the open stairwell, and his head throbbed. He sat leaning in the kitchen, staring out the window at the mound of dirt that made the entry, and sipped his coffee. The envelope lay on the table in front of him.

He jerked upright, his headache forgotten, and suddenly he knew. The reason was there. There had been no room for error, and everything had been planned down to the last detail.

He jumped up from the table, splashing coffee out of his cup and onto his slacks. He got the phonebook out of the drawer under the telephone and, flipping through it, found the correct page. He ran his finger down the column until he found the number he wanted, and grabbing the phone, he dialed the number, listening anxiously as it rang.

"Good morning, Greene Realty, may I help you?"

"Hello," he said to the female voice. "Could I speak to Mr. Greene, please?" He grabbed paper towels and wiped up the spilled coffee.

"Just a moment, sir." The phone went dead.

A moment later, she was back on the phone. "I'm sorry, sir, Mr. Greene said . . . I mean, Mr. Greene is not in the office at present. May I take a message?"

Shit, Henry thought. She saw my name on her caller ID. He would have to get a burner phone for such uses. Also, it was obvious Greene was there and didn't choose to talk to him. "No, I guess not. I'll call back another time."

He hung up and went back to the table. Greene had anticipated his call, knew he would call, and didn't want the encounter. He grabbed his keys, and getting the Lincoln, headed toward town. He drove the twelve-mile trip to Greene's office in nine minutes, just in time to see Greene coming out to get in his car. Henry pulled up behind it, blocking it, and got out just as Greene opened the door. "Mr. Greene, I'm glad I caught you coming into your office. I called a short while ago, but you had apparently not got here yet."

He grabbed the realtor's hand and shook it. "I just have a couple of questions. So why don't we go to your office and take care of them before your day gets hectic." He took Greene's arm and steered him back toward the door of his office. "It's cold out here, and it may take a few minutes."

Greene closed his car door, trying to smile, but he looked ready to flee.

They went into the office, passed the obviously perplexed receptionist, and to Greene's inner office. Once inside, Henry closed the door and indicated Greene should take his chair, while he sat in the chair opposite.

Henry smiled at the ashen face in front of him. "As I said outside, I have some questions. I'm sure you will be candid in your answers."

"Of course," Greene stuttered. "Of course I will."

"That's good to hear. The first thing I'd like to know is, how many deals did Hampstead turn down for that house before he accepted mine?"

"Why, none. That is, none that that offered what he wanted."

"I'll come back to that in a minute. When I initially called you, you told me the house was newly listed. How long did the ad run in before I called you?"

Sweat started to bead on Greene's upper lip. "Well, I think three. He called me just shortly before you did to say I should entertain your offer when you called but not to let you know he knew you would call."

Henry smiled. "Did it run anywhere else?"

"I don't know. I suppose he could have listed it by owner at some point. I never saw it in the MLS."

"Now, I'm going to ask the question I asked before. This time, think about it. You didn't give me the correct answer before."

"Now wait a minute," Green sputtered, sweat appearing on his forehead. "You can't threaten me. I will . . ."

Henry smiled at the sweating realtor. "Shut up, Mr. Greene. I haven't threatened you. Yet."

Greene's mouth snapped shut.

"That's better," Henry said smiling. He knew his smile was unnerving the man. "Now, one more time, how many times did you turn down offers on the house prior to mine?"

Greene was starting to look a little green. "I don't have to answer these questions."

Henry, still smiling, leaned forward, his forearms on the desk. In a low voice, he said, "That's true, Mr. Greene. You don't have to answer my questions. You also don't have to get the shit beat out of you. You don't have to have an accident on your way home tonight. You don't have to have your office burnt to the ground. There are a lot of things you don't have to do. But, one thing you should know is that if you do answer my questions, I will give you a thousand dollars. If you don't, one of those other things might happen. Now, one more time, how many offers did you turn down?"

Greene cleared his throat and clasped his trembling hands down in his lap while thinking about the options Henry had given him. After deciding the thousand dollars might be the best, he said, "Listen, Mr. Jenkins, I didn't turn down the offers, Hampstead did. He just told me he would have the final say on any offers made. He took yours."

Henry reflected on that momentarily then said, "You are trying to avoid answering my question, Mr. Greene, and my patience is growing thin. I'm going to ask only one more time. How many, and how many offered more than I did?"

Sweat rolled down Greene's jowls and soaked into his shirt collar. "There were four. All were more than yours. His responses were they were black or foreigners or had too many kids, and they would destroy the house."

Henry digested this information. Was Greene apprehensive because he thought he might lose his realtor's license or was he afraid of Hampstead? "Tell me something, Mr. Greene. Why didn't you want to answer my questions?"

Greene pulled a handkerchief from his pocket and mopped his brow. "Hampstead said not to discuss the sale with anyone."

"Discuss what about the sale?"

"I don't know. He just said that discussing it with anyone could be dangerous. Now, I don't know who is more dangerous, him or you."

Henry stood, more sure now of his conclusions about Hampstead. For some reason, the man steered him to buying the house on Hunters Trail.

Going toward the door he said, "Thank you, Mr. Greene. Our conversation has been enlightening."

"Wait. What about the thousand dollars?" You said if I answered your questions, you would give me a thousand dollars."

Henry stopped at the door and turned. "You're right. I did say that, and I will but not right now. You see, Mr. Greene, you have proven yourself to be less than trustworthy. You were asked by Hampstead not to discuss the sale, and you did, with me. That tells me you might do the same with someone else. As such, that thousand dollars is the proverbial carrot on a stick. I wouldn't want our little tete-a-tete to become known to anyone. If, when I have completed what I need to accomplish, I find you have not repeated our conversation, I will indeed give you that thousand dollars. If, at any time, I find you have divulged it, one or more of the other options may come into play. Now, you have a nice day."

He left the office, got into the Lincoln, and headed back toward Hunters Trail, this time at a more sedate speed.

His mind reeled with his newfound knowledge. Had Hampstead been one of the men who killed Mary and Linda? Surely not. The man was in his seventies and certainly not in good health. As big as he was, Henry knew Mary could have defended herself against the rickety old man. Also, even though Hampstead was weird, he didn't strike Henry as the type who would do what was done to his wife and daughter, even with help.

But Hampstead knew something. It was obvious he had kept an eye on Henry. He knew Mary and Linda were killed. He knew he needed a house. He knew Henry had gone to Denver, 'out west' he had said. Did he know where or for what reason? Henry doubted it. Frank played his cards too close to the chest. He even knew he wanted a house like the one on Hunters Trail. Henry thought that could have been guesswork, but he doubted it. Could he have overheard a conversation Henry had had? With who, Fred, Sheila, Lt. Cameron? Had he somehow bugged Henry's phone? If so, for what purpose? Did he have some tie to the killers? Or, did the killers have something on him?

The appraised value of the house had been much more than Henry had paid, yet Hampstead had rejected higher offers. Was that to ensure Henry got the house?

It seemed obvious to Henry now that Hampstead wanted him to bring his 'prisoners' here if he caught them. He had set everything up for that eventuality. He encouraged it by stocking the shelter, providing bounding equipment, even providing tranquilizer guns instead of real firearms to encourage letting them live.

What he hadn't anticipated was Henry finding the key in the magnetic box or finding the hidden panel with the extra shackle keys. He also would not be expecting Henry to do away with the outside entrance to the shelter, or he wouldn't have left the keys there.

As far as that entrance and his intention to close it off, Henry now saw that as a problem. If his conclusions were correct, Hampstead, or someone, was keeping an eye on him. If he destroyed the entrance now, they would know that he knew. His thoughts now were that Henry was going to find the perpetrators, and that he was going to confine them in the shelter. He gambled that Henry was not a killer.

Well, he was partially right. Henry wasn't a killer. Killing them was an easy out for them. He needed them to live every day knowing, suffering for what they did. However, when he caught them, and he would, they would be confined in the shelter.

His newly acquired knowledge also told Henry that there were possibly other keys hidden that he hadn't found. So, if he did find the men, and he did confine them, they, or someone (Hampstead), could just let them out again.

Even with knowledge of these developments, Henry gained ground. He could now narrow the scope of his search to someone Hampstead knew. He knew he would have to revise some of his immediate plans, and he knew he was going to need some help with the new ideas that were coming to mind.

He pulled the car into the garage and, closing the door, went into the house. Then getting the envelope from the table, he resealed it and, going downstairs, put it back in the recess and locked the panel. Next, he put the key back in the magnetic box and returned it to its original spot under the shelf. Finally, he picked up the tools he had taken outside and carried them back to the workshop then locked the shelter door and returned to the kitchen.

He would still seal the entrance, but that would come a little later, and when that later came, it would have to be done quickly. He picked up the phone. He scanned the yellow pages and found the number for a building supply company. He called and ordered some things he would need delivered and, giving them a credit card number, hung up. Next, he called a more familiar number.

"Frank's Auto, may I help you?"

"Yes, you can," Henry responded. "This is Henry Jenkins. Is Mr. Alessio in?"

"Just a moment, sir. I'll check."

That moment became four minutes when Frank came on the phone. "Mr. Jenkins, how can I help you? Car problems?"

"No, no, nothing like that. I have a unique situation here that I am unfamiliar with and need someone with experience to help me."

"Well, as they say, discretion is a virtue. That being said, can you give me an idea of the type of experience needed?"

"Let's just say, for the moment, I'd like a sound system. I believe I have most of the materials needed on hand. One thing is an intercom system. The others are probably better seen than me trying to explain on the phone."

"I see. Well, I can't tell you the cost until I get a man out there, but if you have the basics, I'll send someone to do the job for a nominal fee."

"That is not a problem. I believe I have most of the tools, and any that I lack, I can pick up at the local hardware or electronic store."

"Good. I'll have someone out there Monday. Good day, Mr. Jenkins."

So Henry knew some of the items he would have to get: an intercom system, a burner phone, maybe more than one, and tools to change the locks. He hadn't seen those in the basement. He had ordered thirty-seven concrete blocks and two bags of mortar earlier. Those were to be delivered Monday morning. He would pick up door replacement locks for the front and back doors and would have the garage door opener reprogrammed.

Jumping in the car, he made the second trip of the day to Pittsburgh. He picked up the tools and door locks he needed at the hardware store. Next, he bought three burner phones at the AT&T store in the mall and an intercom system at Best Buy. Then he ate dinner at a Denny's restaurant before he drove back home. By that time, it was six o'clock.

He picked up the phone and called Brenda.

"Hi, lover," she said. "Did you miss me?"

"More than you know. Would you like to come over?"

"I just got home, and I want to take a quick shower, is seven-thirty all right?"

"Or you could come here and take a shower with me. I just got home too."

"Ooh, I like that idea. How about half an hour then?"

"Much better, I'll see you then."

While he waited for her, Henry changed the bed linens and fluffed the pillows, carrying the old linens to the laundry and putting them in the washer. Next, he got the fire going in the bedroom and brought wine and glasses from the kitchen. And finally, he found some mood music on a television channel (thank you, Dish Network) and turned it low enough to just be heard.

He surveyed the room and, finding it satisfactory, poured himself a glass of wine. Then, he lay back on the bed to wait for his favorite redhead.

Brenda showed up promptly at seven and breezed into the bedroom. Henry stood up to share a very long, very seductive kiss.

Brenda held him close. "I missed this. I missed our horizontal refreshment and, now you tell me, that after this evening, I'll get to miss our vertical refreshment in the shower."

"Boy, you sure do miss a lot."

Brenda smiled. "I wouldn't miss it if we did it every day, all day."

He laughed. "We'd both be dead in a month or in the mental wing of the hospital."

"Hey, I could take that kind of crazy." She started undressing. "Now, you promised me a shower, and I can't wait to lather you up and rinse you off."

He followed suit, and soon, they were both in the shower. As promised, she soaped him all over as he did the same for her. After half an hour of mutually assured cleanliness, they rinsed each other off. Then, he held her against the wall, her legs wrapped around his waist as they built each other's desires.

Henry withdrew before he climaxed to Brenda's dismay. "But, you weren't finished."

Henry patted her bottom. "I'll finish in the bedroom. I've got a lot more to do before I'm done."

"Oh, I like the sound of that," she said stepping out and grabbing a towel. "What do you have in mind?"

Henry picked up another towel and began drying her off as she did the same for him. "I guess you'll just have to wait and see."

In the bedroom, Brenda got on the bed while Henry poured them each a glass of wine and handed one to her.

"To us," he said clinking her glass.

"To the wonderful times you give me," she replied, sipping hers. "Oh, while I'm thinking of wonderful times, I still have your key. Which, I guess you noticed since I let myself in."

Henry ran his fingers over her nipples. "Just keep it for now. You only come when I call you, and it saves you waiting for me to let you in."

He continued his exploration of her body with his eyes, mouth, and hands to her extreme pleasure and soft moaning. Then he entered her, first him on top then her.

Afterward, satiated and weak from their concerted effort, they lay back sipping their wine.

"It really is nice being here with you like this," she said. "I could never have believed sex could be this good or carried on for so long."

"I'm glad. I know you completely satisfy me. I just wonder, every time, if I am going to be able to get out of bed the next morning."

She laughed. "Well if you find you can't, I'll be happy to get a rise out of you."

"And no doubt you could, sweetheart."

He thought for a moment then said, "Tomorrow is Sunday. If you don't have to work, maybe we could see how resilient we are."

She threw her arm around him and planted several kisses on his chest. "I don't, and I think that is just the best idea you could ever come up with."

The next day was a repeat of the night before, except much longer and punctuated by breaks for breakfast, lunch, and dinner fixed in the kitchen. Brenda didn't feel it necessary to get dressed to go out.

"It's such a waste of time," she said, "putting on clothes, driving ten miles, then driving back and getting naked again. We would have wasted at least three or four hours. Just think how many times you could make me climax in three or four hours."

That evening, as they both lay totally exhausted by the day's activities, Brenda leaned over and whispered, "Seven."

Henry laughed when she told him that was the number just in the time they had saved by staying in and staying naked. "You mean you kept track?"

She grinned. "Hey, time in life is precious. One needs to get the most out of that time, and you have definitely given me the most I could ever wish for. If I had kept track of every one, it would have been a good bit higher."

She sat up, "But now, as with all good things, this must come to an end. As much as I would like to spend the night cuddling with you, I have a very early appointment tomorrow. So, regrettably, I am going to have to spend the night alone, in my own bed."

Henry smiled and kissed her. "Well, I must say you have given me the best, if most tiring, day I can remember. That said, I'm really glad I got to spend this time with you. And, who knows, maybe we could go two or three days sometime."

She got up and smiled as she wiggled into her panties. "I'll hold you to that, mister."

After she dressed, Henry bid her a goodnight with wonderful dreams, assuring her his would be, and she went out closing the door behind her.

As he drifted off to sleep a short time later, he hoped his dreams would be about her and not the nightmares of the past several months.

# CHAPTER 33

**M**onday arrived cloudy, but at least it wasn't snowing. The delivery of concrete blocks and mortar arrived at eight o'clock, and Henry had them offloaded in the garage behind the Cadillac. Darrell Franklin arrived from Denver just as the delivery truck was leaving and had to wait until it pulled out of the driveway.

He rang the doorbell, and Henry answered, putting his finger to his lips. The man introduced himself. "Mr Jenkins, I'm Darrell. I understand you have some work to be done."

"I do," Henry said, stepping aside. "Why don't you come on into the kitchen, and we'll discuss my projects."

The man sat, declaring, "Christ, I thought home was cold. This place isn't any better." Then as an afterthought, "But at least it ain't snowing."

Henry smiled. "Thank God for that. Would you like something to drink? I got coffee brewing, or something different if you prefer."

"Coffee sounds great. Thank you."

Henry poured two coffees and gave one to his visitor then sat down. "Darrell, due to the nature of the work I need done, I'll have to see some ID, and I'll have to call to confirm you're the right man."

"Sure, no problem." He tossed his driver's license to Henry and sipped his coffee while Henry made the requisite call to Frank.

After getting confirmation, he returned the license. "Sorry, just a little paranoid lately. I hope you can tell me if that paranoia is unfounded."

Darrell put his finger to his lips and shook his head. "Okay, do you want to show me? I understand it was a couple of trees out back you need removed?"

"Yes." Henry was glad the man was quick on his feet. "I certainly wouldn't want them to fall on the house during a storm. Bring your coffee, and I'll show you."

They stepped out back and closed the door. "Thanks for that. I wasn't sure how much I could say. Now, here's my problem. I don't know if my house or phone is bugged. There is a man who seems to know a lot more about me and my activities than I am comfortable with. I expect I've been followed, at least at times, but that is something I can handle."

Darrell nodded. "In that case, it's good you didn't say anything inside. I can scan for listening devices. Anything else?"

"As a matter of fact, yes, but if you can check for bugs, we can discuss the other things inside if it's clear."

"That's fine. Let me get my equipment, and we'll do a scan. It shouldn't take too long."

Darrell went out to the rental car and, retrieving a black plastic covered box, reentered the house. He put his finger to his lips for silence, turned the gadget on, and began going room to room scanning the walls and the furniture, as well as the vents, smoke detectors, and phones. When he had completed his survey of the upstairs, he pulled Henry into the living room and said, "The phone has one, so don't use it. I would suggest you not pull it out. Just disconnect the phone and put it outside or in the garage so that it's useless. And don't use the other house phones; they're interconnected. Other than that, this floor is clean."

Henry disconnected the phone and put it in a box in the garage then returned to Darrell. "Now, let's see what we have in the basement."

They went downstairs with Darrell scanning the stairway and the rec room with no indications. In the workshop, he pointed to a place above the workbench and again put his fingers to his lips.

Henry opened the shelter door, and Darrell scanned the tunnel and the shelter, indicating two bugs in the shelter, and even one in the bathroom. Motioning to Henry, they went back and upstairs.

"Well, sometimes paranoia is warranted," he said. "Do you want me to get rid of them?"

"Not now. As long as the rest of the house is clear, I'll leave them. Removing them now would let him know that I know. I don't want that." He smiled. "Besides, I'm the only one that goes in there, and I don't talk to myself, at least not yet."

They sat back down at the table with another cup of coffee.

"Now," Henry said, "my other concerns. I would like an intercom system installed between the rec room and the shelter. I have that in the garage. You noticed the entry at the end of the shelter? I would like that, and the shelter, wired with explosives so I can, at some point, collapse them but not right now. I will need the explosives hidden in the walls or ceiling so they don't show. I have plastic explosives and wiring in the basement. I don't know what else you will need, but I can get it. I want to change the locks on the doors, but I can do that while you work in the basement. However, I will need you to reprogram the garage door openers as I don't know how."

Darrell nodded. "Well, let me see the plastic and wiring, and I'll determine what else I might need."

Henry nodded, and they went back downstairs. He opened the cabinet, and Darrell inspected the plastic explosives, the wiring, and the detonator caps. He rummaged through the cabinet, as well as the shelves, looking for other hardware, and then motioned Henry back out of the shelter.

Once more in the kitchen, he said. "Okay, I'm going to need a couple of things that I didn't see down there. I'll make you a list, and then I'll get started while you go to the store." While he made the list, he continued, "It looks like I've got about three days' work here. I trust you have a room available for me to stay in?"

"I do, and food if you don't want to go out somewhere to eat."

"That will be great." He handed Henry the list. "The more time I have here, the sooner the job gets done."

Henry stood up and, reaching in his pocket, withdrew the laser key, handing it to Darrell. "You'll need that to unlock the shelter door," he explained. "On the pegboard, count over six holes from the right and twelve down from the horizontal line, and point the laser there."

Darrell nodded. "Yeah, I saw you open it, interesting mechanism."

Henry excused himself and headed out.

Once in Pittsburgh, Henry spent the next four hours shopping for the items on the list. His purchases took him to an electronics store, Best Buy, and a hardware store. When he returned, Darrell was sitting at the table drinking coffee. He sat the items Darrell had listed on the table and looked quizzically at his benefactor.

Darrell looked at the purchases and then said, "I have wired the stairwell. I believe you will have a hard time finding the plastic or the wires. With your purchases, I should be able to complete the project. The lead shielding is a plus as I can peel it back, knock a hole in the blocks, put in the plastic, and fold back the lead shielding. I will mold it so you can't see where I opened it. If you would like, I can show you in the stairwell."

Henry nodded in the affirmative and followed Darrell down to the basement. Once in the stairwell to the outside, he directed his gaze to where Darrell pointed. Henry could see nothing to indicate where the explosives or the wiring had been installed. That was great. If he couldn't see it, he was sure Hampstead wouldn't either. After the examination, they went back to the rec room where Darrell said, "I don't think anyone will be able to see the change. Now with your purchases, I will be in the workshop for a while. I have to make a switch, so you can set the stuff off. When I am done, I will explain it to you and show you how to operate it."

He watched as Darrell took items he had purchased from the bags into the workshop, examined them, and laid them on the work bench.

Then utilizing the wire strippers, soldering iron, and various items Henry had gotten from an electronics shop, he began assembling some type of push button switch.

Henry looked at the time and went upstairs. While Darrell was busy in the basement, Henry replaced the locks on the exterior doors and the one to the basement. He would have to let Brenda know of the change and give her a new key. She would be shocked if she came over and hers no longer worked.

To Henry, replacing the locks had been surprisingly easy. So with that completed, he went up to the kitchen and prepared some dinner for himself and Darrell. By the time it was ready, Darrell was back upstairs, and they sat and ate while he explained the switches he had made to Henry.

Darrell laid two push button switches on the table then picked one up. "It's a real simple switch and, as such, a dangerous one. All you have to do is push this button to detonate the explosives. I have put guard covers on them, so you don't inadvertently push one, but be assured, you don't want to be in the room when you do. The reason there are two is so that one collapses the stairwell and the other the shelter. I have marked them so you will know which is which. You will need to be on your back porch to assure you are close to detonate them, but don't go out into the yard when you do it. You might end up in a hole. I would keep the switch where no one else is going to find it and push the button to see what happens."

Henry figured he would keep them in the hidden compartment in the car. That way, he would be the only one to know where they were.

"Tomorrow," Darrell continued, "I will start placing the explosives in the shelter itself, which will take me a couple of days. I'll place them such that, as I said, it will collapse the shelter separate from the outside entry. It will be confined, so it doesn't damage the house, but it will take out about half the tunnel going to it. The way I'm doing it, both the shelter and the stairwell will collapse in on themselves. So you won't have any debris cleanup to contend with. The issue then will be the very large hole in your back yard. I would suggest you be ready to have about twelve truckloads of dirt ordered to fill it because it will be very obvious."

He finished eating and said, "Now, the scanner I used to search for bugs I'm going to leave with you. You know where the current ones are, but you might want to scan the place sporadically to assure no new ones have been placed. The ones in the shelter will be destroyed with the explosion. The one in the workshop can be smashed, or you can put a couple of drops of sulphuric acid on it. The acid will eat through the diaphragm in a few hours and disable it."

He slid his chair back and stood up. "Thanks for the meal, and if you don't have any questions, I'm going to go back downstairs and put in the intercom system. I know you want it in the shelter. I assume the other end will be in the rec room?"

Henry nodded. "Yeah, but somewhere so it won't be obvious."

Nodding, Darrell went back downstairs, and Henry cleaned up in the kitchen.

Darrell, as promised, finished Wednesday afternoon. He quietly showed Henry where the charges had been placed and explained, outside the room, how he had placed everything behind the lead shielding so it was undetectable. He had also reprogrammed the garage door openers and the cars to them.

"One final thing," he said, "when you blow the stairwell, the mike in the shelter will pick it up. So you will want to keep that in mind. Now," he said pulling out his phone, "let me talk to the boss for a minute, and we'll determine the cost."

He talked to Frank detailing what he could over the phone. Henry listened to the one-sided conversation. "Yes, sir, we removed a couple of trees Mr. Jenkins was concerned with, removed the stumps, and back filled the holes. No, sir, Mr. Jenkins had or purchased everything I needed except for the item I brought with me. Yes, sir, it was good I brought it. I have told him I would leave it with him for future use. Thank you, sir, I will tell him. Yes, I'm flying out this afternoon, and I'll see you tomorrow."

He disconnected and turned to Henry. "The cost of my work will be seven thousand. That includes the labor, flight, and rental car."

Henry nodded. "Fine, let me get that for you." He went to the bedroom, took the cash from his briefcase, and returning to the kitchen, handed it to Darrell. "Thank you for your efforts. I really appreciate it. I would have had no idea how to do it."

Darrell smiled as he pocketed the money. "That's why I have a job. Now, if you have any trouble with my work, call Mr. Alessio, and we will get it straightened out."

Henry smiled. "If there's any trouble with it, I might not be able to call."

Darrell laughed as he walked out the door. "That could be true. Good day, Mr. Jenkins."

When he was gone, Henry took the switches and put them in the Lincoln. Then, he decided that he still had some time to do a little detective work.

He looked at the time, four o'clock. He pulled out of the garage and headed for Pittsburgh. He hoped his favorite realtor was still in his office. He wouldn't call because he didn't want Don Greene to jump in his car and leave.

Twenty minutes later, he pulled into the lot beside Greene's yellow Lexus. When he went in the office, Greene was looking in a file cabinet. "I'll be right with you," he said and then turned. "Oh, it's you. What do you want?"

Henry smiled. "Good afternoon, Mr. Greene. I just need a little information. This time, I'll pay up front."

Greene sighed and sat down at his desk. "What is it this time, more threats?"

Henry shook his head and pulled some money from his pocket as he sat down. Leaning his arms on the desk, he peeled three hundred-dollar bills from the stack and laid them on the desk.

Greene eyed the money and looked at him.

Henry tapped the bills. "For that, I need the answer to a question. Did Hampstead live in that house before I bought it?"

Greene shook his head. "I don't think so. He didn't buy it until August."

Henry added another bill to the pile. "Did anyone live there?"

He nodded, "A couple of guys, I think."

Another hundred landed on the growing stack. "Tell me more."

Greene looked at the largess. "Hampstead bought the house in August from some guy in England who inherited and wanted to unload it. I never saw him. I dealt through his attorney. When Hampstead told me he wanted to sell it a couple of months later, I went out there, and there were two guys loading stuff into a van. I figured they had been living there. Hampstead was there too."

"Did they have a black van?"

Henry saw him eye the money and laid another bill on top.

"Yes, they did. I don't know what kind it was though."

Henry laid four more bills on the stack. "That makes one thousand dollars. Where does Hampstead live?"

Greene reached for the money, and Henry put his hand on it. "First, answer the question."

Greene got up and went to the file cabinet he had been perusing when Henry came in. Pulling out a folder, he sat down and copied an address from the file and handed it to Henry.

Henry took the address and lifted his hand from the money.

Greene grabbed it before Henry could change his mind.

Henry put the address in his pocket and stood. "Thank you for your time, Mr. Greene. Just remember, no one knows about our conversations. There are still other options."

He left the office, closing the door softly behind him.

It was now after six and dark, so he was done for the day. His search could continue tomorrow.

Returning to the house, he called Sheila and talked to her for an hour. He told her he felt he was making progress, but it was too early to call in the police. No, he was not in any danger (was he?). Yes, he would back off if things got too hot. No, he really couldn't tell her anything at present. Yes, he was eating enough if not three meals a day. Yes, he was getting enough sleep. He missed her too and would call her, probably next Tuesday or Wednesday.

He hung up, showered, and went to bed.

During the night, it snowed two inches.

# CHAPTER 34

He had a hard time seeing through the mist, but he could see the woman's silhouetted form lying tied to the bed. One of the guys was drawing the barrel of the pistol down her cheek and across her breasts, almost lovingly, caressing her with it. The woman was weeping hysterically. The man using her was growling at her to shut up, spitting the words at her.

The mist obscured their faces. Henry saw a gun lying on the table next to him and started to reach for it, but something cold was gripping his arms, preventing him. The woman was screaming with the pain of her violation, begging him to help her.

A second guy held her arms pinned to the bed, laughing at her anguish as the other pounded into her unrelentingly.

Henry swiveled his head around to see who, what, held him. Hampstead stood behind him, a sardonic grin showing decayed, yellow teeth in the wasted, pasty face.

The woman screamed, and the guy raised the gun, forcing it between her teeth.

Henry jerked his arm free and lunged for the gun in the man's hand, but he pulled the trigger before Henry could reach him.

Henry bolted upright in bed. The pillow where he had been lying was soaked with sweat, and his head pounded like he had a hangover, even though he had had nothing to drink the night before. Stumbling into the bathroom, he took three aspirin and climbed into the shower to let the needle spray drive the pain from his head.

When he came out and dressed a half hour later, the headache had receded, and the dream was just a distant memory.

Going into the kitchen, Henry dumped coffee and water into the coffee maker and punched the on button then put bread in the toaster to complete his breakfast. When they were ready, he slathered butter on the toast and carried it and a cup of black coffee to the table where he could sit and look out at the new fallen snow.

The snow was overall unblemished, marred only by bird tracks and the slight depressions going up across the back yard. He drank his coffee and stared at them. Were the depressions made by some large animal crossing the yard while it was snowing? Maybe they weren't prints, or if they were, the snow had almost obliterated them. Had someone been in the yard during the night?

He took his coffee and went to the side window. The depressions came up from the road along the woods and then angled into the yard toward . . . toward the shelter entrance? He returned to the back window and looked out. The depressions did, in fact, appear to go to the mound.

Well, he reasoned, it certainly looked like tracks, probably a bear. They had been seen in the region before, but it wouldn't hurt to check it out.

He set his coffee on the counter and went downstairs. Getting the laser key, he opened the door and proceeded to the shelter, turning on the lights as he went. Once in the shelter, and remembering the microphones, he quietly looked around, but nothing appeared to be disturbed or missing. He breathed a sigh of relief as he walked around and surveyed the shelves. Whatever it was, it must have gone around the entry and on out into the woods behind.

Henry walked to the stairwell, to the outside entry, and looked up. The plastic explosives were undisturbed in the recesses. However, on the top three steps, there appeared to be water. Did the entry leak? He doubted that it did. It was too well built and was, or had been, powder dry up until now. He walked up and examined them more closely. If they were footprints, they had dried to the point they were indistinguishable. He unlocked and opened the outside door enough to get his head through. The snow depression showed the door had been opened even though someone had tried to smooth it out.

Pulling the door shut and locking it, he went back down and into the shelter. Nothing appeared to be missing. Everything was just as he had left it. Why would someone come in and just do nothing? Were they trying to get in the house? It was good he changed the lock at the top of the basement stairs.

He was about to go back upstairs when he looked at the cabinets. He got the keys and, as quietly as possible, unlocked and opened the doors. At first glance, nothing appeared to be missing. He felt under the lower shelf. The key was still there. He stood looking at the shelf with the drugs on it and decided everything was as it should be then realized what was missing. The level in several of the drug containers was down about half an inch.

Henry closed and locked the cabinet doors, pondering who the miscreants might be. Hampstead? He didn't think the old man would be out traipsing around the place in the snow. Greene had said two guys had been living in the house. It was probably them, or one of them. But, what was the relationship to Hampstead? Were they related? There must be some tie. How else would they know how to get in the shelter? As for the drugs, if they broke in for the drugs, why didn't they take all of them? That was probably one question he could answer. They were hoping he would not notice the reduction. Too many questions and no answers, he thought as he went back upstairs.

His coffee was cold, so he poured it out and got another cup. His toast was also cold, so he tossed it out back for the birds. While he was cleaning up in the kitchen, he decided to drive out to the address Greene had given him. He didn't know that the drive would accomplish anything, but it was better than sitting around achieving nothing.

Turning off the coffee pot and putting his cup in the dishwasher, he collected his wallet and keys, put on a coat and hat, and headed for Pittsburgh.

Hunters Trail had not been plowed. Nor had any cars been on the road recently to pack down the six inches of snow the area had received. The heavy Lincoln, however, had no problem and drove almost as if the roads were dry, packing the snow under the oversized tires.

He rounded a curve on the country road to see a pickup bearing down on him. The driver had lost control, and the vehicle was sliding toward him sideways. He glanced down, put his thumb on the switch for the front bumper, and activated it just before impact. He felt the thud of the extended bumper lock into place just as the pickup connected.

The impact slowed Henry down, but the heavy car continued another twenty feet before coming to a stop and shoving the pickup back in the direction it had come. Henry retracted the bumper and got out of his car.

The driver of the other vehicle got out and, holding onto the truck and a liquor bottle, came to where Henry was standing. "For Chris' sake man, why didn't you stop?"

Henry looked at the inebriated man. "Sir, I believe you slid into me. I had control of my car. Also in your state, you shouldn't even be on the road."

The man looked at the side of his truck. The side was crushed just about the height of Henry's headlights. The door was sprung and the fender was crushed into the tire, which was slowly going flat. He then looked at Henry's car, which exhibited no damage at all. "Look at my truck, man. You totaled it."

Henry, who had at first felt bad about the accident, was now irritated with the drunk. "I believe you've got that wrong, fella. I didn't do anything. You slid into me. Now, if you need a ride somewhere, I can take you, but you need to get your facts straight."

"I'll show you facts, asshole," the man said. He tried to swing at

Henry but lost his balance and fell against the truck. Holding onto the truck, he started around to the driver's side.

Henry watched, first with amusement, and then with alarm, when he saw the rifle in the rear window gun rack. He didn't know if the guy was going for the weapon or not, but he had no desire to be around to find out.

Getting back into the Lincoln, he put it in gear, but the truck was blocking the road. The driver was fumbling with the gun rack and trying to get the rifle loose.

Henry hit the switch and felt the bumper extend once more. Accelerating, he moved forward against the truck and shoved it off the side of the road. As he pulled away, he could see the man's legs flaying as he tried to right himself in the seat of the truck. The rifle was still in the rack.

He smiled as he retracted the bumper and continued down the road. By tomorrow, the guy would probably be wondering what had happened.

Henry sat in a Wendy's having some lunch while he scanned the city map. Hampstead's street, if Henry was correct, was about four miles southwest of the city. Henry had unsuccessfully searched for a phone number for the man, but that could be nothing more than a restricted number. Still, he thought sarcastically, Hampstead wouldn't need a phone. He was psychic. He could just beam into someone's mind and know what's happening.

It started snowing again while he was in the restaurant, and he sat watching it while he finished his lunch. Mary had loved the snow. That was the main reason they had stayed in Pennsylvania's mountainous region. After Henry had received his inheritance, he suggested they move south, but Mary wanted to stay where they had four distinct seasons. Besides, Mary had argued, and Henry agreed, Clarksville was a lot safer place to raise a daughter than was some large city in South Carolina or Georgia or Florida. In Clarksville, you didn't even have to lock your doors at night or take the key out of the ignition.

In Clarksville, the biggest crimes committed were kids stealing cigarettes down at the drugstore or jimmying the pinball machines in the TipTop restaurant to get free games. The last major crime in Clarksville was in 1973, when Jory Claiborne's wife, Helen, shot Jory because he came in drunk one time too many and with lipstick and the smell of perfume on him. Helen had castrated him with a shot to the testicles. After that, Jory lost his desire for booze and women. And apparently, Helen lost her desire for Jory because she ran off with Spud Wilkins a month later. They never were heard from again, and Jory became a tenor in the church choir.

Henry got up and dumped his trash as he thought: Well Mary, I guess Clarksville's 'safe' days are a thing of the past.

Once more in his car, Henry headed for the address Greene had given him. The snow fall was getting heavier. Henry slowed to twenty miles an hour so he could read the street signs at the intersections. If it got any worse, he'd have to call off his search and go home. As it was, the snow was getting deeper. Much more, and he would have to quit anyway. The car might be heavier, but it wasn't a snow plow.

The next street sign appeared through the snow. Kemper. Henry cut sharply right. The car started to slide but regained traction. Thank God for all-wheel drive and the weight, he thought. He eased down the street trying to see the house numbers through the heavy downpour without success. Buttoning his coat, he got out and started walking down the street. He pulled his hat down tighter on his head and donned his gloves against the cold and blowing snow. The snow stuck to his hat and coat as he walked, turning them white. He could barely see the house numbers.

Number 615 loomed out of the snow on the right side. Hampstead's house, number 617, was next. He tried to see it through the blizzard but could not. Getting closer, he saw not the house but a van sitting in the driveway. He sharply inhaled the cold air and snow. His heart beat faster as he neared it.

The van was a dark green Dodge Ram, but it did not have the heart-shaped windows in the back. In fact, it had no windows at all, just paintings on the sides. Still, the windows could have been removed and filled in as he had been informed. Walking up to the front, he looked at the snow covered bumper. With a gloved hand, he wiped the snow away on the driver's side. Nothing. Disappointed, Henry turned and walked back to his car. He was sure when he saw the van it would be the right one, but nothing was the same: color, windows, bumper, all different.

Opening the car door he knocked the snow from his boots and climbed in closing the door. He doffed his hat and coat and threw them on the passenger side floor. His clothes were wet, and he was cold. He started the engine and, putting the heat on high, sat watching the snow begin to melt and run down the windshield. The snow had slacked off some, but it was unlikely anyone would come out now and see his car idling by the curb. He sat staring at the van, thinking. Where was he right now, as far as a solution? What did he know? What was his next move?

He knew, he was sure, Hampstead was involved. How and for what purpose, he didn't know. Why and to what extent, he didn't know. One thing he was sure of, though, he was involved.

Next, who were the people living in the house before Henry bought it? Were they the ones that killed Mary and Linda? Was Hampstead protecting them? If he was, why?

And, where was the van? Was that it and had it been changed and repainted? Was it no longer on the road? Was that it sitting in the driveway in front of him with new bumpers and new paint?

Finally, how was he going to find the answers? If he just went up and asked Hampstead, two things would undoubtedly happen: First, the man would lie, and second, he would know that Henry knew. If that happened, Henry would be in danger. And, if there are two things I don't like, he thought, it's pain and death, especially if I am the recipient of either.

So, where did he go from here? He could try to find out about Hampstead and whoever else lived in the house, if anyone. Hampstead, at his age, was probably retired, but he had to have a history. He could also find out about the van and its owner. Surely, Hampstead didn't own it. It looked more like a toy for a younger person, especially with the paintings of a nude girl with ankle-length blond hair twined about her on each side.

The snow had slackened even more, and Henry figured he had better move before one of the locals questioned the car idling at the curb. Putting the gear selector in drive, he eased away from the curb and headed toward Pittsburg. He figured the easiest way to start getting information was to find out where Hampstead hung out. To do that, he was going to have to follow him, learn his patterns of coming and going, and find out where he spent his time.

That, however, was for another day. The snow was starting to pick back up, and he had one more task to accomplish before it got dark.

On the way through the city, he picked up two small bells and two spools of two-pound test fishing line at a Walmart. Then stopping at Home Depot, he bought a package of drill bits. He hadn't seen any in his shelter, neither as small in diameter as he wanted or as long as he wanted. He also bought some small eyelet screws. With his shopping complete, he drove back to the house.

It was still snowing when he got home. He was going to have to work fast. Finding a drill in the basement, he inserted the smallest drill bit and drilled two holes in the lower part of the window frame in his bedroom, one on each side. He could fill them when they were no longer needed, and they were small enough that little air, if any, would come through. Opening the spools, he fed fishing line from each through each of the holes he had drilled and then went outside.

On the outside, he screwed two eyelets in below the holes and two about six inches up from the ground and directly below the others. That completed, he pulled the fishing line from one hole down through the eyelets and walked back into the woods on the left of the shelter where he tied the end of the line to a tree, also about six inches from the ground. Then he walked back to the house, got the other line, and repeated the process, only this time, going to the right of the shelter. When that was done he went back to the bedroom, and playing out about twenty additional feet of line on each spool, he cut it and tied one line to each bell. With that complete, he played the lines out along the wall and laid the bells on the floor under the bed.

Now, he reasoned, if someone came through the yard, they would snag the line and pull the bell across the floor. If he was home, he would hear it, and if he was out, he would see the bell was moved. Although not foolproof (an animal could snag it), it wasn't bad. The line was virtually invisible, and one would have to become entangled in it to know it was there. It was also smarter than an alarm system or motion lights, which would warn anyone away before he had a chance to see them.

Placing the lines around the baseboard would keep anyone (Brenda) from accidently catching their foot on it.

Thinking of Brenda, he picked up the phone and dialed. She answered immediately.

"Hi, Henry, I'm glad you called. I was lying here with nothing to do and was thinking about you and us. I would tell you what I was thinking, but I'm not into phone sex . . . yet."

Henry laughed. "Well, if we got together you could tell me or show me. Would you like some company?"

"I would love your company. Would you like me to come over?"

"I don't think you would want to be out driving in this. It's really getting pretty bad out there. I could come there."

"Hey, I'm a Pennsy girl. I grew up in this stuff. Besides, I have four-wheel drive. I will have to drive a little slower, though, and I've got to get dressed unless this is a come as you are party. Can you give me an hour?"

"I'll give you as much time as you need, as long as you get here safely. Some idiot slid into me this morning. I wouldn't want the same thing to happen to you."

"Oh, are you all right?"

"I'm fine. I don't know how he's going to feel when he sobers up."

"Did it do much damage to your car?"

Oops, Henry thought to himself. "No, none, he just kind of glanced off of my bumper and slid off the road. Anyway, just take your time coming and be safe."

Henry could hear the smile in her voice. "As long as you promise to do the same when I get there. I'll see you soon. Bye." She hung up.

While he waited, he glanced out the back window. The snow was already covering his tracks to the woods. With the snow and drifting, they would be completely covered in a couple of hours. He took a shower and, putting on a robe, got wine and glasses that he carried to the bedroom. Then he lit the fireplace and, remembering an important fact, went back to the front to wait.

When Brenda pulled into the drive, he waited then opened the door just as she started to insert her key. "I figured I'd better open the door for you. I forgot to tell you I changed the locks."

"Oh, no," she pouted, "you don't want me to surprise you anymore?"

He laughed and handed her a new key. "Hardly. I just felt it prudent. I don't know how many keys to the old locks are floating around out there, and I would hate to have an unwelcome visit in the middle of the night."

She smiled. "That makes sense." She put the key on her key ring and took the old one off. "And thank you for making me an invited guest."

She handed him the old key and slipped her hand inside his robe and against his stomach. When he flinched, she laughed. "You know the saying, 'cold hands, warm heart.'"

He pulled her to him. "Then yours must be on fire."

They went to the bedroom where their sexual encounter not only met but surpassed the previous ones.

Afterward, Brenda still breathing heavily said, "Wow, I don't know that we can ever beat that one."

Henry, also out of breath, replied, "Maybe not, but I'd sure like to try."

Brenda rose up on one elbow. "Really, right now?"

He laughed. "Well maybe not right now, maybe not even tonight. I don't want to go to the ER or to explain that I'm there because of our bedroom antics."

He held her caressing her back. "You are going to spend the night, aren't you?"

"I'd love to, darlin', but no. I'm really sorry, but I've got too much to do tomorrow, and I will need an early start. Maybe next time."

Henry feigned disappointment. "Now it's my turn to say wow. I was sure with the weather you would be with me in the morning."

She kissed along his jaw and down his neck. "Can I get a raincheck for next time?"

"As many as you want, sugar. As many as you want."

After they had dressed, Henry walked her to the front door and kissed her goodnight. "I'll call you tomorrow to see if you have any free time."

"Oh, I'm sure I can find time for you, tiger. Why don't you call me after five? I think I'll be done by that time."

Henry went out with her and brushed the snow from her windows. The falling snow was down to a few flurries, but the wind had picked up some. "Be careful driving back. With this wind, the snow will be drifting. If you get stuck, give me a call. And give me a call when you get home, so I know you're safe."

She smiled as she ducked into the car. "I will, I won't, I will, and I will."

Henry smiled and stepped back as she pulled away then went back into the house.

An hour later, she called to let him know she had made it home with no mishaps. "See, it was silly of you to worry."

"That's all right, sweetheart; I'd rather be silly than sorry. Goodnight."

"Goodnight, Henry."

# CHAPTER 35

Henry sat in the Lincoln, across the intersection from Kemper Street, as he had every evening for the past two weeks. Brenda had come over to Hunters Trail to spend the night with him on a few occasions and had even stayed the whole weekend, though he went out in the evenings and came back at about ten o'clock when Hampstead apparently went to bed. Each night with her was better than the one before, and he looked forward to the next one.

Now he sat reminiscing about those times while he watched the house on Kemper. Hampstead had gone out three times in the evenings during that period with Henry following at a discrete distance. Twice he went to a grocery store about a mile away, and once to a pharmacy five blocks over. Other than that, he had stayed home.

Henry had copied down his license number but had been unable to find out anything from the DMV, who apparently did not give any information to civilians. Also, the van that he had seen in the driveway the first day had not returned, at least while Henry was there.

The snow had, for the most part, melted with several days in the forties, but the night air was still damned cold. Henry took a drink of coffee from his thermos and slouched deeper into his seat. He had been sitting here for over two hours and was thinking of starting the car to warm up when the headlights of a vehicle pulled into the opposite end of the street.

He was instantly alert as the vehicle slowed and turned into the driveway at Hampstead's. It was a van. At this distance and in the dark, he couldn't tell if it was the same one he had seen before, but it was definitely a van.

Two figures got out and went up to the house. A moment later, the door opened, and they went in. Henry, who had been getting drowsy, was wide awake, but the cold and his excitement made him shiver. He downed the last of his coffee and hoped the two figures were not going to spend the night.

As the minutes ticked by, he hunched over the steering wheel and pulled his coat closer around him. Looking at his watch, the red numerals told him it was 9:43. They had been in the house over a half hour.

Henry was going to start the car to warm up the interior when the two figures stepped out onto the porch. He stayed his fingers against the start button and waited. There was a short dialogue between those two and one in the house, then the two figures got into the van and backed out of the driveway. Henry waited until they had come up the street toward him and then turned left onto Hazelton before he started his car. It was definitely the same van he had seen before. He waited until they were a block down and then pulled out to follow.

Three blocks down, the light changed to red, and the van stopped. Henry hadn't wanted to get too close, but to stop in the middle of the block would have been obvious. He let the Lincoln drift closer, hoping the light would change. Seeing the van's license plate, he grabbed a pen and began jotting down the number. As he did so, the left turn light changed to green. Seeing the traffic beginning to move out of his peripheral vision, he accelerated before he looked up and bumped into the van before realizing the through light was still red. That's also when he noticed the police cruiser at the other side of the intersection.

"Shit! Damn!" He cursed his carelessness. He couldn't afford to let the guys in the van see who he was, and he damned sure didn't want Pittsburgh's finest questioning him with them there.

The doors to the van opened. Henry rotated the holders to show the Maryland tags. The flashing lights of the cruiser came on, and the car started to pull across the intersection. He hoped the windows were dark enough that the cop couldn't see his face. As he backed away from the van and swung the steering wheel to the left to get around it, he noticed something that caused his heart to pump even more adrenalin into his system. The right rear bumper had the same curious Q-shaped dent in it that he had seen on the left front of the one leaving his house.

The tires squealed as he jerked the shift lever in drive and mashed the accelerator to the floor. When they gained traction on the salt-covered road, the Lincoln shot forward, pressing Henry into the seat. He tore around the van, scraping the door and barely missing the driver. Having seen the dented bumper, he was sorry he didn't hit him.

The Lincoln gained speed through the intersection as the police cruiser started across. Henry swung the wheel to the right but not soon enough to miss the city car. The bumper connected with the left fender, driving it in and up, buckling the hood. The cop's expression would have been comical if Henry hadn't been so scared that he felt his bladder might let go at any second.

The Lincoln barely shuddered as it barreled past the cruiser, ripping the fender loose from the disabled car. Henry swung the wheel left and tore off down the street. In his rearview mirror, he saw the two men jump back into the van. Henry drove as fast as possible through the city streets, weaving in and out of traffic and hoping he wouldn't hit anything or anybody. Remembering the siren under the hood, he found the switch and turned it on. He knew one thing. He had to get out of the city as quickly as possible. He had already broken several traffic laws, and he was sure other cops were already after him. The van was visible in his rearview mirror. That was another vehicle he had to lose, at least for now.

Going past the stadium, he turned on to Penn Avenue and accelerated again. If he was correct, Route 28 was two blocks ahead.

At Butler, he made a left and went across the 31st Street bridge doing seventy miles an hour. Seeing the flashing lights coming toward him, he swung right onto Route 28. The Lincoln slid into a car parked at the curb. He jerked the wheel around and hit the accelerator. The car shot forward.

The van made the corner and came after him. A moment later, two sets of flashing lights came into view behind them. The van made a right at the next street and disappeared. Henry knew they didn't want a confrontation with the police any more than he did.

He passed the last traffic light, leaving the city behind him but not the pursuing police cars. The road ahead was dark and, for the most part, unfamiliar to Henry, who wanted badly to slow down but knew he couldn't. He hadn't driven ninety miles an hour since he was a teenager, and the speed scared him. A glance in the mirror told him he now had three police cars baring down on him, and he depressed the accelerator down even more. When he went through Aspinwall, the speedometer read 97.6 MPH.

As the Lincoln went into the turn, Henry prayed it wouldn't slide. He pulled through the curve and into the straight section of road knowing his nerves couldn't take much more of this. The police cars were getting closer, proving to him that either they were better drivers or just as stupid as him. He knew he would have to lose them, and outrunning them didn't appear to be an option. If he could get far enough ahead, he could go off on an alternate route until he felt safe. Also, he was heading toward Clarksville, and he sure as hell didn't want to go where he was known.

Three sets of S curves would be coming up soon, if he remembered correctly. If he could lose them there, he would be all right. He was doing well over a hundred, and a glance in the mirror told him he was finally gaining a little ground. He dared a look away from the road to quickly scan the console. Taking one hand from the steering wheel, he placed it against two of the switches and slowed down for the upcoming curve.

He had decelerated to sixty, knowing the cruisers were again gaining on him. As he went into the second set of curves, he saw the lead cruiser coming up behind him and threw both switches.

Oil and tetrahedrons sprayed out behind the Lincoln. Henry flipped the switches to the closed position and slowed even more as the first car came around the curve followed closely by the other two.

The lead car hit the oil and sharp jacks, and Henry watched as it slid off the road, its tires rapidly deflating. It went up the embankment and, as if in slow motion, rolled over and down onto the top of the second cruiser. The third, unable to stop, crashed into the others, and all three came to a jumbled stop, their sirens growling to silence.

Henry switched off his own siren and accelerated back to sixty as he left the final curve. At New Bethlehem, he bore left on Route 861. From there, he took Routes 68 and 422 to interstate 79 South. He switched to the Iowa tags, just in case. He would need to stop shortly and inspect the damage to his car. Right now, however, he had to think.

Why was the dent on the back bumper of the van? Was it a different vehicle? He didn't think so. That would be too much of a coincidence. Could the bumpers be reversed? If that was the same van, apparently so. Were the two men in the van the ones he was looking for? He had seen the driver when he went around the van. The guy looked to be around thirty years old and muscular. Certainly not a person Henry would want to get in a fight with. He was about six foot and had long, dirty hair and sported a scraggly beard.

He hadn't got a chance to see the other guy. He wished he had. He had jotted down the license number for the van. With that, he might be able to get the name and address of the owner.

Route 79 took him close to Pittsburgh again, but he hoped all the police were looking for him to the north of the city. He certainly didn't want to have to evade them again. Matching his speed to the posted speed limits, he drove south and crossed into West Virginia. Bypassing Morgantown and Fairmont, he stopped in Clarksburg and found a service station. While the pump worked to fill the car with diesel fuel, he surveyed the damage incurred by his blunder. There was no major damage to the car, but the paint had been scratched up pretty good on the sides from scraping other vehicles, and he had broken the plastic headlight lens and one of the side markers on the front when he hit the cop car.

"Need those replaced?" the attendant asked as he looked at the car. "Looks a little banged up. Did you run into some brush?"

Henry shook his head, "No, the lights still work, and I'm sure you don't have the outer covers. I'll get them replaced later. And, yeah, I got on some narrow roads and tangled with the brush on the sides."

"Yep, that can happen around here if you aren't careful. Hey, you must have one helluva gas tank on this thing to take that much fuel."

"Yeah, it's pretty big. I do a lot of driving. Tell me something, is there a motel in town?"

"There's a Sheraton up on Main Street, just down passed the courthouse. There used to be the Town House Motel out on Route 50, toward Salem, but it burnt down. I was never inside, but it looked pretty nice from the outside until a couple of druggies lit one of the rooms on fire and burnt the whole thing to the ground. Before it was a motel, it was a church, but it was converted." The kid laughed at his pun. "There's a story about that church too."

"Yeah, I'm sure there is." He handed the kid another ten and got in his car. "Thanks, lad, you've been a big help."

The kid looked at the bill. "Thank you. You stop back." He waved and turned toward the station.

He smiled as he pulled away from the pumps. He had been in a lot of states over the years, and the people in West Virginia were probably the friendliest overall. He drove to the Sheraton and got a room. It was two-thirty and the evening's exertion had worn him out. He climbed into the king-size bed and contemplated his next few days. Tomorrow, rather later today, he would head for Denver. The car had become too obvious over the last few hours and needed some changes. Even with different tags, the car was still gray and would certainly draw the attention of the police and the guys in the van if they saw it. However, that was for another day. He would call Frank later to let him know he was coming, but right now, he needed sleep.

He turned on his side and thought about turning off the TV, but his breathing became slow and even, and the television droned on as he slept.

# CHAPTER 36

H enry woke at ten o'clock Friday morning to at least a sunny day, if still a cold one. He started coffee in the small pot and picked up the complimentary newspaper outside his door. As expected, there was nothing about his case, and the police chase and wreck was not newsworthy in the Clarksburg Exponent. One item did catch his eye, however, and he read the article.

The headline read, "Woman found murdered in Pittsburgh." In the smaller print below was the following. "Police were called to a home in Pittsburgh, at 9:15 p.m. last night, where gunfire had been heard and reported by a neighbor. Upon entering the home, police found the woman on the floor in the bedroom of the home. Police stated the woman had gunshot wounds to the back."

Henry stared at the paper. Gunshot wounds, could it be the same guys that had killed Mary and Linda? It had happened a short time before he saw the van at the house, enough time for them to commit the murder and get to Hampstead's. He continued reading. She was deceased when police arrived and found the front door ajar. When questioned, police spokesman Lieutenant Corey Michaels said he could provide no further information at this time. There would be a news conference this afternoon at three o'clock.

"Three o'clock?" Henry said aloud. "That's no good. I'll be on my way to Denver at three o'clock." He flipped to the inside front page of the paper and found the number for the editorial editor. Using one of the burner phones, he dialed the number and waited.

"Clarksburg Exponent/Telegram, how can I help you?"

"Could you connect me with the reporter covering the murder of the woman in Pittsburgh?"

"Do you have information concerning the murder?"

"I may have. Could I speak to the reporter please?"

"Just a moment, sir."

He was put on hold for several minutes as the reporter was located.

"Diane Murphy, may I help you?"

"Maybe, are you covering the home invasion murder in Pittsburgh?"

"Yes, do you have information about it?"

"I could have, depending on what is said at the press conference this afternoon. I'm going to be leaving here shortly and will be out of earshot of the conference. If I call you back about four o'clock, can you tell me what was said?"

"Well, you're going to have to give me something if you want something from me."

Henry thought for a moment. "Okay, if anyone saw a vehicle pull away from the house, I have reason to believe it may be a van. If you tell me what is said at the conference, I can give you more information."

"All right, sir. Call me back after four. What is your name?"

"That's not important, Diane. At what number can I reach you when I call?"

She gave him her number and asked, "Can I have your number?"

Henry chuckled. "Nice try but no. I'll talk to you after four." He hung up.

He quickly scanned the rest of the paper, got his luggage, dropped the key card on the dresser, and headed for Denver.

By the time he got to Lawrenceville, Indiana, it was after four o'clock and Henry was getting hungry. It was also time to fill the gas tank and call Diane Murphy. He filled the tank at the Exxon station and then found a restaurant. He decided to call the reporter before he went in. He dialed the number and waited.

"Diane Murphy, may I help you?"

"Yes, I talked to you earlier about the murder in Pittsburgh."

"Oh, yes, and you are going to share your information with me?"

"If I find it is the same as the prior information I have, yes."

"All right. This is the short version of what was discussed at the news conference. The woman was thirty-one years old, lived alone, and had no known relatives living in the area. She had been raped, bludgeoned, and shot three times in the back. She had duct tape on her mouth and had her hands bound behind her."

"That sounds familiar. What about a vehicle. Did anyone see anything?"

"Yes, the neighbor that heard the gunshots saw a dark colored van go down the street before the cops arrived at the scene. She didn't know the make, and it was too dark to see the color. She did say she thinks it had something painted on the side."

She paused, "Now your turn. What do you have for me?"

"I can tell you that there was a previous double murder, not too far away, that seems to fit the same M.O. There was also a dark van involved in that. If you do a little research, I think you will find they are the same. That's all I can tell you for now. I hope it helps."

"Yeah, thanks, I think I can take it from here. Are you sure you can't give me your contact information?"

"If I find you discover the similarities I believe to exist, I'll call you again."

"All right, I appreciate that. Oh, there is one more piece of information that the police shared. The woman was an interior designer named Brenda Cartier."

Henry dropped the phone, shaking violently. "No, no, no, no, no! That can't be true! That's not possible! Not her, not Brenda!" He laid his head on the steering wheel and a great guttural sob escaped his throat.

Diane Murphy heard the lament from the phone lying on the floor. "Sir, sir, can you hear me? Talk to me, sir. Sir, I need you to talk to me. Do you know this woman? Sir?"

Henry grabbed the burner phone and disconnected the call. Then he removed the sim card and broke the phone in half. He wanted to talk to no one, especially this reporter, right now. This was his fight.

How had they known of his tie to Brenda? Had they seen her coming to the house? It was almost impossible, considering the number of women in Pittsburgh, that they had randomly selected her. Henry buried his face in his hands. This was his fault. If he hadn't gotten involved with her, this wouldn't have happened. If he had ended it when he intended, she would be alive now. Their prurient desires had sent this beautiful, vivacious woman to an early grave. He anguished for over an hour before he let anger overcome his remorse.

He would need two more days to get to Denver, whatever time it would take Frank to fix the car, and then three days back. Then, then the perverted sons-of-bitches would know what pain and anger and revenge felt like. He didn't want to kill them. He wanted to do such damage to them that they would wish every day for death.

His desire for food had disappeared. He pulled out of the lot and headed west. His next two days of driving cooled his anger to a very slow and determined burn.

# CHAPTER 37

Tuesday. Henry sat in Frank's gas station reception area and perused a twenty-year-old *Playboy* magazine. His anger, sorrow, and hatred had cooled to a calculated plan during his trip. Frank, according to the receptionist, would not be in until nine o'clock. Henry looked at his watch. It was 9:15.

The phone on the desk buzzed, and she picked it up. She listened for a moment, relayed some messages then said, "Mr. Jenkins is here to see you." There was a pause. "Just a moment, sir, I'll check."

She lowered the phone and said, "Are you the one with the Lincoln?"

Henry nodded. "Yes, I'm Henry Jenkins."

She relayed the message and hung up. "Someone will be with you shortly."

The shortly was immediately. The door to the shop swung open, and a skinny guy with a pinched face stuck his head in. "Mr. Jenkins, would you come with me?"

The man pushed the door open and Henry followed him into the shop. As they strode toward the elevator, the man said, "I'm Weasel. The boss told me to bring you up to the office."

Henry smiled. The nickname certainly fit him.

They got off the elevator, and Henry walked over to where Frank sat at the desk. Frank was on the phone and motioned Henry to take a seat. Weasel stood by the door.

When Frank got off the phone, he looked at Henry. "I would think you would have called before driving this far. It must be pretty important."

Henry nodded. "It is, to me anyway. I was right in the middle of something and ran into a problem."

"I see." Frank returned, jotting some figures on the pad in front of him. "Figuratively or literally?"

"Well, I ran into a police . . ."

"Whoa," Frank interrupted, "I don't want to know what you did. That implicates me. I just want to know what you need."

Henry nodded. "Sorry. The car got scratched up and a couple of lens covers are damaged. I would like to get the color changed, the lenses replaced, and the Maryland and Iowa plates changed, as well as the tanks refilled."

Frank picked up the phone and pounded in three numbers with a beefy finger. "Fred," he said a moment later, "when can you get the Henry Jenkins' Lincoln in for a color change?"

He listened for a moment then said, "No, a complete change. It'll have to be stripped down to the metal and repainted." He looked at Henry. "What color? Blue," he said to the phone. "Okay, that's fine."

He hung up the phone and looked at Henry. "He says he can start it tomorrow morning and will have it ready by Friday."

"That's great," Henry responded. That would give it time for things to cool down in Pittsburg before he returned Monday night or Tuesday morning.

"Not too great," Frank said, punching numbers into a calculator. "If my people have to do a rush job, which yours is, I have to pay them more. That means you have to pay more."

He pulled the paper from the machine and handed it to Henry. "That will cost you eleven thousand five hundred."

Henry frowned, "That must be one hell of a paint job."

Frank laughed, "My people do good work. The car has to be stripped to the metal and primer coated. Then there're four coats of paint and the clear coat, each one is baked on, plus replacement lenses and fluids. I'm assuming you want an oil change while you're here. On top of that, we need to come up with two license plates and associated material for those."

Henry sighed. "Well, it's got to be done. A question, though, do you have a loaner I can use?"

Frank shook his head. "I don't do that. If something happens, it ties us together. I can, however, have a rental here in a few minutes if you need one." He pulled a folder from his desk and pulled out a couple of pages. "Mr. Wiesel, would you take care of that while we talk?" He held the paper out to the man.

Wiesel took the papers and left.

Henry looked at Frank. "I'll need to get my briefcase out of the car, so I can give you the money. And, as I didn't reserve a place to stay, I'll need to call my brother."

Frank stood. "I'll give you the room. Just hit this button (he pointed to a button on the phone), and I'll be back up."

Henry dialed Fred's number, and after three rings, Midge answered.

"Hello, Midge," he said, expecting a barrage of obscenities from her. "This is Henry. Is Fred home?"

"Hi, Henry, no, I'm sorry. He's at work. Can I have him call you when he gets home?"

Her voice was soft, almost pleasant, and Henry wanted to pull the phone away from his ear and stare at it in amazement. "No, but thanks anyway Midge. Just tell him I called and will try to reach him this evening.

"Henry, I don't know what time he'll be in. I could have him call you at home."

"No, I'm not home. I'm in Denver and haven't got a motel yet."

"Oh, you are? Then why don't you come by for dinner this evening and stay with us?"

Henry wanted to say who the hell are you and what have you done with Midge. Instead, he said, "That sounds nice, Midge, but I'm kind of busy. Just tell Fred I'll call him later, okay?"

"All right, Henry, I'll tell him. And Henry, we'd love to have you here if you change your mind."

"Thanks Midge, bye." Henry hung up the phone and stared at it. "Damn!"

He pushed the button on the phone, and Frank reentered immediately. To Frank he said, "Well, I guess I'll catch Fred later."

Frank looked at him for a second then said, "Three zero five."

"Huh?" Henry looked perplexed.

"Dial three zero five. That's Fred's extension."

He stared a Frank. "Fred works here?"

Frank nodded. "If he didn't, you'd never have gotten the work done here."

Henry dialed the extension.

"Fred here," came the voice on the phone.

"Fred, Henry. I didn't know you worked for Frank."

Fred laughed. "Hank, how are you? And, no, we don't advertise where we work, but I've been here about four years. So, what's happening with you?"

"I just wanted to tell you I'm in town, and maybe we could meet up later. By the way, what's with Midge? She was so nice on the phone I was wondering if it was even her."

He laughed again. "I'll tell you later. Now, it's obvious you're in Frank's office, or you wouldn't have my extension, so let me talk to him for a minute."

He handed the phone to Frank who listened for a moment then hung up. "Fred's coming to get you to go to lunch, and judging the time, your rental is probably out front. I'll take this opportunity to tell you your car will be ready Friday. Just bring the rental back here, and they'll pick it up. Now, for the money, just give it to Fred. He'll get it to me. No sense making another trip up here."

Fred stuck his head in the door and Frank motioned. "Here's your escort. We'll see you Friday."

Henry got on the elevator and they went down and to the Lincoln. He got his briefcase and turned the keys over to a man who immediately took the car around the building and inside. He counted out the money for Frank, and Fred took it to his office and locked it in a drawer.

Returning to Henry, they went out, got in the rented Camaro, and pulled away from the lot.

"Why didn't you tell me you worked for Frank when I called about having the work done?"

Fred smiled. "Well, Hank, I didn't know if he wanted to do it, for one thing. For another, and as I mentioned before, the operation can be outside the law at times. So I don't advertise. Then, after you told Frank your name was Davis or whatever you said, I had to convince him you were okay. It kinda pissed him off when you lied to him."

Henry grinned, "Yeah, I got that. Thanks for your help."

He pulled in the lot of the Chinese restaurant Fred suggested and went inside. When they were seated Fred asked, "So what happened to the car?"

Henry told him about his experiences in Pittsburgh.

Fred listened to his brother's report of his efforts, then said, "Hank, old buddy, you're fixin' to fuck up. You're looking for people who will kill you, just like they did your girlfriend. I'm really sorry about her. I know that's gotta be devastating on top of what happened to Mary and Linda, but none of that is your fault. I would say these guys know who you are and know you are looking for them. They'll do whatever they have to do to be left alone to pursue their brand of drug induced fun. You're also screwing with the cops who will shoot you and ask questions later if you get in their way. Then you put dynamite charges in your yard that will blow your ass away."

Henry looked surprised. "How do you know about that?"

"There's not much in my organization that I don't know about."

"Well, you must be pretty high up."

"High enough," Fred responded. "So tell me, what is the bomb shelter for? Darrell Franklin tells me it's pretty elaborate."

"If, no when, I catch them, it will be their new home for a long time. It will also be where they will learn the error of their ways."

"So why do you want to destroy the entrance?"

"Initially I felt it was too obvious, sticking up in the back yard, so I was getting rid of it for that reason. There's another entrance through the basement, and I didn't need it. Later, when I found Hampstead was setting me up, I decided to seal it off to prevent him getting in. I know he is somehow tied to these guys, and I believe he would free them at some point."

Fred sat quietly in thought for several moments then said, "Hank, murder, justified or not, is murder. There are prison terms for it, and burying someone alive is worse. I understand wanting revenge. I really do. I'd probably consider it myself in similar circumstances. At least think about the consequences if you get caught. The justice system hates vigilante justice, and when it is premeditated, the penalty is even worse. I don't want to have to visit you in some prison."

"No lectures, Fred, I know the consequences of getting caught. I just made a promise, and I won't go back on it. I'm willing to take that chance. Anyway, enough of that, tell me about Midge. I talked to her on the phone, and she was actually nice. I couldn't believe it was her."

Fred laughed. "After our get together last time, she had a slight attitude adjustment, as the song goes."

"Just like that?" Henry asked.

"Well, maybe a little persuasion on my part. I won't go into detail. Let's just say the results were gratifying. She's gone on a diet, changed some of her mannerisms, even quit drinking. That, in itself, has been amazing. She really was packing it away there for a while. Now, she goes to meetings almost every night, but that's okay with me. She's like a different person since she quit." He paused then said, "Why don't you come over and stay with us? At least, come to dinner. Then if you decide, you can stay with us while you're in Denver. It will save you a buck or two and, with the way you're spending money, you could use a freebie."

Henry grinned. "Okay, but no lectures."

"No lectures," Fred promised.

After lunch, Henry dropped Fred back at work and went shopping. He hadn't brought any clothes with him, and he sure couldn't live in the ones he had on for a week. If I keep taking these jaunts, he thought, I should keep a 'go bag' in the car. When he finished shopping, he threw his purchases in the trunk and thought about driving over to Fred's, but he was still leery of Midge's attitude change. He would give Fred time to get home first. Instead, he found a movie theater with a matinee and watched Jason Stratham wipe out about a hundred guys single handedly.

At five o'clock, he drove to Fred's. He had hoped Fred would be home, but when he got there, Fred's car was not in the driveway, and he thought about leaving.

"Oh, what the hell," he said aloud. "I guess I can give it a shot". He got out of the car and went up to the house. In hindsight, his fears were completely unfounded. Midge was a gracious host and showed genuine remorse over the deaths of Mary and Linda.

"Henry, I don't know what to say. This is just so terrible and unspeakable. I realize now that I have not been much of a sister-in-law in the past, and my actions were more than deplorable. Maybe I was just a little jealous of what you had, and my drinking brought out the bitch in me. But I really did love you and your family. I know it is much too late for Mary and Linda, but I do hope sometime in the future you can forgive me for my past actions."

"Thanks, Midge. I appreciate that more than you know."

Fred came in as Henry and Midge sat at the kitchen table drinking coffee and chatting about Midge's new program.

He clapped Henry on the shoulder as he walked past. "I'm going to grab a beer. Do you want one?"

Henry shook his head. "No, thanks, Fred. Since Midge isn't, I don't want to drink in front of her."

"No, please, Henry, just because I quit doesn't mean you can't have a beer with Fred."

"Thanks Midge, maybe later. Anyway," he said directing his conversation to Fred, "how bad is the car?"

Fred drank from his bottle then said, "We can talk about that stuff after Midge goes to her meeting. No sense boring her with shop talk."

Dinner was enjoyable, as was the rest of the week with Midge and him catching up on the years they had tried to avoid each other. Henry didn't tell her about his plans, nor did he mention Brenda. That was stuff only Fred needed to hear.

On Friday morning, he told Midge goodbye and promised he would stay with them the next time he came to Denver. He hugged her for the first time ever and told her he really enjoyed their time together. Then he got in the Camaro and followed Fred back to Frank's Auto.

At Frank's, he turned the keys to the Camaro over to one of Frank's employees in exchange for the key to the Lincoln, now painted a dark blue. They had removed the California and Iowa tags and replaced them with ones for Nebraska and Ontario, Canada. The associated registrations, insurance, and driver's licenses had been traded and were in the hidden compartment with the pistol.

When he got in and started the car, Fred leaned in the window. "Hank, I know it won't do me any good to ask you to let it go, turn it over to the police. So I won't. I know full well that once your mind is set, you'll do your best to finish what you start. I just want to say, be careful. If these guys even think you know who they are, they'll kill you. I don't want to have to come to Pennsylvania to bury you. If you need anything that I can help you with, call me."

Henry smiled. "Thanks, Fred. I know you care, and I'll be okay."

Fred shook his head. "Don't be so sure. From what you've told me, the old man knows more than I would be comfortable with. He's set it up, so if you catch them, he can release them. It seems to me, you're alive right now because he doesn't know all you know, and I get a feeling, old or not, he'll try to kill you.

"Just watch your step, Hank. The car is safe. Just stay inside unless you're 100 percent sure you're on solid ground, and when you're home, find something to protect yourself with."

"I will, Fred. Not to worry. Everything will be fine."

He put the car in gear and held out his hand. "Take care, Fred, and tell Midge I really did enjoy our visit."

Fred shook his hand and stepped back. "I will, little brother. You drive safe."

Henry pulled forward as Fred yelled after the departing car, "And think!"

# CHAPTER 38

Henry pulled into the garage on Hunters Trail at ten o'clock Monday morning. The first thing he did was call Sheila, who was almost frantic over his long absence. It took over an hour, but he finally appeased her frustrations, told her several lies about what was going on, and convinced her as to how much he had missed her. Well, the missing her part was true even though the missing Brenda part was just as strong. He hung up thinking, women. But he would have been just as worried if their roles were reversed.

Next, he went to the bedroom. He looked at the bed and immediately visualized the beautiful redhead lying there, beckoning. He shook his head as anger filled it and an ache engulfed his heart. He looked, noticing the bells were still where he had placed them and left the bedroom.

He found the license number he had jotted down for the van. Then he looked up the phone number for and called the Pennsylvania DMV, using one of his burner phones. As the phone rang, he ran a plausible story through his mind.

"Yes, ma'am," he said with a southern drawl when a female voice answered. He hoped the fake accent would be convincing. "My name is Dexter Walthorpe from down in Montgomery, Alabama. I have a slight problem, and I hope y'all can be of assistance in helping me to resolve it."

"Yes," came the frazzled reply. "What is it?"

"Well, ma'am, I was pulling into a parking space down at Heinz Field, that's the stadium you know, and my bumper hit the car next to me, and it put a pretty big ding in the door, you know? So anyway, I went on in, and then when I came out, I stood around for, oh, I don't know, almost two hours, but nobody came out for that car. So I left, you know?

"Then, this morning I went back out there, I figured I would put a note for the owner, but the car wasn't there, you know? I'm sorry, ma'am, I keep calling it a car. It was one of them vans, you know, the ones all fixed up with pictures on 'em and everything. Anyway, ma'am, I just feel awful about it."

"Just what is it you need, Mr. Walthorpe?" She sounded slightly exasperated.

Henry smiled. "Well Ma'am, I don't mean to be no trouble, you understand, but I did write down that license number for the car before I left. So I figured, if you could be so kind as to find out the name for me, I could call them poor folks and tell them how sorry I am and pay them for the damage or give them my insurance information."

"What is the license number, sir."

He gave her the number. "I really appreciate this, ma'am. I feel awful bad about not finding those folks . . ."

"Please hold on, sir." He was put on hold.

A few minutes later, she came back on the line. "Sir, I'm not supposed to do this, but with you being out of state and all, I guess it can't hurt. That license number belongs to a Gilbert S. Francis of Pittsburgh, Pennsylvania." She gave him a street address.

Henry wrote the information down. "Ma'am, I surely do appreciate this information you gave me, and I'm sure Mr. Francis will never forget it, you know? Why, if it had been my car that that happened to . . ."

"Yes, sir, I understand," she interrupted. She cut the connection.

Humph, he thought smiling, she doesn't like southerners. Well, he had a name and address. That is, if the guy still lived there or the van wasn't stolen. He put the paper in his pocket and went downstairs. Right now, he had something to do.

Unlocking the door to the shelter, he went to and unlocked one of the cabinets. He saw that no more of the drugs had disappeared during his absence. That, along with no movement from the bells, assured him no one had been in the house while he was in Denver.

He removed the guns, shackles, and tranquilizer darts from the cabinet and relocked it. Then carrying them upstairs and out to the garage, he placed the rifle and leg irons in the left compartment in the trunk. After loading darts into the two handguns and taking four more out of the box, he put the remaining ones in with the rifle and closed the compartment door and the trunk lid. Taking the guns forward, he placed them, along with the handcuffs, in the compartment under the dash.

"Now, Henry, old boy," he said aloud, "It's time to see if you can find one Gilbert S. Francis."

He had no problem finding the address. He had been very close to it when he turned up Route 28 just a short time ago. After locating the building, he decided to get some lunch. The van wasn't in sight, and the Lincoln, with its new paint job, would stand out sitting in the parking lot.

Henry wondered, as he ate, how he could make the car less shiny. His thoughts were soon answered. As he sipped at his second cup of coffee, it started snowing. He sat with his coffee in the warmth of the restaurant as the snow fell gently, silently outside. With the cold temperature, the snow immediately stuck, and he knew the salt trucks would be out coating the roads with their loads of calcium.

Most drivers, including Henry, normally cursed the mixture of salt and muck that coated their vehicles after a snowfall. However, this time, he looked forward to the residue that would mask the newness of the paint and make the Lincoln less obvious.

The clouds and snow made for a dreary day, and after driving around for a couple of hours, Henry decided the car was dirty enough and the day was dark enough to drive back to Francis's apartment.

Sitting in the car with nothing to do would have been extremely boring, so he had brought an old Steven King novel about a kid that started fires with her mind to read while he sat. He read until it was too dark to see then dozed as he waited.

Shortly after six o'clock, the van pulled into the lot, and one guy got out. Henry sat up in his seat and watched the lone figure cross the lot and go into the apartment building. He wanted to grab the pistol and go after him. Instead, he sat in the car and contemplated his plan of attack.

For one thing, he wasn't sure if this was the right man. The hair was long and brown, as Cameron had indicated, but a lot of people had long brown hair. Also, this could just be a guy who had borrowed the van. The best idea, at least for the present, was to follow the guy, find out his haunts, and ask some questions.

At a quarter to eight, the man came out, got in the van, and drove toward downtown. Henry followed, this time at a safe distance. The van made four stops during the evening and at two a.m. returned to the apartment. Henry drove back to Hunters Trail.

# CHAPTER 39

Cursing the little amount of sleep he got, he was up at six thirty and drank two cups of coffee in the time it took him to shower and get dressed. He hadn't shaved in well over a week, and the bristle on his face had begun to resemble a beard. Looking at it in the mirror for a couple of seconds, he decided to keep it, for now, and returned to the kitchen.

Pouring a third cup of coffee in a carry out cup, he took it with him as he climbed into the Lincoln. Shortly thereafter, he was heading down Route 28, and his timing could not have been better. The van pulled onto the highway a quarter mile ahead of him. Maintaining his distance, he followed it to a used car lot on the south side of the city and watched as the guy parked it and went inside the three bay garage that read 'Painting, Body Work, and Insurance Repairs.'

He sat a block away, watching the building until he was reasonably sure the guy worked there and was not just stopping by. Then he put his car in gear and drove to the first stop he had made the night before.

The sign in the window of the dilapidated building said it was 'Harry's Pub and Pool,' and a smaller one in the window said it was closed and would open at two p.m.

He then drove to the second place, a brick building with no windows named 'The Shamrock Club' with a big green neon clover leaf as a background, and parked his car. This one was open, and he went inside.

The inside was dingy and smelled of stale beer and urine. A worn-out looking barmaid wiped the bar with a worn-out looking bar rag. The only customer was a grungy looking guy who appeared he was still sitting there from the night before.

Henry sat down on the cleanest looking bar stool and ordered a draft. When the girl (Henry couldn't tell if she was twenty-five or forty) brought the glass and set it down, sloshing beer on the counter, Henry laid a hundred dollar bill on the counter.

She looked at it and whined, "I can't cash that, buddy. I just opened. You got anything smaller?"

"I'll tell you what," he said, leaving the bill on the counter, "you answer a couple of questions for me, and it's yours."

The girl eyed the C note with new interest and Henry with suspicion. "Like what?"

Henry smiled. "I'm trying to locate someone, and I think, maybe, you can help."

Her eyes narrowed. "Are you a cop or something?"

He laughed. "No, I'm not a cop. This guy just has something I want to buy, and I don't know where to find him." He didn't know if his reason would wash or not, but it was something to say.

The girl eyed the money again. "So, what is it you want to know?"

Henry smiled what he hoped was a disarming smile. "A guy comes in here, named Gilbert Francis. Do you know him?"

The girl shook her head. "I don't know that name."

Henry tried again. "He drives an emerald green van with pictures of a nude woman on the sides."

He saw a spark of recognition in the woman's eyes. "Oh, you mean Snowman. What do you want to know?"

"Where do I find him?"

She was again suspicious. "Are you sure you ain't a cop?"

Henry pulled out a driver's license and slid it across the bar. "As the license says, I'm Bill Donaldson from Maryland. I'm not a cop. I just want to buy something from him."

The woman, more at ease, slid the license back. "He was in last night, but he ain't sellin' right now. Said he'd have some more stuff comin' in on about Saturday or Sunday."

Henry nodded, trying to keep the elated expression he was sure showed on his face from showing. "Yeah? That's too bad. Well, tell me something else. What happened to the black van he used to have?"

She picked up the bill and put it in her pocket. "That's all you paid for, mister. Besides, I still don't know you ain't a cop."

Henry pulled another hundred from his pocket and laid it on the counter. "I told you, I'm not a cop. What about the van?"

She sighed and the hundred disappeared to join the first. "That's it, the green one. He said he thought the cops were startin' to get suspicious about something, and he had it redone."

Henry suppressed his jubilation. "Where does he get his stuff?"

The girl picked up her bar rag. "I don't know, and you're getting too nosey." She started to turn away.

Henry laid another hundred on the counter. "Just that question, and I'm done. Where does he get his drugs?"

She turned back, procrastinating over the money. The money won. "I don't know, up north somewhere. He talks about him and his buddy coming down through the mountains somewhere. It must not be too far away, 'cause it doesn't take very long to get them. Now, that's all. I don't know who you are, and if he found out I talked to you, he'd kill me. He told someone he had killed some people before and more than once. I don't want to be next."

"No, I don't want you to be next either. The money is yours, and thanks for the information."

Henry left the beer untouched and stood up. The guy down the bar still sat there, staring longingly at his empty glass. Henry buttoned his coat and went out, sure now that 'Snowman' was the one he was looking for.

His next stop was a place called 'The Eagle's Nest,' situated seven miles south of the city. The atmosphere was no better that the Shamrock, but there were several people in the bar. Henry felt instant discomfort when he went in as several turned to look at him. It was definitely a 'redneck' bar for the good-ole-boys. There were no women, and the bartender was a beefy, red-faced, three-hundred-pounder with arms as big as Henry's thighs.

Henry slipped onto a stool and ordered a draft. Sipping it as he looked around the bar, his gaze settled on a guy sitting by himself. Taking his glass, he walked around the bar and seated himself next to the scrawny, blond-haired man. "Mind if I ask you a question, fellow?"

The man looked at him, and his eyes reminded Henry of the guy who had had his henchmen kill that actress, Sharon Tate. What was his name, Manson? But it couldn't be him. He died in prison. "Depends on what the fuck you ask, man."

Henry smiled, "Fair enough. Do you know Snowman?"

The eyes shifted to someone in the back, and Henry suddenly felt he shouldn't be here and his luck had just run out. "Hey, Willie, this jerk-off wants to know if I know the Snowman."

Henry winced inwardly and stared at the man's protruding Adam's apple. "Look friend, I don't want to cause any trouble. I just wanted to . . ."

"What do you want to know about the Snowman for, asshole?"

The voice came from behind and to Henry's left. He turned to face a short, stocky man with biceps that were twice the size of his own. He sure didn't develop them from lifting the pool cue he held in his hand. This was apparently Willie.

"Hey look, I don't want no trouble. I just wanted to catch up with him. I was told he hung out here sometimes."

"Who are you, asshole?"

"My name's Donaldson, Bill Donaldson. I'm not a cop or anything." He pulled the driver's license from his pocket to show Willie. "I'm just looking to buy some stuff from him."

The man with the wild eyes pulled the license from his hand as Willie jammed the butt of the cue stick into his stomach, driving the breath from his lungs in a tremendous whoosh.

"We don't like outsiders here, fuckhead," Willie with the stick said.

The stick slammed down across his back as he doubled over from the previous blow to his stomach, and a wave of nausea gripped him.

"We also don't like shitheads we don't know coming in here asking questions."

Henry wanted to tell them to forget it, he'd just leave. Just let him go. But, he couldn't draw breath in his lungs, and he was getting dizzy. The beer he had just drank came back up with a vengeance, spraying the man with the stick.

Through the fog in his brain, he heard laughing and Willie cursing. "The son-uva-bitch barfed on my fuckin' boots."

Henry felt the cue sick connect with his cheekbone and again with his eyebrow, but there was no pain, just a slow fade as his world went from red to gray to black. As his consciousness faded, he thought: No, Sheila, there's no way I'm gonna be in danger. I have my car.

# CHAPTER 40

Henry awoke with a blinding headache and pains where he didn't know he had places. He lay with his eyes closed trying to remember how much he had drank the night before. Then he remembered the beating. He shifted, in a bed? The pain in his stomach, ribs, and back told him they had not stopped wailing on him after he passed out. Opening his eyes, he looked at his surroundings, a hospital room, and swinging his feet around painfully, sat on the edge of the bed.

A nurse opened the door and entered the room. "Mr. Donaldson," they must have his driver's license he showed at the bar, "I must ask you to lie back down. The doctor will be here in a few minutes."

Henry shook his head, and it felt as though his jaw was detached and moving independently of the rest of his face. He moaned and stopped the movement. "What time is it? I've got to get up."

"No, you can't. Let me get Dr. Abernathy." She left the room.

Henry eased himself slowly off the bed and, feeling like he was going to pass out, held on to the wheeled tray by the bed. When the dizziness and nausea passed, he moved to the cabinet by the bed and dragged his clothes from inside. Then he moved back to sit on the bed, feeling every hit he had taken. Gingerly touching his face, he found a bandage over his left eye and one on his cheek. The pain he felt when he took a breath told him he had some damaged ribs. He also had bruises on his arms and legs and a bump on the back of his head the size of an egg that hurt like hell when he touched it. So don't touch it, dummy, he thought.

He had managed to slip into his slacks, an extremely difficult task, and he was pulling his shirt on when an elderly, gray-haired man, apparently the doctor, came into the room followed by a uniformed police officer. Henry continued to dress, grimacing as pain shot through his left shoulder.

"Mr. Donaldson, I'm Dr. Abernathy. I must tell you that it is entirely inadvisable and against my better judgement for you to leave the hospital at this time. You were brought in yesterday with a concussion, contusions, and abrasions, as well as trauma to your head and torso. You were brought in unconscious, and I advise that you stay in the hospital, at least overnight, so we may observe your progress before you leave."

Henry tried a smile that came out as a groan as he buttoned his shirt. "Doc, from what I can tell, I have some scrapes that will heal. What I'd like to know is what is under these bandages?"

The doctor sighed, seeing Henry was not going to stop dressing. "You have two broken and one cracked rib on the right side. You have bruised ribs on the left side. You have three stitches in you left eyebrow. Those won't show once it's healed. The cut on your cheek is long but not deep. It too should be fine once it heals."

Henry nodded, this time slowly so he didn't jiggle anything. "Hell, it doesn't seem bad to me. I don't have double vision, and I expect neither pupil is dilated, or I wouldn't be able to see well. So I expect my staying here is a waste of my time and your bed space."

"The decision is yours, Mr. Donaldson. I cannot keep you here if you don't want to stay. I will ready your release papers and prescribe medication for pain. Meantime, I think this officer wants to talk with you."

Henry, with a lot of discomfort, pulled his socks on as the policeman laid a note pad on the tray and produced a pencil.

"Would you like to tell me what happened, Mr. Donaldson?"

Henry sat back on the bed for a moment to rest. The name he was being called by was on the license he had shown at The Eagle's Nest, and he was sure it could not be tied back to him. "To tell the truth, you probably know more than I do. I think I got mugged."

The officer nodded. "Well, my report says a motorist found you along the edge of I-79 yesterday afternoon, and an ambulance brought you into the hospital. You didn't have any money, and we haven't found a car. Where were you, or better, what do you remember?"

Apparently, they hadn't found him at The Eagles Nest. Well, he could live with that. Also, the men at The Eagles Nest apparently thought he would either die in the cold out on the interstate or from the beating, or both. He slid his feet into his loafers and said, "Hell, all I remember is I was walking down the street, I don't remember which one, and all of a sudden, bam, everything went blank."

He changed the subject. "You say they got my money?" He asked, holding up his wallet. "I still seem to have my wallet."

"Yeah," the officer replied. "When you were found, your license and wallet were alongside, but your money was missing."

"Damn," Henry said. "I had almost eight hundred dollars."

He appeased the officer with as much of his fictitious story as he could. By the time the officer was finished, Henry had completed dressing and signed the release form for the hospital. He picked up his coat and walked out of the hospital followed by the cop.

"Listen," he said, "I obviously don't have any money. Could you drop me off somewhere and loan me a few dollars? I'll get it back to you as soon as I get home."

"Yeah, I can do that Mr. Donaldson. Come on."

He dropped Henry downtown and handed him ten dollars. "You sure you're going to be all right, Mr. Donaldson?"

Henry eased out of the patrol car. "Yeah, sure, no problem, and I appreciate the lift and the loan. I'll get it back to you. By the way, what's your name and precinct number?"

The officer gave him the information. Henry, thanking him, closed the door, and the car pulled away. He flagged down the next cab and told the driver to take him to The Eagle's Nest.

The Lincoln sat where Henry had parked it. Since the car had California tags, he doubted the drunks inside associated it with him. He paid the cab driver nine-fifty and got out. No one was outside the bar when he limped over and, unlocking the door, climbed into the safety of the Lincoln, closing the door behind him.

He felt better, now that he was in the car. He had been apprehensive when the cab had pulled into the lot and even more so getting out to walk to his. Now inside, he started the engine and leaned back into the seat to think while it warmed up.

Apparently, bar hopping was not the best way for him to get information, especially from bars Francis hung out in. He had lost eight hundred dollars, a good bit of skin, and acquired numerous black and blue marks to show how bad his efforts had been. Speaking of money, he reached into the glove compartment, extracted a thousand dollars, and put it in his pocket. There was one thing for sure, he would not go back into The Eagles Nest to ask more questions or to retrieve his money.

He put the car in gear and turning, pulled to the edge of the lot. As he sat waiting for a car to pass so he could pull out, he saw Willie, the one with the cue stick, get out of a brand new pick-up truck and saunter toward the bar.

An idea struck Henry. Touching a button on the dash, he watched the console open and the keyboard lift into position. He punched information into the unit and hit the flash button.

Willie was almost to the door.

Extending the rear bumper, Henry shifted into reverse and the tires squalled as the Lincoln surged backward toward the pick-up. Willie was reaching for the door when he heard the tires screaming on the asphalt. He turned, staring at the car and the flashing sign in the back window, 'For Bill Donaldson.' Staring at the flashing sign, his mouth fell open in horrified amazement as the bumper of the car crashed into his new pick-up, crushing the door, bed, and fender on the passenger side. With the Lincoln continuing its assault, Willie watched the side windows and windshield explode and the camper shell on the back jump from the bed to splinter on the asphalt.

Henry continued ramming the truck, pushing it sideways across the lot. Two of the tires went flat and rolled off the rims as the truck slid off the pavement and into a large oak tree, caving in the driver's side of the vehicle.

Henry pulled the shift lever into low and extended the front bumper. Again pushing the accelerator to the floor, he swung the car toward the front door of the bar. Sudden realization crossed Willie's face as the Lincoln barreled toward him. Clawing the door open, he jumped inside, but the door didn't have time to close before the heavy bumper splintered it, the door frame, and put a large gaping hole in the brickwork. Chunks of wood and brick flew into the bar hitting patrons and smashing tables, bottles, and glasses as the car continued halfway into the building.

The smile on Henry's face was almost festive as he threw the shift lever into reverse, and the car squealed out of the bar, slewing around in the lot. He retracted the bumpers, and leaving long acceleration marks on the asphalt, he turned left on the highway. He held the speedometer at the speed limit until he was well away from The Eagles Nest. He was sure no one was going to be in any mood to follow him for a long time.

He was headed for Hunters Trail. His ribs were on fire, and every muscle in his body seemed to be screaming in agony. He hadn't even noticed while the adrenalin was coursing through his body a short time ago.

He stopped at a pharmacy to fill the pain 'scrips the doctor had given him and then headed for home to soak in the relaxing, turbulent whirlpool bath. The bath, he thought wistfully, that he never gotten to share with Brenda.

Thinking about his retaliation for the beating he had received, and smiling, he reached for the phone by the tub (thank you, Brenda) and dialed Sheila's number. She was elated that he had called. Yes, things were going well with him. No, he was no closer in his quest, as of yet. He would definitely be home as soon as possible. He missed her and couldn't wait to make love to her.

Next, he called Frank's. He told him he would need a security system installed and that he would be at home. No, he didn't have the equipment and didn't know what to get. Yes, he would have the necessary funds to install the home security system.

Hanging up, he eased out of the tub and gingerly dried off and dressed. Standing in front of the bathroom mirror, he gently removed the bandages from his forehead and cheek. The doctor was right. The cut was in his eyebrow and would not show once healed. The cut on his cheek looked bad now, but it was not deep. When the swelling went down and the bruising disappeared, it would not be too noticeable. He tossed the bandages in the trash and left the bedroom. He would heal a lot faster than Willie's truck or The Eagles Nest.

# CHAPTER 41

The next morning, Henry put coffee on to brew and ran, more hobbled, to the street to retrieve the morning paper from the mailbox. The trek was excruciating but moving was probably better therapy than sitting.

Back at the house, he poured a cup of coffee and opened the paper. The front page was the normal news, terrorists in Afghanistan had kidnapped another American and a German. The President would not condone nor tolerate their action. ISIS had killed three more Britains, and communist factions in the Philippines had gunned down four civilian aid workers, including a six-year-old child. On page two and three were articles which drew Henry's interest.

### POLICE HAVE NO SUSPECTS IN SLAYING

Pittsburg police spokesman Lt. Jarrod Banks said yesterday that police had yet to identify a suspect or suspects in the fatal stabbing of interior designer Brenda Cartier. Banks said he could not comment on the open investigation and stated they had some leads but to divulge them would hinder the prosecution of suspects once they were named. Beyond saying Cartier had been raped and then stabbed to death, police would give no further details.

Article two:

### POLICE SEEK MARYLAND SUSPECT IN DISTRUCTION OF POLICE CRUISERS

City police today are continuing their search for the man believed responsible for destroying three city police cruisers and badly damaging another two weeks ago. A spokesman for the Pittsburg police, Mr. Harvey Shackleford, told reporters that the man police sought was a William Donaldson of Fallston, Maryland. Donaldson had been identified by the license plate on his car. He said they had requested information from the Maryland State Police but had not yet received it. Shackleford said Donaldson spread nails and oil on the Route 28 roadway causing the collision of three police cars that were pursuing him for intentionally colliding with a fourth cruiser shortly before. Shackleford was unable to explain how Donaldson was able to spread the nails and oil on the road during the high-speed chase.

Article three:

### MAN HOSPITALIZED AFTER MUGGING

William Donaldson of Fallston, Maryland was the victim of an alleged mugging on Tuesday. Donaldson was taken by ambulance to an area hospital after being found unconscious on Interstate 79. Patrolman Arthur Newhurst, the officer who questioned Donaldson on Wednesday, was unaware of the victim's connection with the destruction of four police cars over two weeks ago. As a result, Donaldson walked away from the hospital before it was determined he was wanted in the earlier incident.

Police believe Donaldson is also responsible for the damage sustained by a Bethel Park bar known as The Eagle's Nest. That bar and a pick-up truck in the parking lot were extensively damaged.

Article four:

## PUB BECOMES DRIVE-THROUGH
## AFTER BEING RAMMED

Police today were continuing an investigation of an incident in which a car rammed into a truck, virtually destroying it, before running through the front of a brick building south of Bethel Park, Pennsylvania on Wednesday. Police said that after the intentional damage, the car went south on Route 19.

According to an eyewitness to the incident, Mr. Willie Adams of South Pittsburgh, the car was idling at the edge of the parking lot for The Eagles Nest when Adams pulled into the lot and parked. Adams said he had just reached for the door of the pub when the spinning tires of the car caused him to turn just in time to see the car barrel across the lot and into his new truck. He said the car pushed his truck into a large oak tree at the perimeter of the lot, buckling the frame. Adams said he had just purchased the truck and had not had time to get insurance for it.

Adams is presently in the hospital recovering from two broken legs he received when the car crashed into the bar. He said that after the car destroyed his truck, it turned and came toward him. He said he dove into the club but not in time to "get out of the way of the (expletive deleted) madman who drove through the front wall of the bar" and hit him, breaking his legs.

Adams said the incident happened so fast, he didn't have time to notice the type or color of the car, but it was a late model coupe with a sign in the back window that was flashing 'For Bill Donaldson.'

Good, Henry thought. He saw my sign. He smiled as he continued reading.

Adams said he had no idea why the man would destroy his truck and didn't know anyone who would have reason to want to harm him.

Jack Mason, the owner of The Eagles Nest, who was in the bar at the time of the incident, said all he saw was Adams diving in the front door followed by the front end of the car coming in behind him. Mason was also not able to identify the type of car involved in the incident. He said all he saw was the bumper coming through the wall and bricks and furniture flying everywhere. He added that when the first brick flew by his head, he hit the floor and stayed there until it was over and the car was back out of the building. Mason said the damage to the building, furniture, and booze would exceed $200,000.

Henry laughed. The whole place, including Willie's truck, wasn't worth that much. And poor Willie had no idea who would want to harm him. He laughed again as he finished reading the article.

Mason said his insurance would only cover part of the damage and certainly not enough to reopen The Eagles Nest. He said he had been operating on a shoestring budget anyway, and with the damage done by that crazy son-of-a-b----, he'd have to close down. "Well, I guess I have one consolation," Mason said. "The dumb bastard destroyed the front of his car when he came through that wall. I don't see how he could have got more than a mile or two down the road, if he got that far."

Police are currently searching for the late model car with a damaged front end. The Eagles Nest and the bar's owner have been cited on numerous occasions for fights and for serving alcohol to minors.

According to the state liquor board, they
were to be closed permanently at the end
of the month.

Henry smiled and thought, I guess I helped them close early. He had looked at the Lincoln when he got home. A cursory inspection revealed only some minor scuffing on the front bumper. His coffee had gotten cold, and he got up to refill his cup when the doorbell rang. He set the cup down and went through the living room. It was time for the man from Frank's to be here. He reached the handle and opened the door.

"Fred!"

Fred stood on the porch, a suitcase beside him. "Hi, Hank, are you going to invite me in or leave me out here to freeze my ass off on the porch?"

Henry laughed, "No, no, come in." He grabbed his brother's hand and the suitcase pulling them inside.

Closing the door, he put the suitcase down by the couch and grabbed Fred's arm. "Come on in the kitchen and get some coffee. What the hell are you doing out this way? Where's Midge? Are you . . . ?"

"Hey, slow down, Hank. I'll be here a day or two to answer your questions. You don't have to get them all in at once. First, let me get a cup of coffee, and then tell me who rearranged your face. And why. By the way, the beard looks pretty good. I could never grow one that didn't look scraggly as crap."

Henry murmured something akin to a thank you as he got another cup from the cupboard, poured coffee into it and his, and sat down at the table.

"So you want to know about my bumps and bruises." He handed Fred the newspaper so he could read the articles Henry had just finished before the doorbell rang.

When he had finished, Henry said, "So, that is where things stand now. I expect I'd better move my butt before Snowman puts two and two together. If, and I think he is the one I'm looking for, he will soon be after yours truly."

Fred shook his head. "Hank, you dumb shit; you're going to get yourself killed. If this man, Snowman, is the one, and his buddies play that rough, you don't stand the chance of a snowball in hell of pulling this off. You ought to just tell the police what you know, and let them handle it."

Henry nodded. "I know. Good reasoning tells me I'm playing with a mighty hot fire, but I think I can do it. I'm going to try anyway. I've got to. So, anyway Fred, what brings you to Pittsburgh in two feet of snow?"

"Well, it's a foot less than what we have in Denver," Fred chuckled. "As a matter of fact, I'm here to install some video equipment, in case your head injury has made you forget your phone call."

Henry thumped his forehead with the heel of his hand and then winced at the pain. "Oh, that's right. I guess I just didn't expect Frank to send you. So, how long will you be here?"

"Oh, I figure the installation will take a couple of days, depending on how you want it set up. So I'll probably stay 'til Sunday and get in some visiting time while I'm here. Midge wanted to come, but I told her you wouldn't be around, and she would be bored."

"Probably a good idea," Henry responded. "I wouldn't want her here right now anyway. It would mean too many questions to answer and most likely with lies. I hope, when this is all over, you can both come for a visit."

"Just so long as it's not a funeral, Hank, old buddy."

"Not yet, Fred. Not yet."

Henry explained his facial damage and bruises to Fred while they had breakfast that Henry fixed.

Afterward, Fred went into Pittsburgh for the equipment he needed to set up the surveillance system. Henry, who didn't feel it would be wise to be seen on the streets in town right now, stayed at the house.

While Fred was gone, he donned some rubber gloves and put a hundred dollars in an envelope, along with a note, thanking Officer

Newhurst for the ten dollar loan and the ride into town. He addressed it to the officer at his precinct. He would have Fred mail it when he got back to Denver. That should throw them off for a bit. He would tell Fred to handle it so as not to leave his prints on it either. The envelope and stamp were self-sticking, so he didn't have to lick them and leave his DNA on it. One, he thought, could never be too careful, and sometimes, paranoia was a good thing.

He then went downstairs and opened the door to the shelter. That done, and his ribs feeling like someone had taken a sledge hammer to them, he laid down on the couch to wait for Fred's return.

He was almost asleep when the doorbell rang. He jumped, then winced with pain, at the sound. He got up and helped Fred move the boxes into the house and down to the basement. Before going into the workshop, he reminded Fred of the listening devices and pointed to where they were located. Fred grabbed the TV remote, and finding a GALA music channel, turned the volume up. Grinning, he whispered, "Always did like loud music. Now, where do you want this?"

Henry rubbed his sore ribs and tried not to inhale too deeply. "Well, I'd like the cameras where I can watch the entire room. But I want them hidden if possible." He pulled back the door, and Fred followed him into the shelter.

Fred looked around and said, below the volume of the music, "Nice layout. I especially like the chains. Gives the place that nice homey touch."

Henry laughed. "You can put them wherever you think best. Darrell hid his wiring behind the lead shielding. I guess you could do the same."

"Yeah, I can do that. What's the room in the corner?"

"That's the toilet."

"Okay, I can put one in there and a couple in here. That should cover everything. Where do you want the monitor?"

"I think it would be best in the workshop. I'll be able to conceal it in there."

"All right. Well, you get out of here and let me get to work. The sooner I get done, the more time we have to visit."

Henry nodded. "Good, and while you're working on this, I think I'll go down in the city and do a little scouting."

Fred followed Henry back upstairs. "Aren't you a little concerned about the police?"

"Not really. The car's a different color, I'll use out of state plates, and the front is not bashed in. I don't think they'll give it a second glance."

He put on his coat with some difficulty and turned to Fred. "Make yourself at home. If you get hungry, there's plenty of food, although the milk may be a bit rancid by this time. I'll pick up some more while I'm out. And, don't forget the bugs."

Fred smiled. "No problem. I have some earplugs and great volume on the radio. So you go play, and I'll get stuff taken care of here."

Henry got in the Lincoln and checked the two handguns to assure they were loaded. As an afterthought, he got the rifle from the trunk and put it under the passenger side seat.

It was still early in the day when he left Hunters Trail, but he didn't know what time Gilbert Francis got off work, and Henry didn't want to miss him. He still had the Steven King novel in the car. So when he found a place to park where he could observe the garage, he read while he waited.

Promptly at five o'clock Francis came out of the garage and got in the van. It was not snowing. As a matter of fact, the weather had warmed, and some of the snow from before had melted making a slushy mess on the streets. But it was overcast, and more snow was called for by Sunday afternoon.

Henry sat across the street until Francis pulled into the traffic, then he pulled to a discrete distance behind him. When the van pulled into the lot of the Shamrock, he drove on past and parked in a grocery store a half block away, where he could watch the building.

He certainly didn't want to confront the man in a populated area and definitely not a place where his friends congregated. He had already determined what he wanted to do, and generally, where he wanted to do it. Now, it was just a matter of time until everything came together.

Thirty minutes after he went in the bar, Francis came out, and Henry sat up in his seat. A moment later, another man joined him. It was the scrawny guy with the weird eyes Henry had first spoke to at The Eagles Nest. They both got in the van and pulled out of the lot. Henry followed them as they made two stops and, deciding they were not going to part, turned his car toward home. Besides, it was almost ten o'clock, and he could spend a little time with his brother before it was time to retire. He stopped by a convenience store and got some milk and bread on the way.

Fred had the cameras installed and was running the wiring in the workshop when Henry came in. He motioned Fred to join him in the rec room and got them a couple of beers. When Fred joined him and closed the door, he said, "Hey, are you about ready to call it a day?"

Fred smiled, reaching for the beer Henry held out. "Yeah, I guess the rest will hold until tomorrow. I'll tuck the wiring in behind the molding and figured I'd put the monitor in the corner cabinet in the workshop. That way, you can lock it up if you want."

"That sounds great. Let's go upstairs. Have you eaten anything?"

"Yeah, I thawed a ribeye and made it into a couple of sandwiches. I'm good."

Once seated in the kitchen, Fred asked, "So what are you going to do once you catch one or both of those guys?"

Henry shook his head. "To tell you the truth, I'm not sure yet. All I do know for sure is that once I catch the first one, I'm not going to have much time to get the second. I don't know how many people are involved. I know at least three. One, Hampstead, doesn't bother me. The other two, that could be a problem. When I've got one, I'm going to have very little time before the second finds out."

"Why the time constraints?" Fred asked.

"Because once I have one, I've got to destroy the outside entrance

273

to the shelter. When Hampstead, or whoever, notices it's gone, I'd better have the second one in my control, or it could be my ass."

Fred agreed. "And it may be more than your ass. When do you expect to catch them?"

Henry shrugged. "As soon as I can. I'd have had one this evening if he hadn't picked up a buddy. I've got to get him alone. I'm just wondering if the guy with him this evening is the other piece of crap I'm looking for."

"Just be careful Hank. Anything I can do to help?"

Henry shook his head. "Not that I know of. This is really something I don't think you should get involved in."

"Well, if you need help, I'm only a phone call away, and you know I'll help."

Henry nodded. "I know. Thanks, Fred. But it's something I need to do myself." He smiled. "Besides, who would I have to visit me if we both ended up in prison?"

# CHAPTER 42

The next afternoon, while Fred continued his work in the basement, Henry dressed for the cold evening air. Getting several items from the workshop and the cabinet in the shelter, he told Fred he would be back later. Then putting the items in the back seat of the Lincoln, he headed toward the body shop and the snowman.

As the evening before, Gilbert Francis walked out of the shop at precisely five o'clock and got in his van. This time, however, he drove through the city and stopped at his apartment. Fifteen minutes later, he was back in the van with a large package he had picked up and was heading north on Route 28.

Henry followed the van as it passed Hunters Trail and headed on toward Clarksville. At first, curious as to where the man was going, realization finally struck him. The barmaid at the Shamrock had said he would have some more drugs Saturday or Sunday. Gilbert Snowman Francis was on his way—where, New York—to pick up his drugs. The package he had stopped for was probably the money to pay for his new stash. Henry thought about the road ahead and said aloud, "Well, Mr. Francis, if I have anything to do with it, this is one pickup you will not be making."

He sat up straighter in the seat and gripped the wheel with both hands in anticipation of his next move. The place for his move was about six miles ahead.

Pressing on the accelerator, he eased closer to the van's taillights. It was well past dark, and snowflakes appeared and disappeared in the headlight beams. For what he had planned, Henry didn't think he would need the rifle, but with one hand, he opened the bolt, placed a dart in the chamber, and shoved the bolt home behind it. He had three miles to go.

He pulled the two handguns from their hiding place and slipped one into each coat pocket. He stuck a flashlight between his legs, so it wouldn't fall from the seat and assured his seatbelt was fastened securely. He had one mile to go.

Watching the road carefully, Henry saw what he had been looking for, a road sign that read Clarksville 10 Miles. He depressed the accelerator and pulled into the other lane. Adrenalin started pumping into his bloodstream. A car coming in the other direction right now would almost certainly mean severe injury or death to anyone involved.

He eased the Lincoln up beside the van and matched speed with it. He could not see the driver through the dark windows. He didn't need to see. His next marker was coming up on the right, a yellow caution sign showing a curve ahead that read Maximum Safe Speed 25 MPH.

Henry eased the nose of the Lincoln slightly ahead of the van. The curve was not what he was waiting for, the sign was. Gripping the wheel even tighter and sucking air into his lungs, he pulled the wheel sharply to the right. A thought flashed in his mind. He wondered what Francis was thinking right now.

The Lincoln's fender slammed into the front of the van, and Henry cut further to the right. He could feel the van trying to cut back into the lane, trying to stay in the road, but the van was no match to the sheer weight of the car. He pushed back, forcing it, further, further . . .

The van went off the road. Henry watched the caution sign buckle and disappear beneath it, and the van was suddenly gone. Henry fought for control of his car, which was precariously close to going off the road too. Finally, the tires gained traction and swerved back onto the pavement. The curve was just ahead, and he pumped the brakes, slowing as quickly as possible without going into a skid.

When he managed to get control of the heavy vehicle, he shifted into reverse and backed past where the van had gone off the road. He pulled off onto the shoulder and put the shift lever in park as he grabbed the flashlight and got out. The cold air hit him when he stood up. He realized he had been sweating and knew it was from the adrenalin and his nerves. His hand, holding the flashlight, was trembling. Putting his other hand in his pocket, he gripped the pistol. He knew he would have to calm down, or he'd never be able to get a good aim when he shot the dart gun. That is, he thought, if he needed to shoot it. The guy might be dead.

Henry walked to the edge of the shoulder and shone his light down the embankment. Forty feet down, the van lay on its top, crushed against a tree. Two of its wheels were still spinning. The flashlight beam played across the broken windshield and door, but he was unable to determine what had happened inside the vehicle.

He really had no great burning desire to go down the snow-covered hill with the man still down there and Henry not knowing his condition. Almost three minutes passed as he played the light back and forth across the van, trying to determine what to do. Finally, deciding he would have to find out, he wrapped his fingers around the pistol grip and stepped up on the edge of the hill. As he did so, he heard a thud in the back of the van. He stopped and listened. A moment later, there was another loud noise, and one of the rear doors abruptly swung open.

Henry, the flashlight in one trembling hand and the gun in the other, waited. A moment later, Francis, the package he had brought from the apartment under his arm, jumped from the van. Slipping in the snow, he fell and grabbed the open door to keep from sliding farther down the hill.

Henry fought the desire to raise the pistol and fire the dart at him, right then, for two reasons. One, at this range, he would probably miss and the guy would run or, if he had a gun, shoot back. Two, if he did get lucky and hit him, he would have to drag the dead weight up the hill. Neither option appealed to him.

Instead, and to throw Francis off guard, he yelled down the embankment. "Hey, fellow, are you okay? I saw that guy run you off the road."

Francis climbed unsteadily up the hill. "I'm okay, but when I find that fucking lunatic, I gonna rip his motherfucking heart out."

Henry smiled, but his smile carried a touch of fear. Francis was halfway up the hill. Shining the light in his face, Henry asked, "Is there anything I can do to help?"

Francis was panting from exertion as he fought through the snow and brush, getting closer to the top. "Yeah, you can get that damned light out of my eyes."

Henry aimed the pistol at Francis's torso. He held the light so he wouldn't see the gun behind it. "Just want you to be able to see to get up the hill, man."

Francis had just reached the crest of the hill.

Henry leveled the pistol. "But I know what you mean, Mr. Francis."

Francis stopped. "Hey, who the hell are you? How do you know my name?"

Henry slowly squeezed the trigger. "You know me, 'Snowman.' My name is Jenkins, Henry Jenkins, of Clarksville." The look on his face told Henry he had the right guy.

The gun bucked in his hand, and the dart lodged in Francis's right chest just above the nipple.

Francis slid backward, clutching at the snow. "You son-of-a-bitch, I should have killed you! I told them I should have killed you."

He started scrambling back up the hill, at the same time struggling to get his hand in his coat. The end of the protruding dart bobbed up and down with his exertions, ignored by the crazed animal that was Francis.

Henry was suddenly very frightened. Francis was apparently reaching for a gun in his coat. Henry had no idea how long it would take for the tranquilizer to take affect or even if it would. He backed away from the shoulder and around the side of his car.

Francis had reached the top of the hill and stood up, pulling a very big gun out of his waist band.

Henry got in the Lincoln and shut the door. Apparently, he was going to have to run the Snowman down. He could always put him back in the van and burn it. That would certainly get rid of him, even if it was not the plan.

Francis stood, his legs spread, facing the car. Slowly, he started to bring the gun up in front of the Lincoln's headlights.

Henry put the shift lever in drive.

The gun seemed to move in slow motion. Rising slowly. Henry watched in fascination as it moved. He held one foot on the brake and the other touching the accelerator, waiting . . .

The bore of the pistol was level with the windshield, and Henry could see the painfully slow movement as Francis began to apply pressure to the trigger. Then the gun started to go down. No, not down. Francis was getting shorter. As Henry watched, his legs began to sag, bending slowly like a character in an animated cartoon. His knees touched the road, the gun still held stiffly in his hands in front of him. Then, just as slowly, he started to lean forward, the gun lowering to the ground. Suddenly, the slow motion action ended. Now totally off balance, Francis pitched forward, smashing his face into the gravel on the shoulder of the road.

Henry suddenly felt weak, so weak that the dart gun was too heavy to hold, and it and his hands fell into his lap. It was too much effort to even raise his hands to the steering wheel. He realized that even in the safety of the armored car, he had been very scared. The adrenalin that had pumped him up was now gone, and its effects were obvious. Even now, with Francis lying there totally out, he was apprehensive about getting out of the car. What if the man was faking? What if he got out of the car, and the man jumped up with that enormous gun?

He sat, staring at the figure lying in front of the car, and decided that wasn't going to happen. When Francis pitched forward, he had apparently broken his nose. Blood was seeping from it into the dirty snow.

Henry hit the trunk release and got out of the car. The strength was returning to his body, and he had to get the man out of the road before a car came by and saw him there. Using his foot, he pushed Francis over on his side and picked up the gun, a .357 magnum revolver. He jammed it into his waist band and grabbing Francis under the arms dragged him around to the trunk of the car. Removing the gas can and plastic explosive he had brought from home, he wrestled the limp body into the trunk.

Next, he got the handcuffs. He cuffed the man's hands behind his back and locked the leg irons to his ankles. Even though he didn't need them in the trunk, Henry didn't know how long the effects of the tranquilizer lasted, and he didn't want any surprises if Francis was awake when he opened the trunk later.

Closing the lid, he picked up the items he had put on the ground. He started to go down the hill to the van when he saw the package Francis had brought from his apartment laying on the ground where he fell. Setting his stuff down for the moment, he got the package and put it and the revolver in the car. Then, taking his tools, he half slid, half fell, down the embankment to the van, praying nothing would blow up just yet.

The van, prior to going down the hill, had been as beautiful on the inside as out. Now, the interior was a jumbled mess. The couch/bed, table, and engine cowling were lying on the ceiling. The upholstery on the walls had been torn lose and hung in tatters. Henry saw several small, white, plastic bags, probably cocaine, and hand rolled cigarettes scattered around. Henry took the lid off the gas can and poured the contents liberally over the interior of the van. Next, he took half the plastic explosive and molded it around the gas filler neck and inserted a fuse. Then, he took the remaining plastic and placed it between the oil pan and the cross brace for the frame of the vehicle and inserted a fuse in it.

Climbing the hill, Henry wondered if he had used enough of the explosive material or too much. He wished he knew more about the stuff. Well, he thought, if it just ignites the gas, I guess that's good enough.

Once more at the car, he got the detonator from the trunk. Francis hadn't moved, and Henry hoped he wouldn't die in the cold before he got him back to Hunters Trail. He got in the car and unwrapped the insulation from the detonator's wires. He took a deep breath and touched the wires together. Nothing. Trying again he sawed the two wires together, still with no result. Then he got an idea. He took the battery from the unit and held it against the heat vent. With the battery in the trunk, it might have got too cold to work, he reasoned. Warming it might revitalize it.

A car came down the road and slowed for the curve. Henry watched it as it wound through the curves, then breathed easier after it picked up speed and went on out of sight.

He felt the battery. The heat vent had done its job, and the battery was comfortably warm. Reinserting it into the case, he leaned back and waited. He wanted to be sure the car that had passed had time to get out of earshot. After three minutes had passed, he picked up the detonator and, with trembling fingers, touched the wires together.

Henry was not ready for the results. The sky flashed daylight bright as the van exploded. Even in the car with the windows closed, he could feel the concussion, and the noise was deafening. The Lincoln, despite it's weight, rocked violently, and debris rained down around him.

Glad he had been in the protective shelter of the car, he waited a few minutes then got out to look down the hill. With the fire that lit up the scene below, Henry had trouble determining that the van had even been a vehicle.

Well, he thought getting back in the car, I guess the newspaper will tell me if I did it right. Right now, I need to get out of here before someone comes along and sees me sitting here. Also, I have a very special cargo I have to get home, and I don't even want to get stopped. He pulled away from the shoulder and, at the first available wide spot, turned back toward Hunters Trail.

The snow was starting to get heavier and was already sticking to the pavement. Henry turned on the windshield wipers and drove cautiously. The hunter, he thought, was returning successfully from the kill.

He pulled into the garage and closed the door. He certainly didn't want anyone, if they were watching, to see him pulling a body from the trunk. Besides, when he was coming up the road, he thought he saw a vehicle sitting back off the road between his house and the neighbor's. He got the package and the revolver from the car and went inside.

# CHAPTER 43

When he went in, he found Fred in the basement watching an old sitcom on the TV and sipping a beer.

Henry tossed the package and the revolver on the couch beside him and plopped into the recliner. "Boy, do I have a surprise for you."

Fred grinned and sipped his beer. "I have no doubt. Can I get you a beer?" He went behind the bar and returned with two beers, handing one to Henry. He sat down and picked up the revolver, turning it over in his hand, examining it. "Where did you get the toy?"

Henry smiled, picking up the package. "A guy I met this evening was kind enough to give it to me along with this package."

Fred laid the revolver on the table saying, "Damned expensive present. I'd say over nine hundred dollars from the looks of it. What's in the package?"

Henry pulled at the wrapping. "That, we are about to find out. The guy also gave it to me. I figured he wouldn't need it anymore."

Getting the wrap open at one end, he dumped the contents on the table.

Fred whistled. "Holy Hell, there must be half a mill there. What does your benefactor have, oil wells?"

Henry shuffled the banded stacks of hundred dollar bills around on the table, "No, not oil wells, something more expensive, drugs."

"Oh shit, Hank, you don't just toy with the idea of getting your ass shot off; you beg for it. Drug dealers don't like people taking their money. If they find you got this, they'll come after you, full force. Where is the guy you got this from anyway?"

Henry continued to count the money. "In the trunk of the Lincoln, last time I checked. His name is Gilbert Francis. The girl at the bar called him the Snowman."

"Dead," Fred asked.

"No, he's not dead." Henry smiled. "Let's just say he's on one hell of a downer."

Fred nodded, "Well, at least he can't get to his contacts to tell them you have their money. I trust he's one of the men you've been looking for?"

Henry finished counting the money. "Fifty stacks, ten thousand per stack, exactly half a mil. Francis must have had one hell of a racket going. To answer your question, yes, as a matter of fact, he is one of those I've been looking for. I did have a lingering doubt about that right up until I caught up with him this evening, but now I know that he is."

Fred drank from his beer and sat it on the table. "You know, Hank, he apparently had a good-size operation going around here, judging from that pile of money. I would expect he got his base capital built up by robbing houses like they did yours. Mary and Linda just happened to be unfortunate enough to be home when they went in, so they had to get rid of the witnesses."

Henry winced at the mention of his wife and daughter.

Fred continued, "The thing is, you don't have much time. As soon as his contacts realize he's not going to show up, they're going to put the word out, and his buddy is going to know what happened or at least guess at it."

Henry nodded. "I know that. That means I have very little time to find him. I've got to get Francis in here, get him to talk, and get the other one before he gets suspicious. My only problem is I don't know how Hampstead fits in and that bugs me."

"Well, let's worry about that later, Hank. Right now, let's get your Snowman in here before he becomes one in the trunk of your car. It's freezing outside, and you'll end up with a corpsicle in your trunk if you leave him there too long."

Henry stood up. "What about the bugs?"

Fred shrugged. "I can take care of that. Do you have any grease?"

"I think there's some Vaseline upstairs."

"That will do. The mikes will still work, but will be so distorted they'll be useless. Anyone listening will just think they've gone bad."

Henry got the Vaseline while Fred accessed the mikes. Then he packed the salve into the diaphragms, wiped the excess off, and closed the covers. He turned to Henry. "Now, that takes care of that. Let's get your boy in here. In the meantime, you can tell me how you convinced him to climb into your trunk."

On the way through the rec room, Fred picked up the revolver and checked the chamber. "Just a little insurance, in case," he said to Henry.

"Well, I thought I was a little innovative for the most part." Henry said as they went up the stairs. "Of course, I did get the shit scared out of me when I shot him with a tranquilizer dart, and he didn't drop immediately. I thought he wasn't going to go down. Anyway, when I left here today, I drove down to where he worked and . . ." He gave Fred a rundown on what had happened and the destruction of the van.

Fred laughed when he had finished. "Cripes, you probably blew away half the hillside using that whole block of plastic. But that's good. They'll be a while trying to identify it."

They were at the car. Henry reached in and hit the trunk release while Fred stood at the back, the revolver in his hand, in case Francis had regained consciousness.

By the time the lid had fully raised, Henry was beside his brother. Francis lay in the same position he had been in since Henry put him in the trunk. "Man, I hope I didn't kill him. I've been told that stuff can kill a smaller animal if it's not healthy."

Fred grabbed his arm. "No great loss if he is, but he's still breathing. Let's get him inside. It's cold out here."

Together, they half dragged, half carried the unconscious man to the shelter and confined him in the chains and shackles Henry had installed. Then taking the handcuffs and leg irons off, they went back to the rec room, closing the door behind them.

Fred tinkered with the back of the TV for a moment then turned it on. "I know you didn't say anything about a monitor in here, but it's convenient, and if you want to disable it at times, I'll show you how to do it."

He sat down and picked up a controller that looked like one for an X-Box game. "This," he said, "controls the direction of the camera." Pointing to the other knobs, he said, "This one controls the focus and this one controls distance. This last one is volume. The audio feature cost a little more, but with your recent financial acquisition, it shouldn't be a problem."

Henry laughed, glancing at the money on the table. "No, I don't think it will hurt my bottom line at all. In fact, this guy has reimbursed me for a lot of my expenditures."

They sat watching the monitor as Fred brought the inert figure on the floor into focus. "What are you planning to do to make him tell you who his partner is?"

"The first thing I'm going to do is castrate the son-of-a –bitch. But I want him awake when I do it. Then if that doesn't work, I'll try a few other things just as reprehensible. Whatever I do, it won't be as bad as what he did to my family."

Fred got a pained expression on his face. "Are you sure you have the stomach for this? I know I wouldn't have."

Henry's face showed loathing as he stared at the monitor. "That piece of garbage did a lot worse to Mary and Linda than anything I could ever do to him. And yes, as long as I have their pictures in my mind, I could disembowel the bastard while he watched and feel good for having done it. To make him tell me who else is involved, I'll do anything necessary, including pulling his teeth and fingernails out with a pair of pliers."

Fred looked at his brother. "Wow!"

Henry continued to stare at the monitor. "If you don't want to watch, that's fine. I understand."

Henry continued to watch the monitor and an idea formed. "Do you have any tape left from the work you were doing?"

Fred nodded. "Yeah, there're some rolls on the workbench."

Henry stood. "Good, I'll be back in a few minutes."

He selected a wide roll from the bench and went into the shelter. Francis still hadn't moved. He pulled his left leg over to one of the rings in the floor and secured it with several loops of tape. Then pulling his right leg to another ring, he did the same. Next, he taped his wrists together and then secured them to the chain coming down from the ceiling.

Francis moaned, starting to come out of the drug induced sleep. Henry carried the remaining tape back to the workbench, went to the refrigerator, and got two beers and, handing one to Fred, settled himself back in the recliner. "Now I'll wait until he's good and awake."

Fred watched the monitor. "Hank, are you sure this is what you want to do? I mean, maybe you ought to turn him over to the police. Let them find the other one."

Henry laughed. "Shit, Fred, they've had months to find this asshole. If I wait for them, I'll probably be killed myself. If I have Francis, the other one will know and want to get rid of me, their only witness. Besides, there's no guarantee their punishment would fit the crime or even come close, and certainly their punishment would never be what they deserve if they get into the judicial system. So, no thanks, I'll take care of it, at least for now. The police can have whatever is left."

The figure on the monitor raised his head and then let it drop back to his chest.

Fred looked at Henry. "So why not get the other one and turn them both over to the police? I'm sure they would stand trial and go up the river, even if they didn't get the death penalty."

"The punishment would never fit the crime, Fred. They'd be back on the street at some point and probably to do the same thing. The recidivism rate for criminals is, I believe, around 80 percent. That doesn't sound like good odds to me. Hell, they might even plead insanity and never see the inside of a prison. They'd go to a psychiatric hospital for a couple of years and then be released as cured."

He paused, "The way I see it, if crime is to be deterred, the punishment has to exceed the crime. In Iran and other eastern countries, if someone steals something, they cut off his hand. If they commit murder or adultery, they are stoned to death. As a result, they have very little crime.

"The point is they have little crime because they show you lose more than the crime is worth. Here, on the other hand, if you steal a million dollars, you maybe get ten to twenty and are out in three. If they don't find the money, you're back on the street a millionaire. If you rape and kill someone, you get twenty-five to life and are back on the street in seven or eight years, if you are convicted at all."

Francis raised his head and looked around, turning his head to examine his bonds.

"So, you see Fred," Henry said standing up, "I've got to take care of this myself."

# CHAPTER 44

Henry walked toward the shelter door and said to Fred, "If it gets too gory for you, you can turn off the monitor." He went into the shelter and closed the door. Francis immediately swung his head around and narrowed his eyes when he saw Henry.

Henry smiled at the man as he got a folding chair and, bringing it close, sat down in front of him. "Good evening, Mr. Francis, or should I call you Snowman? Did you have a nice nap?"

The man glared at him. "Fuck you, Jenkins," he said more loudly than necessary.

Henry continued to smile. "The reason I brought you here is because I need to know who helped you rape and kill my wife and daughter and the lady who redecorated this house. I don't suppose you would be willing to provide me with that information. Would you?"

"I'm not giving you shit, Jenkins," he said again too loudly. "And when they find out I'm here, you can kiss your ass goodbye."

Henry stopped smiling but said in a low voice, "Mr. Francis, if you are talking loudly for the benefit of the microphones in the walls, you can stop. They have been disabled."

Francis's expression changed, telling him he had been doing just that. Henry continued, "So that was it then? I'm glad I was able to clear that up for you."

He let that sink in then said, "And the keys in the compartment in the entryway, they won't do you any good either because as soon as you tell me who helped you, I'm going to seal it up and the keys with it."

Francis smirked. "Then you'll wait 'til Hell freezes over, asshole, because I'm not going to tell you shit!"

Henry smiled again. "Well, as a matter of fact, you are. And, when we're done, you'll be begging to tell me more."

"Don't hold your breath," Francis sneered. "I've been worked over before. And where the hell is my money? My people will kill you, along with everyone you know if they don't get their money."

"Ah, I'm afraid that money, if there was any money, is gone. There was a big explosion where you drove off the road. I'm afraid everything was destroyed."

Henry continued smiling. "Now, if you have been worked over, it was probably deservedly so, and not nearly well enough since you're still alive. But let me explain some things to you, Mr. Francis, so there is no misunderstanding of my thoughts or intentions."

"You are pond scum, Francis. You are the maggots in the rotting, putrid meat in life. You are emotionally bankrupt and morally lower than whale shit. You really don't deserve to live in society, and someone should have crushed your perverted, demented head when you were born. However, there are times in life when a piece of slime such as yourself survives to destroy or corrupt everything around you."

"You listen to me you . . ." Francis began.

Henry reached forward and punched him in the face with his fist. Blood sprayed from his nose. "Don't interrupt me. If you're talking, you aren't listening, and you really need to understand what is going to happen here tonight."

"Now, where was I? Oh yeah, to continue, that's what you did to me, Francis. You destroyed my world and corrupted me to the point where I now am determined to right that wrong. I am at that point where I am going to put an end to the filth you create just by your mere existence."

Francis laughed. "You can hit me all you want. You can even kill me, but when my friends get hold of you, you will wish you had never seen me."

"I'm not going to kill you, Francis, nor will I be killed. You see, you don't have friends, and your partner in crime is going to be in here with you, or instead of you, in a few hours. And the people you stole the money from will take care of you if you get out of here."

"You have big dreams for a dead man, Jenkins, and you know I didn't steal that money, you did."

"Think what you will, Francis, but let me explain what is going to happen to you right now. You see, I have no intention of killing you. That would be too easy. What I'm going to do is put you in a position where you will want death, maybe even beg for death. But if you die, Francis, it will be by a hand other than mine."

"You see, Francis, I really do want you dead, but even more, I want you to live. In death, you would not suffer as I want you to suffer. In death, you cannot hurt as you have caused others to hurt. In death, you wouldn't feel the ridicule, laughter, and humiliating degradation you have caused others."

"I want you to feel those things, Francis. I want those things to be your constant companions. I want you to feel the pain and anguish you have caused others, every minute of every day for the rest of your miserable, disgusting life."

Francis laughed. "Give it your best shot, shithead. You haven't got much time."

"Ah, Mr. Francis," Henry said as he went to the cabinet and, unlocking it, pulled out a surgical case, "That's a fallacy on your part. You see, for what I have planned for you doesn't require a lot of time."

Henry opened the case and pulled out a surgical scalpel, holding it up so Francis could see it. "You raped my wife and daughter. So, the first thing I'm going to do is castrate you, so you won't want to do that sort of thing again."

Francis suddenly realized his vulnerability in the way he was bound, and he strained, uselessly, at the tape that held his legs apart.

Unable to pull his legs together, his courage waned. "Listen, buddy, you got this wrong."

Henry moved over in front of him. "Well, you and I both know that is not true, and I see even the idea has affected a change in your attitude. That's good. Do you want to tell me who helped you in the brutalization and death of my family before, or after, I castrate you, Mr. Francis?"

"Look, Jenkins, I don't know what you're talking about. That wasn't me. I just heard about it. I don't know who did it." He tried unsuccessfully to pull his legs together.

"I'll ask again; do you want to tell me who helped you before, or after, I castrate you, Mr. Francis? It doesn't matter to me."

"Look, Jenkins, I'm telling you, again, that wasn't me. I just heard about it. I don't know who did it."

Henry's smile drew into a thin, unsympathetic line. "Don't give me that bullshit. You were a cocky little bastard until I told you I was going to cut your balls off. Does the idea of being a eunuch not appeal to you, Mr. Francis?"

Sweat began to appear on Francis's brow. "Listen, man, don't do that shit. I swear to Christ, I didn't do nothing."

Henry laughed. "Mr. Francis, Christ doesn't believe you. You should, instead, be begging his forgiveness for your sins." Henry reached forward and unbuckled and unzipped the man's pants and jerked them down to his knees. He wasn't wearing skivvies.

Francis jerked back and forth against his bonds, trying to keep Henry from getting his jeans off. Henry laid the scalpel on the chair he had vacated and turned back to Francis. "Let me tell you something, old sod. You can make this easy or hard on yourself. That scalpel is extremely sharp and, if you keep thrashing around like you are, you may lose more than your balls."

"Please, man," Francis pleaded, "don't do this. I didn't do it."

"Then who, Mr. Francis, who did do it?"

Francis swung his head back and forth violently. "I don't know. I just know I didn't do it."

Henry shook his head. "I guess there is honor among thieves after all. Or is it that you are more afraid of them than me?"

Reaching forward, he grabbed the man's testicle sack in his hand and picked up the scalpel with the other. "Well, Mr. Francis, let's find out how deep that honor goes."

Francis strained to pull his legs together to no avail. "Please don't do this, man. Are you crazy?"

Henry smiled. "Perhaps I am crazy, Mr. Francis. Perhaps you made me crazy. But I am sure of one thing, when I am done with you, you will never have the desire to rape another woman."

"Listen, Jenkins," Francis said, sweat running down onto his shirt collar and staining his underarms. "If I tell you who did it, will you stop this?"

Henry laughed. "Mr. Francis, perhaps I was not clear before. Let me explain again. I know you are one of the people who beat, raped, and murdered my wife and daughter. For that, I am going to castrate you and maim you. You have no options and no deals in that. I will do whatever is necessary to find out who else was involved. You can tell me before or after. But regardless of when you tell me, or how much you tell me, you will feel what my family felt. You will suffer as they suffered. The things I'm going to do to you will leave you drooling for death."

"You see, Mr. Francis, I have no compassion. I only want to hurt, to maim, and destroy you as you did me."

Francis's face was ashen. "Look, man . . . Mr. Jenkins." Tears formed in his eyes. "I was high on flakes, PCP. I didn't know what I was doing. It was the drugs."

Henry went to the cabinet and pulling down a bottle marked aspirin, popped two into his mouth and swallowed them. "Now, Mr. Francis, I'm on drugs. So, what I'm going to do is okay."

He walked over to Francis who was bucking wildly against his bonds.

"For God's sake, man," he screamed.

"Yes, Mr. Francis, for God's sake. And for the sake of every woman you have ever touched or looked at."

Henry grabbed the man's testicle sack in his hand, and with a single swipe of the razor sharp scalpel, separated his testicles from his body.

Holding the severed testicles in his hand and up in front of Francis's eyes, he said, "For my wife."

He let them roll off his hand. Francis's eyes followed them as his manhood fell and hit the floor between his legs with a soft plop.

Francis screamed and babbled about bleeding to death. Henry went to the cabinet to get some compresses, antiseptic and tape to stop the bleeding. He was not ready for Francis to give up.

"Mr. Francis, I don't want you to bleed to death, at least not now. So, if you will hold still for a moment, I'll take care of this. With young bulls, farmers just coated their ball sacks with tar. Unfortunately, I don't have any, so I've got to dress yours."

Francis sagged against his bonds as Henry dressed the wound, but he continued to babble hysterically, drool running down his chin. Henry tugged his jeans up and refastened them.

"Now, Mr. Francis, I am going to give you a few minutes to recover while I prepare for our next little tete-a-tete."

Using the scalpel, Henry cut the tape binding Francis's ankles. He left the tape that bound his wrists to the chain. He walked to the shelves as Francis stood and squeezed his legs together.

The babbling had stopped, but the look of hatred returned to the man's eyes. "You'd better kill me you son-of-a-bitch, because when I get loose, you are a dead piece of shit."

Henry picked up an axe handle from one of the shelves and came back to face Francis.

Francis tried to kick him, but Henry stepped out of range.

Francis again squeezed his legs together; his eyes were narrow slits.

"I take it you aren't ready to tell me who helped you?" Henry asked.

Instead of answering, Francis spat. The spittle ran down Henry's shirt sleeve.

"No, I guess not." Henry said. "Okay, let me explain what I'm going to do now. I'm going to break your arms and legs; not just break them, I'm going to crush the joints so that every movement you make causes you excruciating pain. I'm going to fix you so you will be totally dependent like you do to the people you sell your drugs to. Except you won't be able to take anything that will stop the pain."

He swung the axe handle and, as it connected with Francis's right knee, he heard the joint pop sickeningly. Francis screamed and fainted.

"Shit!" Henry spat. He dropped the axe handle and went to the shelf where he had seen a bottle of ammonia. He opened it and stuck it under his captive's nose until he was jarred back to consciousness.

"What's wrong, Mr. Francis? Can't you stand a little pain? Mary had a fractured skull, a broken jaw, and broken teeth, and you still had to shoot her to kill her. You brutalized and raped my daughter, then shot her twice, and she was still conscious when I found her. Come on, Francis, surely you aren't as weak as a little fifteen-year-old girl, are you? I don't even know what you did to my interior decorator, but I'm sure it was as bad or worse. So, come on, show me you're a big, tough man who can take a little more pain than three helpless women."

He stood up and picked up the axe handle.

Francis tried to turn to keep the weight off the busted knee. Henry swung the club, breaking the other knee. Francis screamed and fainted again. And again, Henry revived him. "Are you ready to tell me who helped you, Francis?"

"You're crazy, man!" Francis hissed through the pain.

Henry smiled as he swung the club twice more, breaking both ankles. "Yes, I'm crazy, Francis. Who is your buddy?" He swung again, shattering the left femur. However, this time, the axe handle splintered and hurt his hand.

Francis screamed with each hit but remained conscious. "Please, please, please . . ."

Henry swung, breaking the right leg between the ankle and knee, and the axe handle broke in half. "Yes, Francis, please, please, please. Please tell me who helped you."

He went to a shelf and returned with a piece of pipe about an inch and a half in diameter and three feet long.

Francis said nothing, clenching his teeth against the pain and watching the new club in Henry's hand.

Again, Henry swung, this time breaking the left shoulder joint and clavicle. Francis did not scream this time. He just grunted and passed out. Henry swung and broke the other arm at the elbow.

He dropped the pipe and went into the rec room to get a beer. Fred sat on the couch, a fifth of bourbon on the table in front of him, a half-filled glass in his hand. The monitor was focused on Francis's inert body. Henry got a glass from the bar, put some ice in it, and poured two fingers of bourbon in it before sitting down.

"Hank," Fred began, "what you do to that guy is your business, but if you aren't careful, he'll go into shock and die on you. I don't see how he's stayed this long, probably the drugs."

Henry drank from the glass and grimaced when the liquor hit his throat. "Well, I'm almost done. I figure he can't walk again, at least without crutches. I just want to be sure he feels it every time he moves, and as soon as I'm done with him, I'll take him somewhere and turn him over to the police. But first, he is going to tell me who helped him, or things will get even worse."

Fred looked at the monitor. "I think he's coming around. He moved a little bit anyway."

Henry nodded. "I saw. I'll give him a few minutes to think, and then I'll go back in."

Henry continued to stare at the monitor. "My God, Fred, I think his hair is starting to turn white." He downed the rest of his drink. "I better get in there. I don't want to lose him before I get what I need."

Henry entered the shelter and picked up the pipe, and Francis followed the movements with partially glazed eyes. Spittle ran from the corner of his mouth. His hair was definitely graying. Henry had always thought that was an old wives tale.

"Mr. Francis," Henry said, standing in front of him, "I'm about done if you tell me who your cohort was. If you're not, I have a lot more in store for you."

Francis stared at Henry drunkenly. His hair seemingly turning whiter as Henry stood there.

Henry waited a moment and then raised the club above his head. The blow broke the man's elbow. Francis's eyes cleared and a gurgling sound came from his throat. His hair was even whiter.

Henry paused. "I'm sorry, Mr. Francis, did you say something? I didn't hear you."

Francis took a deep breath and groaned with the pain it caused. "Darnell Jefferson," he choked out barely above a whisper. "His name is Darnell Jefferson, Hampstead's stepson."

"Well, now." Henry smiled. "Don't you feel better for having told me that?"

He didn't wait for an answer. "Now, just where do I find this Darnell?"

The man's hair was even lighter, and he giggled as he said, "Heh, heh, The Eagles Nest."

Henry shook his head. "No, Mr. Francis, I destroyed the Eagles Nest. Try again."

"You? Heh, heh, it was you? I should've killed you. Heh, heh. I told Hampstead—should've listened—wouldn't listen. Heh, heh, at the Shamrock." Henry stooped in front of Francis, holding the pipe at shoulder height. "What does Darnell look like? How will I recognize him?"

"Heh, heh, heh, strange eyes, heh, heh, heh."

Henry immediately knew it was the guy he had initially spoke to at The Eagles Nest. The one who's eyes reminded him of Charlie Manson. "Is he late twenties, skinny with dirty blond hair?"

"Heh, heh, heh, Darnell, heh, heh."

Henry stood and lifted the pipe. He had no intention of hitting the man again, but apparently, Francis thought he was going to do so. He jerked as much as the bonds and broken bones would allow, screaming with pain and anticipation. His eyes got strangely bright as he yelled, "Yes, hit me, hit me, kill me. Do you hear me, you son-of-a-bitch. Kill me! You know you want to. You said it! You said it, heh, heh, heh."

Henry swung the pipe, the metal connected with his mouth, splitting his lower lip and snapping off several teeth. Francis fainted. His hair was totally white now, except for a small spot at the crown of his head.

Henry laid the pipe back on the shelf and cut the tape holding the man's wrists letting the man fall to the floor. Then he said, "And for Linda."

He walked back into the rec room. "Did you have the volume up, Fred?"

"Yeah, I did, why?"

Henry sat down on the couch and opened a beer. "The name he gave me, Jefferson. I met him at The Eagles Nest. He's the one that got me worked over."

Fred nodded, "I was wondering why you could describe him, but wait a minute, that means he knows you."

"Not necessarily. I used a different name and a different license plate on the car." He sipped his drink and continued, "Listen, I know you have to head for home today and need to get some sleep, but could I get you to help me with something?"

"Sure, I can sleep on the flight home anyway. What do you need?"

"Well, I've got to dump him somewhere," Henry said, pointing to the monitor. "And let the police know. Then, I've got to locate and contain Jefferson, today if I can."

Fred stood up. "Then let's get movin' son. Times a wastin'." He stuck the revolver in his belt once again.

Henry got a blanket in the shelter, and they rolled Francis into it. The man's arms and legs took on almost comical movements as they got him on the blanket. The blood from his split lip had coagulated, but the dried blood on his chin made it look worse than it was.

They carried him to the car and deposited him in the trunk. Then Henry locked the house, and they drove into downtown Pittsburgh.

When Henry turned onto Carson Street, he saw Southside Park across from Duquesne University and decided it was as good a place as any to get rid of his passenger.

Pulling to the curb, he waited until a carload of teenagers passed, giving the Lincoln the once over. Then he hit the trunk release, and he and Fred get out. Fred grabbed one end of the rolled up blanket, while Henry got the other. Together, they carried the bundle to a nearby bench and laid it down. Henry noticed even the hair at the crown of Francis's head was now white.

Getting back in the car, Henry said, "I'm going to call the police from somewhere near, so I can be sure they get him."

"You aren't going to use your cell phone, are you?" Fred asked.

"No, I have a burner phone. They won't know who it is."

He made a U-turn and stopped across the park where they could see the bench, and he dialed 9-1-1 on the burner.

The call connected. "Nine-one-one, what's your emergency?"

Henry affected his southern drawl. "Yes, ma'am. I was driving past, I think y'all call it Southside Park across from the university on, I think it's Carson Street."

"Yes, sir, and what is the emergency?"

"Well, Ma'am, there's a man there wrapped in a blanket, and he looks like he's in real bad shape. It looks like he's bleedin' and stuff."

"All right, sir. With whom am I speaking?"

"Ah, ma'am, I don't want to get involved. I just wanted y'all to know that the condition the guy is in he might die, if he ain't dead already, if someone don't get down here and pick him up. I will tell you one thing. He said he was involved in a rape and murder up in a town called Clarksville and the murder of some interior decorator in Pittsburgh."

"Very well, sir. The police and an ambulance are on the way. Just wait there until they get there."

Henry laughed. "Like that's gonna happen." He hung up.

When he got off the phone, Fred chuckled. "That's the worst southern accent I've heard in a while."

Henry grinned. "Just as long as it doesn't sound like my accent."

Their wait was not long. Within five minutes, a police cruiser pulled up next to the park bench followed shortly by an ambulance.

As the EMTs loaded Francis into the ambulance, Henry eased away from the curb and drove down the street. "Now it's time to pay Mr. Jefferson a visit."

# CHAPTER 45

With traffic very light at almost two o'clock Saturday morning, and bars ready to close shortly, it took only a few minutes to drive to the Shamrock. Henry pulled into the lot, away from the door, and killed his headlights but left the engine running.

"Well, I guess we just wait to see who comes out," he said to Fred. "I sure can't go in there to see if he's in there. He would recognize me."

Fred opened the car door. "Load your dart gun, Henry. I'll bring him out if he's in there. I believe I know what he looks like."

"Are you sure you want to go in there? You know what happened to me."

"Just get your dart gun ready and leave it to me."

Fred shoved the revolver into his waistband and, zipping his jacket, got out of the car. "Just don't shoot me."

"I'll try not to do that," Henry smiled.

As Fred started toward the door, Henry got out the two handguns, making sure they were loaded and the safeties off. He also got the rifle and did the same with it. Then taking his artillery, he stepped around the corner of the building and into the shadows. His tasks were seemingly easier as they progressed.

Fred opened the door and stepped into the dimly lit stench of the bar room. There must have been thirty people in the smoke-filled, dingy room, and it was difficult to see more than ten feet in front of him. He strolled up to the bar and ordered a draft.

After the bartender brought it, he laid five dollars on the bar and, picking up the glass, moved through the throng of people. He sipped the beer as he looked at the patrons, some who returned his gaze with suspicion.

Jefferson was leaning against the wall near the pool table, sucking on a reefer. As Fred started toward him, he inhaled, held the smoke in his lungs for a moment, and then coughed it in Fred's direction.

Fred smiled and walked up in front of him. "Jefferson? Are you Darnell Jefferson?"

"Who the fuck wants to know?" Jefferson spat.

Fred held his smile. "Listen, you scrawny little piece of cat shit, the Snowman asked me to relay a message to you, but with your attitude, I may just shove this glass up your ass instead."

He turned and walked back toward the door.

"Hey Jet," Jefferson called to someone at the table, "I'll be right back."

He walked quickly after Fred and grabbed his arm, "Hey, mister," he whined in a shrill voice, "what did the Snowman say?"

Fred jerked his arm away and swung toward him. "You ever touch me again," he whispered in a low menacing voice, "and I'll break your skinny fucking neck."

Darnell quickly pulled his hand back. "Hey man, I didn't mean nothing. I just got to know what Francis said."

The man Jefferson had yelled at was coming toward them, and Fred cursed under his breath. He certainly didn't want to draw a crowd.

"Just come outside where we can at least breathe. Also, I don't want to compete with the noise in here."

"Yeah, fine. C'mon, Jet. Let's see what this guy wants."

Fred wanted to tell him his friend couldn't come, but knew that would only draw more of his buddies. He shrugged his shoulders and went for the door, sitting his glass on the bar as he went.

When he stepped out the door, he looked toward the Lincoln but did not see Henry. He hoped he was ready. Unzipping his jacket, he stepped off the porch and walked out into the parking lot.

"Hey man, where are you going?"

"I'm not standing there under that light." Fred said. "I don't want to be associated with scum like you two."

Hey, asshole . . ." Jet began.

Jefferson elbowed him, cutting him off. "Save it a minute, Jet. Let's see what he's got."

Fred stopped about twenty feet from the Lincoln and, pulling the magnum from his waistband, turned just as Henry pulled the trigger on the rifle.

The dart stuck in Jefferson's thigh, and the man's eyes widened in surprise then confusion as he looked down to see the red cylinder protruding from his leg.

Jet stared down the bore of the revolver with a similar expression on his face. "Sonuvabitch," he gasped. "You sonuvabitch."

Jefferson, stunned, pulled the dart from his leg and held it up to within a few inches of his face, staring at it perplexed. "What the hell is . . ." The sentence was left unfinished as he pitched forward, crumbling to the ground.

Jet stared at his fallen companion then at Fred just as a dart lodged in the back of his left shoulder. "You rotten bastard, you set us up."

Fred smiled, holding the magnum steady. "Yeah, I guess I did, didn't I? You should have stayed inside."

Jet stared at him as he strained uselessly at reaching the dart in his back. A moment later, he fell beside Jefferson.

Fred jammed the gun back in his waist band, and grabbing Jet, dragged him to a pickup truck parked a few feet away and hefted him into the bed.

Henry got Jefferson and wrestled him into the trunk of the Lincoln, securing him with the handcuffs and leg irons.

Once more in the car, they headed back to Hunters Trail.

Fred laughed. "When I came out of that bar and didn't see you, I thought you, and I, were in a world of trouble."

Henry shook his head. "I didn't want Jefferson to see me when he came out the door, so I stepped around the corner. I didn't expect him to have company."

"Fred nodded. "It worked out all right. I'm just glad he didn't bring five or six of his buddies, and I hope the one I put in the pickup doesn't freeze to death."

"Well, he shouldn't have come outside in the first place."

The rest of the drive to Hunters Trail was spent in reflective meditation.

A half an hour later, and once again in the garage, they hauled Jefferson out of the trunk, still unconscious. They carried him downstairs and into the shelter where they bound him with the restraints.

"You know," Henry said when they were back in the rec room, "that guy you put in the bed of that pickup can recognize you."

Fred shrugged his shoulders. "In a few hours, I'll be on a flight to Denver. I doubt they will be looking for me there."

They rested long enough to have a cup of coffee and then went back into the shelter. Jefferson was still sleeping.

They began removing all the explosive items and drugs from the cabinets. Fred carried the explosives and associated items to the workshop, while Henry flushed all the drugs down the toilet. Next, they removed any items that could be used to open the restraints and checked again to ensure everything had been moved to the workshop.

With that done, Henry got the detonator for the outside entry. "Now I have to collapse the outside entry. Could I get you to change the lock on the door between the rec room and the workshop while I do that?"

"Sure," Fred replied. "Where is the new lock?"

"It's in the garage lying on the hood of the Cadillac. I wasn't going to worry about it, but since Brenda had a key to the house, which they may have gotten when they killed her, I think it might be wise."

"Can't hurt, and better safe than sorry."

Fred headed upstairs, and Henry installed a new battery in the detonator before following him. He walked to the kitchen window where he could see the entry and pulled the insulators from the ends of the wires. Touching the two wires together, he watched ground that had been a hump, sink in on itself with a noise akin to a gunshot. He figured any neighbor who heard the bang would just think someone had shot a rifle or something.

Henry went outside and walked back to where the entry had been. A few clods of dirt peppered the ground around what had been the opening, but most had stayed and fallen into the stairwell. A couple of pieces of wood were exposed, but they would be buried when he smoothed it over. He went back to the house to get the necessary implements.

Fred was still working on the lock installation when he got back inside. "So, how did it go?"

Henry got a mattock and shovel. "Good. I just need to level it off a little bit."

Fred nodded as he tightened the screws. "Darrell does good work. Let me put these tools away, and I'll give you a hand out back."

By ten o'clock, it was snowing again, but the outside work was done. Fred had helped Henry carry the concrete and blocks from the garage down to the workshop before he left for the airport. After he left, Henry sat at the kitchen table with a cup of coffee. He was in pretty good shape as far as the timing and completion of his endeavors were concerned. He still had to get the concrete blocks placed, but the shelter was secure for the moment. Jefferson had the necessities befitting a criminal, and there was a new lock securing the workshop, if Hampstead did happen to come by and get in the house during his absence.

It was time for him to get in touch with Sheila.

# CHAPTER 46

Sheila picked up on the second ring. "Hello."

"Hi, sugar. Could you tolerate my company for a day or two?"

"I'd love it, but it would be even better if it were a year or two, or longer."

Henry told her he would be there in a couple of hours and hanging up, jumped into the shower. He was tired from the night's efforts, but he figured he could at last sleep through the day if he was active. He dressed, put coffee in a carry out mug, and got in the Cadillac. Even though his need for the Lincoln was satisfied, at least for now, there was no need to flaunt his good fortune. There were still police looking for such a car.

It was one o'clock when he got to Clarksville, and Sheila opened the front door as he got out of the car. She greeted him with a very warm, very amorous kiss then stepped back to look at him. "I like your beard. It makes you look . . . dapper? But what happened to your face?"

She touched the area beside the stitches in his eyebrow and the scratch on his cheek. "I told you, you would be hurt. What happened?"

Henry laughed, taking her arm. "Let's go inside, and I'll tell you. It's not, I'm sure, what you think."

In the kitchen, Sheila fixed them some lunch, while Henry fabricated a story to explain the damage to his body.

"I bought this house near Pittsburgh, and I . . ."

"Wait a minute," Sheila interrupted, "are you moving down there?"

Henry smiled. "I hope to do just that, but that depends on you."

Sheila showed her concern as she said, "But that's so far away, Henry. I wouldn't like you way down there. I'd hardly ever see you."

"You would if you moved with me."

Sheila's face brightened. "Are you asking me to go with you?"

"Sounds reasonable to me. Of course, I still have work to do there. So it would be a while before you had to decide if that is something you would like to do."

"I want to see it," Sheila said coming to the table to hug him. "When can we go?"

"Whoa. Wait one. I still have work to do down there before I'm ready for you to see it. It will still be a few weeks."

Sheila's smile dimmed, but Henry could tell she was elated by his intentions. She returned to the skillet of bacon on the stove. "Well, if I must. So tell me about your facial injuries."

"Well, there was this tree in the back yard that was old and half dead. I was afraid it might fall on the house in a storm, so instead of calling someone to remove it, I decided I would be smart and do it myself. Anyway, I was up in the tree, cutting a limb, when it kicked back, hitting me in the head, and knocked me out of the tree."

Sheila's expression was one of worry and concern. "You could have been killed, Henry. Are you sure you're all right?"

"Oh, sure. I got some bumps and bruises and a couple of busted ribs when I hit the ground, but that was several days ago. I'm okay now, or pretty much okay. It still hurts when I take a deep breath. Why? Are you going to be my pretty little nurse and give me some TLC?"

Sheila laughed as she put the bacon on a grill to drain. "I can probably manage that."

Henry smiled. "I like my nurses naked. Especially when they look like you."

She laughed again. "Oh, you're bad. But I might be able to accommodate you with that too."

Putting toast in as she started eggs and hash browns, she asked, "So, how long are you going to stay this time?"

"Just till Monday, sugar. I've got to get back and take care of some details." He walked up behind her and slipped his arms around her waist. Kissing her on her neck, he added, "Besides, if I hang around too long, you'll kick me out."

Sheila, ignoring the smoke coming from the toaster, turned and kissed him. "No, I wouldn't get tired of you that soon, maybe a week, but not two days."

"Better watch that toast," Henry said, patting her bottom. "I like things hot but not that hot."

After they had eaten, they put their dishes in the dishwasher. Then Sheila took Henry's hand and led him into the bedroom. "Now that I have satisfied your hunger," she said smiling as she took off her clothes, "it's time for you to satisfy mine."

Henry followed suit and joined her on the bed. "You only satisfied part of my hunger," he said pulling her to him. "Now it's time for dessert."

An hour later, Henry was lying contentedly caressing Sheila's stomach when the doorbell rang. "Damn it," she said. "The first time in weeks I get what I want, and we get interrupted."

She got up, pulled on a robe, and blew a kiss at Henry. "Don't go away. I'm not done with you yet."

"No chance, sweetheart. With you naked, I may just stay here forever."

"I'll let you," she said as she went down the hall.

A couple of minutes later, she came back to the bedroom with a worried look on her face. "Henry, there's a police detective out there. I think he said his name is Cameron. He wants to talk to you."

Henry swung his feet to the floor and sat up. He knew why Cameron was there, but he wouldn't let on to Sheila. "No problem, sweetie." He said pulling on his slacks. "But while I talk to him, why don't you wait in here?"

Sheila stood by the bed. "What's wrong? What does he want? Is it about those men you're looking for?"

Henry put his hands on her shoulders and kissed her nose. "I don't know what he wants. I'm guessing it is probably about them, but until I talk to him, that's all it is, a guess. So why don't you wait in here and watch TV till He's gone. Then I'll tell you. Okay?"

Sheila nodded but didn't lose the worried expression. Henry kissed her again and, going out of the bedroom, closed the door behind him.

Cameron was standing by the front door when Henry entered the room. He was holding a brown fedora in front of him, turning it slowly by the brim. Henry extended his hand and shook that of the detective.

Henry waved to a chair in the living room. "Come on over and have a seat. No sense standing there by the door."

Cameron returned the greeting and took the offered seat.

"Now," Henry said, "what brings you here today?"

Cameron crossed his legs and sat the fedora on his knee. "I got a call from down in Pittsburgh. It seems they got an anonymous call from someone about a badly beaten man. You wouldn't know anything about that, would you, Mr. Jenkins?"

Henry shook his head, looking steadily into the detectives eyes. "Sorry to say I don't, Lieutenant. Besides, is there some particular reason why I should?"

Cameron eyed him with a look that said he didn't believe him. "You know, Mr. Jenkins, considering the situation we have here, I would have expected you would know something about it. For instance, before I came over here, I did some checking on you. It seems you have purchased a house near Pittsburgh, and according to a place called Cartier Interiors, had some expensive redecorating done. Then the woman who did the work for you was murdered about the same way your wife and daughter was."

Henry acted dumbfounded. "Are you saying Ms. Cartier has been killed? My God, that's terrible. What happened? When did it happen? Do they have any suspects? Do they think it is somehow tied to what happened to my family?"

At the same time, he was thinking, Damn. Someone at Brenda's office had talked to the police. Of course no one had told them not to talk to anyone. And, what about Greene? For a buck, he would tell anyone anything they wanted to know. He hoped the thousand dollar carrot would keep his mouth shut. He knew one thing. He was going to have to get back to the house and finish the needed work there, and quickly.

To Cameron, he said, "Well, as the case may be, I needed a house, and I didn't know there were restrictions on where I could get one."

"Mr. Jenkins, the man who placed the anonymous call in to the Pittsburgh police said the man, a Gilbert Francis, was involved in the Clarksville murders and the Pittsburgh murder. It would go a lot easier on you if you were straight with me."

Henry wanted to laugh. Cameron meant it would be a lot easier on Cameron. He remembered when he was a kid, and he did something he wasn't supposed to do, his dad would tell him it would go a lot easier on him if he came clean. So Henry would admit what he had done, and his dad would beat the shit out of him. After a few confessions, Henry determined straight denial was a hell of a lot better than admission. His dad would yell at him longer, but Henry didn't get his backside dusted.

"Mr. Cameron, I'm glad someone called that knew about our incident, but as I said before, I don't know anything about it. Maybe the caller was someone familiar with this Cartier woman. Also, if this guy, what did you say his name was, Gilbreth? If he is one of the men in our murder, maybe he can give you more information."

Cameron leaned forward. "Mr. Jenkins, I think you do know. Right now, I can't prove it, but if I do, I'll have to take you in. Would you mind telling me where you were yesterday?"

Henry didn't change his expression. "As a matter of fact, I do mind, Lieutenant. You're trying to put me in an incriminating position. One I don't care to be in. If you have one of the men in custody, good. I'm glad you do. But if you are trying to tie me to that, I won't help you. Besides, if Pittsburg has him, why don't you go talk to him?"

Cameron sighed. "It seems the man was beaten so badly the he is in shock, and his mind is slightly haywire. Pittsburgh says he's lucky to be alive. Where is the other one, Mr. Jenkins?"

Henry laughed. "Don't try to catch me up, Lieutenant. I expect if I beat this guy, I would have done the same to the other and would have called the police on both."

"Maybe you did beat them both. Maybe you did, and the other one died. Maybe you hid the body somewhere."

"Oh, come now." Henry was becoming exasperated. "What difference would it make if, as you say, the call was anonymous? And wouldn't it make more sense to report the dead one? He couldn't talk."

"Mr. Jenkins, I could run you in for questioning—hold you for a couple of days, but I'm not going to do that. I will, however, be looking for a way to connect you to this. I know this was your doing. I don't believe anyone else would have castrated the man."

"Wait a minute, Lieutenant. If he raped and killed my wife and daughter, he could have done the same to any number of women, including the interior decorator you told me about. Anyone could have castrated him."

Cameron stood up. "That's true, but it is unlikely that anyone would have known about the murders here."

"I don't know. A lot of people read the newspaper or listen to the news. If he was in a confessing mood, he might have said anything."

Cameron started toward the door. "No, Mr. Jenkins, you're the one that did it. You know it, and I know it. Fortunately, right now, it's not murder. That may change, considering his condition. If he dies, you are number one on my suspect list, and I'll take you in. As it is, I would suggest you stay in town until this is resolved."

Henry, standing, walked over to the door. "According to the law, I am innocent until, or unless, I am deemed guilty by a jury of my peers. Since I haven't been, I'll go wherever I want and anytime I want."

"Perhaps so," Cameron said, planting the fedora on his head, "but to the subject. If you know who the other one is, I expect you should tell me."

Henry snorted. "You've had six months to find them, Lieutenant. The same amount of time I have. Really, even more time. I told you before, either you catch them, or I will. You've got one. What have you done to catch the other?"

Cameron jumped on Henry's statement. "So you do know he's one of them?"

Henry got a pained expression on his face and opened the door. "Oh, come on, Lieutenant, you told me that. I didn't tell you. But I will tell you this. The situation is still the same as when I first talked to you."

Cameron stepped out onto the porch and Henry said, "Good luck, Lieutenant. Tell the boys in Pittsburgh I'm glad they got him."

Cameron stared at him for a moment then turned and strode off the porch without saying anything else.

Henry closed the door and heaved a sigh of relief. He hadn't committed any faux pas in his interview with Cameron. There was one thing, however, he would have to get back to the house. He had told Sheila he would stay until Monday, but that was now out. He would leave bright and early tomorrow.

He returned to the bedroom and smiled at Sheila's concern.

"What did he want?" she asked sitting up and her robe falling open.

Henry sat down on the bed beside her and ran his hand up her leg. "I would tell you, but with your robe open, anything I was going to tell you comes secondary to what I want to do with you right now."

Sheila laughed and pulled the robe closed. "Okay, now tell me."

"He told me they think they have one of the men involved in Mary and Linda's murders and hope to get the other one when they can question him."

"Oh, Henry," she said, squeezing his arm, "I'm so glad. Maybe they'll get the other one now, and you can stop thinking about it so much."

I seriously doubt they will, he thought, but to Sheila he said, "Yes, I think; I hope it will be over soon. Now as much as I hate to tell you this, I can't stay till Monday. I'll have to leave in the morning."

Sheila's face showed her obvious disappointment. "But Henry, tomorrow is Christmas."

"Oh, jeez, sweetheart. I've been so caught up in my own world I didn't even realize it was that time. I'll tell you what, let me get caught up on what I absolutely need to do, and I'll make it up to you. I promise." She lay back on the bed and opened her robe. "Then we had better not waste the time we have, lover."

Henry removed his slacks, and she tossed her robe off the bed then straddled him. He pulled her down onto him and entered her, adoring the nakedness of the beautiful woman above him and the rocking motion of her hips as she moved on him.

An hour later, they lay satiated, basking in the afterglow of their union. "Well," she said, "maybe I could make us some dinner, and then if you're up to it, we could go again before bedtime."

Henry caressed her. "I think I've a little monster on my hands."

She smiled and rolled off the bed. "Maybe."

At six o'clock, Henry sat on the couch reading the newspaper, while Sheila was busy in the kitchen. Henry had offered to help, but she shooed him out. The story about Francis made the front page with the following account.

### MAN NEAR DEATH FOUND IN SOUTHSIDE PARK

Pittsburgh police were called to Southside Park across from Duquesne University at 3:30 a.m. on Saturday to find a man who had been severely beaten. Police arriving at the scene found Gilbert Francis of south Pittsburg wrapped in a U.S. Army blanket, lying on a bench across the street from the University. A police spokesman said Mr. Francis had been surgically altered and that his arms and legs had been broken in several places. The extent of the injuries were still being evaluated at the time this paper went to press.

Police said they had been unable to question Francis and that no motive had been established. Police theorize that due to the nature of the injuries, the incident was a crime of passion. A man, who had called in anonymously, according to police, said Francis was involved in a double rape and murder in Clarksville, Pennsylvania in June, as well as the murder of an interior decorator in Pittsburg two weeks ago. They said the caller did not identify himself and was not at the scene when police arrived. Police are trying to trace the origin of the blanket in which Francis was wrapped.

The Clarksville murders, still unsolved after six months, involved the rape and murder of Mary Jenkins, and her fifteen-year-old daughter, Linda. The daughter had turned fifteen on June twelfth, the day of the incident.

Clarksville police say that is still an open case, but they had no leads until the anonymous call in Pittsburg.

Henry leafed through the paper until he found an article on page eleven headlined,

**EXPLOSION ON ROUTE 28 STUMPS POLICE**

Pennsylvania State police were called to the scene of an explosion on Route 28 north of the city on Wednesday to find a crater six feet deep and almost twenty feet wide.

TFC Marvin Wilshire said it appeared as if a vehicle had exploded after going off the right side of the road and down the embankment. Trooper Wilshire said the vehicle appeared to be a van or SUV. Police have not, at this time, determined if the van lost control and went down the embankment. They said they have not determined the cause of the explosion or if the explosives were in the vehicle or if it was intentionally destroyed after it went off the road. A search was made of the area, but police found no one in or around the site of the explosion. Wilshire said a pyrotechnics expert has been called in to investigate the scene and that a variety of drugs were found at the sight.

Sheila called, telling him dinner was ready, so he folded the paper and went to eat.

# CHAPTER 47

Henry left Clarksville at 10:30 Sunday morning with a promise to Shelia that he would try to call her mid-week. The drive to Pittsburgh seemed overly long even though the speedometer told him he was pushing seventy. At 11:45, he pulled into the garage on Hunters Trail then went back to get the newspaper from the box. As he was walking back to the house, he noticed the footprints in the snow at the edge of the woods by the house.

Clutching the newspaper, he trotted up the driveway and went inside, closing the garage door behind him. Then quickly went downstairs and turned on the television monitor for the shelter. The set brightened and Henry used the joy stick control to scan the room. His heart raced when he didn't see Jefferson, but then he saw the chain going into the bathroom.

He waited almost three minutes before Jefferson left the bathroom, and breathed a sigh of relief when the man shuffled across the room to sit down on a chair.

Leaving the monitor running, he went back upstairs and looked out the kitchen window into the back yard. The footprints in the snow went about halfway back to where the shelter entrance used to be and then in longer strides came toward the back door. He ran through the house looking for any obvious entry point—there were none—before going back to the kitchen.

Henry studied the footprints for a few minutes before going back downstairs and to the workshop. There were scratch marks on the new lock Fred had installed. He opened that door and then going over opened the door to the shelter tunnel with the laser key. Flipping on the light, he went down the hallway to the shelter entrance. The dead bolt he had installed previously was still securely fastened, but he could see scratches on it too where someone had tried to jimmy it open. He rubbed his fingers across the marks thoughtfully and then returned to the workshop, closing the door behind him.

Someone had obviously been here, he thought, but who? Hampstead? The man looked old, tired, and malnourished. Certainly not the type to be out traipsing around in the snow and breaking into houses. But Francis had said he was Jefferson's stepfather, and looks could be deceiving. Was he so fond of his deviant stepson that a seventy-something-year-old man would take such risks? Was he afraid of what would happen if he didn't help him?

Next, how did he get in the house, Henry mused. I changed all the locks. Did they get the key I gave to Brenda? That was the only logical conclusion he could reach. He knew one thing, for sure. Before this day was through, he had a lot of work to do.

He got up from the couch, got in the Lincoln, and drove to Home Depot where he bought another lock for the front door. Returning, he got tools and replaced the lock again. That would eliminate anyone from entering that way.

Retrieving the dart gun and a dart from the Lincoln, he returned to the basement. The monitor showed him Jefferson had not moved. He sat down on the couch and loaded the dart into the gun and shoved the bolt home. He continued to watch the monitor. He did not want to open the shelter door with Jefferson sitting that close to it. The chain allowed the man to come about three feet into the hallway. He might be able to jump him before he could fire the weapon. It was better to wait, Henry thought, until the man made another trip to the bathroom before he opened the door.

He laid the gun on the coffee table and picked up the newspaper to peruse while he waited. Francis had again made the news with the following article.

Pennsylvania State Police today reported that the vehicle, determined to be a Dodge van destroyed by an explosion on Route 28, north of the city last Friday, belonged to a Gilbert Francis. Francis was the same man found beaten and dumped on a park bench near Duquesne University that same night.

TFC Marvin Wilshire, who has been the lead officer investigating the explosion, said a license plate found at the site was determined to be from the vehicle which belonged to Francis. Wilshire said that, as a result of the investigation, it was determined the vehicle had been forced off the road and later destroyed by a military grade plastic explosive. The source of the explosive material is still being investigated. He said the investigation showed that the van was forced off the road and down the embankment, but it was not initially clear if the explosion was caused by Francis or an outside influence.

Francis, found severely beaten and left on a park bench in Southside Park, was taken by ambulance to the University of Pittsburgh Medical Center, where he is currently undergoing physical and psychiatric evaluation. Attending physician, Dr. Mark Henley, said that he cannot divulge any of the injuries or the reason for the

mental evaluation due to doctor/patient
confidentially. Henley did say that while
Francis was coherent, he has not discussed
the situation with police or hospital
personnel.

Elated by that news, Henry cursed as he read further.

Henley, Chief Orthopedic Surgeon at
the center, indicated that Francis is
undergoing surgery to replace severely
broken joints with titanium prosthetics
and with extensive physical therapy, is
expected to regain partial use of his arms
and legs. Henley said, when questioned,
that that might be as high as 90 percent. He
said that, although Francis may never run
a marathon, he would be able to function
physically in a relatively normal manner.

Police, initially believing the incident was
a crime of passion, said after collecting
evidence at the sight of the vehicle, they
now believe the crime was drug related and
that the call made anonymously was to try
to throw the police off course.

Henry threw down the paper with mixed emotions. With the
police thinking the incident was drug related, it took the heat off of
him. However, if through the efforts of modern medicine, Francis was
going to be as good as new, he obviously had not done his job very well.

He sat staring at the monitor. Jefferson was eating from a can of
something he had got from one of the shelves.

At two o'clock, Jefferson again went to the bathroom. Henry
grabbed the gun and quickly unlocked and opened the door to the

shelter. When Jefferson stuck his head out of the john, Henry had the gun aimed and ready.

Jefferson slunk from the bathroom, eyeing Henry warily as he zipped his pants. A growing dark spot on his jeans indicated he hadn't finished when Henry opened the door. He stood for a moment then said, "You're dead motherfucker."

Henry pulled the trigger. As the dart slammed into Jefferson's right side, his expression was much the same as when Henry had shot him at the Shamrock. "You know, Mr. Jefferson, for a man in chains who is about to be castrated, you have a strange sense of what is actually happening or going to happen."

Jefferson yanked the dart from his side and rushed toward Henry. "You bastard! You dirty . . ."

Henry jerked the door closed and stepped back. He heard a muffled thump as Jefferson hit the door and then fell to the floor. While he waited to make sure the man was unconscious, he took the gun into the workshop and laid it on the bench then picked up the tools he needed.

When he next opened the door, Jefferson lay on the floor, the dart clutched in his hand. Henry removed the dart and thought about binding and then waiting to castrate the man until he regained consciousness, as he had done with Francis. Deciding he had too much to do to wait, he removed his testicles with the scalpel and then dressed and bandaged the incision. He flushed the testes down the toilet and cleaned up the room before going back to the workshop, leaving the door open.

While Jefferson slept, Henry removed the peg board and door frame at the workshop and using a chisel and hammer removed the necessary half blocks from the opening. He was mixing mortar in the mortar pan when Jefferson started to awaken.

First, there was groaning noises coming from the room, followed shortly afterward by a long string of obscenities when he realized he was missing part of his manhood. "You sonuvabitch! You miserable bastard! You cut my balls off."

The screaming was close to crying as the man appeared in the doorway at the shelter end of the tunnel.

Henry looked at him, smiling. "Did you think I was joking with you, Mr. Jefferson? How does it feel to know you will never be able to do more than piss out of that thing again?"

Jefferson cupped his crotch with his hands. "You bastard, when I get out of here . . ."

Henry laughed as he interrupted, "Uh-uh, Mr. Jefferson. You see, you're very wrong already. You are never going to get out of there. That room is your home and will, in time, be your tomb."

"Screw you, asshole. I'll get out, and when I do, your ass is mine."

Henry troweled mortar onto the floor of the opening and began placing blocks into the wet mucilage. "Mr. Jefferson, did you ever read *The Cask of Amontillado*?"

Jefferson looked blank. "Huh?"

Henry slathered mortar on another block and laid it in place as he continued. "*The Cask of Amontillado*, Mr. Jefferson, a short story by Edgar Allen Poe. You see, I must apologize, I'm not being innovative here. What I'm doing here is neither new nor creative. I got this idea from that story. You ought to read it, if you have that ability. I believe I saw a book of Poe's works in one of those boxes. That story is probably included. I know you will have plenty of time to find it."

Henry mortared and set the next tier of blocks in place as he talked. "To whet your appetite for Mr. Poe, so to speak, let me explain a bit of the story to you."

"But first, let me explain what I have done so far to assure you will remain a guest in my shelter." Henry set another block in place. "I've destroyed the microphones. You may already know that. I expect your stepfather told you they weren't working or weren't working correctly."

He looked up at Jefferson. "I also destroyed the outside entrance. No one will be able to access your little domain from that side."

He scraped excess mortar from the block. "I can see by your expression that you didn't know that. It was such a nuisance, you see.

People kept coming in there, and then one day, I found this cubby hole with a bunch of keys that fit the shackles. That really bothered me because I thought that even if I got rid of those keys, there might be others."

He began the next tier of blocks. "Anyway, it bothered me so much that I just put some explosives in there and boom. The entry was gone, along with access to any keys."

Henry smiled at Jefferson who was now listening attentively. "It also got rid of that ugly mound of dirt in the back yard. That was really an eyesore anyway. Don't you think? So next, I caught your co-conspirator, the Snowman."

Henry looked at Jefferson and placed another block. "I can see that bothers you too. Now, he can't help you because I broke his arms and legs and left him dying on a park bench. Oh, and I also castrated him. So you see, you are, for now, in better shape than he. The only thing is he will probably live, as he is now in the hospital, and you will surely die here."

Henry put down mortar for the next tier. By the way, did you know someone was down here while I was gone, trying to get you out?"

Jefferson showed some interest at this but said nothing.

Henry nodded. "Well, I guess you could have. Even though the room is soundproof, someone working directly on the door would be heard. The only problem was I had replaced the lock, and whoever it was couldn't get it open. Who was that, Darnell? Was it your stepfather, Hampstead?"

Henry looked at him. "You don't have a very good poker face, Mr. Jefferson. I can tell, from your expression, that it was him. Francis, or if you prefer, the Snowman, told me he was. It's too bad scum like you has relatives. It just makes the job harder. I guess it was my fault, though, he came into the house. I have a burglar alarm. I just forgot to set it when I went away for the weekend. Do you think that was a Freudian slip, Mr. Jefferson?"

He sat another block in place and tamped it down. Straightening, he laid the trowel down and said, "Oh, I was going to tell you about the

*Cask of Amontillado.* Let me grab a beer, sorry you can't have one, and I'll give you a rundown on the story."

Henry got a beer from the refrigerator and, returning, sipped it as he talked. "It seems, in the story, that this one man had dishonored the other. Sounds a bit like our situation, doesn't it, Mr. Jefferson. Of course, in the story, the culprit wasn't quite the piece of garbage you are. He didn't rape and kill innocent women and children. Nor did he pistol whip them and shoot them as they lay dying. But I guess you have to be a real piece of low life shit to do that. Don't you agree?"

"But to the story. The man who had been dishonored took the other to his wine cellar on the pretext of showing him some vintage wine. When he got him down there, he shackled him to a wall and then bricked up the entry. Naturally, the story ended there, but you get the point, I'm sure. The man died of starvation with no one to help him."

Henry smiled. "A horrible way to die. Don't you agree, Mr. Jefferson? The way you're going to die, only more slowly."

Henry saw a glint of perspiration on Jefferson's brow. "I can see you are starting to get the idea of where this is going. So let me confirm it in your mind. I guess—no, I'm sure—you and I are more depraved than Poe's characters. You raped, bludgeoned, and killed my wife and daughter as surely as Francis did. At this point, it doesn't matter what specific role you played. You beat them, trying to bring them down to your level. You humiliated them and subjected them to evils only they could have imagined. But Mr. Jefferson, nothing living or dead could reach the depths 'of depravity where you maintain your serpentine existence."

You see, even to the depths you have brought me in taking care of this situation, I could never reach sinking as low as you."

Henry swigged his beer. "Yet, you certainly helped me to lower my moral values, or at least shown me that I can live my life without remorse for what I have done, am doing, and will do. I gave some thought to just killing you both, but that was letting you off too easy. Then I gave some thought to making you a vegetable, but I find joints can be replaced with titanium. Damned shame, isn't it? Now I'm going to have to start all over with your buddy because the doctors say they can fix him. As a result, for you, I find my present plan is the best. Don't you agree?"

Henry gestured toward the food shelves behind Jefferson. "I figure you have enough food on those shelves to last about two years, if you are frugal. I was going to leave all the drugs that I found in the cabinet, but then, I thought you would just stay high or overdose and die before you had time to reflect on your crimes and how you were going to die."

Henry smiled and picked up the trowel. "Maybe, if you're lucky, you'll go crazy. That would be easier for you. But one thing you can bet on, Mr. Jefferson, your life, and what's left of it, will be spent in this dungeon, alone with your remorse, if you even feel remorse. Some things are sure, you will never hurt anyone again, and every moment you have left, you can remember the acts that put you here."

Henry picked up a block, mortared the ends, and set it in place. "Even Hampstead can't help you now."

Jefferson was perspiring freely now, even though the temperature in the shelter was seventy-two degrees. "Listen, Jenkins. I didn't kill your wife and kid. It was . . ."

Henry whirled around glaring at him. "You are just as guilty as Francis. Your semen was in them. Your DNA was on them. Do you think I would forgive you for your role in that? Only Mary, Linda, Brenda, or God can forgive you, and three of them are dead because you. If you want forgiveness, you better take a hard look to God because you will get none on this earth."

Jefferson straightened up. "The Bible says, 'judge not, lest you be judged.'"

Henry laughed. "Well, I see you know of the Bible even though you don't practice its teachings. The Bible also says and eye for an eye and a tooth for a tooth. I'm only taking the eye and the tooth. I will let God judge me for what I am doing, just as he will judge you when I am done with you."

He strode into the workshop, got the dart gun, and hopping the partial wall, went down the hallway toward the shelter. When Jefferson saw the gun, he started backing away from the door and toward the bathroom. Henry reached for the door and slammed it shut. He breathed a sigh of relief when the lock snapped shut. Two hours later, what had been a doorway was a continuation of the block wall in the workshop.

The next day, he painted the workshop, including the renovated wall, noting that there was no difference in continuity. Removing the locking mechanism from the pegboard, he attached a simple hook latch and hung tools on both sides. He assessed the work and nodded with satisfaction in the result.

Darnell Jefferson had effectively vanished from the face of the earth.

# CHAPTER 48

Henry sat in the rec room two months later. He made the trip to Hunters Trail every couple of weeks to check on his "guest" and to assure himself that nothing was happening at the house. Occasionally, he would bring Sheila with him, and they would stay the weekend. Sheila was impressed with the house and the interior design. She had told Henry she would like to meet the interior decorator, but he informed her that she had died shortly after the work was done. She wanted to know details, but he told her he didn't know. He had just seen the obituary in the paper.

This trip she had not come with him, and he sat watching Darnell Jefferson on the monitor as he flipped through the news. Gilbert Francis was no longer newsworthy, and 'Doonesbury' had nothing controversial to denigrate the President for. Henry noticed that Jefferson had begun to read from the stock of books he had access to. It looked like the one he currently held was the writings of Poe, and Henry wondered if he had read *The Cask of Amontillado* yet.

Henry picked up a pencil and turned to the crossword puzzle in the paper. He gave up when he got down to six letters missing (what the hell was a twelve letter word for wilts disease anyway) and was laying the paper down when the doorbell rang.

He jumped at the unexpected sound then put down the paper and pencil and turned the television to a cable news station. Starting up the steps, he hesitated, and then returning to the table beside the couch, he picked up the magnum and went up the steps. As he did so, he pulled out his shirt tail and stuck the revolver in his waist band, concealing it with his shirt.

A look through the sidelight of the front door told him that Bartholomew Jephthah Hampstead had come to visit.

Assuring himself the revolver was covered, he opened the door. "Mr. Hampstead," he said, looking surprised, "I didn't expect to see you again. What brings you out this way?"

Hampstead snorted. "Cut the crap, Jenkins. You know why I'm here. Can we talk?"

Henry continued with his naïve innocence. "Why certainly, sir. Did you leave something here when you sold me the house that you didn't intend to leave? I can assure you, I have completely renovated the house, and I have found nothing."

Hampstead's normally ashen pallor was even grayer. "May I come in, sir? What I have to say or offer may have beneficial and financial interest to you."

Henry wanted to slam the door in the man's face. Instead, he stepped aside and waved him in. "Certainly, although I see no way we could have financial dealings. I mean, the house was paid for, in cash, and an amount you were quite agreeable with."

Hampstead strode past him and, without hesitation as to where he should go, went downstairs to the rec room with Henry following. He sat down on the couch uninvited.

Henry claimed the recliner and, using the arm as cover, removed the revolver and put it down beside him. "So, Mr. Hampstead, what sort of interesting things have you come to propose to me?"

Hampstead clamped his hands together to stop them trembling and, taking a deep breath, looked at Henry. "Mr. Jenkins. There is no sense playing word games with each other, so I will come straight to the point. I'm here because you've got the boy, and I want him back. You name the price you want."

Henry wanted to grab the gun and shoot him. However, logic

prevailed. "Mr. Hampstead, I'm going to say I really don't have any idea as to what you are talking about. However, for the sake of argument, what amount of money, or the price as you put it, are we talking about?"

Hampstead leaned back on the couch, apparently more at ease with Henry's presumed interest. "As I said, you name it. I was thinking in terms of, say five hundred thousand."

Henry ached to put a bullet between the man's eyes. "So, what you're telling me is that, to you, the rape, mutilation, and murder of my wife and daughter and my friend are worth half a million dollars. Is that what you're telling me? That's the price of their suffering, humiliation, and deaths?"

Henry paused but continued before Hampstead could respond, his voice raised in anger. "You are, with your values, about as deserving of life as those pieces of garbage that committed those crimes. Do you think I married and had a daughter so I could sell their life blood to Francis and Jefferson? Do you think your fucking money can buy back what they, and you by association, have destroyed?"

Henry forced his voice back to a low timbre. "You are sick, Hampstead. You are low and common and don't deserve any better than what they deserve." He settled back in his seat and smiled. "But, Mr. Hampstead, I don't know what you're talking about. As you can see, I am here alone."

Hampstead had leaned forward during Henry's tirade. His hands trembled and he rubbed his arm as he spoke. "Mr. Jenkins, I realize money cannot replace the monumental loss you have incurred or the suffering you must live with. That was not my intention in the offer. The money is not to buy or replace your family, but for me to buy back the life of my stepson. His death by your hand will not, cannot, replace your loss, but if retaliation for your loss is what you intend, you are lowering your own moral values to his."

Henry bolted upright in his chair. "Let me tell you something, you doddering old bastard. I have never beat a woman or raped little children. I have never humiliated nor degraded even an animal the way your stepson did my wife and daughter. And if that wasn't enough, came back to do the same to my friend. So don't give me bullshit about lowering my moral values. My values, regardless of what I might do to them, could never be that low."

Henry glared at the man across from him. "If you want to talk about values, look at your own sick values. You knew what they had done, yet you didn't turn them in to the authorities. You condoned their crimes by doing nothing. You may as well have been there with them."

He leaned back. "How many others, Hampstead? How many others have you helped them rape and brutalize and kill by your inaction? How many others have you tried to pay off, or have paid off, to protect that piece of slime?"

Hampstead rubbed his arm. "Mr. Jenkins, I am not here to discuss your, or my, moral fiber. I am not here to claim guilt or innocence for the boy or myself. I have the money to give you, a million—two million, if necessary. If it is any consolation to you, I will send him out of the country. All I want to do is spare his life."

Henry laughed. "What, so your psychosexual madman can rape and kill children in Europe, or Canada, or Mexico instead of Pennsylvania? Hampstead, you must think I'm a fucking lunatic."

Hampstead inhaled raggedly, continuing to rub his arm. "Let me try to explain something to you, Mr. Jenkins. Its meaning may not have near the impact on you that I would like, but I hope you will at least keep an open mind."

Henry shrugged. "Sure, go ahead. Tell me."

"I was married to my wife, God rest her soul, when the boy was nine. He came from a home where they were beaten almost daily for any perceived infraction and abused continuously. The boy suffered a great deal emotionally and physically during that time. Afterward, we sent him for counseling with some of the best psychiatrists in the country. I'm not saying that should excuse his actions in his adult life, but it certainly would influence how he looks at life. However, I promised my dear wife, who died five years ago from cancer, that I would look after and provide for the boy until I died. That, sir, is all I am trying to do."

Henry, without emotion, looked at the old man, who sat massaging his arm. He wanted to gag or rip down the wall he had constructed and put him in with his 'boy.' Instead, he sat quietly for several minutes willing his body to relax, forcing the adrenalin to stop coursing through his bloodstream. When he was reasonably calm, he spoke softly. "Mr. Hampstead, when I returned home a couple of months ago, I noticed footprints in the snow around the house and indications, in the house, that you were here. How did you get in my house?"

"Sir," Hampstead replied, "I can assure you I took nothing. My only interest here was the boy, and when I found he was inaccessible, I left the way I came in, through an unlocked window in the kitchen which someone had left open."

Henry nodded. That accounted for the footprints onto the back porch. He had opened the window one morning when he overheated a skillet and apparently forgot to relock it. He was just kind of amazed that the old man could navigate through it.

"Another thing, when you sold me the house, you left tools, foodstuffs, and more importantly, a large cache of drugs and explosives here that had more street value than the house was worth. Can you explain that?"

Hampstead continued to rub his arm and shoulder, his pallor was becoming grayer. He again inhaled raggedly and appeared to be in discomfort. "The foodstuff and tools were for practical reasons, Mr. Jenkins. I found out what the boys did after I read the newspaper accounts. I confronted them, and Darnell told me what happened."

"As you might assume, Mr. Jenkins, I am a wealthy man. When I got all the information I could from the boys and the newspapers, I hired some people to investigate you and your life. By the time they were done, I knew you as well as I know myself, and I tried to guess how you would retaliate if you caught them. Because of the way you reacted to situations in your youth, I decided, given the right circumstances, you would react that way again."

My God, Henry thought, do childhood indiscretions follow you all your life?

Hampstead continued. "Anyway, I decided to play a long shot, and when your house burnt, I bought this one for resale to you because I thought it would appeal to you, as you see it did. Then, and continuing to think ahead, much like a chess game, I came up with ideas on how I might influence you in restraining but not permanently harming the boys, hence the restraints and dart guns. I even reduced the amount of fluid in the darts, so they would not be fatal to humans. I might add I didn't consider you would be as violent as you were with the Francis boy."

It seemed Hampstead liked to talk, and Henry had no problem understanding the man and his thinking, so he let him continue.

"As for stocking the shelves; I am not a well man, Mr. Jenkins, and the boys didn't know where the extra keys were. I'm sure you found them, or you wouldn't have taken the extra precaution of destroying the outside entry. In any case, I stocked the shelves to provide provisions for them in case my health failed. There is one more set of keys in that event. However, they would never find them until all their provisions were used up. That is unless you found them, which I'm sure you haven't. I figured, in case that happened, they had enough to sustain them for a year, and then they could let themselves out."

"I bought the restraints at an antique sale with the idea that if you had them, you would use them. I guessed you would enchain the boys for a period of time, and that after some time for them to consider the error of their ways, I would take them off your hands. Apparently, your chess game is as good as mine. Either you thought the situation through, or you got lucky."

"As for the dart guns, I figured you had never killed anyone and probably didn't have the propensity to do so. I figured if you had a ready means to stop them, you would probably not go to a more lethal weapon. I am not a man of violent nature, Mr. Jenkins. I do not believe in willful destruction, in your case or theirs. I was totally devastated by their acts and spent many nights trying to decide how to handle the situation. Perhaps I didn't handle it in the best way but nor did I handle it in the worst."

"I believe they even contemplated killing you. I convinced them that you would let no irreparable harm come to them if they would let me handle the situation. I assured them everything would turn out for the best for all concerned."

"As for the drugs and explosives, those were not mine or my idea. I didn't know they were here until I was moving the boys out after selling you the house. I suggested they leave them, which they did. I found out later that they had come back to retrieve some of them. After that, I hid the keys, so they would have no access."

Hampstead pushed on his chest and grimaced as he coughed. "If I might ask you a question, Mr. Jenkins, when did you become aware I had done these things for your benefit?"

Henry shrugged. "At this point, that doesn't matter. Does it? Tell me instead why they killed the lady that did the interior work here."

Hampstead shook his head. "I don't know what they had in mind, at the time, and would have stopped them had I known. That was all the Francis boy's doing, not Darnell. Francis said as much time as she was spending with you, you must have some attraction to her. He figured, if he killed her, you would be scared enough to back off from your quest."

Henry shook his head in amazement. "That is probably one of the dumbest fucking things I have ever heard. If anything, I would be even more infuriated and more determined to see it through, and even though you would like me to believe it was all Francis, you and I both know it was both of them."

"So, let's look at the facts," Henry began. "Your stepson and Francis brutally and willfully tortured, raped, and killed my wife, daughter, and the woman who redecorated my home. There are probably others, but they can't be my concern, even though Francis and Jefferson will pay for them too. They destroyed my home, not only in their desire to get money, but just for the sake of destruction."

"I don't think it was a first time thing, Mr. Hampstead, and you probably know it's not. It was too well planned, just as it was for Brenda Cartier. I haven't looked into their pasts, nor do I care to do so at this time. If I did, I would probably throw up with what I found. I may do so in the future to lend some closure to anyone else they have harmed. Maybe they hadn't killed anyone before, maybe they had, but drugs don't come free, Hampstead. The money I caught Francis with did not come through charitable contributions. They've lied, stolen, brutalized, and killed to obtain the things they wanted. If I have anything to do with it, and I do, they will never have the ability to do it again."

"Hampstead, you can be assured, I am their judge, jury, and executioner. You call it what you want. You had the opportunity, and the money, to stop them before this started. You could have sent them out of the country. You didn't. No, Hampstead, I won't relinquish my opportunity to give them what they deserve for five hundred thousand, or two million, or any amount of money. As I said before, you are just like them. You had an opportunity to do it right, but for whatever reason, ties, greed, or fear, you chose not to do so."

"That tells me, if you did buy his, their, release, they would be back on the streets, and I would be dead soon after. So, no, Hampstead. The ball is in my court, and I will play it. I will decide the punishment, and I will mete it out as I choose."

"You are scum, Hampstead, just like they are. If I were to look into your past, as you have done mine, I expect I would find a man who got his wealth the same way they did, and you probably did the same things they did when you were younger. I expect you deserve to die just as they deserve to die and probably deserved it long ago."

"The only reason you're sitting here right now is because you weren't in my house with them last June. If you had been, or if I even thought you had been, old man or not, I would kill you. However, I am not one to cure the ills of the whole world nor to expunge vermin like you from it. I'm just cleaning up my world, so it never happens again and, from those two, it won't."

"Hampstead, you said you made a promise to your wife. Well, I made a promise to my wife too that whoever did that to them would never do it to anyone else. I didn't quite keep that promise when it came to Brenda Cartier, but I can keep it now. I don't give a rat's ass about you, your promises, or anything else. Since you have, as you said, psychic abilities, why don't you conjure up your dead wife's spirit and tell her the piece of shit she called a son is finally going to get what he deserves."

Hampstead gasped at the reference to his wife. "Jenkins, I beseech you not to do this thing. I can make you a very wealthy man, and I assure you that no harm will come to you as a result. I just beg you to return my stepson to me. Do what you will, but I pray, give me my son."

Henry laughed facetiously. "You old bastard, I think if I told you to kill Francis, and I'd give you Jefferson, you would do it."

Hampstead grimaced at the tightening in his chest. "If you will agree, I will do that, and I will give you the money."

Henry sneered. "I really should kill you. You're evil and fucking garbage. Let me explain something to you. You lied to me. You told me your wife had a stroke but was alive. Secondly, you set me up, or tried to set me up from the start. I'm still not sure of the reason, unless you're just bat shit crazy. In any event, I found you were setting me up and, as a result, was able to stay a step ahead of you. Third, if we were talking about stealing cookies or killing some kid's pet gerbil, I could be compassionate, but we are not talking about a child's indiscretion. We're talking about rape and murder that was done horrifically. We're talking about drugs that are sold to kids that kill them or turn their brains to mush. We're talking about humiliation and degradation in its basest possible form."

"So my response to you, Hampstead, is no. I don't have your son here as you can see, and even if I did, you'd never get him back."

Hampstead raised his voice. "I know you have him. He's in the shelter."

Henry raised his eyebrow quizzically. "Shelter, Mr. Hampstead? What shelter? I don't know what you are talking about."

Hampstead's complexion grew even more ashen and a tic had developed in his left eyelid. "Yes, you do, Jenkins. You filled in the outside entrance and changed the lock on the inner door to keep me from getting to him."

"Mr. Hampstead, I believe your mind may be playing tricks on you. There was an old root cellar out back which I had filled in because I was afraid a child might wander in there and the roof would collapse. I know nothing about any shelter. Are you sure your advanced age is not making you senile?"

Hampstead's voice was shrill as he jumped up, holding his hand against his chest and striding toward and through the workshop. "Yes, you do. You changed the lock so I can't get him out. You destroyed the outside entry, so I can't get to my keys."

Henry, holding the revolver to his side and slightly behind, followed. "Your keys, Mr. Hampstead? Any keys here would legally become mine with the sale of the house."

"Mr. Hampstead, you tell me you've been in my home when I haven't been here. Let's see, don't they call that breaking and entering? Maybe you should call the police with your theories. I'm sure they would be interested in a closed up shelter entrance, but even more so by a rapist and murderer. Then what would you do, Mr. Hampstead? Would you try to bribe them, let them know you were harboring scum?"

Reaching the pegboard, Hampstead produced a laser key similar to the one he had given Henry and pointed it at the now defunct hole.

Henry let him try it several times, then said, "Excuse me, Mr. Hampstead. What in the world are you trying to do?"

Hampstead pushed the laser button several more times. "You've done something to the lock. It won't open."

Henry reached over and lifted the simple latch. "Is this what you mean, Mr. Hampstead?"

Hampstead grabbed the hinged peg board and swung it around. A strange, wretched noise came from his throat when he was confronted with a block wall behind it, and he grabbed at his chest.

Under other circumstances, Henry might have felt sorry for the man, but right now, all he could think of was that knowing what Francis and Jefferson had done, he had done nothing.

"You've killed him," he rasped, his hand clutching his chest.

"Killed him, Mr. Hampstead?" Henry asked perplexed. "Killed who? I don't understand."

"I know he's in there," Hampstead said as he sagged against the wall, trying to suck air through the tightness in his chest. "You must give him to me."

Henry hopped up on the workbench and sat facing Hampstead, his legs dangling over the side. "That's right, Mr. Hampstead. I'd forgotten. You're psychic. You know all things. Well, perhaps with your psychic abilities, you can tell me how this turns out."

Hampstead reached for his pocket, and Henry picked up the revolver, leveling it on the man's chest. "Uh-uh, Mr. Hampstead. Keep your hand away from the pocket."

Hampstead grimaced and slid slowly, almost comically, to the floor. "For God's sake, Jenkins, let him out."

Henry was tired of the game. "For God's sake, Mr. Hampstead? For God's sake? God has nothing to do with this. When that man was a child, you as an adult were responsible for him. If you coddled him because of prior abuse, you are as guilty as the one who abused him. If you were overly lenient with him, you condoned his actions, maybe even encouraged them. However, when he became an adult, he became responsible. No, Hampstead. God has nothing to do with this. If God were responsible, it would never have happened."

"He stays, Hampstead. He stays there, by himself to reflect on what he has done, and when the time comes, he will die there. It was his choice to do what he has done and yours to allow it. Now, the choices are mine. May you both rot in Hell."

Hampstead, struggling for breath, opened his mouth and looking at Henry, rasped, "And you too, sir."

He shuddered and wet himself as his head slumped forward on his chest.

Henry slid off the workbench and put the gun in the drawer below the top. He walked over to Hampstead and checked the man's pulse at his neck and then at his wrist. He reached into the pocket the man had reached for and pulled out not a gun but a bottle of nitroglycerin tablets. He put the bottle back, and pulling out his phone, dialed nine-one-one.

When the call was answered, he said, "An elderly gentleman who was visiting me in my home has had, I believe, a heart attack. I need an ambulance to come and get him. I believe he is quite dead." Pause, "My name and address?"

He gave them the information and then went back to the rec room to sip a beer and wait for the ambulance.

# CHAPTER 49

Henry heard the siren of the approaching ambulance and went upstairs. When it pulled into the driveway, he opened the door to see it was preceded by an unmarked police car. Henry waited as a man exited the police car and came to the door while the EMTs were getting the stretcher from the back of the ambulance.

"Mr. Jenkins," he said extending his hand, "I'm detective Roberts."

Henry took the proffered hand and said, "I'm not sure I need a police officer. The man just keeled over in my basement."

"It's just routine, Mr. Jenkins. Anytime there is a death in a private home, the police are required to make a report. You say the man is in the basement?"

Henry nodded. "Yeah, you can go on down. The stairs are right there. Just go to the right when you get there. I'll wait for these guys."

The detective walked inside, and Henry waited as the others came to the door and then followed Henry downstairs.

The cop was checking for a pulse when they entered the workshop. "How long ago did this happen, Mr. Jenkins?"

Henry shook his head. "Not that long. I called 9-1-1 within a minute of him collapsing. So that time plus whatever time it took you guys to get here."

The cop straightened and took Henry's arm. "We can go in the other room and let these guys work."

They went into the rec room, and Henry indicated a seat for the cop who sat down with a pad and pencil.

"Mr. Jenkins, can you tell me who the gentleman is and what his relationship is to you?"

"Sure," Henry said sitting down on the recliner. "His name is Bartholomew Hampstead. I think he told me his middle name was Jephthah, or something like that. I don't know how to spell it, although I could find it for you. Mr. Hampstead is the gentleman who sold me this house. He said that he was nearby and thought he would drop in to see how I liked the place now that I had been her for a few months."

"Mm-hmm," the cop said writing on his pad. He looked up at Henry. "Mr. Jenkins, I had the opportunity to talk to a detective downtown and a Clarksville detective on the phone on the way out here. It seems there are a lot of people dying around you for some reason."

Henry nodded sadly. "Yes, sir. I lost my wife and daughter a few months ago. That's true."

Roberts eyed him. "I believe that is not all, from what I gather. It seems the lady who did some work for you also died."

"Regrettably, that is also true."

Roberts looked at his pad. "Then there seems to be some connection with a man that was beaten in Pittsburgh that had the same DNA as one of the people involved in both cases."

"Yes, Mr. Cameron, in Clarksville told me that. Thank God they got him."

"And now, it seems, a friend of his is missing and has been for over two months."

Henry shook his head. "Well, I wouldn't know anything about that."

The ambulance guys brought the stretcher carrying Hampstead through, spoke to the cop, and went upstairs and out. Henry heard the front door close.

Roberts continued. "Well, now it seems this missing friend's name is Darnell Jefferson. Do you know that name, Mr. Jenkins?"

Henry again shook his head. "No, can't say as I do."

Roberts stared at him. "Would it surprise you to know that is the name of Hampstead's stepson, Mr. Jenkins?"

"Really!" Henry acted surprised. "Mr. Hampstead didn't mention that."

"Are you sure, Mr. Jenkins?"

"Oh, absolutely. I would never forget that if he had mentioned it. You said he was this other man's friend, the one who they think murdered my wife and daughter. Do you think this man who's missing is the other one involved in that?"

Roberts frowned. "Mr. Jenkins, my question is do you have something to do with the man being missing?"

"Oh, goodness no, Detective. I know very little about the case, or cases, and you all don't keep me informed on anything."

"Mr. Jenkins, I understand you bought this house from Hampstead after the deaths of your wife and daughter. Why was that?"

"Well, as you know, if you talked to Detective Cameron, my house burned down not long after that, apparently due to some damage caused by the guys that invaded my home. I was looking for another place away from the memories of that, and this house was on the market. Nothing clandestine about that. I would say you could talk to Mr. Hampstead, but as you saw, he is dead. And now, you tell me his stepson is missing, so you can't ask him either."

Roberts frowned again. "I wouldn't try to be cute, Jenkins. You are already a suspect in the beating incident and, as a result of that, the missing man. If it turns out there is anything suspect in Hampstead's death, you can be assured I will be back out here."

"I'm not being cute, Detective, just factual. Instead of looking at me, perhaps you should be looking to see who else these people have raped and/or killed, and who else might despise them."

"I'm looking at you, Mr. Jenkins, because of what you said to Detective Cameron. No cop and no justice system likes vigilante justice. I don't care how justified it might seem to you. With that in mind, can you tell me where you were the night of December twenty-third, the night Francis was beaten?"

Henry laughed, "I can barely remember yesterday, let alone over two months ago. So no, I can't tell you."

Roberts wrote on his pad. "Then can you tell me where you were December twenty-forth, the day Jefferson went missing?"

"Nope, can't do that either."

"So you have no alibi for the time of either incident?"

"Hell, I don't know. Do you know where you are every day of your life?"

"I'm not the one who is a suspect, Mr. Jenkins."

"Well, if I'd known I was going to be one, I would have had someone attached to my hip."

Roberts stood and closed his note pad and stood. "We will find the answers, Mr. Jenkins. You can bet on that. You had better hope it's not you. Do you mind if I look around your house?"

Henry smiled. "No problem. Just as soon as you bring a warrant. If you're looking to hang me out to dry, I'm not going to help you."

Roberts walked toward and then up the steps. "That's fine, Mr. Jenkins. If I find there is any suspicion concerning Hampstead's death, I will be back, and I will have that warrant."

"I have no doubt, Detective. Now you have a good day."

Henry showed him out and closed the door.

# CHAPTER 50

Over a year had passed since Mary and Linda had died. Henry decided, he told Sheila, he didn't really care for the house on Hunters Trail after all, or its location back in the woods, and he planned on selling it when the market picked up.

There were really two very good reasons he didn't want to move there. One, it was where he and Brenda had their love nest. Two, it was where Jefferson was ensconced, and as soon as that situation was resolved, he didn't want to be there any longer. The idea of having the man buried in his back yard had no appeal at all.

He still made the drive down to check on Jefferson sporadically, but most of his time was spent at Sheila's, which suited her just fine.

They had flown out to visit with Fred and Midge in Denver in May. Midge was happy that Henry had found another love interest and, to her, just as sweet and lovely as Mary had been. Henry agreed, and didn't say but thought, and a fantastic lover. Midge asked if there were wedding bells in the future, but they both demurred, and Fred told her it was no business of theirs until or unless they were told.

While the women went shopping, Henry gave Fred the most recent lowdown on his activities over a couple of beers. The police, State, Pittsburgh, and Clarksville had backed off. They said the cases were still open, but they, and Henry, knew not a lot of effort was being put into them. Henry told Fred of his plans for the house at Hunters Trail.

Once Jefferson had finished his life sentence with no parole, Henry would implode the shelter and fill the crater. When that had grown over, he would sell the place. He was sure, with the shelter almost twenty feet underground, no one was going to be digging down that deep.

Then, if things continued to go as he and Sheila planned, they would build a new home somewhere as yet to be determined.

When he had checked the monitor at Hunters Trail on their return home, Henry noted that Jefferson had been using a spoon handle to chip away at the concrete around his restraint eyebolt. He figured the food would run out about fifty years before he got the eyebolt loose.

Also, the food supply was going down much faster than Henry had thought. At least half of it was gone, and Jefferson had picked up weight. He was getting to be almost obese, as a matter of fact. Henry guessed with nothing else to do and no drugs to keep him thin, all he had to occupy his time was eating. He rotated the monitor to look at the rest of the room. The empty food cans and boxes were just thrown over to one corner. A closer look with the zoom lens showed he didn't bother to even rinse out the containers. The smell in there must be horrendous, Henry thought. Well, at the rate he was going, he probably wouldn't have food for more than six to eight more months, and with the unhealthy environment he was creating, his life expectancy might be less than that.

In August, he turned on the monitor at Hunters Trail and got a shock by what he saw. The blue, bloated corpse of Darnell Jefferson lying amid the rancid debris on the floor. He had apparently decided he could not chip away the concrete, so he had sharpened the spoon handle and slit the veins in both arms. He must have bled out in a very short time.

Gagging, Henry ran to the bathroom and retched violently in the toilet. He felt like he upchucked everything he had eaten in a week. The scene in the shelter had been horrific. He didn't even want to go back to turn off the monitor. Catching his breath and splashing cold water on his face and into his mouth for several minutes, he again felt like he could progress with what he had to do.

First, he went to the rec room and turned off then disconnected the monitor. Next, he went through and ripped out the wiring in the rec room, the workshop, and into the wall going toward the shelter. When he had gathered all the material that could possibly belong to the system, he carried it all up and put it in the trunk of his car to be deposited in a dumpster somewhere along the way home.

When that was done, he called an excavating company he had previously contacted and ordered twenty truckloads of fill dirt and three truckloads of topsoil to fill a sinkhole in his back yard. They would be able to deliver beginning at ten o'clock tomorrow. He then got the detonator, put in a new battery, and with a grand wha-woomp, the ground in the back yard suddenly sunk eight feet. Although the underground implosion was muffled by the ground above and made almost no noise, it shook the windows in the house, and he wondered if the neighbors felt the vibration.

The next day, the dirt was delivered as promised and the hole filled and graded over. The site foreman told Henry the slight rise would eventually level out as the dirt settled and found its permanent level. He suggested that Henry go ahead and put down fertilizer and grass seed so it would have a good root system before winter.

Henry had a landscape company come out the following week, for premium pay, to do the work and plant some bushes that would hide the fill. When he saw the completed work, he felt the extra money for the short turnaround was well worth it.

In September, Henry had stopped at a whole foods store. He picked up a couple of items for a recipe Sheila had found on the internet and wanted to try. On his way home, he felt someone was following him and began evasive driving actions down several side streets and alleys around Clarksville. Fifteen minutes later, he was pulled over by the police and arrested for having drugs in the car. Fortunately, he was in the Cadillac and the Lincoln was safe in the garage on Hunters Trail. He was fingerprinted and booked at the Clarksville Police Station, and the car was towed to the impound lot. Once booked, he was allowed his one phone call. That call was to a friend he had known for several years through philanthropic work they had done together. His friend asked to talk to the police captain, and Henry relayed the message.

Captain Fontaine, irritated by the interruption, picked up the phone in his office and snipped, "This is Captain Fontaine. Who is this?"

The man at the other end of the phone call introduced himself, and the captain paled as he heard, and then replied to, the response. "Yes, Governor, how can I help you?"

"Captain, I understand you have Henry Jenkins in custody there."

"Yes, sir, Governor. I see by the report, just laid in front of me, that he was arrested on a drug possession and distribution charge."

"Drugs? What kind of drugs?"

"Well, sir," the Captain hesitated and then replied weakly, "it says here, barley."

"What? Barley? You mean barley, like they use in barley soup?"

"Y . . . yes, Sir. That appears to be the case."

"What kind of a damned operation are you running over there, Fontaine? Explain to me what happened that you pulled him over in the first place."

"Well, sir, Jenkins . . ."

"It's Mr. Jenkins," came a growl over the phone.

"Yes, sir. Mr. Jenkins was acting suspiciously and was pulled over by one of our cruisers."

"How suspiciously?"

"It says here that Mr. Jenkins thought he was being followed and was taking evasive action."

"Well, was he?"

"We didn't see anyone, sir."

"What the hell does that mean, Captain?"

"According to the report, the officer, in an unmarked car, observed Mr. Jenkins maneuvering through several side streets and alleys."

"Are you all lunatics over there?" The Governor fumed. "First, you follow him until you scare the hell out of him, and then arrest him for having barley grain in his car. What were you following him for in the first place?"

"I . . . I don't know, sir. It doesn't say in the report."

"Captain, I want him released, now. And I mean right now. I want you to personally apologize to that man for the harassment he received, and his car had better be setting out front, waiting for him when he walks out that door. Do we understand each other?"

"Yes, Governor. I'll take care of it."

"You'd better hope he doesn't sue your ass for false arrest, Fontaine."

"No, sir. I mean, yes, Sir. I mean, I hope not too, sir."

"And Fontaine. I don't ever want another call that you have done anything to intimidate or harass Mr. Jenkins, understood?"

"One hundred percent, sir."

It took twenty minutes to get the car back to the front of the police station. But that had given the police captain plenty of time to provide a red-faced apology to Henry and then scream at the arresting officer to get his ass into the captain's office.

Lieutenant Cameron and state investigators had 'interviewed' Henry several times over the months in an effort to locate Jefferson. And, "wasn't it strange that Hampstead, who just happened to be Jefferson's stepfather, had had a heart attack and died in Henry's workshop?" However, Jefferson, it seemed, had just disappeared. Henry offered that he would eventually, probably, turn up in Albuquerque or LA or somewhere with a drug cartel in Mexico.

If Francis knew anything, he wasn't talking. Francis also wasn't telling who beat him and left him in the park. Henry reasoned that that was because involving him would bring out the drug money Henry had taken. By keeping his mouth shut, Francis might have a chance to get it back if/when he was freed.

Gilbert Francis had recovered, and his trial for the Clarksville murders had begun last week. Although he admitted, to Henry's surprise, that he and Jefferson (who was still missing) had committed the murders of Mary and Linda, he was not guilty by reason of insanity.

Henry figured he had chosen that course of action because he knew, once back on the street, someone was going to want their five hundred grand. Therefore, he was safer locked up than free until it all blew over and he could retrieve the money or slip away to new climes.

When Henry saw Francis going into the courthouse, he was limping but definitely under his own power. Henry seethed that the orthopedic surgeon had been able to put in all the artificial joints that made him whole again. Oh, well, Henry thought, thanks to the government and ACLU dictating that criminals get better care than victims and veterans.

Francis's trial lasted two weeks. Henry attended every day, and when called, answered what he could about coming home to see the van squealing out of his driveway and finding his family dead.

Considering the evidence the prosecution had, or better didn't have, Francis could have gotten off scott-free if he hadn't admitted to the crime.

Henry wondered if the pistol he had taken from Francis was the one used in the murders and decided to get rid of it when he got a chance to take it apart and toss the pieces.

When the trial ended, Francis was determined by the jury to be not guilty by reason of insanity. Henry, his fists clenched tightly, sat in the second row behind the prosecutor.

The Honorable Harold J. Warren handed down his decision. "Gilbert Samuel Francis, a jury of your peers has found you not guilty of these atrocious acts by reason of insanity. I cannot fault the jury for their verdict due to the options they had and lack of due diligence by the state. It was the only feasible conclusion they could reach. However, it is my personal and considered opinion that you did willfully, and with full knowledge of your actions, bludgeon, rape, and kill Mary Margaret Jenkins and Linda Lea Jenkins. I believe you did so with malice aforethought while attempting to steal money and other items for the purpose of procuring drugs for your own use and resale. I believe you are the most despicable and depraved being that has ever stood before this court, and that for your crimes, you deserve a sentence of no less than death for those crimes. However, due to the verdict of this court, and the current laws of the state of Pennsylvania, I am limited in the scope of the punishment I may direct. Therefore, my decision will be in accordance with those laws."

"Gilbert Francis, you have been deemed insane by your peers. I do therefore order that you be remanded to the custody of the Pennsylvania State Police. They will transport you to the State hospital for the criminally insane where you will be incarcerated until such time that it is determined, by the state of Pennsylvania, that you may safely walk in our society again."

The judge peered at Francis over the half glasses perched on his nose and added, "And, Mr. Francis, I can only pray to God that day never comes."

He banged the gavel on its pad. "This court is adjourned."

Francis, as he was being led out, looked at Henry and grinned.

Henry opened his clenched fists and looked down at his hands. He had held his hands so tightly there was blood in his palms where his fingernails had punctured the skin.

Detective Cameron sat across the room and slightly behind Henry, gazing at him reflectively.

When Henry got home, Sheila was out shopping. He dialed a familiar number in Denver. A few minutes later, he called Fred to telling him he was sending him three thousand dollars to give to Frank Alessio.

# CHAPTER 51

## THREE YEARS LATER

Sheila was in her sewing room altering a pair of slacks. Henry didn't even know people did that anymore in this, everything-is-disposable, throwaway society. She had been dieting to lose, what she said was, an excessive ten pounds. Henry didn't agree but so what. He thought, plus or minus ten pounds, she was still a gorgeous woman that turned him on every time he saw her naked and oft times when she was dressed. They had spent the morning showering and doing each other sexual favors, several in fact, and then had a leisurely brunch.

Now, Henry was lying on the couch alternately watching cable news and dozing. Life since his promise to Mary and Linda had been fulfilled had become somewhat boring. He had started thinking about perusing the job postings in the newspaper, but Sheila had dissuaded him each time by showing him how much more fun life, in the bedroom or at least in the house, could be. However, even their fantastic and often inventive sexual escapades couldn't keep him entertained all the time.

He was again in the dozing stage when the phone rang. He lazily picked it up and punched the 'on' button. "Hello?"

"Mr. Jenkins, Frank Alessio here. I've tried to you call the past few days but got no answer, and I wasn't going to leave a message."

At the sound of Frank's voice, Henry had immediately gone from comfortably sleepy to intently alert. "Yes, Frank. We've been away. I take it you have some information."

Henry's eyes turned to ice as Frank relayed the information. "Yes, I do. I received word a week ago that your man walks tomorrow at 3:30 p.m. Sorry that's such short notice, but as I said, I have been trying to reach you."

Henry shook his head like Frank could see him. "No, no problem. I appreciate the call."

Henry hung up and sat staring at the floor between his knees. In the three years since Francis was sentenced, Henry had had time to come to terms with his loss. Not that he ever entirely put it out of his mind, but he had learned to live with the moments when it suddenly reared up in his head. Now, with the phone call, it was again as vivid as the day it had happened.

Henry had had the lot across the street filled and graded, and it now looked like it should, an empty lot with a For Sale sign on it. Henry even mowed it when he mowed Sheila's lawn to keep it looking neat. With it now being an empty space, the idea of seeing it or maintaining it did not bother him nearly as much as it once had. Twice he had thought the lot was sold, only to have the sales fall through. Now in the hands of another realtor, he was told they had a prospective buyer again, and this one really liked the idea of being at the end of a street where life would be "quieter and safer." One could only hope.

He had sold the house on Hunters Trail six months ago. He had not put it in the hands of Greene Realty, although he did send Greene the money he had promised. He had been selective about who he sold it to, not through racial prejudice—he had ultimately sold it to a retired black Navy Master Chief and his wife—but due to safety considerations. The chief said he was buying it for his wife for putting up with him during his thirty-year Navy career.

Henry decided to sell to them because the chief wanted to put a garden out back and wile away his time weeding instead of digging. Henry didn't care that he would be ripping out the landscaping he had paid to have put in. And he had sold the place for $150,000 more than he had paid for it. All the furniture, artwork and other things Brenda had bought for the house were put into storage for the unforeseeable future.

During dinner, Sheila commented on Henry's reflective mood.

Henry shook away his reverie and said, "I'm sorry, Sheila, what did you say?"

Sheila looked at him pensively. "I said, you seem like you're a thousand miles away."

"I'm just thinking about something I have to do tomorrow."

"We're supposed to go to The Gallery tomorrow to look at a dining room suite."

"I'd really like to go with you, sweetheart, but I'm afraid you'll have to do that by yourself or maybe put it off until Thursday. Something came up that I'm going to have to take care of tomorrow that I can't put off."

"I guess I could put it off. What do you have to do tomorrow?"

Henry didn't like lying to Sheila. As a matter of fact, except for his family situation, and of course Brenda, he couldn't recall ever doing so. However, he could not see her condoning or even understanding what had happened to Hampstead or Jefferson. Even though he had not caused Hampstead's heart attack, he had done nothing to try to save his life. And though he had not killed Jefferson, he would have ultimately been responsible for his death if the man had not killed himself first.

"Well, I got a call from Dan, my lawyer. He said he had some financial stuff he had to run through with me, and he made it sound important. But, you know how lawyers are. To them, everything is important to their billable hours. Anyway, he asked to see me tomorrow, and I told him I would."

"Is that what the phone call was about when I was in the sewing room?"

"Yes," Henry said jumping on the opportunity for plausibility. "As a matter of fact, it was. But I'll tell you what; I have to meet with him at 3:30. If I can make that meeting short and get back here at a reasonable time, we can go look at a table tomorrow evening, okay?"

Sheila smiled. "Okay."

# CHAPTER 52

Wednesday morning dawned heavily overcast and, according to both the newspaper and the woman who gave the weather on the local news channel, rain was expected by mid-morning and would last through the rest of the day.

Henry looked at the newspaper while Sheila fixed them both some breakfast. He did not expect to see anything about Francis's release from prison, and he was not disappointed. Trouble in the Middle East was still brewing, Israel had been bombed by the Palestinians again, North Korea was coming under even heavier sanctions, and the Democrats were still blaming the Republicans for all the ills in America and, with the help of the media, getting away with it.

The want ads didn't have much to pique Henry's interest. He did see one ad for a private investigator and wondered how that type of work might be.

Sheila called Henry to breakfast, and he tossed the paper aside.

After eating, Henry told Sheila he was going to take a shower and headed for the bathroom. He was rinsing soap from his head when Sheila opened the door and stepped into the shower with him. The next half hour was spent with them carefully washing and rinsing each other, paying careful attention to selective parts of each other's bodies. Afterward, they toweled each other dry and then spent the next hour in bed each vigorously bringing the other to a rousing climax.

Afterward, Henry lay back, reflecting on the last three plus years with Sheila. She was a fantastically beautiful and desirable woman. He never tried to compare her with Mary or vice versa because he knew they each had their own qualities, and he pointedly kept them separate.

Although he and Sheila did not keep up the almost daily pace of their sexual enthusiasm as they had initially, they certainly made up for it in the abandonment and freedom of their less frequent commitments.

"I think," Sheila said getting up from the bed, "that I need another shower. You made me all sweaty."

Henry reached out and ran his hand up her leg. "Do you need help?"

Sheila laughed and pushed his hand away. "No, because then I would need another shower." She went into the bathroom and began to run the water.

At ten-thirty, as Henry dressed, he hoped his encounter with Francis would go as planned. When it was over, he would put all of it in the past, where it belonged, and forget it. At eleven o'clock, he kissed Sheila goodbye and, getting the rifle from the Lincoln, put it in the Cadillac before backing it out of the garage. Although he had brought the Lincoln from Hunters Trail, he rarely drove it, especially when going to Pittsburg and seldom into Clarksville.

Last evening, after they had dinner, Henry had gone to the basement where he found a brown bottle far in the back on the top shelf of a cabinet. He had carefully opened a tranquilizer dart and poured some of the liquid from the bottle into the dart and reassembled it. Then he had discreetly carried it upstairs and put it in the coat he would be wearing the next day. As he drove toward the hospital for the criminally insane, he loaded the special dart into the rifle and laid it on the back seat.

As he drove, he reflected on the visit with Fred and Midge in July. The visit had been quite enjoyable. Midge was completely changed from the spiteful woman she had been when Mary was alive. Henry had wished, sadly, Mary could see the difference. However, Midge and Sheila had a wonderful time.

When the women went out, he and Fred discussed Francis and his impending release at some point in time. Fred was less than enthusiastic about Henry waiting for that day.

"Let it go, Hank. It's over. You are rid of two of them, and I doubt this one will bother you. His drug buddies will probably make short work of him anyway for losing their money. You don't have to do it."

"That is an area where we will have to disagree, Fred. I can think of a few scenarios where it could mean my demise and worse. Francis could come after me to get the money back. Francis could convince his distributors that I got their money, and they would come after me. And the third, and most horrible thing, they would come after Sheila to get to me, probably kill her, and kill me anyway if I gave them the money. There is just too much that can go wrong with him meandering the streets."

It had started drizzling when Henry was fifteen minutes from home, and when he stopped twenty feet from the gate of the institution, it was a deluge.

He shut off the ignition and looked at his watch. It was almost three o'clock and thirty minutes till Francis would be coming out the gate. He looked at his surroundings. On his side and down past the gate were two cars. On the opposite side of the street and directly opposite the gate was another car. None had their engines running, and with the downpour, Henry could not see anyone in any of them. The street was practically void of traffic and that was good. He certainly didn't need an audience for what he was doing.

At 3:25, he reached back and got the rifle off the back seat. He then sat back in his seat holding the rifle and forced himself to stop clenching his teeth.

At exactly 3:30, a lone figure stepped through the gate into the steady downpour, his head bent against the driving rain. As he started walking toward Henry's car, Henry noticed even the slight limp he had in the courtroom was almost gone. As he reached for the door handle, he remembered the smug look Francis had given him as he exited the court three years ago and hatred filled his heart and flashed in his eyes.

He pushed the door open and standing, steadied the rifle on the top of the door frame, pointed toward his adversary. Francis, head bent, had still not noticed him and continued toward him.

Across the street, another lone figure, a huge man that looked like a football player stepped out of his vehicle and gazed across the street at Henry. Rain poured off the brim of the familiar brown fedora pulled snugly down on the head of Lieutenant Cameron.

Henry raised the rifle, steadying it on the door frame and taking aim on the figure still walking toward him.

As Henry aimed at Francis, Cameron drew his .44 magnum from his shoulder holster and, holding it in both hands, leaned his forearms against the roof of the unmarked police car, oblivious to the soaking rain.

"Jenkins!" Cameron's voice was like thunder in Henry's ears. "Lay it down!"

Henry did not turn his head from his prey. "You had your chance, Lieutenant. I told you what would happen if your system failed." He started slowly squeezing the trigger.

"Jenkins, don't do it. It's not worth it."

Francis, hearing the exchange, looked up. Rain spattered his face as he gaped at Henry then Cameron and back again. His eyes settled on the rifle in Henry's hands and suddenly realized the danger he was in.

"Jenkins, for God's sake, don't do this."

Francis looked wildly around and, seeing the two parked cars, which might afford some protection, spun on his heels. He slid and nearly went down but gained his footing and started to run toward shelter.

When the firing pin struck the cap, Henry barely felt the recoil, and the explosion of the shell was muted by the pounding rain.

Francis had only taken two steps when the point of the dart went through his coat and shirt and penetrated the disc between the second and third lumbar vertebrae in his back. He was almost to the first car when he screamed and sagged to the ground.

Henry never saw him fall. Just as the dart struck Francis, Cameron's gun erupted with a sound no storm could quell. When the slug tore into Henry's left side, he was thrown violently against the side of the Cadillac and fell to the ground, dazed more by his collision with the car than by the impact of the bullet. When the haziness receded and he could focus his eyes, he lay on the wet pavement. The water running by him in the street was washing the blood away from the jagged exit wound in his right side almost as fast as it flowed from his body. He couldn't feel the pain yet but knew it would come.

"Why did you do it, Jenkins?" Cameron asked as he put something soft under Henry's head. "There were men here to arrest him for the Cartier murder in Pittsburgh."

"Did I get him, Lieutenant?"

Cameron looked down the street at the inert form on the sidewalk and back to Henry. "Yeah, you got him, but a dart gun? If you were going to take a chance on being killed, why, in God's name, did you use a fucking dart gun?"

"I never wanted to kill him, Lieutenant. I didn't want him to die. That was a special dart. I added to it. If it works as I intended, he'll live, but he'll be a mess." He coughed and could feel the pain starting, creeping up his rib cage. He couldn't tell how bad he was hit and didn't want to know.

"You see, just like the first time we talked, I told you if your system let them go, I would stop them. I've stopped them, Lieutenant. It's over."

"You said them, Jenkins. Did you kill Jefferson?"

Henry tried to laugh, but it came out as a groan. "He's dead, but I didn't kill him. He slit his wrists when he determined he was a waste of human life. But you don't have to worry about him anymore."

"Where is he, Jenkins? Where is the body?"

"It . . . it doesn't . . . matter," Henry said through the pain.

Darkness was pressing on his eyelids, and the pain was horrendous. "With Francis out of commission, that's three, and that's all."

Cameron slapped his cheek to keep him awake. "Stay with me, Jenkins. The ambulance is on its way. What do you mean three? Who's the third, Hampstead?"

Henry tried to nod but couldn't. Ye . . . yeah . . . was trying to pro . . . pro . . . tect them. . . knew about it . . . all along."

"Did something you did have anything to do with his heart attack?"

"N . . . no . . . just died. Couldn't . . . take . . . loss . . . son."

"One thing, Lieu . . . lieutenant. Tell . . . Sheila . . . why I . . . I had to . . . do . . . it." Darkness was closing in rapidly. ". . . know . . . Lieu . . . resentments . . . do . . . kill."

Another police car and two ambulances pulled up. The attendants put Henry on one stretcher and Francis on another and shoved them into the vehicles. The ambulance Henry was in flew past the other one that had come for Francis.

Lieutenant Cameron waited until Francis was taken away and a rollback truck had loaded Henry's car to take it to the police impound lot. The rain had finally stopped.

He walked over and talked for a while to the uniformed officers then got in his car to go back to the station. They could wrap things up here, and he had a ton of paperwork to complete.

# CHAPTER 53

Lt. Cameron knocked on the door then stood quietly waiting for it to open. He had changed out of the wet clothes he had on earlier and now wore a brown suit. The rain had not returned, but the sky was still a threatening gray.

The door opened, and Cameron looked down into the pretty face of the well-built woman with the dark, almost black, shoulder-length hair.

"Mrs. Jenkins. Mrs. Sheila Jenkins." She looked like the woman he had seen before, but he wasn't sure.

Sheila looked at him noncommittally but didn't correct him. "May I help you?"

Cameron twisted the brim of the almost dry fedora between his hands. Like every other time it had happened, he didn't want to be here. In fact, he dreaded this part of his job. However, it was his responsibility to tell her, and he never shirked his responsibilities, no matter how distasteful. This, to Cameron, was one of the worst.

"Mrs. Jenkins," he held out his I.D. folder showing his badge and credentials, "I am Lieutenant James Cameron of the Clarksville Police Department."

Even though the man had broken the law, and it was his job to stop him, Cameron understood how Henry must have looked at the situation, and he could not help feeling a little sorry for him and now her.

A frown appeared on Sheila's brow and her left eyebrow arched. "Yes, I remember you now. What do you want? Henry isn't here right now."

"Yes, ma'am. I know that. That's why I'm here." He paused, taking a deep breath. "Mrs. Jenkins, there was a shooting this afternoon and ..."

"Where is he? Sheila interrupted, timorously, her heart suddenly trying to beat its way out of her chest. "Where is Henry! Is he all right?"

Cameron looked down at his hat then back at Sheila. "Mrs. Jenkins, your husband was shot at 3:36 p.m. this afternoon. He is in shock trauma in Pittsburgh. I'm terribly sorry."

Cameron had started carrying the magnum five years ago after he had been shot in the arm by a man with a .357 caliber revolver because the nine millimeter police issued Glock he had carried didn't have the range, accuracy, or stopping power to stop the man he was chasing.

Now, he wished he had had the smaller Glock to stop Henry. But, 20/20 hindsight wasn't worth a damn. Jenkins was in the hospital with half his guts shot through and not expected to survive the night.

He grabbed Sheila's shoulders as her knees began to buckle, and she started to fall.

"Mrs. Jenkins, I have a police cruiser out front. If you want, I can take you down to Pittsburgh. With lights and siren, I can get you there much quicker."

During the drive to the hospital, Cameron related the sequence of events leading up to the shooting. Sheila was alternately furious with the man who shot Henry to understanding that he was doing his job. After all, hadn't she warned Henry this would happen? Even though she was so scared that Henry might not make it that she was nauseated, she was also angry with him for deceiving her.

Cameron had to pull to the side of the road twice on the way to Pittsburg so she could throw up.

## The Pittsburg Press
## Thursday, September 5

Pennsylvania State Police on Wednesday reported that in a shooting at the Pennsylvania State Mental Institution for the Criminally Insane, Henry Jenkins of Clarksville, Pennsylvania was critically wounded by off-duty

Clarksville police detective James Cameron. State police spokesman Rick Turner said Jenkins was shot after Jenkins shot and wounded another man, Gilbert S. Francis, of Pittsburg. Turner said Jenkins shot Francis

with a tranquilizing gun normally used in subduing animals. Turner said the incident occurred as Francis was released from the Institution after serving three years for the rape and murder of Mary Jenkins and Linda Jenkins, the wife and daughter of Jenkins.

In a report filed by detective James Cameron, Jenkins was warned three times to lower his weapon before Cameron fired his own service revolver but not in time to prevent the shooting of Francis. Cameron said the motive for the shooting of Francis was to avenge the prior murders of Jenkins' wife and daughter. According to the police report, Jenkins indicated a second man, Darnell Jefferson, also of Pittsburgh and alleged accomplice of Francis in the killings, was dead. However, he was not able to tell the police how he knew this information or where the body could be found.

A third man, the stepfather of Jefferson, Bartholomew J. Hampstead, who died in the Pittsburgh home of Jenkins' was, according to Jenkins, also involved in the Clarksville case.

Lieutenant Cameron, on administrative leave, as is common in shooting incidents, was unavailable for comment.

### The Pittsburgh Press
### Friday, September 6
### Man Shot with Dart Gun Paralyzed

Hospital spokesman, Dennis Cloud, told this reporter today, that Gilbert Francis, the man shot with a tranquilizer dart as he left the state mental hospital on Wednesday was paralyzed from the neck down with no chance of recovery.

Cloud, the chief neurosurgeon at the hospital, said two factors complicated any chance Francis would have for recovery. He said the tranquilizing dart, which lodged between the vertebrae in Francis' spine punctured the spinal cord, causing paralysis of the lower limbs. He said the major damage, however, was from sulfuric acid that had been added to the tranquilizing liquid in the dart.

Cloud said that by the time an analysis of the fluid was made to determine the contents, irreparable damage had been done. He said excellent work by hospital staff in determining that mixture was all that gave them time to save his life. Cloud further stated that Francis was unable to move or speak and was currently in a medically induced coma.

Francis, twenty-nine, had been sentenced to three years to the mental institution after being judged mentally insane in the double rape murders of Mary and Linda Jenkins in Clarksville four years ago. Henry Jenkins, the husband and father of the two women, shot Francis upon his release from that institution.

Jenkins was subsequently shot and critically wounded in the incident by an off-duty Clarksville police officer.

**The Pittsburgh Press**
**Wednesday, May 29**
**Man Charged in Shooting**

Henry David Jenkins of Clarksville, Pennsylvania was arraigned yesterday in the shooting of Gilbert S. Francis of Pittsburgh. Jenkins has been charged with the attempted first degree murder of Francis in a revenge shooting outside a Pittsburgh mental facility last September. Francis, had just been released from the facility after serving three years for the rape and murder of Jenkins' wife and daughter. Jenkins shot Francis as he exited the facility grounds.

Jenkins was subsequently shot and critically wounded by off-duty police detective, James Cameron. Jenkins spent two months in a Pittsburgh hospital following extensive, lifesaving surgery. Jenkins is currently out on bail as he awaits trial in the shooting.

Cameron, who resigned from the Clarksville police force shortly after the incident, was not available for comment.

**The Pittsburgh Press**
**Thursday, December 4**
**Trial Begins in Shooting**

The trial began today in Pittsburg in the case of the State/v/Henry David Jenkins. Jenkins is the accused in the attempted first degree murder of Gilbert S. Francis.

The state prosecutor in the case, Bentley Samuelson, said "the state will prove that Jenkins, with four years of premeditation, did willfully and with full knowledge and intent, gun down Francis in an act of revenge."

Daniel G. Domerugue IV, the attorney for Jenkins, has entered a plea of not guilty by reason of insanity. Domerugue said he would show "not only was his client so bereaved and distraught by the death of his family that he was unaware of his actions, but he further stated that his client never had the intention of killing Francis as was evidenced by the use of a tranquilizing dart instead of a bullet.

The trial is expected to last three weeks.

**The Pittsburgh Press**
**Thursday, December, 18**
**Trial Continues in Dart Gun Shooting**

James Cameron, formally a detective with the Clarksville Police department, took the stand today in the trial of Henry Jenkins of Clarksville.

Cameron, who resigned from the police force shortly after the shooting to go into his own business as a private investigator, testified that he had no knowledge of the contents of the tranquilizing dart used by Jenkins in the shooting of Gilbert Francis last September. To the chagrin of the state's prosecutor in the trial, Cameron further testified that Jenkins didn't appear "particularly rational" during the interviews he had with the defendant.

When questioned on reports he had written during his time as a detective on the police force, Cameron stated, "In my reports on the subject, I didn't write my opinion, only what was said. Now you are asking for my opinion, and that is what I'm giving you."

As he left the bench and walked past the defendant, Cameron was heard to whisper, "Good luck, Jenkins. I hope you make it."

# CHAPTER 54

It was Christmas Eve, or more precisely, Christmas Eve Day. Henry sat in the coffee shop across the street from the courthouse talking to Sheila and Dan. The jury had been out, this was the third day, and they were all starting to get tired of the wait, even though Dan had said the longer they were out, the better the chances for Henry.

"If they don't reach a decision by one o'clock," Dan said, "the judge may possibly ask them to stay, but since it's Christmas Eve, there are two other options: recess until after Christmas or declare a hung jury. If they opt for a hung jury, we may have to start all over again."

Henry ran his index finger around the rim of his cup, gazing out of the window of the restaurant. Prison, he thought, a hell of a place to spend Christmas.

"I hope they do something. You're costing me a fortune, and my ass . . . sorry Sheila, my butt hurts from sitting all day. Those aren't the most comfortable chairs in the world."

Dan smiled. "As for the money, you pay me that much because I'm good. As for the chair, if you had listened to me in the first place, you wouldn't be sitting in it."

Sheila held Henry's hand and smiled at him. "Let's just hope they finish today and with a good decision. We need to have you in physical therapy, not in a courtroom."

Henry squeezed her hand. "The therapy you have been giving me at home is better than any I get at the center."

Sheila reddened, glancing at Dan then back to Henry. "Shush, you're embarrassing me."

Dan laughed as a man from the court came over and put a hand on his shoulder. "Dan, the jury is back in."

Dan looked at his watch and got up. "You guys head on back. I'll pay the tab and be right with you."

In the courtroom, Sheila sat behind Henry and put her hand on his arm. "Good luck, Henry."

Henry smiled, looking more confident than he felt. "It will be okay. Don't you worry." He glanced around the room. Francis sat at the prosecutor's table in a motorized wheel chair that was controlled by head movements. He had only been in court three times. Dan had told Henry that Francis was on pain medication daily to reduce the pseudo-pain in his arms, legs, and back. He was unable to talk, and his health care workers were unsure of his short-term memory, although he did seem to be able to remember things prior to being shot.

Henry watched the jury file in and take their seats. Each one glanced at Henry as they sat down, and Dan had said that was a good thing. Even though he didn't think he would spend too much time locked up if convicted—Dan had put on a damn good, if not excellent, defense—he was still apprehensive about the outcome.

The judge banged his gavel, and the murmur in the courtroom subsided. "Ladies and gentlemen of the jury, have you reached a verdict?"

The jury foreman stood with a paper in his hand. "We have, Your Honor."

The judge looked at the jurors. "In coming to a decision regarding this case, you were given these options: guilty, guilty but insane, not guilty by reason of insanity, and not guilty. Would you state your verdict at this time?"

The foreman read from the paper in his hand, "We the jury, in the case of the state of Pennsylvania versus Henry David Jenkins . . ."

Henry could feel beads of moisture forming on his head and wished he would read faster. The suspense was driving him nuts, and, if possible, he could hear Sheila holding her breath.

"... find the defendant ..."

The foreman looked up at Henry, and he wanted to scream at him to get on with it.

"... not guilty."

Sheila had her arms around him before he could even sag in his chair in relief.

Somewhere, a million miles away, he thought he heard the judge dismiss the jury and the case as he hugged Sheila and then Dan.

He had physical therapy on Monday, and the doctors had assured him if he was diligent with that, he would be good as new.

The plastic surgeon had promised they could grow skin in a lab and the skin grafts would completely hide the scar tissue from the gunshot wounds and surgery.

Sheila, on the way out of the courtroom, was already promising her own physical therapy as soon as they got home, and Henry patted her bottom to reflect his approval.

As he walked past Francis, he returned the smile the man had given him four years ago in a similar setting.

It looked like it was going to be a pretty good Christmas after all.

THE END